RULED *By* *The* BOSS

CHANTELLE SHAW

ABBY GREEN

LOUISE FULLER

MILLS & BOON

RULED BY THE BOSS © 2024 by Harlequin Books S.A.

The publisher acknowledges the copyright holders of the individual works as follows:

ACQUIRED BY HER GREEK BOSS
© 2017 by Chantelle Shaw
Philippine Copyright 2017
Australian Copyright 2017
New Zealand Copyright 2017

First Published 2017
Third Australian Paperback Edition 2024
ISBN 978 1 038 90123 1

CLAIMED FOR THE DE CARRILLO TWINS
© 2017 by Abby Green
Philippine Copyright 2017
Australian Copyright 2017
New Zealand Copyright 2017

First Published 2017
Third Australian Paperback Edition 2024
ISBN 978 1 038 90123 1

KIDNAPPED FOR THE TYCOON'S BABY
© 2017 by Louise Fuller
Philippine Copyright 2017
Australian Copyright 2017
New Zealand Copyright 2017

First Published 2017
Third Australian Paperback Edition 2024
ISBN 978 1 038 90123 1

Published by
Harlequin Mills & Boon
An imprint of Harlequin Enterprises (Australia) Pty Limited
(ABN 47 001 180 918), a subsidiary of HarperCollins
Publishers Australia Pty Limited
(ABN 36 009 913 517)
Level 19, 201 Elizabeth Street
SYDNEY NSW 2000 AUSTRALIA

MIX
Paper | Supporting
responsible forestry
FSC® C001695

Printed and bound in Australia by McPherson's Printing Group

CONTENTS

Acquired By Her Greek Boss
Chantelle Shaw

MILLS & BOON

Visit the Author Profile page at
millsandboon.com.au for more titles.

Chantelle Shaw lives on the Kent coast and thinks up her stories while walking on the beach. She has been married for over thirty years and has six children. Her love affair with reading and writing Harlequin stories began as a teenager, and her first book was published in 2006. She likes strong-willed, slightly unusual characters. Chantelle also loves gardening, walking and wine!

DEDICATION

For Pippa Roscoe,

Thank you for being a wonderful editor,
for giving great advice, for the laughs we've
shared and your understanding—and occasional
tear-mopping—when I've struggled with a book!

Best wishes always,

Chantelle

CHAPTER ONE

'CAN I HELP YOU?' Alekos Gionakis said curtly, when he strode into his office on Monday morning and found an unknown woman making coffee with his espresso machine.

In the past month he'd had four temporary PAs, all of whom had proved inadequate to the task of organising his hectic schedule. But this morning his super-efficient personal assistant was due back at work after her holiday and Alekos was looking forward to his life running smoothly again. The idea that Sara might have delayed her return for some reason, and he would have to manage for even one more day with yet another temp, cast a dark cloud over his mood.

His rapier glance skimmed over the woman's hair that fell in loose waves around her shoulders and seemed to encompass every shade of brown from caramel to latte. Her delightfully curvaceous figure was packaged in a dusky pink blouse and a cream pencil skirt that was a good two inches shorter than knee length.

Moving his gaze lower, Alekos felt a jolt of masculine appreciation at her shapely legs, which were enhanced by her high-heeled shoes with cut-out sections at the front that revealed her bare toes. He noticed her toenails were varnished a flirty shade of hot pink that was more suited to a beach than to Gionakis Enterprises' prestigious offices in Piccadilly.

'Good morning, Alekos.'

He frowned at the sound of the familiar voice. Low-toned and melodious, for some reason it made him think of a cool, clear mountain stream.

'Sara?' Her *voice* was recognisable, but everything about his PA's appearance was definitely not. His brain was not playing tricks on him, Alekos realised when she turned her head. Even though she was standing several feet away from him, he was struck by the intense green of her eyes. They were her only remarkable features—or at least that had been true when Sara's style of workwear for the past two years had been a navy blue skirt and jacket, which she'd teamed with a plain white shirt, buttoned primly all the way up to her throat in the summer, or a black roll-neck sweater in colder weather.

Smart, practical and frankly unnoticeable was how Alekos would have described his PA's appearance before she had inconveniently decided to take a month's holiday in Spain. When he'd objected, she had reminded him that she hadn't used any of her annual leave since she'd started working for him, apart from one day to attend her mother's funeral. Sara had looked even more washed out than she usually did. Alekos was not renowned for his sensitivity, but he'd acknowledged that caring for her terminally ill mother must have been a strain and he'd reluctantly agreed to her taking an extended holiday.

He had vaguely imagined her on a scenic coach tour of Spain to visit places of historical and architectural interest. He knew she liked history. No doubt the majority of the other people on the tour would be pensioners and she would strike up a friendship with a spinster, or perhaps a widow who was travelling alone and who would be grateful for Sara's innately kind nature.

Alekos's rather cosy picture of his PA's holiday plans had been disrupted when she'd told him that she was going away on a YFS trip—which stood for Young, Free and Single. As their name suggested, the tour operator specialised in holidays for people in the twenty-something age bracket who wanted to spend every night clubbing, or partying on a beach. The media often reported scenes of drunken debauchery by Brits in Benidorm. When he had pointed out that a better name for the holiday company would be AFS—Available For Sex—Sara had laughed and, to Alekos's astonishment, told him she was looking forward to letting her hair down in Spain.

His eyes were drawn back to her hair. He visualised her as she had looked every weekday for the past two years. She had always worn her nondescript brown hair scraped back from her face and piled on top of her head in a no-nonsense bun that defied gravity with the aid of an arsenal of metal hairpins.

'You're wearing your hair in a new style,' he said abruptly. 'I was trying to work out why you look different.'

'Mmm, I had it cut while I was away. It was so long, almost waist length, and I was fed up of having to tie it up all the time.' She ran her fingers through the silky layers of her new hairstyle. In the sunshine streaming through the window, her hair seemed to shimmer like gold in places and Alekos felt an un-expected tightening sensation in his groin.

'And I finally ditched my glasses for contact lenses. Although I must admit they're taking a while to get used to.' Sara sounded rueful. 'My new con-tacts make my eyes water sometimes.'

Alekos was relieved that she wasn't fluttering her eyelashes at him seductively, but she was blinking presumably because her contact lenses felt strange. Without the thick-rimmed glasses he was used to seeing her wearing, her cheekbones were more no-ticeable and her face was prettier than his memory served him.

He wondered if she'd had some sort of surgical procedure to her lips. Surely he would have remem-bered the fullness of her lips—and, *Theos,* that faint pout of her lower lip that tempted him to test its softness with his own mouth. He forced his mind away from such a ridiculous idea and reminded him-self that this was Miss Mouse, the name that one of his legion of leggy blonde mistresses had unkindly christened Sara.

The nickname had suited her plain looks but not her dry wit that frequently amused Alekos, or her sharp mind and even sharper tongue that he had come to respect, because Sara Lovejoy was the only woman he had ever met who wasn't afraid to state her opinion—even if it was different to his.

'I'll put your coffee on your desk, shall I?' Without waiting for him to reply, Sara walked across the room and placed a cup of coffee on the desk in front of Alekos's chair. He could not help himself from focusing on the sensual undulation of her hips as she walked, and when she leaned across the desk her skirt pulled tighter across the curves of her buttocks.

Alekos cleared his throat audibly and tightened his fingers on the handle of his briefcase as he moved it in front of him to hide the evidence that he was aroused. What the blazes was the matter with him? For the first time in a month he had woken in a good mood this morning, knowing that Sara would be back and between them they would clear the backlog of work that had built up while she'd been away.

But work was the last thing on his mind when she turned to face him and he noticed how her pink silk shirt lovingly moulded the firm swell of her breasts. The top two buttons on her blouse were undone, not enough to reveal any cleavage but more than enough to quicken his pulse as he visualised himself removing her shirt and her lace-edged bra that he could see outlined beneath the silky material of her top.

He forced his gaze away from her breasts down to her surprisingly slim waist and cleared his throat again. 'You...er...appear to have lost some weight.'

'A few pounds, as a matter of fact. I expect it was down to all the exercise I did while I was on holiday.'

What sort of exercise had she done on a young, free and single's holiday? Alekos was not usually prone to flights of imagination but his mind was bombarded with pictures of his new-look PA discarding her inhibitions and enjoying energetic nights with a Spanish Lothario.

'Ah, yes, your holiday. I hope you enjoyed yourself?'

'I certainly did.'

Her grin made him think of a satisfied cat that had drunk a bowlful of cream. 'I'm glad to hear it,' he said tersely. 'But you are not on holiday now, so I'm wondering why you've come to work wearing clothes that are more suitable for the beach than the office.'

When Alekos spoke in that coldly disapproving tone, people tended to immediately take notice and respond with the respect he commanded. But Sara simply shrugged and smoothed her hand over her skirt.

'Oh, I wore a lot less than this on the beach. It's perfectly acceptable for women to go topless on the beaches in the French Riviera.'

Had Sara gone topless? He tried to banish the vision of his prim PA displaying her bare breasts in public. 'I thought you went to Spain for your holiday?'

'I changed my plans at the last minute.'

While Alekos was registering the fact that his ultra-organised PA had apparently changed her holiday destination on a whim, Sara strolled towards him. Why had he never noticed until now that her green eyes sparkled like emeralds when she smiled? He was irritated with himself for thinking such poetic nonsense but he could not stop staring at her.

Along with her new hairstyle and clothes, she was wearing a different perfume: a seductive scent which combined spiky citrus with deeper, exotically floral notes that stirred his senses—and stirred a lot more besides, he acknowledged derisively when he felt himself harden.

'So, where do you want me?' she murmured.

'What?' He stiffened as a picture leapt into his mind of Sara sprawled on the leather sofa with her skirt rucked up around her waist and her legs spread wide, waiting for him to position himself between her thighs.

Cursing beneath his breath, Alekos fought to control his rampant libido and realised that his PA was giving him an odd look. 'Shall I sort out the pile of paperwork on my desk that I presume the temp left for me to deal with, or do you want me to stay in here and take notes from you?' she repeated patiently.

She put her hands on her hips, drawing his attention to the narrowness of her waist that served to emphasise the rounded curves of her breasts. 'I understand that the temp I arranged to cover my absence only lasted a week, and HR organised three more replacements but you dismissed them after a few days.'

'They were all useless,' he snapped. Glancing at his watch, Alekos discovered that he had wasted ten minutes ogling his PA, who normally did not warrant more than a five second glance. He felt unsettled by his awareness of Sara as an attractive woman and was annoyed with himself for his physical response to her. 'I hope you are prepared for the fact that we have a ton of work to catch up on.'

'I guessed you'd have me tied to my desk when I came back to work,' she said airily.

Alekos's eyes narrowed on her serene expression, and he was thrown by the idea that she knew the effect she was having on him. His mental vision of her tied, face down, across her desk made his blood sizzle. He felt confused by his inability to control his response to her.

This was dull, drab Sara—although, admittedly, he had never found her dull when she'd made it clear, soon after he'd promoted her from a secretary in the accounts department to his PA, that she wasn't going to worship him like most women did. But her frumpy appearance had been one reason why he had chosen her. His position as chairman of GE demanded his absolute focus and there was no risk of him being distracted by Miss Mouse.

Alekos had become chairman of the company, which specialised in building luxury superyachts, two years ago, following the death of his father, and he had decided that Sara's unexciting appearance, exemplary secretarial skills and excellent work ethic would make her his ideal PA.

He walked around his desk, lowered his long frame into his chair and took a sip of coffee before he glanced at her. 'I need to make a few phone calls and no doubt you will have plenty of stuff to catch up on, so come back in half an hour and bring the Viceroy file with you.'

'Aren't you forgetting something? The word *please*,' Sara reminded him crisply when he raised his brows questioningly. 'Honestly, Alekos, no wonder you frightened off four temps in as many weeks if you were as surly with them as you're behaving this morning. I suppose you've got woman trouble? That's the usual reason when you come to work with a face like thunder.'

'You must know by now that I never allow my relationships to last long enough for women to become troublesome,' Alekos said smoothly. He leaned back in his chair and gave her a hard stare. 'Remind me again, Sara, why I tolerate your insolence?'

Across the room he saw her eyes sparkle and her mouth curve into a smile that inexplicably made Alekos feel as if he'd been punched in his gut. 'Because

I'm good at my job and you don't want to sleep with me. That's what you told me at my interview and I assume nothing has changed?'

She stepped out of his office and closed the door behind her before he could think of a suitably cutting retort. He glared at the space where she had been standing seconds earlier. *Theos*, sometimes she overstepped the mark. His nostrils flared with annoyance. He could not explain the odd sensation in the pit of his stomach when he caught the drift of her perfume that still lingered in the room.

He felt rattled by Sara's startling physical transformation from frump to sexpot. But he reminded himself that her honesty was one of the things he admired about her. He doubted that any of the three hundred employees at Gionakis Enterprises' London offices, and probably none of the three thousand staff employed by the company worldwide, would dream of speaking to him as bluntly as Sara did. It made a refreshing change to have someone challenge him when most people, especially women, always said yes to him.

He briefly wondered what she would say if he told her that he had changed his mind and wanted to take her to bed. Would she be willing to have sex with him, or would Sara be the only woman to refuse him? Alekos was almost tempted to find out. But practicality outweighed his inconvenient and, he confidently assumed, fleeting attraction to her, when he reminded himself that there were any number of women who would be happy to help him relieve his sexual frustration but a good PA was worth her weight in gold.

The day's schedule was packed. Alekos opened his laptop but, unusually for him, he could not summon any enthusiasm for work. He swivelled his chair round to the window and stared down at the busy street five floors below, where red London buses, black taxis and kamikaze cyclists competed for road space.

He liked living in England's capital city, although he much preferred the current June sunshine to the dank drizzle and short days of the winter. After his father's death it had been expected by the members of the board, and his family, that Alekos would move back to Greece permanently and run the company from GE's offices in Athens. His father, Kostas Gionakis, and before him Alekos's grandfather, the founder of the company, had both done so.

His decision to move the company's headquarters to London had been mainly for business reasons. London was closer to GE's growing client list in Florida and the Bahamas, and the cosmopolitan capital was ideally suited to entertain a clientele made up exclusively of millionaires and billionaires, who were prepared to spend eye-watering amounts of cash on a superyacht—the ultimate status symbol.

On a personal front, Alekos had been determined to establish himself as the new company chairman away from his father's power base in Greece. The grand building in Athens which had been GE's head-quarters looked like a palace and Kostas Gionakis had been king. Alekos never forgot that he was the usurper to the throne.

His jaw clenched. Dimitri should have been chairman, not him. But his brother was dead—killed twenty years ago, supposedly in a tragic accident. Alekos's parents had been devastated and he had never told them of his suspicions about the nature of Dimitri's death.

Alekos had been fourteen at the time, the youngest in the family, born six years after Dimitri and after their three sisters. He had idolised his brother. Everyone had admired the Gionakis heir. Dimitri was handsome, athletic and clever and had been groomed from boyhood to take over running the family business. Alekos was the spare heir should the unthinkable happen to Dimitri.

But the unthinkable *had* happened. Dimitri had died and Alekos had suddenly become the future of the company—a fact that his father had never allowed him to forget.

Had Kostas believed that his youngest son would make as good a chairman of GE as his firstborn son? Alekos doubted it. He had felt that he was second best in his father's eyes. He knew that was still the opinion of some of the board members who disapproved of his playboy lifestyle.

But he would prove those who doubted his abilities wrong. In the two years that he had been chairman the company's profits had increased and they were expanding into new markets around the globe. Perhaps his father would have been proud of him. Alekos would never know. But what he knew for sure was that he could not allow himself to be distracted by his PA simply because her sexy new look had stirred his desire.

Turning away from the window, he opened a document on his laptop and resolutely focused on work. He had inherited the company by default. He owed it to Dimitri's memory to ensure that Gionakis Enterprises continued to be as successful as it had been when his father was chairman, and as Alekos was sure it would have been under his brother's leadership.

Sara ignored a stab of guilt as she passed her desk, piled with paperwork that required her attention, and hurried into the bathroom. The mirror above the sink confirmed her fears. Her flushed cheeks and dilated pupils betrayed her reaction to Alekos that she had been unable to control.

She felt as though she had been holding her breath the entire time she had been in his office. Why was it that she'd managed to hide her awareness of him for two years but when she had set eyes on him this morning after she hadn't seen him for a month her pulse-rate had rocketed and her mouth had felt dry?

The sensation of her heart slamming against her ribcage whenever she was in close proximity to Alekos wasn't new, but she had perfected the art of hiding her emotions behind a cool smile, aware that her job depended on it. When Alekos had elevated her to the role of his PA over several other suitably qualified candidates for the job, he had bluntly told her that he never mixed business with pleasure and there was no chance of a sexual relationship developing between them. His arrogance had irritated Sara and she'd almost told him that she had no intention of copying her mother's mistake by having an affair with her boss.

During the eighteen months that she had worked in the accounts department before her promotion, she'd heard that the company's board members disapproved of Alekos's playboy lifestyle, which attracted the wrong type of press interest, and she understood why he was determined to keep his relationship with his staff on a strictly professional footing. What Alekos wanted from his PA was efficiency, dedication and the ability to blend into the background—and plain, conservatively dressed Sara had fitted the bill perfectly.

In truth she would have worn a nun's habit to the office if Alekos had required her to because she was so keen to secure the job. Her promotion to personal assistant of the chairman of Gionakis Enterprises had finally won her mother's praise. For the first time in her life she had felt that she wasn't a disappointment to Joan Lovejoy. The surname was a misnomer if ever there was one because, as far as

Sara could tell, there had been no love or joy in her mother's life.

She'd wondered if her mother had loved the man who'd abandoned her after he had made her pregnant. But Joan had refused to reveal Sara's father's identity and only ever made a few oblique references to him, notably that he had once been an Oxford don and it was a pity that Sara hadn't inherited his academic brilliance.

Sara had spent most of her life comparing herself to a nameless, faceless man who had helped to create her but she had never met—until six weeks ago. Now she knew that she had inherited her green eyes from her father. He was no longer faceless, or nameless. His name was Lionel Kingsley and he was a well-known politician. She'd been stunned when he had phoned her and revealed that there was a possibility she might be his daughter. She had agreed to a DNA test to see if he was really her father but she had been sure of the result before the test had proved it. When she looked into a mirror she saw her father's eyes looking back at her.

For the first time in her life she felt she was a whole person, and so many things about herself suddenly made sense, like her love of art and her creativity that she'd always suppressed because her mother had pushed her to concentrate on academic subjects.

Lionel was a widower and had two grown-up children. Her half-siblings! Sara felt excited and nervous at the thought of meeting her half-brother and half-sister. She understood Lionel's concern that his son and daughter from his marriage might be upset to learn that he had an illegitimate daughter, and she had told herself to be patient and wait until he was ready to acknowledge publicly that he was her father. Finally it was going to happen. Lionel had invited her to his home at the weekend so that he could introduce her to Freddie and Charlotte Kingsley.

Sara had seen pictures of them and discovered that she bore a striking resemblance to her half-siblings. But the physical similarities between her and her half-sister did not apply to their very different dress styles. Photographs of Charlotte wearing stylish, figure-hugging clothes had made Sara realise how frumpy she looked in comparison. The smart suits she wore to the office reflected the importance of her role as PA to the chairman of the company and she had reminded herself that if Alekos had wanted a decorative bimbo to be his PA he wouldn't have chosen her.

The new clothes she had bought while she had been on holiday did not make her look like a bimbo, Sara reassured herself. The skirt and blouse she was wearing were perfectly respectable for the office. Shopping in the chic boutiques on the French Riviera where her father owned a holiday villa had been a revelation. Remembering the photos she'd seen of her stylish half-sister had prompted Sara to try on colourful summery outfits. She had dropped a dress size from plenty of swimming and playing tennis and she loved being able to fit into skirts and dresses that showed off her more toned figure.

She ran her fingers through her new layered hairstyle. She still wasn't used to her hair swishing around her shoulders when she turned her head. It made her feel more feminine and, well...*sexy.* She'd had a few blonde highlights put through the front sections of her hair to complement the natural lighter streaks from where she had spent a month in the French sunshine.

Maybe it was true that blondes *did* have more fun. But the truth was that meeting her father had given her a new sense of self-confidence. The part of her that had been missing was now complete, and Sara didn't want to fade into the background any more. Travelling to work on the Tube this morning, she'd wondered if Alekos would notice her changed appearance.

She stared at her flushed face in the mirror and grimaced. All right, she had *hoped* he would notice her, instead of treating her like a piece of office furniture: functional, necessary but utterly uninteresting.

Well, she had got her wish. Alekos had stopped dead in his tracks when he'd seen her and his shocked expression had changed to a speculative gleam as his eyes had roamed over her. Heat had swept through her body when his gaze lingered on her breasts. She felt embarrassed thinking he might have noticed that her nipples had hardened in a telltale sign that he excited her more than any man had ever done.

Her decision to revamp her appearance suddenly seemed like a bad idea. When she'd dressed in dowdy clothes she hadn't had to worry that Alekos might catch her glancing at him a dozen times a day, because he rarely seemed to notice that she was a human being and not a robot. Remembering the hot, hard gleam in his eyes when she had been in his office just now sent a tremor through her, and a little part of her wished she could rush back home and change into her safe navy blue suit. But when she'd returned home from her holiday she'd found that all her old clothes were too big, and she'd packed them into black sacks and donated them to a charity shop.

There was no going back. The old Sara Lovejoy was gone for ever and the new Sara was here to stay. Alekos would just have to get used to it.

CHAPTER TWO

AT EXACTLY NINE THIRTY, Sara knocked on Alekos's door and took a deep breath before she stepped into his office. He was sitting behind his desk, leaning back in his chair that was half turned towards the window, and he was holding his phone to his ear. He spared her a brief glance and then swung his gaze back to the window while he continued his telephone conversation.

She ordered herself not to feel disappointed by his lack of interest. Obviously she must have imagined that earlier he had looked at her with a glint of desire in his eyes. Just because she had a new hairstyle and clothes did not mean that she had become Alekos's fantasy woman. She knew his type: elegant blondes with legs that went on for ever. In the past two years a steady stream of models and socialites had arrived in his life and exited it a few months later when Alekos had grown bored of his affair with them.

Sara had hoped she would be able to control her reaction to Alekos but her heart leapt wildly in her chest as she studied his profile. Slashing cheekbones, a square jaw shadowed with dark stubble and eyes that gleamed like polished jet all combined to give him a lethal magnetism that women invariably found irresistible. His thick black hair had a habit of falling forwards across his brow and she was tempted to run her fingers through it. As for his mouth... Her eyes were drawn to his beautiful mouth. Full-lipped and sensual when he was relaxed and utterly devastating when he smiled, his mouth could also curve into a cynical expression when he wished to convey his displeasure.

'Don't stand there wasting time, Sara.' Alekos's voice made her jump, and she flushed as she registered that he had finished his phone call and had caught her out staring at him. 'We have a lot to get through.'

'I was waiting for you to finish your call.' She was thankful that two years of practice at hiding her reaction to his smouldering sensuality allowed her to sound calm and composed even though her heart was racing. The way he growled her name in his sexy accent, drawing out the second syllable... Saraaa...was curiously intimate—as if they were lovers. But of course they were not lovers and were never likely to be.

She forced herself to walk unhurriedly across the room, but with every step that took her closer to Alekos's desk she was conscious of his unswerving gaze. The unholy gleam in his eyes made her feel as if he were mentally undressing her. Every centimetre of her skin was on fire when she sat down on the chair in front of his desk.

It would be easy to be overwhelmed by him. But when she had been promoted to his PA she'd realised that Alekos was surrounded by people who always agreed with him, and she had decided that she could not allow herself to be intimidated by his powerful personality. She'd noted that he did not have much respect for the flunkeys and hangers-on who were so anxious to keep on the right side of him.

She had very quickly proved that she was good at her job, but the first time she had disagreed with Alekos over a work issue he'd clearly been astounded to discover that his mousy assistant had a backbone. After a tense stand-off, when Sara had refused to back down, he had narrowed his gaze on her deter-mined expression and something like admiration had flickered in his dark eyes.

She valued his respect more than anything be-cause she loved her job. Working for Alekos was like riding a roller coaster at a theme park: exciting, intense and fast-paced, and it was the knowledge that she would never find a job as rewarding as her current one that made Sara take a steadying breath. She could not deny it was flattering that Alekos had finally noticed her, but if she wanted to continue in her role as his PA she must ignore the predatory glint in his eyes.

She held her pencil poised over her notepad and

gave him a cool smile. 'I'm ready to start when you are.'

Her breezy tone seemed to irritate him. 'I doubt you'll be so cheerful by the time we've finished today. I'll need you to work late this evening.'

'Sorry, but I can't stay late tonight. I've made other plans.'

He frowned. 'Well, change them. Do I need to remind you that a requirement of your job is for you to work whatever hours I dictate, within reason?'

'I'm sure I don't need to remind you that I have always worked extra when you've asked me to,' Sara said calmly. 'And I've worked *unreasonable* hours, such as when we stayed up until one a.m. to put together a sales pitch for a sheikh before he flew back to Dubai. It paid off too, because Sheikh Al Mansoor placed an order for a one-hundred-million-pound yacht from GE.'

Alekos's scowl did not make him any less gorgeous; in fact it gave him a dangerous, brooding look that turned Sara's bones to liquid.

'I can stay late every other night this week if you need me to,' she went on in an effort to appease him. Alekos's bad mood threatened to spoil her excitement about meeting her father after work. Lionel Kingsley's high profile as an MP meant that he did not want to risk being seen in public with Sara. As they couldn't go to a restaurant, she had invited him to her home and was planning to cook dinner for him before he attended an evening engagement.

'Oh, I can't stay late on Friday either,' she said. 'And actually I'd like to leave an hour early because I'm going away for the weekend.' She remembered the plans she'd made to visit her father at his house in Berkshire. 'I'll work through my lunch hour to make up the time.'

'Well, well.' Alekos's sardonic drawl put Sara on her guard. 'You go away for a month and return sporting a new haircut, a new—and much improved, I have to say—wardrobe, and now suddenly you have a busy social life. It makes me wonder if a man is the reason for the new-look Sara Lovejoy.'

'My personal life is none of your business,' she said composedly. Technically, she supposed that a man was the reason for the change in her, but she had not met a lover, as Alekos had implied. She had enjoyed getting to know her father when he had invited her to spend her holiday at his villa in the south of France but she had promised Lionel that she wouldn't tell anyone she was his daughter.

Deep down she felt disappointed that her father wished to keep their relationship secret. It was as if Lionel was ashamed of her. But she reminded herself that he had promised to introduce her to her half-siblings on Friday, and perhaps then he would openly welcome her as his daughter. She pulled her mind back to the present when she realised Alekos was speaking.

'It will be my business if your work is affected because you're mooning over some guy.'

Sara still refused to rise to Alekos's verbal baiting. She tapped the tip of her pencil on her pad and said with heavy emphasis, '*I'm* ready to start work when you are.'

Alekos picked up a client's folder from the pile on his desk, but he did not open it. Instead he leaned back in his chair, an unreadable expression on his handsome face as he surveyed her for long minutes while her tension grew and she was sure he must see the pulse beating erratically at the base of her throat.

'Why did you change your holiday plans and go to France rather than Spain?'

'The holiday company I'd booked with cancelled my trip, but a...friend invited me to stay at his villa in Antibes.'

'Would this friend be the man whose voice I heard in the background when I phoned you with a query from the Miami office a week ago?'

Sara tensed. Could Alekos possibly have recognised her famous father's voice?

'Why are you suddenly fascinated with my private life?'

'I'm merely concerned for your well-being and offering a timely reminder that holiday romances notoriously don't last.'

'For goodness' sake!' Sara told herself not to be fooled by Alekos's 'concern for her wellbeing'. His real concern was he did not want his PA moping about or unable to concentrate on her work because she'd suffered a broken heart. 'What makes you think I had a holiday romance?'

He trailed his eyes over her, subjecting her to a thorough appraisal that brought a flush to her cheeks. 'It's obvious. Before you went on holiday you wore frumpy clothes that camouflaged your figure. But after spending a month in France you have undergone a transformation into a frankly very attractive young woman. It doesn't take a detective to work out that a love affair is probably the cause of your new-found sensuality.'

'Well, of course *you* would assume that a *man* is the reason I've altered my appearance.' Sara's temper simmered. 'It couldn't be that I decided to update my wardrobe for *me*.' His cynical expression fuelled her anger but she also felt hurt. Had she really looked so awful in her navy blue suit with her hair secured in a neat bun, as Alekos had said? It was pathetic the way her heart had leapt when he'd complimented her new look and told her she was attractive.

'You are such a male chauvinist,' she snapped. Ignoring the warning glint in his eyes, she said furiously, 'I suppose you think I altered the way I dress in the hope of impressing you?'

The landline phone on his desk rang and Sara instinctively reached out to answer it. Simultaneously Alekos did the same and, as his fingers brushed against hers, she felt a sizzle of electricity shoot up her arm. *'Oh!'* She tried to snatch her hand away, but he snaked his fingers around her wrist and stroked his thumb pad over her thudding pulse.

'When you dressed to come to work this morning, did you choose your outfit to please me?' His black eyes burned like hot coals into hers.

Sara flushed guiltily. 'Of course not.' She refused to admit to herself, let alone to Alekos, that for the past two years she had fantasised about him desiring her. She stared at his chiselled face and swallowed. 'Are you going to answer the call?' she said breathlessly.

To her relief, he let go of her wrist and picked up the phone. She resisted the urge to leap out of her seat and run out of his office. Instead she made herself stroll across the room to the coffee machine. The familiar routine of pouring water into the machine's reservoir and inserting a coffee capsule into the compartment gave her a few moments' breathing space to bring herself under control.

Why had she goaded Alekos like that? She had always been careful to hide her attraction to him but he must have noticed how the pulse in her wrist had almost jumped through her skin because it had been beating so hard, echoing the thudding beat of her heart.

She could not put off carrying their coffees over to his desk any longer, and she was thankful that Alekos did not glance at her when he finished his phone call and opened the file in front of him. He waited for her to sit down and pick up her notepad before he began to dictate at breakneck speed, making no allowances for the fact that she hadn't taken shorthand notes for a month.

It set the tone for the rest of the day as they worked together to clear the backlog that had built up while Sara had been away. At five o'clock she rolled her aching shoulders and went to the bathroom to brush her hair and apply a fresh coat of rose-pink lip gloss that was her new must-have item of make-up.

In Alekos's office she found him standing by his desk. He was massaging the back of his neck as if he felt as tired from their busy day as she was. She had forgotten how tall he was. He had inherited his six-foot-four height from his maternal grandfather, who had been a Canadian, he'd once explained to Sara. But in every other aspect he was typically Greek, from his dark olive complexion and mass of black hair to his arrogant belief that he only had to click his fingers and women would flock to him. The trouble was that they did, Sara thought ruefully.

Alekos was used to having any woman he wanted. She told herself it was lucky that there had been no repeat of the breathless moments that had occurred earlier in the day, when rampant desire had blazed in his eyes as he'd trapped her wrist and felt the give-away throb of her sexual awareness of him.

He must have heard his office door open, and turned his head in her direction. They had played out the same scene hundreds of times before, and most days when she came to check if he needed her to do anything else before she went home he did not bother looking up from his computer screen as he bid her goodnight. But he was looking at her now. She watched his hard features tauten and become almost wolf-like as he stared at her with a hungry gleam in his eyes that excited her and filled her with illicit longing.

Something tugged in the pit of her stomach, tugged hard like a knot being pulled tighter and tighter, as if an invisible thread linked her body to Alekos. And then he blinked and the feral glitter in his eyes disappeared. Perhaps it had never been there and she had imagined that he'd stared at her as if he wanted to devour her?

'I'm just off now.' She was amazed that her voice sounded normal when her insides were in turmoil. 'I'll finish typing up the report for the shareholders first thing tomorrow.'

'Did you remember that we are attending the annual dinner for the board members on Thursday evening?'

She nodded. 'I'll bring the dress I'm going to wear for the dinner to work and get changed here at the office like I did for the Christmas party.'

'You had better check with the restaurant that they won't be serving seafood. Orestis Pagnotis is allergic to it and, much as I'd like to have the old man off my back, I'd better not allow him to risk suffering a possibly fatal reaction,' Alekos said drily.

'I've already given the restaurant a list of the dietary requirements of the guests.' She smiled sympathetically. 'Is Orestis still being a problem?'

He shrugged. 'He's one of the old school. He joined the board when my grandfather was chairman, and he was a close friend of my father.' Alekos gave a frustrated sigh. 'Orestis believes I take too many risks and he has the support of some of the other board members, who fail to understand that the company needs to move with the times rather than remain in the Stone Age. Orestis's latest gripe is that he thinks the chairman should be married.'

Alekos muttered something in Greek that Sara guessed was not complimentary about the influential board member. 'According to Orestis, if I take a wife it will prove that I have left my playboy days behind and I will be more focused on running GE.'

Her heart dipped. 'Are you considering getting married?'

Somehow she managed to inject the right amount of casual interest into her voice. She knew he had ended his affair with a stunning Swedish model called Danika shortly before her holiday, but in the month she had been away it was likely that he had met someone else. Alekos never stayed celibate for long.

Perhaps he had fallen in love with the woman of his dreams. It was possible that Alekos might ask her to organise his wedding. She would have to pin a smile on her face and hide her heartache while she made arrangements for him and his beautiful bride—she was certain to be beautiful—to spend their honeymoon at an exotic location. Sara pulled her mind away from her unwelcome thoughts when she realised Alekos was speaking.

'I'll have to marry eventually.' He sounded unenthusiastic at the prospect. 'I am the last male Gionakis and my mother and sisters remind me at every opportunity that it is my duty to produce an heir. Obviously I will first have to select a suitable wife.'

'How do you intend to *select a suitable wife*?' She could not hide her shock that he had such a cavalier attitude towards marriage. 'Will you hold interviews and ask the candidates, who are your potential brides, to fill out a detailed questionnaire about themselves?' She was aware that her voice had risen and Alekos's amused smile infuriated her further.

'Your suggestion is not a bad idea. Why are you so outraged?' he said smoothly.

'Because you make marriage sound like a…a cattle market where finding a wife is like choosing a prize heifer to breed from. What about love?'

'What about it?' He studied her flushed face speculatively. 'Statistically, somewhere between forty and fifty per cent of marriages end in divorce, and I bet that most of those marriages were so-called love matches. But with such a high failure rate it seems sensible to take emotion out of the equation and base marriage on social and financial compatibility, mutual respect and the pursuit of shared goals such as bringing up a family.'

Sara shook her head. 'Your arrogance is unbelievable. You accuse some of GE's board members of being stuck in the Stone Age, but your views on marriage are Neolithic. Women nowadays don't sit around twiddling their thumbs and hoping that a rich man will choose them to be his wife.'

'You'd be surprised,' Alekos murmured drily. 'When I decide to marry—in another ten years or so—I don't envisage I'll have a problem finding a woman who is willing to marry a multimillionaire.'

'Well, I wouldn't marry for money,' Sara said fiercely. Deep inside her she felt an ache of regret that Alekos had trampled on her silly dream that he would one day fall in love with her. Realistically, she knew it would never happen but hearing him state so emphatically that he did not aspire to a marriage built on love forced her to accept that she must get over her embarrassing crush on him.

'You would prefer to gamble your future happiness on a fickle emotion that poets try to convince us is love? But of course love is simply a sanitized word for lust.'

'If you're asking me whether I believe in love, then the answer is yes, I do. Why are you so sceptical, Alekos? You once told me that your parents had been happily married for forty-five years before your father died.'

'And therein proves my point. My parents had an arranged marriage which was extremely successful. Love wasn't necessary, although I believe they grew to be very fond of each other over the course of their marriage.'

Sara gave up. 'You're just a cynic.'

'No, I'm a realist. There is a dark side to love and I have witnessed its destructive power.'

A memory slid into Alekos's mind of that fateful day twenty years ago when he'd found Dimitri walking along the beach. His brother's eyes had been red-rimmed and he'd wept as he'd told Alekos he had discovered that his girlfriend had been unfaithful. It was the last time Alekos had seen Dimitri alive.

'Love is an illusion,' he told Sara harshly, 'and you would do well to remember it before you rush to give away your heart to a man you only met a few weeks ago.'

After Sara had gone, Alekos walked over to the window and a few minutes later he saw her emerge from the GE building and walk along the pavement. Even from a distance he noted the sexy wiggle of her hips when she walked and a shaft of white-hot lust ripped through him.

He swore. Lusting after his PA was so unexpected and he assured himself that his reaction to Sara's transformation from dowdy to a very desirable woman was down to sexual frustration. He hadn't had sex since he'd split from his last mistress almost two months ago.

'What are you looking for?' Danika had asked him when he'd told her their affair was over. 'You say you don't want permanence in a relationship, but what do you want?'

Right now he wanted a woman under him, Alekos thought, conscious of his erection pressing uncomfortably against the zip of his trousers. A memory flashed into his mind of Sara leaning across his desk with her skirt pulled tight over her bottom. He imagined her without her skirt, her derrière presented for him to slide her panties down so that he could stroke his hands over her naked body. In his fantasy he had already removed her blouse and bra and he stood behind her and slid his arms round her to cup her firm breasts in his hands…

Theos! Alekos raked his hand through his hair and forced his mind away from his erotic thoughts. Sara was the best PA he'd ever had and he was determined not to damage their excellent working relationship. She was the only woman, apart from his mother and sisters, who he trusted. She was discreet, loyal and she made his life easier in countless ways that he had not fully appreciated until she had taken a month's holiday.

If he made her his mistress he would not be able to continue to employ her as his PA. Office affairs did not work, especially after the affair ended—and of course it would end after a few months at most. He had a low boredom threshold and there was no reason to think that his surprising attraction to Sara would last long once he'd taken her to bed.

Alekos turned his thoughts to the party he was

due to attend that evening. Perhaps he would meet a woman who would hold his attention for more than an hour. He received many more invitations to social functions than he had the time or the inclination to attend, but he had a particular reason for accepting an invitation to a party being given by a wealthy city banker. Alekos knew that a Texan oil baron would be included on the guest list. Warren McCuskey was looking to buy a superyacht to keep his wife, who was twenty years younger than him, happy, and Alekos was determined to persuade the billionaire Texan to buy a yacht from GE.

From his vantage point at the window he continued to watch Sara standing in the street below. She seemed to be waiting for someone. A large black saloon car drew up alongside her, the rear door opened and she climbed into the car before it pulled away from the kerb.

He was intrigued. Why hadn't Sara's 'friend' got out of the car to greet her? Earlier, she had been oddly secretive about her boyfriend. And what was the real reason for her attractive new look? Alekos couldn't remember the last time a woman had aroused his curiosity and it was ironic that the woman who had fired his interest had been under his nose for the past two years.

CHAPTER THREE

ON THURSDAY EVENING, Alekos checked the gold watch on his wrist and frowned when he saw that he and Sara needed to leave for the board members' dinner in the next five minutes. Usually when she accompanied him to work functions she was ready in plenty of time. He was annoyed that she had not been waiting for him when he'd walked out of the private bathroom next to his office, where he had showered and changed.

He wondered what she would wear to the dinner. He remembered that a few months ago it had been a particularly busy time at work and Sara had stayed at the office until late, only dashing off to change for the staff Christmas party ten minutes before it was due to start. She had emerged from the cloakroom wearing what he had supposed was a ball gown, but the long black dress had resembled a shroud and had the effect of draining all the colour from her face.

He had been tempted to order her to go and buy something more cheerful. The shop windows were full of mannequins displaying party dresses for the festive season. But then he'd remembered that Sara was grieving for her mother, who had recently died. For once he had studied her closely, and her pinched face and the shadows beneath her eyes had evoked a faint tug of sympathy for his PA, who reminded him of a drab sparrow.

Alekos turned his thoughts to the present. The board members' dinner was a prestigious event that called for him to wear a tuxedo, but he refused to be clean shaven. He glanced in the mirror and grimaced as he ran his hand over the trimmed black stubble on his jaw. No doubt his nemesis Orestis Pagnotis would accuse him of looking more like a pirate than the chairman of a billion-pound company.

Behind him the office door opened and Sara stepped into the room. His jaw dropped as he stared at her reflection in the mirror, and he was thankful he had his back to her so that she couldn't see the betraying bulge of his erection beneath his trousers.

The drab sparrow had metamorphosed into a peacock. Somewhere in Alekos's stunned brain he registered that the description was all the more apt because her dress was peacock-blue silk and the long skirt gave an iridescent shimmer when she walked. The top of the dress was high-necked and sleeveless, leaving her shoulders bare. A sparkling diamanté belt showed off her slender waist.

From the front, the dress was elegant and Alekos had no problem with it. But when Sara turned around to check that the espresso machine was switched off, he saw that her dress was backless to the base of her spine. A hot haze of desire made his blood pound through his veins.

'You can't wear that,' he rasped, shock and lust strangling his vocal cords. 'Half the board members are over sixty and I know for a fact that a couple of them have weak hearts. If they see you in that dress they're likely to suffer a cardiac arrest.'

She looked genuinely confused. 'What's wrong with my dress?'

'Half of it is missing.'

'Well, technically I suppose that's true. But I don't suppose the sight of my shoulder blades will evoke wild lust in anyone.'

Don't bet on it, Alekos thought grimly. He would not have believed that a woman's bare back could be so erotic. The expanse of Sara's skin revealed by the backless dress invited him to trace his fingertips down her spine and then spread his hand over her tempting nakedness.

Theos, what he actually wanted to do was stride over to her, sweep her into his arms and ravish her thoroughly and to their mutual satisfaction on top of his desk. That particular fantasy had been a common theme for the past four days, which had frankly been torturous. Sara had turned up for work each morning wearing outfits that had sent his blood pressure soaring. Her stylish skirts and blouses had hugged her curvy figure without being too revealing, and somehow the hint of her sexy figure beneath her clothes was much more exciting than if she had worn a miniskirt and boob tube.

He checked the time again and realised they would have to leave immediately or risk being late for the dinner. 'God knows what the board members will make of you dressed like a glamour model in a men-only magazine,' he growled as he held the door open and then followed Sara into the corridor. 'You know how conservative some of them are.' He shoved his hands into his pockets out of harm's way, but he could not control the hard thud of his heart, or the hard throb of another part of his anatomy, he acknowledged derisively.

'Nonsense, they'll think I'm wearing a perfectly nice dress,' she said serenely. 'The board members like me. They know I work hard and I would never do anything that might harm the company's image.'

Alekos had to admit she was right. Even his main critic Orestis Pagnotis approved of Sara and had remarked to Alekos that he should consider marrying someone as sensible and down-to-earth as his PA.

The trouble was that Sara no longer looked like his sensible PA. She looked gorgeous and unbelievably sexy, and while Alekos certainly had no thoughts of marrying her he couldn't deny that he wanted her—badly. He was not used to denying himself. But the rules he had made about not getting personally involved with any member of his staff meant that she was forbidden. To a born rebel like himself the word *forbidden* acted like a red rag to a bull. It was a fact of life that you wanted most what you couldn't have, Alekos brooded when they were in the car on the way to the dinner. It was also true that rules were made to be broken.

The restaurant was at a five-star hotel on Park Lane and a private dining room had been booked for the board members' dinner.

'Alekos!' A high-pitched voice assaulted Alekos's ears as he walked into the private function suite, and he swore silently when a young woman ran over to him and greeted him enthusiastically by kissing him on both his cheeks.

'Zelda,' he murmured as he politely but firmly unwound her arms from around his neck. Orestis Pagnotis's granddaughter was as exuberant as a young child but there was nothing childlike about the eighteen-year-old's physical attributes. Alekos was surprised that Orestis had allowed his granddaughter to wear a gold clingy dress with a plunging neckline. But he knew that Zelda was her grandfather's favourite grandchild—a fact she used shamelessly to get her own way.

Zelda had developed a crush on Alekos the previous year when he had spent a few days meeting with some of GE's senior board members aboard the company's flagship yacht, *Artemis*. One night, Alekos had found the teenager waiting for him in his bed. He had managed to persuade her to return to her own cabin and had done his best to avoid her since then.

But the gods were ganging up against him to-

night, he decided as Zelda linked her arm possessively though his and he had no choice but to escort
her into the salon, where champagne cocktails and
canapés were being served. He looked around for
Sara and his temper did not improve when he saw her
chatting with the new whiz-kid CFO. Paul Eddis was
in his early thirties, and Alekos supposed that women
might consider his blond hair and rather delicate fa-
cial features attractive. Sara certainly looked happy
in his company, and Eddis was staring at her with a
stunned expression on his face as if he couldn't believe his luck that the most beautiful woman in the
room was giving him all her attention.

The evening went from bad to worse when they
were called to take their places for dinner and Alekos discovered he was seated next to Zelda. Sara had
arranged the seating plan and he'd specifically asked
her to put him on a different table from Zelda. Had
Sara decided to have a joke at his expense? Alekos
glared across the room to where she was sitting at
another table. But she was facing away from him and
white-hot fury swept through him when he noticed
the waiter ogling her bare back.

He forced himself to eat a little of his cheese souf-
flé, which was as light as air but tasted like card-
board in his mouth. 'Shouldn't you be at school,
studying for exams?' he muttered to Zelda as he
firmly removed her hand from his thigh.

'I've left school.' She giggled. 'Well, the headmis-
tress insisted I leave because she said I was a bad

influence on the other girls. But I don't need to pass exams because I'm going to be a model. Pappoús is paying for me to have my portfolio done with a top photographer.'

'If you don't behave yourself, perhaps your grandfather will refuse to fund your modelling career.'

'Oh, Pappoús will give me anything I ask for.' Zelda leaned closer to Alekos. 'If I don't behave, will you punish me?' she said artfully.

He would like to punish his PA for putting him through an uncomfortable evening. Alekos's furious black gaze bored into Sara's shoulder blades. And yes, they could send a man wild with desire, he discovered. The hellish meal ended eventually but as the band started up and he strode away from the table—ignoring Zelda's plea to dance with her—he was waylaid by Orestis Pagnotis.

The older man glared at Alekos with his gimlet gaze. 'Keep away from my granddaughter. Zelda is an innocent young woman and I will not allow you to corrupt her, Alekos. I've always been concerned that your womanising ways would bring the company into disrepute. I'm sure I don't need to remind you that you need the support of *every* member of the board to implement the changes you want to make within GE.'

Alekos struggled to keep his temper under control. 'Are you threatening me?'

'I suggest you think hard about what I've said,' Orestis warned.

Sara stood up as Alekos approached her table. 'What's wrong? You don't look like you're enjoying the party.'

'I wonder why that is?' he snapped. 'Do you think it could be because you placed me next to Zelda Pagnotis at dinner, after I'd expressly asked you to seat her away from me? Or perhaps it's because Orestis believes that I have designs on his granddaughter, who he thinks is as innocent as a lamb, incidentally.'

'I didn't seat you next to her.' Sara looked puzzled. 'When we arrived I even popped into the dining room to check that the seating plan had been set out as I had organised it… Zelda must have switched the name cards around.'

Alekos's frustration with Orestis's manipulative granddaughter, and his anger with Orestis for threatening to withhold his support at the next board meeting, turned to a different kind of frustration as he stared into Sara's guileless green eyes. Across the room he saw Zelda heading purposefully in his direction. He caught hold of Sara's hand.

'Dance with me,' he ordered, pulling her towards him. She gave him a startled look, but Alekos was too stunned by the fire that ignited inside him when he felt her breasts pressed against his chest to care.

It was impossible to believe that this was the same Sara who had held herself stiffly and ensured that no part of her body touched his when he'd felt duty-bound to ask her to dance with him at the Christmas party. This Sara was soft and pliant in his arms and he was conscious of the hard points of her nipples through his shirt and the surprising firmness of her thighs beneath her silk dress as she moved with him in time to the music.

'I noted that you made sure you were sitting next to Paul Eddis at dinner,' he bit out. The memory of watching Sara leaning her head towards the CFO when they had sat together for the meal evoked an acidic sensation in his gut. *Theos*, was it *jealousy* that had made him want to walk over to Eddis and drag the guy out of his seat? Alekos had never been possessive of a woman in his life, but he felt a burning urge to drape his jacket around Sara's shoulders and hide her naked back from view. 'You are meant to be on duty this evening, not flirting with other members of GE staff, or the waiters.'

Twin spots of colour stained her cheeks and he could tell she was fighting to control her temper. The thought excited Alekos more than it should. He wanted to disturb her composure like she disturbed him.

'I haven't flirted with anyone. You're being ridiculous.'

'Am I?' Alekos succumbed to the demon called temptation and slid his hand up from her waist to her spine. The bare skin of her back was as smooth as silk but, unlike cool silk, her skin was warm and as he spread his fingers wide he felt the heat of her body scald him. 'You must be aware that every man in this room desires you,' he taunted her.

Her eyes widened and he thought he might drown in those mysterious deep green pools. 'Even you?' she taunted him right back.

Her refusal to be cowed by him had earned Alekos's respect when she'd been his prim, plain secretary. But now her sassy tongue shattered the last vestiges of his restraint.

'What do you think?' he growled as he pressed his hand into the small of her back so that her pelvis came into contact with his. The hard ridge of his arousal could leave her in no doubt of the effect she had on him.

'Alekos...' Sara licked her dry lips. Her intention had been to remind him that they were on the dance floor in full view of GE's board members and senior executives. But, instead of sounding crisply efficient in her best PA manner, her voice emerged as a breathy whisper as if she were starring in a soft porn movie, she thought disgustedly.

'Sara,' he mocked, mimicking her husky tone. The way he said her name in his sexy accent, curling his tongue around each syllable, made her toes curl. When she had danced with him at the Christmas party she'd been so tense, terrified he would guess he was all of her fantasies rolled into one. But he'd caught her off guard when he'd pulled her into his arms just now. Dancing with him, her breasts crushed against his broad chest and her cheek resting on the lapel of his jacket, was divine. Beneath her palm she could feel the hard thud of his heart and recognised that its erratic beat echoed her own.

Every day at the office for the past four days had been a refined torture as she'd struggled to hide her awareness of him. It had been easier when he hadn't noticed her, but since she had returned to work after her holiday she'd been conscious of a simmering sexual chemistry between her and Alekos that she had tried to ignore. To be fair, he had seemed as if he was trying to ignore it too and a lot of the time they had been so stiff and polite with each other, as if they were strangers rather than two people who had built up a comfortable working relationship over two years.

But sometimes when she'd stolen a glance at Alekos she'd found him staring at her in a way that made her uncomfortably aware of the heaviness of her breasts and the molten heat that pooled between her thighs. That heat was inside her now, flooding through her veins and making each of her nerve endings ultra-sensitive. She was intensely conscious of his hand resting on her bare back. His touch scorched her skin as if he had branded her, and when she stumbled in her high-heeled shoes he increased the pressure of his fingers on her spine and held her so close that she could feel the muscles and sinews of his hard thighs pressed up against hers.

'Sara...look at me.' His voice was low and seductive, scraping across her sensitised nerves. Impossible to resist. She jerked her gaze upwards as if she were a marionette and he had pulled her strings. Her heart lurched as she was trapped by the dark intensity of his eyes. This had been building all week, she realised. Every searing glance they had shared had throbbed with sexual tension that was now threatening to erupt.

His face was so near to hers that she could feel his warm breath graze her lips. She had never been so close to his mouth before and, oh, God, its sensual curve compelled her to lean into him even closer and part her lips, inviting him to cover her mouth with his.

But she must not allow Alekos to kiss her. Certainly not in front of the board members of GE and the senior executives. Her sudden recollection of their situation shattered the spell he had cast on her. It was acceptable for Alekos to dance with his PA, but not to ravish her in public as the sultry gleam in his eyes warned her that he wanted to do.

The band finished playing and Sara took the opportunity to step away from him, murmuring an excuse that she needed to visit the ladies' room. She resisted the urge to glance back at him as she hurried across the dance floor but she felt his dark eyes burning between her shoulder blades, exposed by her backless dress. Luckily, the bathroom was empty and she stood at a basin and held her wrists under the cold tap to try and cool her heated blood. Thank goodness she had stopped him before he had actually kissed her.

The dull ache in the pit of her stomach mocked her for being a liar. She had wanted him to kiss her more than she'd wanted anything in her life. But her common sense reminded her that if he *had*, they would have crossed the line between employer and employee into dangerous territory.

She knew she couldn't put off returning to the party for much longer but she whiled away a few more minutes by checking her phone for messages. Her heart missed a beat when she saw that she had a text from her father.

Five minutes later, Sara stared at her white face in the mirror and willed herself not to cry. Not now, when she must go back and smile and chat to the party guests as her job demanded. She would have to wait until later, when she was alone, before she could allow her tears to fall. She read Lionel's text one more time.

After considerable thought I have decided that it would be unfair to tell Frederick and Charlotte that they have a half-sister at this time. They were very close to their mother and are still mourning her death. The news that many years ago I was unfaithful to my wife will, I fear, be a great shock to my son and daughter. I hope you will understand my decision. It is not my intention to upset you, Sara, but I must protect Freddie and Charlotte and allow them time and privacy to grieve for their mother. Unfortunately, my position as an MP and public figure means that any revelation that I have an illegitimate daughter would attract a great deal of press interest.

In other words, her father had decided that protecting the feelings of the children from his marriage was more important than publicly acknowledging that *she* was his daughter, Sara thought painfully.

Was it because she was as much of a disappointment to her father as she had been to her mother? All her feelings of self-doubt came flooding back. Maybe she wasn't clever enough, or pretty enough, for her famous father.

And maybe, Sara thought grimly, she should have worn the boring black ball gown to the dinner that she'd bought last year specifically to wear to work functions. The dress was a sensible classic style that did not draw attention to her. Instead tonight she'd worn a daring dress that she had secretly hoped would capture Alekos's attention. What had she been hoping for? Did she really want an affair with Alekos when she knew it would mean the end of her job? She'd felt the evidence of his desire for her when he had held her close while they were dancing. But she did not kid herself that his interest in her would last any longer than with his numerous other mistresses.

Alekos wasn't her knight in shining armour. And neither was her father, she acknowledged bleakly. Her mother had taught her that the only person she could rely on was herself. It was a lesson she was determined not to forget.

* * *

'Where the hell have you been hiding for the last twenty minutes?' Alekos demanded when Sara joined him at the bar. 'I looked everywhere for you.'

'Why, did you need me for some reason?'

'You should know I need my PA to be on hand at all times,' he growled. While Sara had done her disappearing act from the party he'd been forced to hide behind a pillar to avoid Zelda Pagnotis. Alekos feared no man, but an eighteen-year-old girl who was determined to get her claws into him spelled trouble. Sara sat down on a stool and he wondered if he had imagined that she seemed determined not to make eye contact with him.

'Do you want a drink?' He caught the barman's attention and ordered an orange juice, which he knew was Sara's usual choice of drink.

'Actually, I'd like a whisky and soda, please,' she told the barman. 'Make it a double.'

Alekos gave her a close look and noted her face was pale. Tension emanated from her and he wondered if she was in the grip of the same sexual tension that made his muscles feel tight and his blood thunder through his veins. He had tried to convince himself he'd imagined the chemistry that had simmered between them on the dance floor. But his body clenched as he breathed in her perfume. His reaction to her, the way his manhood jerked to attention beneath his trousers, mocked his assumption that his fascination with her was a temporary aberration.

He frowned when she picked up her glass and threw back her drink in a couple of gulps. 'Is something the matter? You seem on edge.'

'I've got a headache,' she muttered.

'If you didn't before, you soon will have after downing a double whisky,' he said drily.

She slid off the bar stool and picked up her purse. 'Seriously, I... I don't feel well and I need to go home.'

Out of the corner of his eye, Alekos spotted Zelda making her way over to the bar. 'I'll drive you,' he told Sara quickly.

She shook her head. 'I'll call a cab. You don't need to leave the party early on my account.'

'It's fine.' He didn't tell her he was glad of an excuse to leave. 'You are my responsibility and of course I'll take you home if you're not feeling well.'

Alekos had driven himself and Sara to the dinner party in his sports car, and so he hadn't had a drink. As soon as they had escaped the busy roads of central London and reached the motorway he opened up the powerful engine. Twenty minutes later, he turned off into a quiet suburb and drew up outside the nondescript bungalow where she lived.

'Thank you for the lift,' she said when he walked round the car and opened her door.

'No problem.'

On the few previous occasions when he had driven her home, she had asked him in for coffee but he had always declined. Tonight she did not issue an invitation but, perversely, Alekos was curious to see inside her home, thinking that he might learn more about the woman who had worked closely with him for two years but about whom, he realised, he knew very little.

'Goodnight.' Sara turned to walk away from him, but she caught her heel on an uneven paving slab and stumbled. *'Ouch.'*

'Are you all right? That's what comes of knocking back a double whisky when you're not used to drinking spirits,' he told her impatiently.

'I've just twisted my ankle a bit. *Alekos…*' her voice rose in protest when he scooped her up into his arms and strode down the garden path to the front door '…really, it's nothing. I'm fine.'

'Give me your key.'

He heard her mutter something beneath her breath but she obviously realised it was pointless to argue with him and dug inside her handbag and gave him a key. He shifted her in his arms so that he could open the front door and carried her into the narrow hallway.

'You can put me down now.' She wriggled in an attempt to make him set her on her feet. The friction of her breasts rubbing against his chest had a predictable effect on Alekos's body. The hunger he had tried to ignore since he had danced with her at the party ignited into an inexorable force that burned in his gut.

'You shouldn't walk in high heels if you've sprained your ankle.'

'I don't suppose it is sprained.' Tension edged into her voice. 'It was kind of you to bring me home but will you please go now?'

He ignored her request and continued walking down the hall, past the sitting room and a small functional kitchen. Both rooms were painted an insipid beige which matched the beige carpet. There were two doors on the opposite side of the hall. 'Which is your room?'

'The second door. I can manage now, thanks,' Sara said when he shouldered the door and carried her into her bedroom. She flicked the light switch and Alekos was surprised by the room's décor. The walls were covered with murals of exquisite, brightly coloured flowers and the floral theme extended to the curtains and bedspread. The single bed was piled with stuffed toy bears and a large pink rabbit, which he guessed were relics from her childhood. The room was a vibrant and startling contrast to the otherwise characterless house.

'You obviously like flowers,' he murmured. 'Who painted the murals?'

'I did.'

'Seriously?' He was amazed. 'You're very talented. Did you study art?'

'No,' she said shortly. 'My mother thought I would be wasting my time going to art school. It was her idea that I trained as a secretary because it's a more reliable career.'

* * *

Sara wished Alekos would leave. She considered struggling to force him to put her down, but his arms around her were like iron bands and she did not relish an undignified tussle. It was bad enough that he believed she had been affected by alcohol and it was the reason she had tripped and hurt her ankle. He had probably only carried her into the house because he'd felt it was his duty not to leave her sprawled in the gutter. But she did not want him in her bedroom. It was her personal space, and when her mother had been alive it had been the only place where she had been able to indulge the creative side of her nature that she'd recently discovered she had inherited from her father.

Her father who had refused to tell her half-siblings that she was his daughter.

Every word of the text her father had sent her was imprinted on her memory. She told herself it was understandable that Lionel Kingsley cared more about his children from his marriage than for the illegitimate daughter whose existence he had only been aware of for a few months. But it felt like a rejection and it hurt. She had no other family. Her mother had grown up in a children's home, and after Joan had died Sara had felt completely alone until she had met her father.

The tears she'd managed to hold back while she had been at the party filled her eyes and slid down her face. She brushed them away with her hand and swallowed a sob but she felt so empty inside, knowing that she would not now meet her half-brother and half-sister at the weekend. And maybe never, she thought bleakly. Perhaps her father regretted finding out about her.

'Sara, why are you crying? Does your ankle hurt?' Alekos sounded terse. Sara knew he hated displays of emotion as much as she hated displaying her emotions in front of anyone. Even when her mother had died she'd accepted Alekos's rather stilted words of sympathy with quiet dignity and had sensed his relief that she'd kept her emotions out of the office.

But she could not stop crying. Perhaps the whisky she'd drunk at the party had loosened her grip on her self-control. Her father's text had left her utterly bereft and the sense of loneliness that she'd always felt—because she'd never had a strong emotional bond with her mother—now overwhelmed her and she turned her face into Alekos's chest and wept.

Somewhere in her haze of misery she acknowledged that the situation was undoubtedly Alekos's worst nightmare. She remembered an occasion when one of his ex-lovers whom he'd recently dumped had stormed into his office in floods of tears and accused him of breaking her heart. Alekos had literally shuddered in disgust at his ex's undignified behaviour. What must he think of her? Sara wondered. But her tears kept coming. It was as though a dam inside her had burst and allowed her pent-up emotions to escape.

She expected Alekos to stand her on her feet before he beat a hasty retreat from the house. But he didn't. Instead he sat down on the edge of her bed and cradled her in his lap. She was aware of the muscled strength of his arms around her, and the steady beat of his heart that she could hear through his chest was oddly comforting. It was a novelty to feel cared for, even though she knew Alekos's show of tenderness wasn't real. He did not care about her. He'd reminded her when he'd offered to drive her home from the party that she was a member of his staff and therefore his responsibility.

But it was nice to pretend for a few minutes that he actually *meant* the gentle words of comfort he murmured. His voice was softer than she'd ever heard it, and she could almost fool herself that it was the intimate voice of a lover caressing her senses like the brush of velvet against her skin. Gradually her harsh sobs subsided and as she drew a shaky breath she inhaled the spicy musk of Alekos's aftershave mixed with an indefinable male scent that was uniquely him.

In that instant she became conscious of his hard thighs beneath her bottom and the latent strength of his arms around her. Heat flared inside her and she felt a sensuous heaviness in her breasts and at the molten heart of her femininity.

She could not have said exactly when she sensed a change in him, only that she became aware that his breathing became irregular and his heartbeat beneath her ear quickened and thudded hard and fast. Desire stole through her veins as she lifted her head away from his chest. Her heart lurched when she saw the fierce glitter in his eyes.

'Sara—' His voice throbbed with a raw hunger that made her tremble as she watched him lower his face closer to hers. She stared at his mouth. His sensual, beautiful mouth. So often she had imagined him kissing her with his mouth that promised heaven. 'You're driving me crazy,' he growled before he covered her lips with his and the world went up in flames.

CHAPTER FOUR

HE HAD WANTED to kiss Sara all evening. All week, if he was honest, Alekos admitted to himself, remembering how he had barely been able to keep his hands off her at the office. By the end of each day his gut had felt as if it were tied in a knot, and punishing workouts at the gym after work had failed to relieve his sexual frustration.

There was only one way to assuage the carnal hunger that ignited inside him and made him shake with need. The ache in his groin intensified when Sara parted her lips beneath his and her warm breath filled his mouth. He kissed her the way he'd fantasised about kissing her when he'd first caught sight of her wearing her backless dress. At the party he'd struggled to concentrate on his conversations with the other guests, when all he could think about was running his hands over Sara's naked back. Now he indulged himself and stroked his fingertips up her spine before he clasped her bare shoulders and pulled her even closer to him.

If she had offered the slightest resistance, perhaps he would have come to his senses. But his heart slammed into his ribs when she wound her arms round his neck and threaded her fingers into his hair. Her eager response decimated the last vestiges of his control, and he groaned as he dipped his tongue into her mouth and tasted her. She was nectar, sweet and hot and utterly intoxicating. In the far recesses of his mind Alekos was aware that he should stop this madness. Sara was his secretary, which meant she was off-limits. But it was impossible to associate the beautiful, sensual woman who had driven him to distraction over the past few days with his plain PA who had never warranted a second glance.

She shifted her position on his lap and he groaned again as her bottom ground against his rock-hard erection. He couldn't remember the last time he had felt so turned on. He felt as if he was going to explode and the faint warning voice inside his head was drowned out by the drumbeat of his desire to feel Sara's soft curves beneath him.

He manoeuvred her so that she was lying on the bed and he stretched out on top of her before capturing her mouth once more and kissing her with a deepening hunger that demanded to be appeased. Trailing his lips down her throat, he slid his hand behind her neck into the heavy silk of her hair and discovered that three tiny buttons secured the top of her dress. Three tiny buttons were all that prevented him from pulling the top of her dress down and re-

vealing her ripe breasts that had tantalised him when
they had been pressed against his chest. Urgency
made his fingers uncooperative. He swore beneath
his breath as he struggled to unfasten the buttons
and something soft fell across his face.

Lifting his head, Alekos found himself eye to eye
with a large pink rabbit. The incongruousness of
making love to a woman on a narrow single bed
adorned with stuffed animals catapulted him back
to reality. This was not any woman. This was Sara,
his efficient, unflappable PA, who apparently had
an unexpected liking for cuddly toys. He was only
here in her bedroom because she had shockingly
burst into tears.

Usually, when faced with a weeping woman, Alekos's instinct was to extricate himself from the situation as quickly possible. But Sara's tears had had an
odd effect on him and inexplicably he'd found himself trying to comfort her. He had no idea why she
had been crying. But he remembered that in the car
when he'd driven her home she had read a text message on her phone and had looked upset.

Memories pushed through the sexual haze that
had clouded Alekos's mind. Sara had hurried out
of the office at the beginning of the week to meet
someone. She had admitted she'd spent her holiday
with a male 'friend' at his villa, and she had returned
from the French Riviera transformed from a frump
into a gorgeous sexpot. At the start of this evening
she had seemed happy, but something had happened

that had caused her to act out of character and she'd gulped down a double whisky as if it was no stronger than milk.

The most likely explanation Alekos could think of for Sara's distress was that her holiday romance was over. So what the hell was he—*the consolation prize*? He rolled away from her and sat up, assuring himself he was glad he had come to his senses before any harm had been done. Before he'd made the mistake of having sex with her. A kiss was nothing and there was no reason why they couldn't put it behind them and continue with their good working relationship as they had done for the past two years.

He stared at her flushed face and her kiss-stung mouth that tempted him to forget everything and allow the passion that had sizzled between them moments ago to soar to its natural conclusion. But apart from all the other considerations to them sleeping together—and there were many—Alekos did not relish the idea that Sara wanted someone else and he was second best. *Theos*, he'd spent much of his life feeling second best to his dead brother and believing that, in his father's opinion, he was inferior to Dimitri.

'Alekos.' Sara's soft voice made his gut clench. She sat up and pushed her hair back from her face. She looked as stunned as he felt, and oddly vulnerable. For a moment he had the ridiculous idea that having a man in her bedroom was a new experience for her. 'We…we shouldn't have done that,' she said huskily.

He was well aware of that fact, but he was irritated she had pointed it out. 'It was just a kiss.' He shrugged, as much to emphasise the unimportance of the kiss to himself as well as to her. 'Don't look so stricken, Sara. It won't happen again.' Anger with himself for being so damned weak made him say harshly, 'It wouldn't have happened at all if you hadn't practically begged me to kiss you.'

'I did no such thing.' Fiery colour flared on her cheeks. 'You kissed me. One minute you were comforting me because I was upset, and the next...'

Alekos did not want to think about what had happened next. Remembering how he had explored the moist interior of Sara's mouth with his tongue, and the little moans she had made when he had kissed her, caused his erection to press uncomfortably against the restriction of his trousers.

'Ah, yes, you were upset—' he focused on the first part of her sentence '—I'm guessing that the reason you were crying was because your holiday lover has dumped you. Your eagerness to kiss me was because you're on the rebound from the guy in France who has rejected you.'

'There was no holiday lover,' she said tightly. 'The "guy in France" was my *father*. I spent my holiday at his villa.' Sara's bottom lip trembled. 'But you're right to think I feel rejected. I'm starting to believe my father regrets that he got in contact with me. Until recently I didn't know about him, or that I have a half-brother and half-sister.' Tears slid down her cheeks. She gave a choked sob and covered her face with her hands, and so did not see Alekos's grim expression.

He had never seen Sara cry until tonight and his abhorrence of emotional displays meant that he really didn't want to stick around. But the fact that she was crying in front of him suggested something serious had happened to upset her. Why, even when she had come to work one Monday morning just before Christmas and told him that her mother had died at the weekend she had kept her emotions in check.

He felt an odd tug in his chest as he watched Sara's body shudder as she tried to regain control of herself. Ignoring a strong temptation to leave her to it, he pulled the dressing table stool next to the bed and sat down on it before he handed her some tissues from the box on the bedside table.

'Thanks,' she said indistinctly. Her tears had washed away most of her make-up, and again Alekos was struck by her air of innocence that he told himself he must have imagined.

'What did you mean when you said you think your father regrets contacting you? Had there been a rift between the two of you?'

She shook her head. 'It's complicated. I met my father for the first time six weeks ago. When my holiday plans to Spain fell through he invited me to stay at his villa in Antibes. He wasn't there for the whole time, but he came to visit me and we began to get to know each other. I pretended to anyone who asked that I was employed as a housekeeper at the villa because my father was worried about the media.' Her voice broke. 'I'm a scandal from his past, you see, and he doesn't want his other children to find out about me.'

'But why would the media be interested in your father?'

'Because he's famous. I promised I would keep my relationship to him secret until he is ready to publicly acknowledge that I am his illegitimate daughter.'

She was her father's shameful secret, Sara thought miserably. And from the text that Lionel had sent her earlier, it seemed as though she would remain a secret and never meet her half-siblings. She hadn't revealed her father's identity to anyone, not even her closest friend, Ruth, who she had known since they were at primary school. But the truth about her father that at first had been such a wonderful surprise had become a burden she longed to share with someone.

She blinked away yet more tears. Her head ached from crying and she wished she could rest it on the pillows. But if she did that, Alekos might think she was inviting him to lie on the bed with her and kiss her again. She darted a glance at him and heat ran through her veins as she remembered the weight of him pressing her into the mattress and the feel of his muscular thighs as he'd ground his hips against her pelvis.

Of course she hadn't 'practically begged him to

kiss her', as he'd accused her, she assured herself. But she hadn't stopped him. She bit her lip. Alekos had been the one to draw back, and if he hadn't... The tugging sensation in the pit of her stomach became a sharp pull of need as her imagination ran riot and she pictured them both naked, their limbs entwined and his body joined with hers.

She flushed as her eyes crashed into his glittering dark gaze and she realised that he was aware she had been staring at him.

'Why did you only meet your father for the first time recently?'

'He wasn't part of my life when I was growing up.' She shrugged to show him it didn't hurt, even though it did. 'My mother was employed as my father's secretary when they had an affair. He was married with a family, but he decided that he wanted to try and save his marriage and ended his relationship with Mum. She moved away without telling him that she was pregnant. She refused to talk about him and I have no idea why, in the last week of her life, she wrote to him and told him about me.'

She sighed. 'My father found out about me six months ago, but his wife was ill and he waited until after she had died before he phoned and asked if we could meet. He said he was glad he had found me. He'd assumed that my mother had told me his identity. Now I'm wondering if his reason for finding me was because he feared I might sell the story about my famous father to the newspapers. If the press got hold of the story it could damage his relationship with his children from his marriage. And I imagine the scandal that he'd had an affair, even though it was years ago, might harm his political career.'

Alekos's brows rose. 'Your father is a politician?'

Sara felt torn between her promise to protect her father's identity and what she told herself was a selfish need to unburden her secret to *someone*. But to Alekos? Strangely, he was the one person she trusted above all others. The tabloids made much of his playboy reputation, but she knew another side to him. He was dedicated to GE and worked hard to make it a globally successful business. He was a tough but fair employer and he was intensely protective of his mother and sisters. He guarded his own privacy fiercely, but could she trust that he would guard hers?

'It's vital that the story isn't leaked to the media,' she cautioned.

'You know my feelings about the scum who are fondly known as the paparazzi,' he said sardonically. 'I'm not likely to divulge anything you tell me in confidence to the press.'

She snatched a breath. 'My father is Lionel Kingsley.' It was the first time she had ever said the words aloud and it felt strange. Alekos looked shocked and she wondered if she had been naïve to confide in him. Now he knew something about her that no one else knew, and for some reason that made her feel vulnerable.

He gave a low whistle. 'Do you mean the Right Honourable Lionel Kingsley, MP—the Minister for Culture and the Arts? I've met him on a few occasions, both socially and also in his capacity as Culture Secretary, when I sponsored an exhibition of Greek art at the British Museum. As a matter of fact he was a guest at a party I went to earlier this week.'

'It sounds as though you have a lot more in common with my father than I do,' Sara muttered. She didn't move in the exalted social circles that Alekos and Lionel did, and she would definitely never have the opportunity to meet her father or her half-siblings socially. She tried to focus on what Alekos was saying.

'What has happened to make you think your father regrets finding you?'

'I was supposed to go and stay at his home at the weekend so that I could meet my half-siblings. But Lionel has decided against telling Freddie and Charlotte about me. It's only two months since their mother died. They were very close to her, and he's worried about how they will react to the news that he had been unfaithful to his wife.'

She pressed her hand to her temple, which had started to throb. 'I get the impression that I'm a complication and Lionel wishes he hadn't told me he is my father. His name isn't on my birth certificate and there's no possibility I could have found out I'm his daughter.'

She swung her legs off the bed and stood up.

Alekos also got to his feet and her small bedroom seemed to be dominated by his six-feet-plus of raw masculinity.

'You should go,' she said abruptly, feeling too strung out to play the role of polite hostess. 'What happened just now…when we kissed…' her face flamed when he said nothing but looked amused, damn him '…obviously it can never happen again. I mean, you have a strict rule about not sleeping with your staff. Not that I'm suggesting you want to sleep with me,' she added quickly, in case he thought she was hinting that she hoped he wanted to have an affair with her.

Hot with embarrassment, she ploughed on, 'It was an unfortunate episode and I blame my behaviour on the whisky I drank earlier.'

'Rubbish.' Alekos laughed softly. 'You're not drunk. And I haven't had a drink all night. Alcohol had nothing to do with why we kissed. It was chemistry that ignited between us and made us both act out of character.'

'Exactly.' Sara seized on his words. 'It was a mistake, and the best thing we can do is to forget it happened.'

He deliberately lowered his eyes to her breasts, and she fought the temptation to cross her arms over her chest and hide her nipples that she was aware had hardened and must be visible jutting beneath the silky material of her dress. Somehow she made herself look at him calmly.

'Do you think it will be possible to forget the passion that exploded between us?' he murmured.

'It has to be, if I am going to continue as your PA.' She sounded fiercer than she had intended as she fought a rising sense of panic that the memory of Alekos kissing her would stay in her mind for a very long time. 'And now I really would like you to leave. It's late, and I'm tired.'

He checked his watch and said in an amused voice, 'It's a quarter to ten, which is hardly late. We left the dinner early because you said you were feeling unwell.'

To her relief he said no more and walked over to the door. 'I'll see myself out. And Sara—' his gaze held hers and his tone was suddenly serious '—your secret is safe with me. For what it's worth, I think your father should feel very proud to have you as his daughter.'

Alekos's unexpected compliment was the last straw for Sara's battered emotions. She held on until she heard the front door bang as he closed it behind him before she gave in to the tears that had threatened her composure since he had *stopped* kissing her.

Yes, she was upset about her father, but she was horrified to admit that she was more hurt by Alekos's rejection. She couldn't forget that he had been the one who had come to his senses. But what did her tears say about her? Why was she crying over a man who hadn't paid her any attention for two years?

He had only noticed her recently because she'd re-vamped her appearance.

Alekos's interest in her was a passing fancy, but he could very easily break her heart if she allowed him to. She wished she *had* been drunk tonight, she brooded. At least then she could forgive herself for responding to him the way she had. Instead she only had her foolish heart to blame.

It took all of Sara's willpower to make herself stroll into Alekos's office the next morning and give him a cheerful smile before she turned her attention to the espresso machine.

His eyes narrowed when she walked over to his desk and placed a cup of coffee in front of him. She had resisted the urge to wear the beige dress that still lurked in the back of her wardrobe—a remnant of her previous dreary style. Out of sheer bravado she had chosen a bright red skirt and a red-and-white polka-dot blouse. Red stilettos and a slick of scarlet lip gloss completed her outfit. Her layered hairstyle flicked the tops of her shoulders as she sat down composedly and waited for him to give her instructions for the day.

'You're looking very perky. I trust you are feeling better?'

The gleam in his dark eyes was almost her undoing, but she had promised herself that she wouldn't let him rattle her and so she smiled and said coolly,

'Much better, thank you. I'm just sorry that you had to leave the dinner early last night because of me.'

'I'm not,' he murmured. The gleam turned to something darker and hotter as he skimmed his gaze down from her pink cheeks to her dotty blouse, and Sara was sure he was remembering the passion that had exploded between them in her bedroom.

She was conscious of the pulse at the base of her throat beating erratically and said hurriedly, 'Shall we get on? I thought you wanted to go through the final details for the Monaco Yacht Show.'

Alekos's sardonic smile told her he had seen through her distraction ploy, but to her relief he opened the folder in front of him. 'As you know, GE is one of the top exhibitors at the show, and we will be using the company's show yacht to give tours and demonstrations to potential clients interested in buying a superyacht. I've heard from the captain of *Artemis* that she has docked in Monaco and the crew are preparing her for the show. You and I will fly out to meet the rest of the sales team, and we will stay on board the yacht.'

For the rest of the morning, work was the only topic of conversation and if Sara tried hard she could almost pretend that the events of the previous night hadn't happened. It helped if she didn't look directly at Alekos but on the occasions when she did make eye contact with him the glittering heat in his gaze caused her stomach to dip. Alekos had called it *chemistry*, and its tangible presence every time she stepped into his office simmered between them and filled the room with a prickling tension that seemed to drain the air from Sara's lungs.

She was relieved when he left for a lunch appointment and told her he did not expect to be back until later in the afternoon. But, perversely, once he had gone she missed him and couldn't settle down to her work because she kept picturing his ruggedly handsome face and reliving the feel of his lips on hers. It was just a kiss, she reminded herself. But deep down she knew that something fundamental had changed between her and Alekos. She had hidden her feelings for him for two years, but it was so much harder to hide her desire for him when he looked at her with a hungry gleam in his eyes that made her ache with longing.

He returned just before five o'clock and seemed surprised to find her still at her desk. 'I thought you wanted to leave early tonight.'

'I'm not going to visit my father at his home in Berkshire now, so I thought I might as well catch up on some filing,' she said in a carefully controlled voice. She was embarrassed that she had cried in front of Alekos last night and was determined to hide her devastation over her father's change of heart about introducing her to her half-siblings.

His speculative look gave her the unsettling notion that he could read her thoughts. 'I've been thinking about your situation and I have an idea of how to help. Come into my office. I'm sure you would rather not discuss a personal matter where anyone walking past could overhear us.'

Sara didn't want to have a personal discussion with him anywhere, but he held open his office door and she could not think of an excuse to refuse. Besides, she was intrigued that he had actually thought about her. 'What idea?' she said as soon as he had shut the door.

He walked around his desk and waited until she was seated opposite him before he replied. 'On Sunday evening I have been invited to the launch of a new art gallery in Soho.'

'I'm up to speed with your diary, Alekos.' She hid her disappointment that he had brought her in to discuss his busy social schedule. But why would he be interested in her problems?

He ignored her interruption. 'The gallery's owner, Jemima Wilding, represents several well-established artists, but she also wants to support new talent and the gallery's launch will include paintings by an up-and-coming artist, Freddie Kingsley.'

Sara's heart gave an odd thump. 'I didn't know that my half-brother was an artist.'

'I believe Freddie and Charlotte both studied art at Chelsea College of Art. Charlotte is establishing herself as a fashion designer. She will be at the gallery launch on Sunday to support her brother, along with Lionel Kingsley.'

'Why are you telling me this?' She could not keep the bitterness from her voice. Alekos was emphasising what she already knew—that she did not belong in the rarefied world that her father and half-siblings, and Alekos himself, occupied.

'Because my idea is that you could accompany me to the gallery launch to meet your half-siblings. I realise you won't be able to say that you are related to them, but you might have a chance to talk to your father in private during the evening and persuade him to reveal your true identity.'

Her heart gave another lurch as she tried to imagine meeting Freddie and Charlotte. Would they notice the physical similarities she shared with them? Probably not, she reassured herself. They were unaware that they had an illegitimate half-sister. Alekos was offering her what might be her only opportunity to meet her blood relations. Common sense doused her excitement. 'It would look strange if you took your PA to a private engagement.'

'Possibly, but you wouldn't be there as my PA. You would accompany me as my date. My mistress,' he explained when she stared at him uncomprehendingly.

For a third time Sara's heart jolted against her ribs. 'We agreed to forget about the kiss we shared last night.' She flushed, hating how she sounded breathless when she had intended her voice to be cool and crisp.

His eyes gleamed like hot coals for a second before the fire in those dark depths was replaced by a faintly cynical expression that Sara was more used to seeing. 'I don't remember agreeing to forget about it,' he drawled. 'But I'm suggesting that we *pretend* to be in a relationship. If people believe you are my girlfriend it will seem perfectly reasonable for you to be with me.'

'I can see a flaw in your plan.' Several flaws, as it happened, but she focused on the main one. 'You have made it clear that you would never become personally involved with any member of your staff. If we are seen together in public it's likely that the board members of GE will believe we are having an affair. They disapprove of your playboy reputation and might even decide to take a vote of no confidence against you.'

'That won't happen. As you said yourself, the board members approve of you. They think you are a good, stabilising influence on me,' he said drily.

Sara remembered the many glamorous blondes Alekos had dated in the past. 'I'm not sure your friends would be convinced that you and I are in a relationship,' she said doubtfully.

'They'd have been convinced if they had seen us together last night.' His wicked grin made her blush. 'The plan will work because of the sexual chemistry between us. There's no point in denying it.' He did not give her a chance to speak. 'It is an inconvenient attraction that we might as well use to our advantage.'

So she was an inconvenience! It was hardly a flattering description. 'Why are you willing to help me meet my half-siblings? You've never taken an interest in my personal life before.'

He shrugged. 'You're right to guess I am not being entirely altruistic. Zelda Pagnotis will also be at the gallery launch. She is a friend of Jemima Wilding's daughter, Leah. You saw how Zelda followed me around at the board members' dinner, how she changed the name cards around so that she was seated next to me.' Frustration clipped his voice. 'Her crush on me is becoming a problem, but if she believes that you are my girlfriend it might persuade her to move her attention onto another guy.'

'Are you saying you need me to protect you from Zelda?'

'Orestis thinks I want to corrupt his granddaughter,' Alekos growled. 'Of course nothing could be further from the truth, but I guarantee Orestis won't disapprove of you being my mistress. He's more likely to be relieved.'

'But why don't you flaunt a genuine mistress in front of Zelda? There must be dozens of women who would jump at the chance to go on a date with you.'

'I don't happen to have a girlfriend at the moment. If I invite one of my exes to the gallery launch there's a risk they will read too much into it and believe I want to get back with them.'

'What it is to be Mr Popular,' Sara murmured wryly. Alekos's arrogance was infuriating, but he had a point. In the two years that she had been his

PA she'd realised that women threw themselves at him without any encouragement from him.

He hadn't needed to encourage her to kiss him last night. She flushed as she remembered how eagerly she had responded to him. But he had called a halt to their passion even though he must have sensed that she wanted him to make love to her. Now he was asking her to pretend to be in love with him, and she was afraid she would be too convincing.

'What do you think of my idea, Sara? It seems to me that it will be an ideal solution for both of us.'

She looked into his dark eyes and her heart gave a familiar swoop. 'I need time to think about it.'

He frowned. 'How much time? I'll need to let Jemima know that I am bringing a guest.'

Sara refused to let him browbeat her into making a decision. Although she longed to meet her half-siblings she was worried about how her father might react to seeing her at a social event. 'Phone me in the morning and I'll give you my answer,' she said calmly. She stood up and walked over to the door, but then hesitated and turned to look at him.

'Thank you for offering to help me meet my half-siblings. I appreciate it.'

Alekos waited until Sara had closed the door behind her before he strode over to the drinks cabinet and poured himself a double measure of malt Scotch. Her smile had hit him like a punch in his gut. He'd always known he was a bastard, and Sara had confirmed it when she'd said that she appreciated his help.

He raked his hair off his brow. Sara had no idea that her revelation about her father's identity was a very useful piece of knowledge that he intended to use to his advantage. His keenness to attend the gallery launch had nothing to do with an interest in art and everything to do with business. Alekos knew that the Texan oil billionaire Warren McCuskey was on the guest list. He also knew that McCuskey and Lionel Kingsley were close friends.

The story went that many years ago both men had been amateur sailors competing in a transatlantic yacht race, but the American had nearly lost his life when his boat had capsized. Lionel Kingsley had been leading the race but had sacrificed his chance of winning when he'd gone to McCuskey's assistance. Three decades later, Warren McCuskey had become one of the richest men in the US and the person who had the most influence over him was his good friend, English politician Lionel Kingsley—who, astonishingly, happened to be Sara's father.

Alekos was aware that networking was a crucial part of business, and the best deals were forged at social events where the champagne flowed freely. He'd heard that McCuskey was considering splashing out some of his huge fortune on a superyacht. At the party on Sunday evening, Sara would want to spend time with her father, and it would be an ideal opportunity for him to ingratiate himself with the Texan billionaire.

He took a swig of his Scotch and ignored the twinge of his conscience as he thought of Sara and how he planned to use a fake affair with her for his own purpose. All was fair in love and business, he thought sardonically. Not that he knew anything about love. GE was his top priority and he had a responsibility, a *duty*, to ensure that the company was as successful as it would undoubtedly have been under Dimitri's leadership. He secretly suspected that his brother had thrown his life away because of a woman. But Alekos would never allow any woman close to his heart and certainly not to influence his business strategy.

CHAPTER FIVE

THE LIMOUSINE CAME to a halt beside the kerb and Alekos prepared to step out of the car, when Sara's voice stopped him.

'I don't think I can go through with it.' Her voice shook. 'You didn't say the press would be here.'

He glanced out of the window at the group of journalists and cameramen gathered on the pavement outside the Wilding Gallery. 'There was bound to be some media interest. Jemima Wilding is well-known in the art world and naturally she wants exposure for her new gallery. I suspect she leaked the names on the guest list to the paparazzi,' he said drily.

The chauffeur opened the door but Sara did not move. 'Doesn't it bother you that photos of us arriving together might be published in the newspapers and give the impression that we are…a couple?'

'But that's the point.' Alekos stifled his impatience, realising he needed to reassure her. When he'd phoned Sara on Saturday morning, she had said she would pretend to be his mistress and accompany him to the gallery launch. Now she seemed to be having second thoughts. 'You want to meet your half-siblings, don't you?' he reminded her of the reason she had agreed to his plan.

'Of course I do. But I'm worried my father will be angry when he sees me. He might think I came here tonight to put pressure on him to tell Charlotte and Freddie about me.'

'Then we will have to put on a convincing act that you are my girlfriend and you are at the party with me.'

'I suppose so.' She still sounded unsure. Alekos watched her sink her teeth into her soft lower lip and was tempted to soothe the maligned flesh with his tongue. But such an action, although undoubtedly enjoyable, would be wasted here in the car where they couldn't be seen.

Glancing out of the window again, he noticed a young woman, wearing a skirt so short it was not much more than a belt, standing in the glass-fronted lobby of the gallery. He gritted his teeth. Zelda Pagnotis was an irritating thorn in his side, but unless he took drastic action to end her crush on him the teenager could become a more serious problem and cause a further rift between him and her grandfather.

'Thank you, Mike,' Alekos said to the chauffeur as he climbed out of the car and held out his hand to Sara. After a few seconds' hesitation she put her fingers in his and stepped onto the pavement. She stiffened when he slid his arm around her waist and escorted her over to the entrance of the art gallery. As Alekos had predicted, the paparazzi took pictures of him and Sara, and she pressed closer to him and put her head down as the flashbulbs went off around them when they walked into the building.

A doorman stepped forwards to take her coat. It had been raining earlier when the car had collected her from her house and Alekos hadn't seen what she was wearing beneath her raincoat until now.

Theos! He tore his eyes from her and glanced around him, thinking he had spoken out loud. But no one was looking at him. He returned his gaze to her and stared. 'Your dress…'

'Is it all right?' Her tongue darted out to moisten her lips. The gesture betrayed her nervousness and sent a shaft of white-hot desire through Alekos. 'Is my dress suitable?' she said in an undertone. 'Why are you staring at me?'

'It's more than suitable. You look incredible.' He ran his eyes over her bare shoulders, revealed by her emerald silk strapless dress, down to the rounded curves of her breasts that made him think of ripe peaches, firm and delicately flushed, tempting him to taste them. Lowering his gaze still further, he noted how the design of the dress drew attention to her slim waist before the skirt flared over her hips and fell to just above her knees.

Forcing his eyes back up her body, he noted how her layered hair swirled around her shoulders when she turned her head, and the hot ache in his groin intensified when he imagined her silky hair brushing across his naked chest as he lifted her on top of him and guided her down onto his hard shaft.

'Theos.' This time he spoke aloud in a rough voice as he curved his hand behind her neck and drew her towards him. He saw her eyes widen until they were huge green pools that pulled him in.

'Alekos,' she whispered warningly, as if to remind him that they were not alone in the lobby. But she didn't pull away as he lowered his face towards hers.

'Sara,' he mocked softly. And then he covered her mouth with his and kissed her, long and slow, and then deep and hard when she parted her lips and kissed him back with a sweet intensity that made his gut twist and made him want to sweep her up in his arms and carry her off to somewhere where they could be alone.

The low murmur of voices pushed into his consciousness and he reluctantly lifted his head and snatched oxygen into his lungs. Sara looked as stunned as he felt, but he had no intention of admitting that what had just happened was a first for him. He had *never* kissed a woman in public before. As he stepped away from her he caught sight of Zelda Pagnotis hurrying out of the lobby wearing a sulky expression on her face.

'First objective of the evening completed,' he told Sara smoothly, keen to hide the effect she had on him. 'Zelda can't doubt that we are having an affair.

I've just spotted Lionel Kingsley and his son and daughter. Are you ready to meet your half-siblings?'

Sara could feel her heart hammering beneath her ribs as she walked with Alekos into the main gallery. She was excited that in a few moments she would meet her half-brother and half-sister for the first time, but she was still reeling from the sizzling kiss she had shared with Alekos.

While she'd been in his arms she had forgotten where they were, or why he had brought her to the art gallery. But when he had lifted his mouth from hers, she'd seen Zelda Pagnotis walk past them and realised that Alekos had deliberately kissed her in view of the teenager. *First objective completed.* She recalled his words ruefully. What an idiot she was to have believed that he'd kissed her because he desired her.

She looked ahead to the group of people Alekos was heading towards and her heart beat harder when she saw her father. Lionel was frowning as he watched her approach and her hesitant smile faltered. *She shouldn't have come.* The last thing she wanted to do was alienate her father. Her steps slowed and she felt a strong urge to run out of the gallery, but Alekos slipped his arm around her waist and propelled her forwards.

A tall woman with purple hair detached from the group and greeted them. 'Alekos, darling, I'm so glad you were able to come this evening. That was quite an entrance you made,' she said in an amused voice that made Sara blush. 'You must be Sara. I'm Jemima Wilding. I'm so pleased to meet you. Alekos, I think you and Lionel Kingsley have met before.'

'We have indeed.' Lionel shook Alekos's hand. 'Your financial support of the Greek art exhibition last year was much appreciated. But actually we met very recently at a party earlier this week.' He glanced at Alekos's hand resting on Sara's waist. 'You were unaccompanied on that occasion.'

'Yes, unfortunately Sara had another commitment,' Alekos said smoothly. He tightened his arm around Sara's waist as if he guessed that her heart was fluttering like a trapped bird in her chest. 'This is Sara Lovejoy.'

To Sara, the silence seemed to last for ever and stretched her nerves to the snapping point. But in reality Lionel Kingsley hesitated infinitesimally before he shook her hand. 'I am delighted to meet you... Miss Lovejoy.'

'Sara,' she said thickly. Her throat felt constricted and she smiled gratefully at Alekos when he handed her a flute of champagne from a passing waiter.

Lionel introduced the other people in the group, starting with a stockily built man with a rubicund face. 'This is my good friend Warren McCuskey, who flew to London from Texas especially so that he could attend the gallery launch and support my son Freddie's first exhibition.'

Sara greeted Warren with a polite smile, but her

heart was thumping as Freddie Kingsley stretched his hand towards her. She prayed no one would notice her hand was trembling as she held it out to him.

Her half-brother smiled. 'Pleased to meet you, Sara.'

'I...' Emotion clogged her throat as Freddie closed his fingers around hers. His handshake was firm and his skin felt warm beneath her fingertips. Her secret drummed in her brain. Freddie was unaware that the blood running through his veins was partly the same as her blood. She swallowed and tried to speak but the lump in her throat prevented her.

Alekos moved imperceptibly closer, as if he understood that her emotions were balanced on a knife-edge. There was something comforting about his big-framed, solid presence at her side and, to her relief, she could suddenly breathe again.

'It's lovely to meet you,' she told Freddie softly. Her half-brother was taller than she had imagined, his brown hair curled over his collar and his smile was wide and welcoming. She looked into his green eyes and recognised herself.

He gave her a puzzled look. 'Have we met before? Your face seems familiar.'

'No, we've never met.' Sara was conscious of her father standing a few feet away and wondered if she was the only person in the group who could sense Lionel's tension.

Freddie shrugged. 'You definitely remind me of

someone but I can't think who. Are you interested in art, Sara?'

'Very. I'd love to see your work.'

She followed Freddie over to where six of his paintings were displayed against a white wall. Even to her untrained eye she could tell that he was a gifted artist. His use of intense colour and light made his landscapes bold and exciting.

'My brother is very talented, isn't he?'

Sara turned her head towards the voice and discovered her half-sister standing next to her.

'I'm Charlotte Kingsley, by the way. I really like your dress.' Charlotte grinned and murmured, 'I really like your gorgeous boyfriend too. And he seems very keen on you. Even when he is talking to other people he can't keep his eyes off you. Have the two of you been together long?'

'Um…not that long.' Sara experienced the same difficulty speaking that had happened when she'd met Freddie. She felt an instant connection with Charlotte which made her think that maybe they could become friends. But perhaps her half-siblings would hate her if they learned that she was the result of Lionel Kingsley's affair with her mother.

She chatted for a few minutes and then slipped away to a quiet corner of the gallery, needing to be alone with her churning emotions. It was obvious that Charlotte and Freddie were deeply fond of each other. Sara felt a pang of envy as she watched them laughing together. Her childhood had been lonely because her mother hadn't encouraged her to invite school friends home. She had longed for a brother or sister to be a companion, unaware that growing up in Berkshire had been her half-sister, who was a year older than her, and her half-brother, three years her senior.

Tears gathered in her eyes and she quickly blinked them away when Lionel walked over to join her. She glanced around the gallery, searching for Alekos. Her instinctive need for his protection was a danger that she would have to deal with later. She saw him chatting with the Texan, Warren McCuskey, and her heart gave a silly skip as she realised that Alekos must have purposely given her and her father a few minutes of privacy.

'Sara, it's good to see you.' Lionel's smile allayed her concern that he was annoyed she had come to the party. 'I had no idea you were dating Alekos Gionakis. I thought you worked for him?'

'I'm his PA, but recently we...we've become close.' She felt her face grow warm. Lying did not come naturally to her. But she had to admit that Alekos's idea for her to pretend to be his girlfriend had allowed her to meet her half-siblings, and maybe she had a chance of persuading her father to reveal her identity to Freddie and Charlotte.

'Gionakis is an interesting man. He is knowledgeable of the arts but I've heard that he's a ruthless businessman.' Lionel lowered his voice so that he couldn't be overheard by anyone else. 'Sara, if Joan had told me she was pregnant I would have offered her financial support while you were a child. I regret that you did not grow up in a family.'

'I have a half-brother and half-sister who are my family, and I would love to get to know Charlotte and Freddie if only you would tell them I am your daughter,' Sara replied in a fierce whisper.

Her father looked uncomfortable. 'I will tell them when the time is right. Maybe if they got to know you first it would help when I break the news that I once cheated on their mother.' He looked round and saw Alekos approaching. 'Does Gionakis know of our relationship?'

Sara hesitated. 'Yes. But I know Alekos won't say a word to anyone,' she said hurriedly when Lionel frowned.

'You must love him to trust him so much.'

Love Alekos! Sara found she could not refute her father's comment. Her heart gave a familiar lurch as she watched Alekos walk towards her. He looked outrageously sexy, wearing a casual but impeccably tailored light grey suit and a black shirt, unbuttoned at the neck. His thick hair was ruffled as if he'd raked it off his brow several times during the evening, and the dark stubble shading his jaw added to his dangerous magnetism.

Of course she was in love with him; she finally admitted what she had tried to deny to herself for two years. She loved Alekos, but he'd told her he did not believe in love. Just because you loved someone didn't mean you could make them love you back. Her mother had discovered the truth of that when she had fallen in love with Lionel Kingsley.

'I told you my plan would work.' Alekos knew he sounded smug but he didn't care. He'd had a couple of drinks at the gallery launch and, although he was certainly not drunk, he felt relaxed and pleased with how the evening had gone. He leaned his head against the plush leather back seat of the limousine as they sped towards north London. His thoughts were on Warren McCuskey. The Texan billionaire was definitely interested in buying a superyacht and Alekos had used all his persuasive powers to convince him to commission a yacht from GE. He was confident he was close to finalising a deal with McCuskey. He could taste success, smell it.

He could also smell Sara's perfume. The blend of citrusy bergamot and sensual white musk, that had tantalised him every day at the office, filled the dark car and his senses. Suddenly he didn't feel relaxed any more. He felt wired up inside, the way Sara always made him feel lately. He was conscious of the hard thud of his heart and the even harder ache of his arousal that jerked to attention and pushed against the zip of his trousers.

'I don't think Zelda will continue to be a problem now that she believes you are my mistress,' he drawled, more to remind himself of the reason why he had spent most of the evening with his arm around

Sara's waist. She'd fitted against his side as if she belonged there. He frowned as he remembered how, every time he'd leaned towards her, he'd inhaled a vanilla scent in her hair that he guessed was the shampoo she used.

'Good. That's one problem solved at least.' She sounded distracted.

Alekos glanced at her sitting beside him. She had put her coat on before they'd left the gallery, but it was undone and he could see the smooth upper slopes of her breasts above the top of her dress. 'Is there another problem?' he said abruptly.

'There might be.' She flicked her head round to look at him and her hair brushed against his shoulder, leaving a trail of vanilla scent. 'Alekos, we need to talk.'

Talking to Sara was not uppermost in his mind. But if he told her of his erotic thoughts about her she would probably slap his face. The car pulled up outside her house. 'Invite me in for coffee and you can tell me what's troubling you.'

'All right,' she said after a moment's hesitation. 'But I only have instant coffee. Will that do?'

As Alekos followed her into the house he regretted his suggestion. He detested the insipid brown liquid that the English insisted on calling coffee. But, more pertinently, he couldn't understand why he had suggested to Sara that she could confide in him what he assumed was a problem with her private life. He was about to tell her not to worry about the coffee but she showed him into the sitting room, saying, 'I'll go and put the kettle on.'

It was difficult to imagine a room more characterless than the one he was standing in. The neutral décor was joyless, as if whoever had chosen the beige furnishings had found no pleasure in life. It was a strangely oppressive room and Alekos retreated and walked down the bungalow's narrow hallway to the kitchen.

Sara had taken off her coat and she looked like a gaudy butterfly in her bright dress against the backdrop of sterile worktops and cupboards. She had also slipped off her shoes and he was struck by how petite she was without her high heels. The sight of her bare feet with her toenails varnished a flirty shade of pink had an odd effect on him and he felt his gut twist with desire. He searched for something to say while he struggled to control his rampant libido.

'How come your bedroom is so colourful, while the rest of the house is…' he swapped the word *drab* for '…plain?'

'My mother didn't like bright colours. Now Mum has gone I've decided to sell the house. The estate agent advised me not to redecorate because buyers prefer a blank canvas.' She placed a mug on the counter in front of him. 'I made your coffee extra strong so it should taste like freshly ground coffee.'

Alekos thought it was highly unlikely. But remembering Sara's brightly coloured bedroom brought back memories of his previous visit to her home when he had kissed her and passion had ignited between them. There was barely enough space for the two of them in the tiny kitchen but he didn't want to suggest they move into the sitting room, which was as welcoming as a morgue. He sipped his coffee and managed not to grimace. 'What did you want to talk about?'

'Lionel thinks it would be a good idea if I could mix with Charlotte and Freddie socially so they can get to know me before he tells them I am their half-sister. He intends to use his association with you—namely your support of art projects—to invite us both to his villa in Antibes, where he's planning to celebrate his birthday.' Sara tugged on her bottom lip with her small white teeth, sending Alekos quietly to distraction as he imagined covering her lush mouth with his.

'Go on,' he muttered.

'I couldn't tell my father that I had pretended to be your girlfriend tonight so I could meet my half-siblings. Lionel believes we are genuinely in a relationship and we would have to continue the pretence if you accept his invitation.'

'Who else has your father invited to his villa?'

'Charlotte and Freddie and my father's close friend Warren McCuskey. By the way, thanks for chatting to Warren at the gallery while I spoke to my father privately.'

'You're welcome.' Alekos ignored the irritating voice of his conscience, which reminded him he was an unprincipled bastard. It was a fact of life that you couldn't head a multimillion-pound business and have principles. He'd seized his chance to grab McCuskey's undivided attention while Sara was talking to Lionel. 'When is your father's birthday?'

'Next weekend. I'd mentioned that we will be in Monaco for the yacht show and he said that Antibes is only about an hour's drive away. But I did warn him that we will be busy with the show and might not have time to visit him.'

'Our schedule for the three days of the show is hectic. But how about if I arranged a birthday lunch for your father and his guests aboard *Artemis* for next Sunday? That way we can catch up on paperwork in the morning, and you'll be able to spend time with Lionel and your brother and sister in the afternoon.' It would also be an ideal opportunity to give Warren McCuskey a demonstration of GE's flagship super-yacht, but Alekos kept that to himself.

'Would you really be prepared to do that on my behalf?' Her smile stole his breath and he shrugged off the niggling voice of his conscience. Sara caught her lower lip between her teeth again. 'But will you mind having to keep up the pretence that I am your girlfriend?'

Alekos dropped his gaze from her mouth to the delectable creamy curves of her breasts cupped in her silk dress, and he was surprised that the thud of his heart wasn't audible. 'I think I can put up with pretending that we are lovers,' he drawled.

He smiled when he heard her breath rush from her lungs as he wrapped his arm around her waist and drew her towards him so that she was pressed against his chest, against his heat and the hardness of his arousal that ached. *Theos,* he had never ached so badly for a woman before.

'Alekos,' she whispered. Her green eyes were very dark and he saw her uncertainty reflected in their depths as he lowered his head. 'What are you doing?'

'Rehearsing for when we meet your father,' he growled before he slanted his mouth over hers and kissed her like he'd wanted to do, like he'd been burning up to do since he had kissed her in the lobby of the art gallery. The difference was that that had been for Zelda Pagnotis's sake, or so Alekos had assured himself. But this time it was lust, pure and simple, that made him cup Sara's jaw in his palm and angle her head so that he could plunder her lips and slide his tongue into her mouth to taste her sweetness.

Without her high-heeled shoes she was much smaller than him and Alekos lifted her up and sat her on the kitchen worktop, nudging her thighs apart so that he could stand between them. The fact that she let him gave him the licence he needed to capture her mouth and kiss her again, hard this time, demanding her response as the fire inside him burned out of control.

Her shoulders were silky smooth beneath his hands. He traced his fingers along the delicate line of her collarbone before moving lower to explore the upper slopes of her breasts. Touching wasn't enough. He had to see her, had to cradle those firm mounds in his hands. With his lips still clinging to hers, he reached behind her and unzipped her dress. The green silk bodice slipped down and he helped it on its way, tugging the material until her breasts popped free. His breath hissed between his teeth as he feasted his eyes on her bare breasts, so pale against his tanned fingers, and at their centre her nipples, tight and dusky pink, just waiting for his tongue to caress them.

With a low growl Alekos lowered his mouth to her breast and drew wet circles around the areola before he closed his lips on her nipple and sucked. The soft cry she gave turned him on even more and he slid his arms around her back and encouraged her to arch her body and offer her breasts to his mouth. Every flick of his tongue across her nipple sent a shudder of response through her and when he transferred his attention to her other breast and sucked the tender peak she made a keening noise and dug her fingers into his hair as if to hold him to his task of pleasuring her.

He was so hard it hurt. His erection strained beneath his trousers as he shifted even closer to her, forcing her to spread her legs wider so that her dress rode up her thighs and he pressed his hardness against the panel of her knickers. Knowing that a fragile strip of lace was all that hid her feminine core from him shattered the last of his restraint and he groaned and cupped her face in his hands.

'Let's go to bed, Sara *mou*. This kitchen is not big enough for me to make love to you comfortably.' He doubted that her single bed would offer much more in the way of comfort and remembering her collection of child's soft toys strewn on her bed was a little off-putting. But the only other room was that soulless sitting room and he quickly dismissed the idea of having sex with her there.

He eased back from her and looked down at her naked breasts with their reddened, swollen nipples. 'Come with me,' he said urgently. If he did not have her soon he would explode.

Bed! Sara stiffened as Alekos's thick voice broke through the haze of sexual excitement he had created with his mouth and his wicked tongue. When he had sucked her nipples she'd felt an electrical current arc from her breasts down to the molten core of her femininity. She'd been spellbound by his magic, enthralled by the myriad new sensations induced by his increasingly bold caresses. But his words brought her back to reality with a thud.

On the opposite wall of the kitchen she could see her reflection in the stainless steel cooker splashback that her mother had religiously polished until it gleamed. Dear heaven, she looked like a slut, with her bare breasts hanging out of the top of her dress and the skirt rucked up around her thighs. She pictured Joan's disapproving expression and shame doused the heat in her blood like cold water thrown on a fire.

'Men only want one thing,' her mother had often told Sara. *'Once you give them your body they quickly lose interest in you.'*

Sara assumed that was how her father had treated her mother. It was certainly true of Alekos. She knew about all the gorgeous blondes who had come and gone in his life, because he'd given her the task of arranging an item of jewellery from a well-known jewellers to be sent to his mistresses when he ended his affair with them. Who would choose a pretty trinket to be sent to a mistress who was also his PA? She didn't know whether to laugh or cry.

'We can't go to bed,' she told him firmly. 'You know we can't, Alekos. We shouldn't have got carried away like we did.' She watched his expression turn from puzzlement to shock at her refusal before his eyes narrowed to black slits that gleamed with anger.

'Why not?' he demanded, his clipped tone betraying his frustration. 'We are both unattached, consenting adults.'

'I work for you.'

He dismissed her argument with a careless shrug of his shoulders. 'This evening we gave the impression that we are having an affair and tomorrow's papers will doubtless carry pictures of us arriving at the art gallery together.'

'But we were only pretending to have a relationship. You don't really want me.'

'It's patently obvious how much I want you,' Alekos said sardonically. 'And you want me, Sara. Don't bother to deny it. Your body doesn't lie.'

She followed his gaze down to her bare breasts and silently cursed the hard points of her nipples that betrayed her. Red-faced, she yanked the top of her dress back into place. 'We can't,' she repeated grittily. But her resolve was tested to its limit by the feral hunger in his eyes. 'If we had an affair, what would happen when it ended?'

'I see no reason why you couldn't carry on being my PA. We work well together and I wouldn't want to lose you.'

Alekos wouldn't want to lose her as his PA, but that was all. She could not risk succumbing to her desire for him because she would find it impossible to continue to work for him after they were no longer lovers. It would be torture to know he was dating other women after he'd finished with her. And she *would* know. In the two years she had been his PA she'd learned to recognise the signs that he was having regular sex.

She felt emotionally drained from the evening. Meeting her half-siblings had made her long to be part of a family. But she certainly wasn't going to sleep with Alekos to ease the loneliness she had felt all her life. 'I think you had better leave,' she told him huskily, praying he wouldn't guess she was close to tears.

'If you really want me to go, then of course I accept your decision,' he said coldly, sounding faintly incredulous that she had actually rejected him. 'But in future I suggest you do not respond to a man so fervently if you don't intend to follow it through.'

'Are you accusing me of leading you on?' Her temper flared. 'That's a foul thing to suggest and grossly unfair. You came on to me.'

'And you hated every moment when we were kissing, I suppose?' he mocked. 'It's a little too late to play the innocent victim, Sara.'

'I'm not trying to imply that I'm a victim.' But if he knew how innocent she really was he would run a mile, she thought grimly. She suddenly remembered that they had travelled from Soho to her house in Alekos's limousine. 'If I had invited you to stay the night, what would your chauffeur have done? Would he have slept in the car?'

Alekos shrugged. 'We have an arrangement. Mike knows to wait for a while…' He did not add anything more but Sara understood that his driver had been instructed to leave after a couple of hours if Alekos went into a woman's house and did not reappear. No doubt it was an arrangement that had been used on many occasions. Sara got on well with Mike and she would have felt so embarrassed if she'd had to face him after Alekos had spent the night with her. It brought home to her that she could not sacrifice her job, her reputation and her self-respect for a sexual liaison with her boss.

But when she followed Alekos down the hall and he opened the front door she had to fight the temptation to tell him that she had changed her mind and wanted him to stay and make love to her. Love had nothing to do with it, she reminded herself. At least not for Alekos. And she had sworn she would not make her mother's mistake and fall in love with a man who could never love her.

'Goodnight,' she bid him in a low voice.

'Sleep well,' he mocked, as if he knew her body ached with longing and regret that would make sleep impossible. As she watched him stride down the path she thought that at least she would be able to face him in the office tomorrow morning with her pride intact.

But pride was a poor bedfellow she discovered later, as she tossed and turned in her single bed. Her nipples still tingled from Alekos's ministrations and the insistent throb between her legs was a shameful reminder of how close she had come to giving in to her desire for him.

CHAPTER SIX

MONACO WAS A playground for millionaires and billionaires, and for the last three days the tiny principality had hosted the iconic yacht show, which this year had taken place in June rather than its usual date in September. Some of the world's most impressive superyachts were moored in the harbour, the largest and most spectacular being the two-hundred-and-eighty-foot *Artemis* from leading yacht brokerage and shipyard, Gionakis Enterprises.

On Sunday morning, Alekos made his way through Port Hercules in the sunshine. Now that the show was over, the huge crowds that had packed the waterfront had gone and his route to where *Artemis* was moored was no longer blocked by yacht charter brokers, who had been keen to tour the vessel and discover the superlative luxury of her interior.

Gone too were the glamour models and hostesses who were synonymous with the prestigious show. Monaco surely boasted more beautiful women wearing minuscule bikinis that revealed their tanned, taut bodies than anywhere else in the world, Alekos thought cynically. He could have relieved his sexual frustration with any of the numerous women who had tried to catch his eye, but there was only one woman he wanted and she had studiously kept out of his way.

After the frenzy of the past three days, Alekos's preferred method to unwind had been to go for a fifteen-mile run along the coast. Now he felt relaxed as he boarded *Artemis* and walked along her deck, with nothing but the cry of gulls and the lap of water against the yacht's hull to break the silence. His sense of calm well-being was abruptly shattered when he entered the small saloon which he had been using as an office and found Sara sitting at a desk with her laptop open in front of her.

She was dressed in white shorts and a striped top and her hair was caught up in a ponytail with loose tendrils framing her face. Without make-up, the freckles on her nose were visible and she looked wholesome and utterly lovely. Alekos felt his gut twist.

'Why are you working already? I told you I was planning to go for a run and you could have a lie in this morning.'

'I woke early and decided to get the report about the show typed up,' she said, carefully not looking directly at him. 'I thought you wouldn't be back for another hour or so.'

'Is that why you started work at the crack of dawn,

hoping to have finished the report before I came back, so that you could avoid me like you've done since you arrived on Wednesday?'

She flushed. 'I haven't avoided you. We've worked together constantly every day.'

'During the day we were surrounded by other people, and you took yourself off to bed immediately after dinner every evening. I can't believe you usually go to bed at nine p.m.,' he said drily.

The colour on her cheeks spread down her throat and Alekos wondered if the rosy blush stained her breasts. 'I was tired,' she muttered. 'The past few days have been incredibly busy.'

'I don't deny it. And because I came to Monaco a couple of days before you did, this is the first chance we have had to discuss what happened after we attended the art gallery launch last week.'

Now she did look at him, her eyes so wide and full of panic that she reminded him of a rabbit caught in car headlights. 'There's nothing to discuss. We...we got carried away, but it won't happen again.'

'Are you so sure of that?' Alekos deliberately lowered his gaze to the hard points of her nipples, outlined beneath her clingy T-shirt, and grinned when she crossed her arms over her chest and glared at him. He did not know why he took satisfaction from teasing her but he suspected it was to make him feel less bad about himself. He couldn't comprehend why he had come on to her so strong last Sunday evening. It was not his style. And she had rejected him! *Theos*—that was a first for him.

What was it about Sara that fired him up as if he were a hormone-fuelled youth instead of a jaded playboy who could take his pick of beautiful women? All week he had racked his brain for an answer while he'd been alone each night in the opulent master suite on *Artemis*, whereas at last year's show he'd enjoyed the company of two very attractive—not to mention inventive—blondes.

The only reason that made any sense—but did not make him feel good about himself, he acknowledged grimly—was simply that he wanted Sara so badly because she had turned him down. He wanted to see her sprawled on his bed, all wide-eyed and flushed with sexual heat, and he wanted to hear her beg him to make love to her because his ego couldn't deal with rejection.

She was watching him warily, and for some reason it angered him. She had been with him all the way the other night, right up until he'd suggested they go to bed. Even though she had said no, he'd sensed he could have persuaded her to change her mind. But he'd never pleaded with a woman to have sex with him before, and he had no intention of starting with his PA, who clearly had a hang-up about sex.

He leaned across the desk and tugged her arms open. Ignoring her yelp of protest, he drawled, 'It will help to make the pretence that we are lovers more convincing if you drop the outraged virgin act when your father and his guests arrive.'

Her eyes flashed with anger and she clamped her lips together as if to hold back a retort. Alekos wondered how much resistance she would offer if he attempted to probe her lips apart with his tongue. Lust swept like wildfire through him and he abruptly swung away and strode over to the door, conscious that his running shorts did not hide the evidence of his arousal.

'As you are so keen to work, you may as well type up the financial report for the shareholders. It will keep you busy until lunchtime, and as you are so averse to my company you won't want to join me for a swim in the pool, will you?' he murmured, and laughed softly at her fulminating look.

They had lunch on one of the yacht's four decks, sitting at a table set beneath a striped canopy that provided shade from the blazing Mediterranean sun. Lionel Kingsley, his son and daughter and Warren McCuskey had boarded *Artemis* at midday, and Alekos had instructed the captain to steer the yacht out of the harbour and drop anchor a couple of miles off the coast.

They were surrounded by blue, Sara thought as she looked around at the sparkling azure ocean which met a cornflower blue sky on the horizon. A gentle breeze carried the faint salt tang of the sea and lifted the voices and laughter of the people sitting around the table. She popped her last forkful of the light-as-air salmon mousse that the chef had prepared for a main course into her mouth and gave a sigh of pleasure.

After her run-in with Alekos earlier in the morning, her nerves had been on edge at the prospect of them having to act as though they were a couple. She'd fretted about the lunch, knowing that she had lied to her father about being Alekos's girlfriend and, even worse, not being truthful to Charlotte and Freddie that she was their half-sister.

But she need not have worried. Alekos had been at his most urbane and charming, although his eyes had glinted with amusement and something else that evoked a molten sensation inside her when he'd slipped his arm around her waist as they had walked along the deck to greet Lionel and his party. 'Showtime, Sara *mou*,' Alekos had murmured before he'd kissed her mouth, leaving her lips tingling and wanting more, even though she knew the kiss had been for the benefit of the interested onlookers.

Recalling that kiss now, she ran her tongue over her lips and glanced at Alekos sitting across the table from her. Heat swept through her when she discovered him watching her through narrowed eyes, and she knew that he was also remembering those few seconds when his lips had grazed hers. She tore her gaze from him when she realised that Charlotte was speaking.

'An office love affair is so romantic. When did

you and Alekos realise that there was more to your relationship than you simply being his PA?'

'Um...' Sara felt her face grow warm as she struggled to think of a reply.

'It was a gradual process,' Alekos answered for her. 'Obviously, Sara and I work closely together and to begin with we were friends before our friendship developed into something deeper.'

He sounded so convincing that Sara almost believed him herself. It was true that friendship had grown between them over the last two years. But that was where fact ended and her fantasy that he would fall in love with her began, she reminded herself.

Keen to change the subject, she turned to Freddie. 'Tell me what it was like at art school. It must have been fun. I would have loved to study for an art degree.'

'Why didn't you, if it is a subject that you say you have always been interested in?'

She shrugged. 'My mother wanted me to find a job as soon as I'd finished my A levels. There was only the two of us, you see, and she struggled to pay the bills.'

'Couldn't your father have helped?'

Sara froze and was horribly aware that her father had broken off his conversation with McCuskey and was waiting tensely for her to respond to Freddie's innocent question.

'No...he...wasn't around.'

'Luckily for me, Sara joined GE,' Alekos said

smoothly. 'I realised as soon as I met her that she would be an ideal person to organise my hectic life.' He rang the little bell on the table and almost instantly a steward appeared, pushing the dessert trolley. 'I see that my chef has excelled himself with a selection of desserts. My personal recommendation is the chocolate torte.'

Following his words, there was a buzz of interest around the table over the choice of dessert and the awkward moment passed. Sara gave Alekos a grateful look.

'After lunch I thought you might like to use the jet skis,' he said to Charlotte and Freddie. 'Or if you prefer an activity that involves less adrenalin there is snorkelling equipment, or the glass-bottomed dinghy is a fun way to view marine life.'

'You've got one heck of a boat here, Alekos,' McCuskey commented. 'Is it true there is a helipad somewhere on the yacht?'

'The helipad is on the bow and there is a hangar below the foredeck which is specially designed. I could give you a tour of *Artemis* if you'd like to see all of her many features.'

'I surely would,' the Texan said enthusiastically.

Sara had never had as much fun as she did that afternoon. The sea was warm to swim in and, with Charlotte and Freddie's help, she soon got the hang of snorkelling. Alekos joined them later in the day and when they took the jet skis out Sara rode pillion behind him and hung on tightly to him as they sped across the bay. With her arms wrapped around his waist and her cheek resting on his broad back, she allowed herself to daydream that it was all real—that she and Alekos were lovers and her half-siblings accepted her as their sister.

'Dad and Warren are driving back to Antibes. But Charlotte and I are meeting up with some friends in Monte Carlo this evening,' Freddie said as they stood on deck and watched the glorious golden sunset. 'Why don't you and Alekos come with us?' He put his head on one side as he studied Sara's face. 'It's bugging me that you remind me of someone, but I can't think who.'

Alekos slid his arm around her waist. 'What do you say, *agapi mou*? Would you like to go to a nightclub?'

'Yes. But I don't mind if you'd rather not,' she said quickly, unaware of the wistful expression in her eyes.

'I want to do whatever makes you happy,' he assured her.

Sweet heaven, he was a brilliant actor, but it was all pretend, Sara reminded herself firmly. She must not allow herself to be seduced by the sultry gleam in Alekos's dark eyes and the velvet softness of his voice that made her wish for the moon even though she knew it was unreachable.

Monte Carlo at midnight was a blaze of golden lights against a backdrop of an ink-black sky. Sara followed Alekos out of a nightclub that apparently was *the* place to be seen and to see celebrities. She had spotted a famous American film star and a couple of members of a boy band, but she'd only had eyes for Alekos.

They had met up with Charlotte and Freddie's friends, and Alekos had arranged for their group to use a private booth in the nightclub. He had stayed close to her all evening, draping his arm around her shoulders when they had sat in the booth drinking cocktails, and drawing her into his arms on the dance floor so that her breasts were crushed to his chest and she was conscious of his hard thigh muscles pressed against her through the insubstantial black silk dress she had chosen to wear for a night out.

He led her over to a taxi and opened the door for her to climb inside. 'My feet are *killing* me,' she complained as she flopped onto the back seat.

Alekos slid in beside her and lifted her feet onto his lap. 'Your fault for wearing stilts for shoes,' he said, inspecting the five-inch heels on her strappy sandals. Sara caught her breath when he curled his fingers around her ankles and unfastened her shoes before sliding them off her feet. While they had been in the nightclub they had continued the pretence of being lovers in front of her half-siblings. But now it seemed way too intimate when he trailed his fingertips lightly up her calves. 'Did you enjoy yourself tonight?'

'It was the best night of my life,' she said softly.

'And the best day.' Her eyes were drawn to him. In the dark taxi his chiselled profile was shadowed and the sharp angles of his face were highlighted by the glow from the street lamps. 'Thank you for making it possible for me to spend time with Charlotte and Freddie, and with my father earlier today. I hope you weren't too bored showing Warren McCuskey around *Artemis*. I guessed you had offered to give him a tour of the yacht so that I could have time alone with Lionel.'

'Yeah, I'm all heart,' he drawled. His oddly cynical tone made Sara dart a look at him, but the taxi drew up to the jetty and he climbed out of the car. She couldn't face putting her shoes back on, and while she stood contemplating whether to walk the short distance along the jetty in bare feet Alekos scooped her up in his arms and carried her up the yacht's gangway.

'Thanks.' She silently cursed how breathless she sounded and hoped he couldn't feel the erratic thud of her heart. 'You can put me down now.'

He continued walking into the main saloon before he lowered her down. She curled her toes into the soft carpet. Every sensory receptor on her body felt vitally alive and she was intensely aware of Alekos, of the spicy scent of his aftershave, the heat of his body and the smouldering gleam in his dark eyes. It all felt like a wonderful dream—staying on a luxurious yacht, spending time with her half-siblings and dancing the night away with a man who was so handsome it hurt her to look at him.

'I wish tonight didn't have to end.' She blurted out the words before she could stop herself and flushed, thinking how unsophisticated she sounded.

'It doesn't have to end yet. Will you join me for a nightcap?'

'Um…well, I shouldn't. It's late and we both have to be up early in the morning. You're flying to Dubai to visit Sheikh Al Mansoor, and my flight to London is at ten a.m.'

'I realise that it's three hours past your bedtime,' he said drily. 'But why not live dangerously for once?'

Alekos had simply invited her to have a drink with him. This was not a defining moment in her life, Sara told herself firmly. 'All right.' She ignored the warning in her head that sounded just like her mother's voice, and sided with the other voice that urged her to stop hiding from life and *live*. 'Just one drink.'

'Sure. You don't want to overdose on excitement.' He gave her a bland smile as he ushered her out of the main saloon and towards the stairs that led to the upper decks. When she hesitated he murmured, 'There is champagne on ice in my suite.'

Sara had never been in the master suite before and its opulent splendour took her breath away. The décor of the sitting room and the bedroom she could see beyond it was sleek and ultra-stylish while the colour scheme of soft blue, grey and white was restful.

Not that she felt relaxed. Quite the opposite as she watched Alekos slip off his jacket and throw it onto a chair before he strolled over to the bar. His white silk shirt was unbuttoned at the throat, showing his dark olive skin and a glimpse of black chest hairs. His hair fell across his brow and the dark stubble on his jaw gave him a rakish look that evoked a coiling sensation in the pit of her stomach.

The sliding glass doors were open and she stepped outside onto the private deck and took a deep breath. On this side of the yacht facing away from the port there was only dark sea and dark sky, lit by a bright white moon and stars like silver pins studding a black velvet pincushion.

Alekos's footfall was silent but she sensed he was near and turned to take the glass of pink fizz he handed her. 'Kir Royale, my favourite drink.'

'I know.' He held her gaze. 'Why were you looking sad?'

Sara sighed. 'Charlotte and Freddie both talked a lot about their happy childhoods, and how much their parents loved each other. Lionel's wife suffered from multiple sclerosis for several years and he cared for her devotedly until her death two months ago.' She bit her lip. 'If Lionel reveals that I am his daughter, all their memories of growing up in a happy family will be tainted by the knowledge that their father cheated on their mother.'

She placed her glass down on a nearby table and curled her hands around the deck rail, staring into the empty darkness beyond the boat. 'I'm afraid that my half-siblings will hate me,' she said in a low voice.

'I don't believe anyone could hate you, Sara *mou*.'

The gentleness in Alekos's voice was unexpected and it tore through her. 'I'm not *your* Sara.'

He smiled at her fierce tone. 'Aren't you?' He uncurled her fingers from the rail and turned her to face him. Sara trembled when he drew her unresisting body closer to his—so close that she could feel his heart thundering as fast as her own.

Of course she was his. The thought slipped quietly into her head. It wasn't complicated; it was really very simple. She had been his for two years and she could not fight her longing for him when he was looking at her with undisguised hunger in his eyes that made her tremble even more.

'I want you to be mine, and I think you want that too,' he murmured. She felt his lips on her hair, her brow, the tip of her nose. And then his mouth was there, so close to hers that she felt his warm breath whisper across her lips, and she couldn't deny it, couldn't deny him when it would mean denying herself of what she wanted more than anything in the world—Alekos.

Maybe it was because she had made him wait that explained the wild rush of anticipation that swept through him, Alekos brooded. And perhaps it was the lost, almost vulnerable expression on her lovely face moments ago that had elicited a peculiar tug on his heart.

The haunted look in her eyes should have warned him to back off while he still retained a little of his sanity. But it was too late. His desire for her was too strong for him to fight. Sara had driven him to the edge of reason for too long and the feel of her soft curves pressing against his whipcord body, and the little tremors that ran through her when he smoothed his hand down her back and over the taut contours of her bottom decimated his control.

He took possession of her mouth and gave a low growl of satisfaction when she parted her lips to allow his tongue access to her sweetness within. This time she would not reject him. He felt her desperation in the way she kissed him with utter abandon, and her response fuelled his urgency to feel her naked body beneath his.

He liked the little moan of protest she made when he ended the kiss and lifted his head to stare into her green eyes with their dilated pupils. She was so petite he could easily sweep her up in his arms, but he stepped back and held out his hand. 'Will you come and be mine, Sara?'

He liked that she did not hesitate. She put her fingers in his and he led her into the bedroom. His heart was pounding faster than when he'd gone for a fifteen-mile run that morning. And he was already hard—*Theos*, he was so hard; his body was taut with impatience to thrust between her slim thighs. The sight of her wearing a bikini when they had swum in the sea earlier in the day had driven him to distraction, and he had suggested using the jet skis to hide the embarrassing evidence of his arousal that his swim shorts couldn't disguise.

Most women would have played the temptress and given him artful looks as they performed a striptease for his benefit. Sara simply stood at the end of the bed and looked at him with her huge green eyes. Her faint uncertainty surprised him. She was, after all, a modern single woman in her mid-twenties and he assured himself that this could not be new for her. It was difficult to picture her as the drab sparrow who he had barely noticed in his office but, remembering the old style Sara, he thought it was likely that she hadn't had many lovers.

But he did not want her to be shy with him. He wanted her to be bold and as eager as he was. His hunger for her was so intense and he sensed that this first time would not last long. He needed her with him all the way, which meant that he must turn her on by using all his considerable skill as a lover.

'I want to see you,' he said roughly. The bedside lamps were switched off but the brilliant gleam from the moon silvered the room and gave her skin a pearlescent shimmer as he pulled the straps of her dress down, lower and lower until he had bared her breasts.

'*Eísai ómorfi.* You are beautiful,' he translated, realising he had spoken in Greek. His native tongue was the language of his blood, his passion, and he groaned as he cradled her breasts in his hands, testing their weight and exploring their firm swell before he was drawn inexorably to their dusky pink crests that jutted provocatively forwards, demanding his attention.

She shivered when he flicked his thumb pads over her nipples, back and forth before he rolled the tight nubs between his fingers until she gave a low cry that corkscrewed its way right into his gut. Giving her pleasure became his absolute focus but when he lowered his head to her breast and closed his mouth around her nipple, sucking hard, she bucked and shook and her undisguised enjoyment of what he was doing to her drove him to the brink.

'Sara, I have to have you now. I can't wait,' he muttered as he straightened up and sought her lips with his, thrusting his tongue into her mouth to tangle with hers. Next time he would take it slow, he promised himself. But he was fast losing control and the drumbeat of desire pounding in his veins demanded to be assuaged.

He would have liked her to undress him, maybe knelt in front of him to pull his trousers down and then taken him in her mouth. His body jerked at his erotic fantasy and he swore beneath his breath. There was no time for leisurely foreplay and he fought his way out of his clothes with none of his usual innate grace, while she stood watching him, her eyes widening when he stepped out of his boxers. She stared at his rock-hard arousal, and the way she swallowed audibly made him close his eyes and offer a brief prayer for his sanity.

'Alekos…' she whispered.

'If you have changed your mind. Go. Now,' he gritted.

'I haven't. It's just…' She broke off and ran her fingertips lightly, almost tentatively over his proud erection.

He grabbed her hand and lifted it up to his chest where his heart was thundering so hard he knew she could feel it. 'Playtime's over, angel.' He tugged her dress over her hips and it slithered to the floor. A pair of black lacy knickers were all that hid her femininity from him and he dealt with them with swift efficiency, sliding them down her legs before he lifted her and laid her on the bed.

The strip of soft brown curls between her thighs partially shielded her slick heat from his hungry gaze. He lifted her leg and hooked it over his shoulder, then did the same with her other leg, and his laughter was deep and dark when she gasped in protest.

'Beautiful,' he growled. She was splayed in front of him, open and exposed, and he had never seen anything as exquisite as he lowered his head and placed his mouth over her feminine heat.

'*Oh.*' She jerked her hips and clutched his hair. It crossed his mind that maybe she hadn't received pleasure this way before, and the possessive feeling that the thought elicited rang a faint alarm bell in his mind. He had never felt possessive of any woman and Sara was no different than any of the countless lovers he'd had since his first sexual experience when he was seventeen.

She squirmed beneath him. 'You can't…' She sounded scandalised, but there was something else in her guttural cry, a note of excitement that made Alekos smile.

'Oh, but I can,' he promised. And then he bent his head once more and probed his tongue into her slick heat, straight to the heart of her. Her hoarse moans filled his ears and her sweet feminine scent swamped his senses. She tasted of nectar and he licked deeper, sliding his hands beneath her bottom to angle her hips so that he could suck the tiny nub of her clitoris.

The effect was stunning. She gave a keening cry, bucking and writhing beneath him so that he gripped hold of her hips and held her fast while he used his tongue to drive her over the edge. She shattered. And watching her climax, her fingers clawing at the satin bedspread as her body shook, fired his blood and his need.

Theos, he had never *needed* a woman before. His brother had been needy for the woman who had broken his heart, but Alekos had learned from Dimitri's death that needing someone was a weakness that made you vulnerable. Although he was loath to admit it, right now he needed Sara the same way he needed to breathe oxygen.

Somehow, Alekos retained enough of his sanity to take a protective sheath from the bedside drawer and slide it over his erection. And then he positioned himself between her spread thighs once more and his need was so fierce and consuming that the flicker of apprehension in her eyes did not register in his mind. Not until it was too late.

He could hear the sound of his ragged breaths and his blood thundering in his ears. His fingers shook as he stroked them over her moist opening and found her hot and slick and ready for him. He was so close to his goal and with a groan he thrust his way into her and froze when he felt an unmistakable resistance.

She could not be a virgin.

But the evidence was there in the sudden tension of her muscles and the way she went rigid beneath him. His brain told him to halt and withdraw, but his body was trapped in the web of his desire. A sense of urgency that was more primitive and pressing than logical thought overwhelmed him. His shock at discovering her innocence was followed by an even greater shock as he realised that he was out of control. His body was driven by a fearsome need that drove him to move inside her and push deeper into her velvet heat.

Somewhere in the crazy confusion of his mind he was aware that she had relaxed a little and she flattened her hands against his chest and slid them up to his shoulders, not pushing him away but drawing him down onto her. She shifted her hips experimentally to allow her internal muscles to accommodate him, and just that small movement blew his mind. With a sense of disbelief Alekos felt his control being stretched and stretched. Everything was happening too fast. He closed his eyes and fought against the heat surging through his veins, but he couldn't stop it… He couldn't…

He let out a savage groan as his control snapped and he came hard, his body shuddering with the force of his climax. Even as the tremors still juddered through him, shame at his lack of restraint lashed his soul. How could he have been so weak? How could Sara have made him so desperate?

And what the hell was he going to do with her now?

CHAPTER SEVEN

'WHY DIDN'T YOU tell me it was your first time?'

Alekos's voice sounded…odd, not angry exactly, but not pleased either. And perhaps his gruff tone was to be expected, Sara acknowledged. He had been anticipating a night of passion with a sexually experienced mistress, but instead he'd found himself making love to a woman whose sexual experience could be documented on the back of a postage stamp.

'It was my business,' she said huskily, finding it hard to speak past the lump that inexplicably blocked her throat.

'But now you have made it my business too.' He said something in Greek that she thought it was best she did not understand. 'I'm sorry I hurt you.' He sounded remorseful and again there was that odd tone in his voice that was not quite anger but might have been regret.

'You didn't really. I mean, just a bit at first but then it was…okay.'

'You should have told me,' he said more harshly this time.

She sighed. 'I was curious.' Not the full truth but it would do. She wanted to cry—perhaps every woman felt emotional after her first sexual experience—but she was determined to wait until she was alone before she let her tears fall.

Alekos's weight was heavy on her, pressing her into the mattress and making her feel trapped. She didn't want to look at him, but there was nowhere else *to* look when his body was still joined with hers. His dark eyes that only moments ago had blazed with desire were now chips of obsidian and his beautiful mouth was compressed into a hard line. It was impossible to believe that his lips had ever curved into a smile of sensual promise.

She pushed against his chest. 'Can we talk about this some other time, and preferably not at all? We're done, aren't we?' She bit her lip. 'To be honest, I don't understand why people make sex such a big deal.'

She could not hide the disappointment in her voice. The discomfort she'd experienced when Alekos had pushed his powerful erection into her had only lasted a few moments. The stinging sensation had faded and been replaced with a sense of fullness that had begun as pleasant, and when he'd moved, and pushed deeper, had become a tantalising throb that she had wanted to continue.

But it had ended abruptly. Alekos's ragged breaths had grown hoarser before he'd made a feral growl that sounded as if it had been ripped from his throat as he had slumped forwards and she'd felt his hot breath on her neck.

He was still on top of her. Still *inside* her. There was too much of him for her fragile emotions to cope with, and now he was frowning, his heavy brows meeting above his aquiline nose.

'No, we are not done, Sara *mou*. Nowhere near.'

'I'm not your Sara.'

He laughed softly and the rich sound curled around her aching heart. Tenderness from Alekos was something she hadn't expected and it was too beguiling for her to bear right now.

'I have indisputable proof that you are mine. Am I hurting you now?' he murmured. He shifted his position very slightly and she felt something bloom inside her, filling her once more so that her internal muscles were stretched. While she was stunned by the realisation that he was hardening again, he bent his head and captured her mouth in a slow, sensual kiss that started out as gentle and, when she responded because she couldn't help herself, became deeper and more demanding.

She was breathless by the time he trailed his lips over her cheek to her ear and nipped her lobe with just enough pressure that she shivered with pleasure that was not quite pain. He moved lower, kissing his way down her throat and over the slopes of her breasts before he flicked his tongue across one nipple and rolled the other peak between his fingers, making her gasp at the sheer intensity of the sensations he was creating.

He played her body the way a skilled musician wrung exquisite notes from an instrument, his touch now light, now masterful, and always with the utmost dedication to giving her pleasure. And all the while he moved his hips unhurriedly, sometimes in a gentle rocking motion, sometimes circling his pelvis against hers.

Each movement resulted in his erection growing harder within her and stretching her a little more, filling her until she was only aware of Alekos— the warmth of his skin, the strength of his bunched shoulder muscles beneath her hands, the power of his manhood pushing into her, pulling back, pushing into her, pulling back, in a steady rhythm that made her want more of the same.

He looked down at her and his mouth curved into a slow smile as he slid his hands beneath her bottom and encouraged her to arch her hips to accept the thrust of his body.

'Does that feel good?'

'Yes.' It felt amazing but she was suddenly shy, which was ridiculous, she told herself, when she was joined with him in the most intimate way possible.

'Tell me if it hurts.'

'It doesn't.'

'Tell me what you want.'

Oh, God, how could she tell him that his relentless rhythm was driving her mad? How could she tell him what she wanted when she didn't know? She stared up at his handsome face and thought she would die of wanting him. 'I want you to move faster,' she whispered. 'And harder. Much harder.'

'*Theos*, Sara…' He gave a rough laugh. 'Like this?' He thrust deep and, before she had time to catch her breath, he thrust again. 'Like this?'

'Yes…*yes.*'

It was unbelievable, indescribable. And so beautiful. She learned his rhythm and moved with him, meeting each thrust eagerly as he took her higher, higher. He possessed her utterly, her body and her soul, and he held her at the edge, made her wait a heartbeat before he drove into her one final time and they exploded together, her cries mingled with his hoarse groan as they shattered in the ecstasy of their simultaneous release.

Sara came down slowly. A heavy lethargy stole through her body, making her muscles relax and blocking out the hundreds of thoughts that were waiting in the wings of her mind, preparing to lambast her with recriminations. Alekos moved away from her and moments later she heard a click that she guessed was the door of the en suite bathroom closing. She wondered if it was her cue to leave. What was the protocol when you had just lost your virginity to your boss?

Oh, God, it was better not to think of that. Better

not to think at all, but to keep her eyes closed and that way she could pretend it had all been a dream. Hovering on the edge of sleep, she was aware that the mattress dipped and she breathed in the elixir that was Alekos—his aftershave, sweat, the heat of his body.

In her dream she turned towards his warmth and curled up against him, her face pressed to his chest so that she felt his rough chest hairs against her cheek. In her dream he muttered words in Greek that she didn't understand as he slid his arm beneath her shoulders and pulled her close to him.

Alekos knew he was in trouble before he opened his eyes. The brush of silk on his shoulder and a faint vanilla scent were unwelcome reminders of his stupidity. Lifting his lashes, he confirmed that the situation was as bad as it could get. Not only had he had sex with Sara, but she had slept all night in his bed. *Theos*, in his *arms*.

He hardly ever spent an entire night with a lover. Sharing a bed for sleeping suggested a level of intimacy he did not want and could lead to mistaken expectations from a woman that she had a chance of being more than his mistress. Last night he had intended to leave Sara in his bed and go and sleep in another cabin.

He could not explain to himself why he had climbed back into bed after he'd visited the bathroom. Alarm bells had rung in his head when she'd snuggled up to him, all soft and warm and dangerously tempting. He'd been tired and had closed his eyes, promising himself he would get up in a couple of minutes, and the next he'd known it was morning.

He swore beneath his breath. Sara was still asleep and he carefully eased his arm from beneath her. The sunlight filtering through the blinds played in her hair and made the silky layers burnish myriad shades of golden brown. With her English rose complexion and her lips slightly parted she looked innocent, but of course she wasn't, thanks to him, he acknowledged grimly.

What had he been thinking when he'd made love to her, not just once but twice? But that was the trouble. *He hadn't been capable of rational thought.* His actions had been driven by desire, by his need for Sara that in the crystal clarity of the-day-after-the-night-before shamed him. Discovering that she was a virgin should have immediately prompted him to stop having sex with her. But he had been unable to resist the slick, sweet heat of her body, and he'd come—*hell*, he'd come so hard. Even now, remembering the savage intensity of his release caused his traitorous body to stir.

Failing to satisfy a lover was a new experience for him and Sara's obvious disappointment had piqued his pride. He grimaced. His damnable pride was not the only reason he'd set out to seduce her a second time. He'd convinced himself it was only fair that he should gift her with the pleasure of an orgasm. Despite her inexperience, she had been a willing pupil and he'd found her ardent response to his lovemaking irresistible.

It was that thought that compelled him to slide out of bed and move noiselessly around the bedroom while he dressed. In his mind he replayed the last conversation he'd had with his brother when he was fourteen.

'Why are you so upset just because your girlfriend cheated? You can easily find another girlfriend. Women love you.'

'No other woman could ever replace Nia in my heart,' Dimitri had said. 'When you are older you'll understand, Alekos. One day you will meet a woman who gets under your skin and you'll be unable to resist her. It's called falling in love and it's hellish.'

He wouldn't visit hell for any woman, Alekos had vowed years ago as he'd watched his brother weeping. Love had brought Dimitri to his knees. Had it also been ultimately responsible for his death? The question had haunted Alekos for twenty years.

There was no danger he would fall in love with Sara. But his weakness last night served as a warning he could not ignore. He didn't know why she had chosen to lose her virginity with him, and he did not want to know what hopes she might be harbouring about them making their pretend affair a reality.

One thing he knew for sure was that he needed to get the hell off the yacht before she woke up. A short, sharp lesson might be brutal but it was best to make it clear that all he'd felt for her was lust. He still felt, he amended when she moved in her sleep and the sheet slipped down to reveal one perfect rose-tipped breast. She was peaches and cream and he wanted to feast on her again. The strength of his desire shocked him and he strode over to the door, resisting the urge to look back at her.

Sara would probably expect to find him gone when she woke up. She knew he was planning to fly to Dubai to take part in a charity polo match organised by his friend Sheikh Al Mansoor. Kalif had brought one of his cousins to Monaco to visit the yacht show, and the three of them would fly to Dubai on the Prince's private jet. There was no reason why he should feel guilty for abandoning Sara, Alekos assured himself. After all, she was his PA and she had arranged his diary around his ten-day trip to stay at Kalif's royal palace.

Deep down, Alekos acknowledged that he was running away, and the unedifying truth did not make him feel good about himself. He was running scared, his conscience taunted him. Sara had made him lose control and it had never happened before. No woman had ever got under his skin and he hoped—*no*, he was sure—that distance would allow him to put his fascination with her into perspective. He'd responded to the chemistry between them. That was all. When he returned to the London office in ten days' time she would no doubt be as keen as him to forget about their night of passion.

* * *

Sara was woken by a *thud-thud* noise that she recognised was a helicopter's rotor blades. She opened her eyes and frowned as she looked around her. This was not her cabin on *Artemis*. This was… *Dear, sweet heaven!* Memories of the previous night flooded her mind. Last night she'd had sex with Alekos and he had not been pleased when he'd discovered it was her first time.

She turned her head on the pillow and, finding she was alone in the bed, assumed he was in the bathroom. Her thoughts flew back to last night. It had been over fairly quickly and she'd felt underwhelmed by the experience. But then Alekos had made love to her a second time, and nothing she'd ever read about sexual pleasure came close to the incredible orgasm that had exploded through her body like an electrical storm and left her shaking in its aftermath.

It had been just as good for Alekos. His harsh groan before he'd slumped on top of her had told her he'd reached his own nirvana. But what would happen now? Where did they go from here?

It suddenly seemed a good idea to get dressed before she faced him. Muscles she'd been unaware of until this morning tugged as she slid out of bed and scooped up her dress and knickers from the floor where they had scattered. The memory of his hands on her body and his mouth on her breasts and—*dear God*—between her legs when he'd bestowed a shockingly intimate caress, caused heat to bloom on her cheeks and she felt even hotter inside.

When he'd realised she was inexperienced he had tempered his passion with tenderness that had captured her heart and made her hope— *No*, she must not go down that road, she told herself firmly. Just because Alekos had made love to her with exquisite care and made her feel beautiful and desirable, she must not hope he might fall in love with her. *But he might*, whispered a little voice in her head.

The sound of rotor blades was becoming fainter, as if the helicopter was flying away. Sara frowned. Who could have been delivered to the yacht by helicopter? As far as she was aware, no guests were expected. Alekos was taking a long time in the bathroom. Struck by a sudden sense of foreboding, she knocked on the bathroom door and when he didn't answer she tried the handle and found it unlocked and the room empty. She ran over to the sliding glass doors and out onto the deck. Looking up, she saw that it was the *Artemis* helicopter flying away from the yacht and her heart dropped faster than a stone thrown into a pool as she realised that Alekos must be on board.

She remembered she'd arranged for the pilot to fly him to the airport at Nice, and from there he would travel to Dubai. Of course she wouldn't have expected him to change his plans, but why hadn't he at least woken her to say goodbye? Because he was reluctant to face her after last night, she thought bleakly. She felt sick to think that Alekos had used her for sex. She heard her mother's voice: *'Once you've given a man what he wants you won't see him for dust.'*

Choking back a sob, Sara hurried back to her own cabin on the deck below, praying she wouldn't bump into any of the yacht's crew. She had things to do: clothes to pack, paperwork to stow in her briefcase before she was due to leave *Artemis* and travel to the airport with members of GE's sales team. Keeping busy stopped her from brooding on the fact that Alekos had abandoned her.

Laden with her suitcase and laptop, she descended to the main deck and forced a smile when she saw her father's friend Warren McCuskey walking up the gangway onto the yacht.

'I'm afraid you have just missed Alekos. He left early for an appointment.'

'Not to worry. I'll call him with the news he's been wanting to hear.' The Texan laughed. 'I've gotta hand it to your guy—he's a damned good salesman. When I met him a couple of months back I happened to say that my wife, Charlene, fancied us having a boat, and since then Gionakis hasn't missed a chance to try and persuade me to buy a yacht from GE. The day after we met at the art gallery in London he invited me to visit *Artemis* while she was in Monaco. By lucky coincidence I'd arranged to stay at Lionel's place in Antibes.'

'Did you say you had met Alekos *before* the gal-

lery launch?' Sara strove to sound casual while her
brain reminded her that Alekos did not operate on
'lucky coincidences'. He'd known Warren would be
staying at her father's villa because she'd told him.

'Sure. And, like I said, he used every opportunity
to use his sales tactics on me. But what really sold
me on the idea of buying a yacht from his company
was when he said that you are Lionel's daughter.'

Warren mopped his sunburned brow with a handkerchief and so did not notice the colour drain from
Sara's face. 'Lionel is my closest friend, and if Gionakis is going to be his son-in-law I'll be happy to buy
a boat from him.'

'Alekos told you that he and I are getting married?' she said faintly.

'Not in so many words. But I can tell when a fella
is in love. He couldn't keep his eyes off you at lunch
yesterday. I was impressed with this yacht and I've
decided to buy her.'

'You want to buy *Artemis*?' Sara was stunned.
The superyacht's price was two hundred million dollars, making her one of the most expensive yachts
ever built. Alekos had seen a business opportunity
when she'd told him that Lionel Kingsley was her father. No wonder he had suggested they could pretend
to be having an affair so that she could attend functions with him and socialise with her father. He had
been aware that Warren McCuskey was Lionel Kingsley's close friend; it was fairly common knowledge.

Alekos had been *so* helpful talking to Warren to

give her time alone with her father, she thought cynically. She had believed his offer to help her had been genuine, out of kindness. But Alekos wasn't *kind*. He was a ruthless businessman and, unforgivably, he had betrayed her secret and told Warren that Lionel was her father.

Idiot, she thought bitterly. Why had she given herself to Alekos, knowing he was a notorious womaniser and heartbreaker? The answer—that she was in love with him—filled her with self-disgust. Did she really have so little self-worth to love a man who only loved himself?

'If you speak to Alekos, will you pass on a message?' Warren said.

'Oh, I'll give him a message, don't you worry.' She disguised her sardonic tone with a bland smile. The Texan would be shocked if he knew she intended to tell Alekos he was an arrogant, manipulative bastard. Beneath her outwardly calm exterior she was seething. Alekos had played her for a fool but she would never give him the chance to humiliate her again.

After the cloudless blue skies and golden sunshine of Monaco, the typical British summer weather of rain and a chilly wind that whipped along Piccadilly did nothing to lift Sara's spirits. It was strange to be back in the office without Alekos and she felt annoyed with herself for missing him as she tried to focus on work.

'Sara, do you have a minute?' Robert Drummond, the CEO, stopped by her desk on Friday afternoon.

'Of course. What's up, Bob?' She noticed he seemed tense. 'Can I get you a coffee?'

'No, thanks. Remind me, when will Alekos be back?'

'He's due in the office next Wednesday. His trip to Dubai is a private visit but I can contact him if necessary.' She hadn't heard from Alekos since they had left Monaco but she had not expected to, and luckily there had been no work issues that required her to phone him.

The CEO frowned. 'Keep this to yourself. There has been some unusual trading activity of the company's shares in recent days. It's probably nothing to be concerned about but I'll keep my ear to the ground and talk to Alekos when he's back.'

After Bob had gone, Sara drummed her fingertips on her desk, wondering if she should call Alekos. She was still his PA for now and it was her job to alert him of anything that might affect the company. Her phone rang and her heart leapt into her throat when she saw his name on the caller display.

'Sara, I need you to come over immediately.' Alekos's sexy Greek accent was more pronounced than usual, making the hairs on her body stand on end. Damn the effect he had on her, she thought bitterly.

'You want me to come to Dubai?' She was pleased that she sounded cool and composed.

'I returned to London earlier than planned,' he

said tersely. 'I'm working from home. I've sent Mike to collect you, so go and wait in the car park for him.'

She stared at the envelope on her desk containing her letter of resignation. The sooner she gave it to Alekos the better.

'Sara—' he sounded impatient, and nothing like the sensual lover who had spoken to her tenderly when he'd made love to her '—did you hear me?'

'Yes.' She dropped the envelope into her handbag. 'I'm on my way.'

CHAPTER EIGHT

ALEKOS'S LONDON HOME was a penthouse apartment next to the river with stunning views of the Thames, Tower Bridge and the Shard.

His valet opened the door to admit Sara into the hallway and her tension racked up a notch when she heard a female voice from the sitting room. Did he have a woman here? Maybe someone he'd met in Dubai. It was only four nights ago that he had slept with *her*. She was tempted to hand the letter in her bag to the valet and ask him to deliver it, but just then the sitting room door opened and Alekos's mother came out to the hall. When she saw Sara she burst into tears.

'No, no, Sara,' she sobbed, 'you must not allow Alekos to work. The doctor said he has to rest.'

Sara had met Lina Gionakis a few times and had found her to be charming but excitable. She frowned. 'Doctor? Is Alekos unwell?'

'He could have died,' Lina said dramatically.

'Rubbish.' Alekos's gravelly voice made Sara's

pulse race as she followed his mother into the sitting room and her gaze flew to him, sprawled on a sofa by the window. He was wearing faded denim jeans, a cream shirt undone to halfway down his chest and no shoes. She dragged her eyes from the whorls of black hairs that grew thickly on his chest and stared at his bare feet. There was something curiously intimate about seeing his feet that reminded her of when he'd stripped in front of her before he had undressed her in his bedroom on *Artemis*.

Pink-cheeked, she jerked her gaze up to his face and did a double take when she saw he was wearing a black eye patch over his right eye.

'Polo,' he said drily, answering her unspoken query. 'I was hit in the eye with a mallet during a match.'

'The doctor said you are lucky you were not blinded in your eye.' Lina wrung her hands together. 'Promise me you will wear a helmet and faceguard in future. What if you had fallen from your horse? A head injury can be fatal. Polo is such a dangerous sport and you know I couldn't bear it if I lost another son.'

'Mana, I am not a child.' Alekos was clearly struggling to control his impatience with his mother and he looked relieved when the valet returned with a tea tray. 'Sit down and Giorgos will serve you tea and cakes while I go over a few things with Sara.'

He strode out of the room and Sara followed him into his study. 'Is your eye injury serious?'

'Not really. The blow from the mallet caused a blood vessel in my eye to rupture and my vision is blocked by a pool of blood covering the iris and pupil. The condition is called a hyphema and it shouldn't result in long-term harm.' He shrugged. 'It's fairly painful and I have to use eye drops and wear the patch for a few weeks. But I'll live,' he added sardonically.

'Your mother is very upset. What did she mean when she said she couldn't bear to lose another son?'

Alekos leaned his hip against the desk and folded his arms across his chest. But, despite his casual air, Sara sensed a sudden tension in him. 'I had an older brother,' he said abruptly. 'Dimitri died…in an accident when he was twenty-one. My mother still mourns him and, as you saw just now, she is terrified of losing me or one of my sisters.'

'I'm not surprised after such a tragic event. You've never mentioned your brother to me.'

'Why would I?'

Why, indeed? she thought painfully. Alekos was an intensely private man who guarded his personal life and his family. He would not choose to confide in his PA, not even one he'd had sex with. It was a timely reminder that she meant nothing to him and she opened her handbag and gave him the letter.

'What's this?'

'My formal notice of resignation. I can't continue to work for you after we…' Colour flooded her cheeks. 'After what happened a few nights ago.'

'We had sex,' he said bluntly. 'It's too late now to be embarrassed about it.'

'But I am embarrassed. We both behaved unprofessionally and that's why I have to leave my job.'

'*Theos*, Sara.' Impatience was etched onto his hard features. 'Why are you getting so worked up because we spent one night together? It didn't mean anything.'

She felt a knife blade pierce her heart. 'You made that very clear when you left the next morning without saying a word.'

Dark colour streaked along his cheekbones. 'You were asleep.'

'You made me feel like a whore.' She drew a shuddering breath and would have laughed at his astonished expression if she hadn't wanted to cry. 'It would have been less insulting if you'd left a cheque for my sexual services on the pillow.'

'You wanted me as much as I desired you,' he said grimly. 'Don't pretend you were the innocent one in this.'

Alekos's words hung in the air. He must have thought she was a freak when he'd discovered she was a twenty-four-year-old virgin, she thought painfully. She had been stupidly naïve to have fallen for the well-practised seduction routine of a playboy. 'When you read the letter, you will see that I have requested to leave earlier than the three months' notice my contract stipulates. It will be easier if I go as soon as possible.'

She turned and walked over to the door, but his harsh voice made her hesitate.

'Damn it, Sara. Where's your loyalty? You can't leave me now when I need you.'

'I'm sorry about your eye, but you said there will be no long-term damage.' She fought the insidious pull on her emotions. Alekos did not need her; he simply wanted to avoid the inconvenience of having to employ another PA. 'And how dare you throw my loyalty in my face after you showed me no loyalty at all?' She breathed hard as her anger with him exploded. 'I told you that Lionel Kingsley is my father in absolute confidence. How could you betray my secret to Warren McCuskey?'

'I didn't...'

She ignored him and continued. 'You were determined to sell a yacht to Warren and you knew that Lionel has a lot of influence over him. When you learned that I was Lionel's daughter you suggested we could pretend to be a couple so I could meet my half-siblings. But the real reason was to give you access to Warren, and your manipulation worked,' she said bitterly. 'One reason why Warren has decided to buy *Artemis* is because you let him think you are in love with me—his best friend's secret daughter.'

'I didn't tell him.' Alekos's voice was as sharp as a whiplash and made Sara flinch. 'Warren asked me if I knew you were Lionel's daughter, and I said yes because it would have looked odd if you

hadn't told me when we were supposedly in a relationship.'

She looked at him uncertainly. 'Then how did
Warren know?'

'It's likely that Lionel confided in his closest
friend.'

Sara had to acknowledge the truth of what Alekos said but it didn't ease the hurt she felt. 'You still
used my relationship with my father to your advantage to promote GE.'

He did not deny it. 'There is no room for sentiment in business. Which is why I need you to carry
on being my PA, for now at least.' He straightened
up and walked towards her, and his face was grim-
mer than Sara had ever seen it.

'GE is the target of a hostile takeover bid. In the
past few months a large amount of company shares
have been bought, seemingly by several smaller companies. I received a tip-off that these companies are
all owned by one individual who has accumulated
a significant number of GE's shares. In business,
an unwanted takeover bidder is known as a black
knight. If the black knight acquires fifty-one per
cent of GE's shares he will be able to appoint a new
management team and board of directors, and effectively take over the company.'

'Do you know how close the black knight is to
acquiring fifty-one per cent?'

'Too damned close. It will be more difficult for
him now he's out in the open. Instead of buying up

shares stealthily through his various companies, he will have to try to persuade GE's shareholders to sell stock to him.'

'Are you saying that if this black knight does manage to buy enough shares, you could lose the company that your grandfather set up?' Looking closely at Alekos, Sara saw evidence of the strain he was under in his clenched jaw and the two grooves that had appeared on either side of his mouth. Despite his cavalier treatment of her, she felt a tug on her soft heart. 'There must be something you can do to stop him.'

'There are various strategies which I am already putting in place, but my best hope—only hope, to be brutally honest—is if I can convince the shareholders, many of whom are board members, not to sell their shares and remain loyal to me.' He raked his hair off his brow. 'As you are aware, I haven't always had the support of every member of the board. In fact, the black knight is a board member.'

'Orestis Pagnotis,' Sara guessed.

'Actually, no, it's Stelios Choutos. He doesn't like the new direction I am taking GE and his takeover bid is backed by an American hedge fund. Fortunately, Warren McCuskey's decision to buy *Artemis* will win me a lot of support from shareholders. An injection of two hundred million dollars into the company's coffers couldn't have come at a better time.'

'I'm sorry about your problems, but I still intend

to resign. I don't see what use I can be.' Sara's heart jolted when Alekos moved to stand between her and the door. The patch over his eye made him look even more like a pirate and his rugged good looks were a dangerous threat to her peace of mind.

'I need to have people around me who I can rely on and trust. If you are really determined to walk away from your job for no good reason I'll allow you to leave after you've served one month's notice. The future of GE will have been decided by then,' he said grimly. 'I'll pay you a full three months' salary. But in return I will expect you to be at my call constantly while I fight to save my company.'

Sara warned herself not to be swayed by his admission that he trusted her. But didn't she owe Alekos her loyalty while GE was under threat? She bit her lip, torn between feeling it was her duty to help him and the knowledge that if she stayed in her job and saw him every day it would be harder to fall out of love with him.

'All right,' she agreed before she could change her mind. 'I'll stay on for one month. But I want six months' salary.'

The extra money would pay for the college art course she wanted to do. Instead of having to wait until she had sold her mother's house, she would be able to start the art course in the new term in September. She had never made any demands on Alekos and had put him on a pedestal, always doing her best to please him. The result was that he'd treated her badly. He had made it clear that she did not matter to him, and she realised that she had wasted two years of her life loving him when he did not deserve her love. It was time she started to value herself, Sara decided.

'I guess I shouldn't be surprised that you are as mercenary as most other women,' Alekos said in a hard voice. 'I've admitted I need your help.'

'There is no room for sentiment in business,' she quoted his words back to him coolly. 'If you want me, you're going to have to pay for me.'

Alekos felt as if his head was going to explode. His eye injury had caused him to suffer severe headaches, but he hadn't taken any of the strong painkillers he had been prescribed because they made him feel drowsy and he'd needed to have all his wits about him at a crucial meeting with a group of shareholders.

He pinched the bridge of his nose to try and control the pain in his head. Behind him, the staccato click of stiletto heels on the marble-floored foyer of GE's offices in Athens sounded as loud as gunshots. He dropped his arm as Sara came to stand beside him and saw her frown when she darted a glance at his face.

He knew he did not look his best. For the past two weeks he'd survived on patchy meals, not enough sleep and too much whisky, while he'd criss-crossed the globe to meet with shareholders and tried to persuade them to back his leadership of GE. Since Stelios Choutos had issued GE with a formal notice of an intended takeover bid the battle lines had been drawn. Shareholders either supported the company's current chairman or the disgruntled board member Stelios. So far, Stelios was winning.

Now Alekos had brought the battle to GE's birthplace in Greece. He stared at the blown-up photographs on the wall of his grandfather and founder of the company, Theo Gionakis, his father, Kostas, and brother, Dimitri. Failure was not an option he would consider. But maybe he *was* second best, as he was certain his father had thought. He wasn't the true Gionakis heir. Self-doubt congealed in the pit of his stomach.

'Why are there photos of your grandfather, your father and your brother above the reception desk, but not a picture of you?' Sara asked.

'They are all dead,' he said bluntly. 'The photo gallery is of past chairmen. Although my brother never actually became chairman, my father had his picture placed here after Dimitri died.' Alekos's jaw clenched. 'If my brother had lived to take over from my father, maybe GE would not be under threat.'

'Surely you don't believe that?'

'I have no way of knowing whether I am as good a chairman as I have no doubt Dimitri would have been.'

He felt Sara's eyes on him but he carefully avoided her gaze. It was easier, he'd found, if he did not look directly at her. That way his heart did not thump quite so hard and he could kid himself that the effect she had on him was a temporary aberration. For the past two weeks he had spent virtually every waking hour with her while they had worked together to save the company. When he was alone in bed at night it was his fantasies about making love to her, fuelled by erotic memories, rather than worry about GE that kept him awake.

He glanced at a message on his phone. 'The helicopter is waiting for us on the helipad. Let's go.'

'Go where?' she asked as they rode the lift up to the roof of the building. 'I know you have a home in Athens, and I assumed I would check in to a hotel.'

'You will stay with me. It'll be easier if you are on the same premises when we have to work late,' he countered the argument he could see brewing in her green eyes. *Theos*, she could be stubborn. But he was damned glad she was on his team.

Sara had impressed him with her dedication to GE. She'd accompanied him on his tour of cities around Europe, as well as to the US and the Far East. They had clocked up thousands of air miles to visit GE's shareholders and at every boardroom meeting, every dinner, every long evening spent in hotel bars Sara had invariably charmed the shareholders with her warmth and grace and personable nature.

She was an asset to the company and he did not want to lose her as his PA. He dismissed the thought that he did not want to lose her at all. She was not his, and perhaps this inexplicable possessive feeling was because he had been her first lover.

They boarded the helicopter and it took off, flying over Athens and out over the coast. 'I thought we were going to your house?' Sara said.

'We are. It's down there.' Alekos pointed to a small island just off the mainland. 'I own the island. Its name is Eiríni, which means *peace* in Greek.'

The helicopter hovered above the many trees that covered the island. From the air, Eiríni appeared like an emerald jewel set amid a sapphire-blue sea and some of his tension eased. This was home, his private sanctuary, and it occurred to him that Sara was the only woman, apart from his mother and sisters, who he had ever brought here. When they landed, he pulled in deep breaths of the fresh sea air mingled with the sweet scent of the yellow mimosa bushes that lined the path leading up to the house. But, as always, the scent that filled his senses was the evocative fragrance that was Sara.

He led her from the baking sun into the cool entrance hall of the house, where they were met by his housekeeper. 'Maria will show you to your room,' he told Sara. 'Feel free to explore or use the pool and we'll meet for dinner in an hour.'

She took a small bottle of pills out of her bag and gave it to him. 'You left your painkillers on your desk back in Athens. If I were you, I'd take the necessary dose and try to rest for a while.'

Her soft voice washed over him like a mountain

stream soothing his throbbing head and her gentle smile made something twist deep inside him. He wanted to lie on a bed with her and pillow his head on her breasts. But that was too needy, he thought grimly. Needing someone made you vulnerable.

'Stop fussing—you sound like my mother.'

'If I had been your mother when you were growing up, I would have sent you to your room until you'd learned some manners.'

The softness had gone from her voice and Alekos heard a note of hurt that her cool tone couldn't hide. *Theos*, what the hell was wrong with him that he couldn't even be civil? As Sara turned to follow the housekeeper he caught hold of her arm.

'I'm sorry.' He raked his hair off his brow. 'I'm under a lot of strain, but that's no excuse for me to take my bad mood out on you.'

She held his gaze, and he had a feeling she knew his secret fear that his father had been right to doubt his abilities. 'You're a good chairman, Alekos, and I believe you will win the backing of the shareholders.'

'Let's hope you're right,' he said gruffly.

When Alekos woke it was dark, and a glance at the bedside clock showed it was ten p.m. *Ten!* He jerked upright and discovered that his headache had mercifully gone. After showering, he had taken Sara's advice and swallowed a couple of painkillers before he'd stretched out on the bed for twenty minutes. That had been three hours ago. She must have thought he'd abandoned her—again.

Leaving her on *Artemis* when he'd rushed off to Dubai had not been his finest hour, he acknowledged. He had been stunned to discover she was a virgin, but what had shaken him even more was the intensity of the emotional and physical connections he'd felt with her when they had made love.

He stood up, thinking he should get dressed and go and find her. Maybe it was the painkillers that had caused his sleep to be fractured with unsettling dreams about his brother, but a more likely reason was his ever-present dread that he could lose GE, which should have been Dimitri's by birthright.

His trousers were on the chair by the window. He was about to put them on when he happened to glance at the beach. The full moon shone brightly on the sand and on Sara. Alekos frowned as he watched her walk along the shoreline. She was wearing a long floaty dress, and when a bigger wave swirled around her ankles she stumbled and fell. *Theos*, what was she doing going into the sea alone at night? He stared across the beach and his heart crashed into his ribs when he could no longer see her.

Swearing, he tore out of his room and took the stairs two at a time. The back door was open and he ran outside and sprinted across the sand. 'Sara, *Sara...*' His breath rattled from his lungs when he saw something in the shallows. It was her dress. *'Sara?'* He ploughed through the waves. 'Where are you?'

'I'm here.' She swam out from behind some rocks and stood up and waded towards him. 'What's the matter?'

Her calm tone turned his fear to fury. *What the hell are you doing swimming on your own in the dark?'* he bellowed as he splashed through the water and grabbed hold of her arm. 'You bloody fool. Don't you have *any* common sense?'

'*Ow!* Alekos, you're hurting me. Why shouldn't I swim? It's not dark—there's a full moon.' She tried to pull free of him but he tightened his grip and dragged her behind him back to the shore. She kicked water at him. 'Let go of me. You're a control freak, do you know that?'

He tugged her closer to him so that her breasts, barely covered by her wet bra, were pressed against his heaving chest. Alekos's lungs burned as if he'd run a marathon. His dream about Dimitri was jumbled in his mind with the reality of seeing Sara disappear into the sea.

'I won't have another death by drowning on my conscience.'

She stopped struggling and stared at him, her green eyes huge and dark in the moon shadow. 'What do you mean?'

He silently cursed his emotional outburst. He knew he should shrug it off and walk back to the house, but inexplicably he found he wanted to tell Sara the terrible secret that had haunted him since he was a teenager. He trusted her implicitly, but he did not want to think of the implications of that right now.

He exhaled heavily. 'My brother drowned in the sea.' Sara drew a sharp breath as he continued. 'He'd gone swimming alone at night and his body was discovered washed up on the beach the next day.'

'Oh, God, how awful. Do you know how it happened? Maybe he had an attack of cramp.'

'Dimitri was a strong swimmer and a superb athlete.' Alekos released Sara's arm and dropped down onto the sand where the waves rippled onto the beach. He loved the sea but he hated it too for taking his brother from him. He hated himself more for his failure. 'It was my fault,' he said harshly. 'I could have saved Dimitri.'

She sat down on the sand next to him. 'Do you mean you were both swimming when your brother got into trouble? I know you would have done your best to save his life,' she said softly.

He shook his head. 'I wasn't with him. At the inquest his death was recorded as an accident. But...' he swallowed hard '... I believe Dimitri took his own life.'

Again she inhaled sharply. 'Why do you think that?'

'Because he told me he wanted to die. My brother was heartbroken when he found out his girlfriend had cheated on him, and he said to me that he didn't want to live without her.' Alekos raked his hair off his brow with an unsteady hand as his mind flew back to the past. Aged fourteen, he hadn't understood why Dimitri had cared so deeply for a woman.

'You'll understand when you fall in love,' Dimitri had told him. *'You'll find out how love catches you when you least expect it and eats away at you until you can't think or sleep or eat for thinking about the woman you love. And when you find out that she doesn't love you, love destroys you.'*

Alekos had vowed when he was a teenager that love would never have a chance to destroy him like it had Dimitri. But for twenty years he'd felt guilty that he had not taken his brother's threat to end his life seriously and he hadn't sought help for Dimitri. His parents had been devastated by their oldest son's death and Alekos hadn't wanted to add to their grief by revealing that he believed Dimitri had committed suicide.

'I had spoken to my brother earlier on the day that he died, and he told me he felt like walking into the sea and never coming back. But I didn't take him seriously. I assumed he'd get over Nia and go back to being the fun, happy guy my brother was—until he fell in love.'

Alekos's jaw clenched. 'Love destroyed him, and I did nothing to save him.' He tensed when Sara put her hand on his arm. Her fingers were pale against his darkly tanned skin. She did not say anything but he sensed compassion in her silence and it helped to ease the raw feeling inside him.

'My memories are of him laughing, always laughing,' he said thickly. 'But on that day I found him crying. I was shocked but I still didn't do anything. I should have told my parents that Dimitri had suicidal thoughts. I didn't understand how my amazing brother, who everyone loved, could really mean to throw away his life and hurt his family over a goddamned love affair.'

'I don't believe you could have done anything, if your brother was determined to take his life,' Sara said gently. 'He may have had other problems you didn't know about. Young men in particular often find it hard to talk about things. But you don't know for certain that he did commit suicide. Presumably he didn't leave a note as the inquest recorded an accidental death.'

'He told me what he intended to do but I've never confided to anyone what I'm convinced was the real reason for Dimitri's death.'

'And so you have kept your guilt a secret for years, even though you don't know for sure that you have anything to feel guilty about. Dimitri's death *could* have been an accident. But even if it wasn't, you were in no way to blame, Alekos. You were young, and you were not responsible for your brother.'

Sara stood up. 'We should go back to the house. It must be late, and there is another meeting with shareholders tomorrow.' She brushed sand from her legs. 'I'm going for a quick swim to wash off the sand but I'll stay close to the shore.'

'I'll come with you.' He jumped up and followed her into the sea. The water was warm and its silken glide over his skin cleansed his body and his mind. The fact that Sara had not judged him and had tried to defend him helped him to view the past more rationally. *Could* it simply have been a terrible coincidence that Dimitri had died soon after confiding that he was depressed? Alekos had never considered the possibility before because he'd blamed himself when he was fourteen and he'd carried on blaming himself without questioning it.

He swam across the bay and back again, once, twice, he lost count of how many times as he sought to exorcise his demons, cutting through the water with powerful strokes until finally he was out of breath.

He watched Sara wading back to the beach. Her impromptu swim meant that she was in her underwear and her wet knickers were almost see-through so that he could make out the pale globes of her buttocks. When she turned to look for him, he saw in the moonlight her dark pink nipples through her wet, transparent bra.

Desire coiled through him, hardening him instantly so that he was glad he was standing waist-deep in the water. But he couldn't remain in the sea all night. He knew from her stifled gasp that she had noticed the bulge beneath his wet boxer shorts when he walked towards her. As he drew closer to her he watched her pupils dilate until they were dark pools, full of mystery and promise, and he asked the question that had been bugging him since the night they had spent together.

'Why did you choose me to be your first lover?'

CHAPTER NINE

SARA KNEW THAT telling Alekos the truth was not an option. Even if she was brave enough, or foolish enough, to admit she loved him, the revelation was not something he would want to hear. She understood him better now that he had told her about the nature of his brother's death. Living with the belief that Dimitri had taken his own life because of a failed love affair explained a lot about Alekos's opinion of love.

'*Love is simply a sanitized word for lust,*' he'd once sneered. The truth was that he blamed love for his brother's death as much as he blamed himself for not preventing Dimitri's suicide—if it *had* been suicide.

She frowned as she examined her own past that, like Alekos, she had allowed to influence her for far too long.

'I grew up being told by my mother that men only want women for one thing. Mum never revealed who my father was but she made it clear that she blamed him for abandoning her when she fell pregnant with me.'

She paused, remembering the brittle woman who she had called Mum and yet she'd never felt any kind of bond between them. Her mother's unplanned pregnancy had resulted in an unwanted child, Sara thought painfully. When she'd been old enough to start dating she had never allowed things to go too far, and when guys had dropped her because she refused to sleep with them it had reinforced her mother's warning that men only wanted sex. 'I'm sure she had loved my father and I think she continued to love him up until her death. I'm certain she never had another relationship after Lionel went back to his wife.'

She stirred the wet sand with her toes. Alekos was standing very close and she was agonisingly aware of him. The moonlight slanted over his broad shoulders and made the droplets of water clinging to his chest hairs sparkle. 'When I finally met my father I realised that he wasn't a bad person. He admitted he'd made a mistake when he'd had an affair with my mother. But she'd known he was married and so it was her mistake too.'

Sara made herself look directly at Alekos. He still had to wear the eye patch and, with a day's growth of dark stubble covering his jaw, he looked more like a pirate than ever. Dark, dangerous and devastatingly attractive. 'I had sex with you because I wanted to. You didn't coerce me or pretend that it meant anything to you—and that's fine because it didn't mean anything to me either.'

'But why me?' he persisted. 'Why not Paul Eddis, for instance? You seemed pretty friendly with him at the board members' dinner.'

She shrugged. 'Paul is a nice guy, but there was no spark between us like there was between you and me.'

'Was?' Alekos said softly. 'I would not use the past tense.' He curved his arm around her waist and tugged her into the heat of his body. The effect on her was electrifying and she was mortified, knowing he must feel the hard points of her nipples. Her brain urged her to step away from him but her body had other ideas and she was trapped by her longing for him when he lowered his head towards her.

'Is this the spark you referred to?' he growled. He kept her clamped against him while he ran his other hand down her spine and lower, sliding his fingers beneath the waistband of her knickers to caress her bare bottom. 'Sexual chemistry enslaves both of us, Sara *mou*.'

She couldn't deny it, not when her body shook, betraying her need for him as he covered her mouth with his and kissed her deeply, hungrily, making the spark ignite and burn. He'd called it *chemistry* and she told herself that was all it was. His story about his brother had touched her heart, but it had also shown her that Alekos would not fall in love with her because he despised love and maybe he was afraid of it.

She could end this now. But why deny herself what she so desperately wanted? Alekos was an incredible lover. True, she had no one to compare him to, but instinctively she knew that when they'd made love it had been magical for him too. She had already decided to leave her job and she had two weeks left to serve of the month's notice period they had agreed on.

Why shouldn't she make the most of the time she had with him and then walk away with her head held high? Her mother had spent her life loving a man she couldn't have. There was no way she was going to do the same, Sara vowed. Knowing that Alekos would never love her freed her from hope and expectation and allowed her to simply enjoy his skill as a wonderful lover.

And so she kissed him back with a fervour that revealed her desire and made him groan into her mouth when she traced her fingertips over his chest and abdomen, following the arrow of black hairs down to where his wet boxer shorts moulded the burgeoning length of his arousal.

His hands were equally busy as he unfastened her bra and peeled the sodden cups away from her breasts so that he could cradle their weight in his palms. 'Beautiful,' he muttered before he bent his head and took one nipple into his mouth, sucked hard until she cried out, and her cry echoed over the empty beach. Then he transferred his lips to her other nipple and flicked his tongue across the tender peak while simultaneously he slid his hand into the front of her knickers and pushed his finger into her molten heat.

Her legs buckled and he tightened his arm around her waist and lowered her onto the sand, coming down on top of her so that his body covered hers. She was aware of him tugging her panties off and her excitement grew when he jerked his boxers down and his erection pushed into her belly. His ragged breaths filled her ears and his male scent swamped her senses. She licked his shoulder and tasted sea salt.

'Open your legs,' he said hoarsely.

She wanted to feel his length inside her and she shared his impatience. But his voice broke through the sexual haze clouding her brain and she remembered something vital.

'We can't here. I'm not on the pill.' Not even her overwhelming desire for Alekos was worth risking an unplanned pregnancy.

He tensed and swore softly as he lifted himself off her and pulled up his boxers before he held out his hand and drew her to her feet. 'I can't go back to the house naked,' she muttered as he began to lead her up the beach. 'One of the staff might see me.'

'None of them sleep here. There is a small fishing village on the island and all the staff return to their own homes every evening.' He scooped her up in his arms and strode across the sand. 'So, are you going to sleep with me, Sara *mou*?' His sensual smile did not disguise the serious tone of his voice.

'I hope not.' She grinned when he frowned. 'I'll be very disappointed if all we do is sleep.'

Laughter rumbled in his big chest. 'Do you know the punishment for being a tease?' He proceeded to tell her exactly how he intended to punish her, so that by the time he carried her into his bedroom and laid her on the bed Sara was shivering with anticipation and a wild hunger that grew fiercer when he slid a protective sheath over his erection and positioned himself between her thighs.

He drove into her with a powerful thrust that made her catch her breath as she discovered again his size and strength. He filled her, fitted her so perfectly as if he had been designed exclusively for her. She pushed away the dangerous thought and concentrated on learning every inch of his body, running her hands over his chest and shoulders, his long spine and smooth buttocks that rose and fell in a steady rhythm.

She arched her hips to meet each thrust as he plunged deeper, harder, faster, taking her higher with every measured stroke. He was her joy and her delight, her master and tutor. Her love.

Terrified she might say the words out loud, she cupped his face between her hands and kissed his mouth.

'Ah, Sara.' His voice sounded oddly shaken, as if

he too felt a connection between them that was more than simply the joining of their mouths and bodies. Don't look for things that are not there, Sara told herself. Enjoy this for what it is—fantastic sex.

Alekos showed her how fantastic, how unbelievably amazing sex could be when he slid his hands beneath her bottom and lifted her hips to meet his devastatingly powerful thrust that hurtled her over the edge and into ecstasy. It was beyond beautiful, and she sobbed his name as pulses of pleasure radiated out from deep in her pelvis. The fierce spasms of her orgasm kept shuddering through her while he continued to move inside her. His pace was urgent now as he neared his own release. And when he came, it was with a groan torn from his throat as his body shook so hard that she wrapped her arms around him and held him tight against her heart.

Another week passed, as tense and turbulent as the weeks preceding it, as Alekos fought to save the business his father had entrusted to him. In many ways it was the worst time of his life. Endless meetings with shareholders at GE's offices in Athens, strategy meetings with his management team and, hanging over him, the possibility he refused to consider— that he might fail. It *should* have been the worst time of his life and the fact that he could smile—*Theos,* that he could actually be happy—was totally down to Sara.

At work she was a calming presence, offering

thoughtful and intelligent suggestions when he asked her advice—which he had found himself doing more and more often. She charmed the shareholders and the board members liked and trusted her. Sara was an asset in the office as his PA, and when they returned to Eiríni each evening she delighted him in her role as his mistress.

Often they walked down to the village and sat on the small harbour to watch the fishing boats unload the day's catch. Later they would return to the house and eat dinner served on the terrace by his housekeeper before they went to bed and made love for hours until exhaustion finally claimed them. Alekos was waiting to grow bored of Sara, but when he woke each morning and studied her lovely face on the pillow beside him he felt an indefinable tug in his chest and a rather more predictable tug of sexual hunger in his groin that he assuaged when he woke her and she was instantly aroused and ready for him.

'Why do you think your father would blame you for GE's problems when you yourself told me that hostile takeover bids are a common threat to businesses?' she asked him one day, after he'd confided that he felt he had let his father's memory down.

'He doubted my ability to run the company as successfully as he believed Dimitri would have done.' Alekos rubbed a towel over his chest after he'd swum in the pool. He sat down on a lounger next to where Sara was sunbathing in a tiny green bikini which his fingers itched to remove from her shapely body that drove him to distraction.

It was Sunday, and after six crazily busy days of working he had decreed that today they would not leave the island. In truth, he would have been happy not to leave the bedroom they now shared, but Sara had murmured that they couldn't spend *all* day having sex.

'Why do you think your father compared you to your brother?'

He shrugged. 'Dimitri was the firstborn son and my father groomed him for his future role as chairman of GE from when he was a young boy. My relationship with my father was much more distant. I was the youngest of his five children, the second son. When Dimitri died and I became my father's heir he made it obvious that I was second best. Sometimes,' he said slowly, 'I wondered if he wished that I had died and Dimitri had lived.'

Sara sat up and faced him, her green eyes bright and fierce. 'I'm sure that's not true. It must have been a difficult time for all the family, but particularly for your parents who were grieving for their son. It sounds like he was very popular.'

'Everyone loved Dimitri.'

'Especially you. I think you were very close to your brother,' she said softly.

'I idolised him.' Images flashed into Alekos's mind: Dimitri teaching him to sail, the two of them kicking a football around the garden, that time when he'd accidentally smashed the glass panes of the greenhouse with a misaimed kick and his brother had taken the blame. He had blocked out his memories of Dimitri because when he'd been fourteen it had hurt too much to think about him. It still hurt twenty years later. And he was still angry. If his brother hadn't fallen in love with some stupid girl he would still be here, still laughing, still Alekos's best friend.

He hadn't spoken about Dimitri in all those years and he did not understand why he had told Sara things that he'd buried deep inside him. He didn't want her compassion, he didn't want to want her so badly that he found himself thinking about her all the time. His crazy obsession with her would pass, he assured himself. Desire never lasted and the more often he had sex with her, the quicker he would become sated with her and then he could move on with his life and forget about her.

He walked back over to the pool and dived in, swimming length after length while he brought his emotions under control. Of course he did not need Sara. She was simply a pleasant diversion from his work problems.

She came to sit at the edge of the pool and he swam up to her. 'How about we have some lunch, followed by an afternoon siesta?'

'Hmm…' She appeared to consider his suggestion. 'Or we could forget lunch and just go for a lie-down.'

'Aren't you hungry?'

'I'm very hungry.' Her impish smile made his gut twist and he pulled her into the water, ignoring her yelp that the water was cold.

He felt angry with himself for his weakness and angry with her for making him weak. 'In that case I'd better satisfy your appetite, hadn't I,' he mocked as he untied the strings of her bikini top and pulled it off, cupping her breasts in his hands and playing with her nipples until she moaned softly.

He was completely in control, and he proved it when he carried her up to the bedroom and placed her face down onto the bed. He made love to her using all his considerable skill until she climaxed once, and when she came down he took her up again and only when she buried her face in the pillows to muffle her cries as she had a second orgasm did he finally let go, and felt the drenching pleasure of his own release.

By the middle of their second week in Greece the situation with GE started to look more hopeful, as increasing numbers of shareholders pledged their alliance to Alekos and refused to sell their shares in the company to Stelios Choutos. Alekos was still tense and Sara knew he would not be able to relax while GE and his position as chairman were still threatened. But, although she continued to be supportive, she had a niggling worry of her own that made her pop to the chemist during her lunch break.

Of course, having bought a pregnancy test, she felt the symptoms that her period was about to start and, although the dull pain low in her stomach was annoying, she felt relieved that she wouldn't need to use the test.

The news came on Friday afternoon. Alekos strode into Sara's office, which adjoined his, and found her standing by the window, gazing up at the iconic Acropolis. She pulled her mind from her thoughts and her heart leapt when she saw the grin on his face.

'We won.' He swept her into his arms. 'Stelios's financial backers have pulled out and I've just had a call confirming he has withdrawn his takeover bid.'

'So it's over? The company is safe and you will continue to be chairman?' She blocked out the re-alisation that the end of the battle for GE meant that her affair with Alekos would also be over.

'I have the unanimous backing of the board, in-cluding Orestis Pagnotis.'

His victory made him almost boyish and he swung her round before claiming her lips in a fierce kiss that deepened to a slow and achingly sweet exploration of her mouth with his tongue. Sara was trembling when he finally released her and she moved away from him while she struggled to regain her composure.

'Congratulations. I never doubted you.'

'I know.' He no longer needed to wear the eye patch now that his injury was completely healed, and his eyes gleamed as he held her gaze. 'Your support was invaluable. We work well together as a team. We'll fly to back to London tomorrow and start focusing on what GE is renowned for, which is to make the best yachts in the world.'

Sara did not say anything then, but when the helicopter flew them to the island and they walked up to the house Alekos slipped his hand into hers. 'You're very quiet.'

'I was thinking that this is our last night on Eiríni—and our last night together. Today was the final day of my notice period,' she reminded him when he frowned. 'I've arranged for a temporary PA to fill my place while you hold interviews and appoint a permanent member of staff.'

He looked shocked, and that surprised her until she told herself he'd been too busy fighting for his company to have been aware that her notice period had finished. She followed him into the sitting room and looked through the glass doors that opened onto the garden where the swimming pool was a brilliant turquoise beneath a cloudless blue sky. She had fallen in love with Alekos's island and it would have a special place in her heart for ever.

Alekos crossed to the bar and poured them both a drink, as he did every evening: a crisp white wine for her and a single malt Scotch with ice for him. Usually they carried their drinks out to the terrace, but this evening he drained his glass in a couple of gulps and poured himself another whisky.

'You could stay on,' he said gruffly. 'Why do you want to leave? I know you enjoy your job.'

'I do enjoy it, but actually I never wanted to be a secretary. I only did it because I needed to help my mother pay the mortgage. Now I'm selling the house and I have plans to do something different with my life.'

'I see.' Alekos did not try to persuade her to stay, nor did he ask about her future plans, Sara noted. She ignored the pang her heart gave and reminded herself that it was time she took control of her life. 'We both know that our affair…or whatever it is we've been having for the past few weeks…was temporary. I think it will be better to end our professional and personal association once we are back in London.'

Once again a flicker of surprise crossed his sculpted features. She was possibly the only woman who had ended a relationship with Alekos before he was ready for it to finish, Sara thought wryly. It was only the thought of her mother's empty life that kept her strong when her treacherous heart and traitorous body both implored her to be his mistress for as long as he wanted her.

'In that case we had better make the most of tonight,' he said in a cool voice that forced her to acknowledge that she really did mean nothing to him other than as a good PA and a good lay. Knowing it helped her to harden her heart when he drew her into his arms and kissed her with such aching tenderness that she could almost believe he was trying to persuade her to change her mind.

It was just great sex, she reminded herself as he undid the buttons on her blouse and slid his hand into her bra to caress her breast. He stripped her right there in the sitting room and shrugged out of his clothes, taking a condom from his trouser pocket before he pushed her back against the sofa cushions. He hooked her legs over his shoulders so that she was splayed open to him and used his tongue to such great effect that she gasped his name when he reared over her and thrust into her so hard that she came instantly.

It was the beginning of a sensual feast that lasted long into the night and Alekos's passion and his dedication to giving her pleasure tested Sara's resolve to leave him to its limits. She wished the night could last for ever, but with the pale light of dawn came a reality that stunned her.

She woke to the sound of the shower from his bathroom and the horrible lurch her stomach gave sent her running into her own bathroom. There could be a number of explanations of why she had been sick, but although she still had an uncomfortable cramping pain in her stomach her period was now over a week late. The pregnancy test took mere minutes to perform and the wait for the result seemed to last a lifetime.

Alekos knocked on the door while she was still clinging to the edge of the basin because her legs had turned to jelly. 'I'll meet you downstairs for break-fast.'

'Sure.' She was amazed that her voice sounded normal. 'See you in a minute.' She almost threw up again at the thought of food, and the much worse prospect of telling Alekos her news. But not telling him was not an option. She wasn't going to make *every* mistake her mother had made, Sara thought grimly.

He found her on the beach, standing on the wet sand where the waves rippled over her bare toes. Alekos remembered how he had seen Sara walk into the sea the night they had arrived on the island, and his body tightened at the memory of how she had come apart in his arms. Sex with her was better than he'd known with any other woman but, *Theos*, he wasn't going to beg her to stay with him. The idea of him pleading with a mistress was laughable but he didn't feel in the mood to laugh, even though he had won the battle to keep GE. Curiously, he hadn't given a thought to the company since Sara had announced her inten-tion to leave him when they went back to London.

'Don't you want something to eat?' he said as he walked up to her. 'The helicopter will be here to col-lect us in a few minutes.'

'I'm not hungry.'

She was pale and he frowned when he saw her mouth tremble before she firmed her lips. The breeze stirred her hair and Alekos smelled the evocative scent of vanilla. 'What…?' he began, unable to rationalise his sudden sense of foreboding.

'I'm pregnant.'

She said the words in a rush, as if they might have less impact. But they left him reeling. He stared at her slender figure, which of course showed no signs yet that a new life was developing inside her. Was it possible she was expecting his baby? He had never thought about fatherhood, apart from in a vague way as an event that he supposed would happen at some point in his future. His family impressed on him the need for him to provide an heir. But this was real. If Sara was telling him the truth, and he had no reason to doubt her, he was going to be a father and he couldn't begin to assimilate the emotions churning inside him. Crazy though it was, he felt a flicker of excitement at the idea of holding his child in his arms. *Theos*, he hoped he would be a good father.

In the years since his brother had died Alekos had become adept at hiding his feelings and his coolly logical brain took charge. 'You're sure?'

'I did a test this morning and it…it was positive. My period is a week late, but I thought…' she bit her lip '… I hoped there was another explanation. We've always been careful.'

Alekos went cold as he recalled that he had been careless that first time when they had been on *Artemis*. His hunger for Sara had been so acute that he'd made love to her a second time immediately after they'd had sex.

He stared out across the sea—flat and calm today, it looked like a huge mirror reflecting the blue sky above, but the idyllic scene did not soothe his tumultuous thoughts. His irresponsible behaviour had resulted in Sara conceiving his child and the implications were huge. He should have taken more care. He should have fought his weakness for Sara. Anger with himself made his voice clipped and cold.

'In that case a damage limitation strategy is necessary.'

She frowned. 'What do you mean by damage limitation?'

'How do you think GE's board members will react to the news that I have fathered an illegitimate child?' he said grimly. 'Once the press get hold of the story—as they undoubtedly will—I'll be accused of being an irresponsible playboy and that kind of reputation will not go down well with the board or the shareholders, especially now, so soon after the hostile takeover bid. There is only one solution. We will have to get married.'

He looked at her stunned expression and ignored the inexplicable urge to enfold her in his arms and promise her that everything would be all right. Instead he drawled, 'Congratulations, Sara *mou*. You've done what many other women dream of and secured yourself a rich husband.'

She flinched as if he had struck her, but then her chin came up. 'Firstly, I have never been *yours*, and secondly I am not any other woman—I'm me, and

I would never marry for money. Your arrogance is astounding. I'm certainly not going to marry you to save your reputation.'

Sara spun round and walked up the beach towards the house. She heard the helicopter overhead and felt glad that soon she would be on it and leaving Eiríni. She wished she could leave Alekos behind. She hadn't expected him to be pleased about her pregnancy. Pleased had not been *her* first reaction when she'd stared at the blue line on the pregnancy test that confirmed a positive result. She felt stunned and scared and very alone, and Alekos's implication that she was a gold-digger who had somehow engineered falling pregnant to snare him was so unfair that tears choked her.

'Would you deny the child its father then, Sara?'

She stopped walking and turned to find he was right behind her, so close that she breathed in his aftershave, mingled with an indefinable scent that was uniquely Alekos. 'You don't want a child,' she muttered.

'It doesn't matter what I want or don't want. The child is my heir and if we marry he or she will inherit not only GE but the Gionakis fortune. If you refuse to marry me I will financially support my child, but in the future I will take a wife and any legitimate children born within the marriage will bear my name and be entitled to inherit my legacy.'

Alekos trapped her gaze with his eyes that were as

black and hard as pieces of jet. 'Will you deny your child its birthright the way you were denied yours, Sara? You told me you wish you'd grown up knowing your father. Can you really deprive your child of the chance to grow up with both its parents?'

CHAPTER TEN

ALEKOS HAD HIT her with an emotional body blow. He had aimed his argument straight at her heart, aware that she would do anything to give her baby a father— even if it meant she had to marry him.

She had tried to dissuade him. During the helicopter flight from the island and when they'd boarded his private jet bound for London, she had offered various suggestions of how they could both have a role in their child's life. But his response had been unequivocal. They must marry before the baby was born so that it was legitimate.

She looked across the plane to where he was sitting in one of the plush leather armchairs and her heart predictably gave a jolt when she found him watching her. He was casually dressed in grey trousers and a white shirt open at the throat, showing his tanned skin that had turned a darker shade of olive-gold from two weeks in the hot Greek sun. His hair was longer, and the black stubble on his jaw reminded her of the faint abrasion marks on her breasts where his cheek had scraped her skin when he'd made love to her numerous times the previous night.

Their last night together, she had believed. Now she wondered if he intended their marriage to include sex, and if—or perhaps that should be when— he tired of her would he have discreet affairs that did not attract the attention of the press or the board members?

'I will make a press statement on Monday announcing our engagement and forthcoming marriage.'

Sara's stomach lurched. 'Why so soon? We should at least wait until I've seen my doctor to confirm my pregnancy. The test showed that I am about five weeks, and I believe a first scan to determine when the baby is due is at around eight to ten weeks.'

'I can't risk the media finding out you are pregnant before I've put an engagement ring on your finger. The board members are jittery after the takeover bid. The news that I am going to marry my sensible secretary and leave my playboy days behind will bolster their confidence in me. For that reason I've made an appointment for us at a jewellers so that you can choose a ring.'

Everything was happening too fast, she thought frantically. Yesterday she'd believed she would never see Alekos again after they had returned to England, but now she was expecting his child and he was bulldozing her into marriage.

'I don't believe a loveless marriage will be good for anyone, including the baby.' She imagined a future where Alekos had mistresses and she became bitter like her mother, and said rather desperately, 'It can't possibly work.'

'My parents did not marry for love and had a very successful marriage.' Alekos opened his laptop, signalling that the conversation was over. It was convenient for him to marry her to keep GE's board members happy, Sara thought. And by becoming his wife she would be doing the best thing for the baby. But what about what was best for her? How could she marry Alekos when she loved him but he would never love her? But how could she deny her baby the Gionakis name? The stark answer was that she couldn't.

The jewellers was in Bond Street and the price tags on the engagement rings made Sara catch her breath. 'Choose whichever ring you want,' Alekos told her. 'I don't care how much it costs.'

But diamond solitaires the size of a rock were not her style, and she finally chose an oval-shaped emerald surrounded by white diamonds because Alekos commented that the emerald matched the colour of her eyes.

'I thought you were taking me home,' she said when the limousine drew up outside his apartment block.

'This will be your home from now on. I'll have your clothes and other belongings packed up and sent over from your house. But I want you here, where I can keep an eye on you.'

She looked at him suspiciously. 'You make it sound like I'm your prisoner. Are you worried I'll leak the story to the press that I am expecting the chairman of GE's baby?'

'*No*. You proved your loyalty to me and to the company when you helped me fight off the hostile takeover.' Alekos raked his hair off his brow and she was surprised to see colour flare on his cheekbones. 'I want you to stay with me because you are pregnant and you need looking after.'

'Of course I don't.' She tried to ignore the tug on her heart at the idea of him taking care of her as if she were a fragile creature instead of a healthy, independent woman.

'You're pale, and you fell asleep on the plane and in the car just now,' he persisted.

'I'm tired because I didn't get much sleep last night.' She blushed as memories of the many inventive ways he had made love to her for hours the previous night flooded her mind. The gleam in his eyes told her he was remembering their wild passion too. 'Alekos…?'

'Yes, it will be a real marriage in every way,' he drawled.

Her face burned. 'How did you know I was going to ask that?'

'Your eyes are very expressive and they reveal your secrets.'

Sara prayed they didn't, but she carefully did not look at him when he showed her to a guest room in his penthouse because she didn't want him to guess she was disappointed that she would not be sharing his bed until they were married.

The following week passed in a blur. News of their engagement was mentioned in most of the newspapers and Sara was glad to hide away in the penthouse to avoid the paparazzi, who were desperate to interview the woman who had tamed the notorious Greek playboy Alekos Gionakis.

Her father phoned to offer his congratulations, but when she asked him if he would attend her wedding with her half-siblings Lionel hesitated for so long that Sara's heart sank.

'Why don't you tell Charlotte and Freddie Kingsley you are their sister?' Alekos asked when he discovered her in tears. He had come home from the office unexpectedly in the afternoon and found her lying on the sofa.

She shook her head. 'I can't betray my father to his children. Perhaps it will be better if he never tells them about me and they won't know that he was once unfaithful to their mother.'

Alekos sat down on the edge of the sofa and studied her face intently. 'You're as white as a sheet. How many times have you been sick today?'

'Three or four.' She tried to shrug off his concern. 'Nausea and tiredness are normal in early pregnancy and I'll probably feel better soon.'

But she didn't. Over the next few days the sickness became more frequent and the dull ache on the
right side of her abdomen that she'd had on and off
for weeks turned into a stabbing pain. Sara had read
that a miscarriage was fairly common in the first
three months of pregnancy and nothing could be
done to prevent nature taking its course.

For the first time since the shock of finding out
that she was pregnant her baby became real in her
mind. She pictured a little boy with black hair and
dark eyes like his daddy and she felt an overwhelming sense of protectiveness for the new life inside her.
'Hang on, little one,' she whispered when she went
to bed early that night, praying that if she rested her
baby would make it through the crucial early weeks
of her pregnancy.

The pain woke her some hours later. A sensation like a red-hot poker scourging her insides was
so agonising that she struggled to breathe. Sadness
swept through her as she realised that she was probably going to lose the baby and when she fumbled
to switch on the bedside light the sight of blood on
the sheets confirmed the worst. But the amount of
blood shocked her and the pain in her stomach was
excruciating. She felt faint, and her instincts told her
something was seriously wrong.

'Alekos...' Dear God, what if he couldn't hear her
and she bled to death, alone and terrified? She called
on every last bit of her fading strength. '*Alekos*...
help me...'

'Sara?' She heard the bedroom door open and the overhead light suddenly illuminated the room. She heard Alekos swear and she heard fear in his voice. 'I'm calling an ambulance.' His hand felt cool on her feverish brow. She tried to speak but she felt so weak. His face swam in front of her eyes as he leaned over her. 'Hang on, Sara *mou*,' he said hoarsely, repeating the plea she had made to her baby. But pain was tearing her apart and she slipped into blackness.

Someone, at some time—Alekos did not know who or when—had come up with the gem of wisdom, *You don't know what you've got till it's gone*. The quote had been painfully apt while he had paced up and down the waiting room while Sara had undergone emergency surgery to stop serious internal bleeding resulting from an ectopic pregnancy.

'An ectopic is when a fertilised egg implants in a fallopian tube instead of in the womb,' the obstetrician at the hospital where Sara had been rushed to by ambulance had explained to Alekos. 'The pregnancy cannot continue but the condition is not life-threatening unless the tube ruptures, which unfortunately occurred in Miss Lovejoy's case.'

An hour-long operation and two blood transfusions later, Sara was transferred to the intensive care ward and a nurse told Alekos she had been lucky to survive. He'd known that, even without much medical knowledge. The sight of her lying pale and lifeless on the blood-soaked sheets was something he would never forget.

It had been much later, when he'd sat by her bed in ITU, steadfastly refusing the nurse's suggestion to go home and get some sleep, when he'd allowed himself to think about the baby they had lost, and the fact that he had very nearly lost Sara. He had spent his life since he was fourteen building a fortress around his heart so that nothing could hurt him like Dimitri's death had. So why were his eyes wet, and why did it feel as if a boulder had lodged in his throat making swallowing painful?

Five days later, he stepped into her room in the private wing of the hospital where she had been moved to after she was well enough to leave ITU and a ghost of a smile curved his lips when he found her dressed and sitting in a chair. He was relieved to see a faint tinge of colour on her cheeks, but she still looked as fragile as spun glass and his stomach twisted.

'You look better.' It was a lie but he suddenly didn't know what to say to her. The little scrap of life that neither he nor Sara had planned for her to conceive was gone. He did not know how she felt about the loss of their child, and he didn't want to face his own feelings. So he forced himself to smile as he picked up her holdall. 'Are you ready to come home?'

She avoided looking directly at him, and that was a bad sign. 'I'm not going to the penthouse with you.'

'I realise it holds bad memories. We can go somewhere else. I'll check with the doctor that you are okay to fly and we'll go to Eiríni.'

'No.' At last she did look at him and wiped away a tear as it slid down her cheek. 'It's not the penthouse. I'm sad that I lost the baby, but we only knew I was pregnant for two weeks. I was just getting used to the idea of being a mother but now…that's not going to happen.' She took something out of her handbag and held out her hand to him. 'I need to give you this.'

He stared at her engagement ring sparkling in his palm and a nerve jumped in his cheek.

'Now there is no baby there is no reason for us to marry,' she said quietly.

Something roared inside Alekos. He felt unbalanced, as if the world had tilted on its axis and he was falling into a dark place. All he had thought about for the past days was Sara and the baby they had lost. *This* scenario had not occurred to him and he didn't know what to say or think or feel.

'There is no need for either of us to make hasty decisions. You've been through hell and need time to recuperate before we think about the future.'

She shook her head. '*We* don't have a future together. Your only reason for deciding to marry me was because I was pregnant with your child.'

'That's not strictly true. There were other reasons that are still valid even though there is no baby.'

'What reasons?' She stared at him and Alekos saw the sudden tension in her body and the faint betraying tremble of her lower lip. For a moment he almost gave in to the urge to put his arms around her and smell the vanilla scent of her hair. He was almost tempted to listen to the roaring inside him. But then he thought of Dimitri walking into the sea, throwing away his life for love, and the fortress walls closed around Alekos's heart.

'My position as chairman of GE will be strengthened if I marry. The board members like and respect you—as I do. I value you, Sara. We are a good team and I am confident that if you were my wife you would run my home as efficiently as you ran my office.'

To his own ears his words sounded pompous and Sara gave an odd laugh. 'You make marriage sound like I would be your PA with a few extra perks.'

'Excellent perks,' he said drily. A lot of women would jump at the chance to live the wealthy lifestyle he was offering. 'You would not have to work and could study art or do whatever you want to do. And let's not forget sex.' He watched her pale cheeks flood with colour and was amazed she could blush when he knew her body as well as his own and had kissed every centimetre of her creamy skin. 'The sexual chemistry between us shows no sign of burning out.'

'And you resent it,' she said slowly. 'The marriage you described is not enough for me. I don't care about your money,' she said quickly before he could speak, 'and I agree the sex is great. But you would tire of

me eventually. I was your PA for two years and I
know the short lifespan of your interest in women.'

'What do you want, then?' he demanded, furious
with her for reading him too well.

'The saddest thing is that you have to ask.' She
stood up and gathered up her handbag. 'My friend
Ruth is coming to pick me up and she's invited me
to stay with her because my mother's house has now
been sold.'

It hit Alekos then that she actually meant it and
something akin to panic cramped in his gut. 'Sara,
we can talk.'

'Until we're blue in the face,' she said flatly, 'but it
won't change anything. I understand why you won't
allow anyone too close. I know you feel guilty because you think you should have done more to help
your brother. But you can't live in the past for ever,
Alekos. Love isn't an enemy you have to fight and I
don't believe Dimitri would have wanted you to live
your life without love.'

'Even though loving someone cost him his life?'
Alekos said savagely.

'You don't know for sure that he did mean to end
his life. You told me you never talked about Dimitri's death with the rest of your family. Maybe you
should. Because a life without love will make you
as bitter and unhappy as my mother was, and how I
would become if I married you.'

Her words stung him. 'I don't remember you
being unhappy when we were on Eiríni.' He pulled

her into his arms and sought her mouth. 'I made you happy,' he muttered against her lips. 'Do you think you'll find this passion with anyone else?'

He kissed her hard and his body jerked when he felt her respond. She was a golden light in his life, and he realised that almost from the first day she had started working for him he had looked forward to her cheerful smile every morning and he'd felt comfortable with her in a way he had never felt with other women. They had been friends before they were lovers but she was prepared to walk away from what they had because he refused to put a label on what he felt for her.

He knew how to seduce her. He knew how to kiss her with a deepening hunger so that she flattened out her bunched fists on his chest and slid her arms up around his neck. Her body melted into him and triumph surged through him, spiking his already heated blood. She couldn't deny *this*.

He couldn't believe it when she wrenched her mouth from beneath his and pushed against his chest. He was unprepared for her rejection and dropped his arms to his sides as she stepped away from him. 'You want me,' he said harshly. 'We're good together, Sara, but I won't beg. If I walk away I won't come back. Ever.'

He held his breath as she stood on tiptoe and brushed her lips gently on his cheek. 'I hope that one day you will find the happiness you deserve. And I hope I will too. I can't settle for second best, Alekos.'

He froze. *Second best*. Was that what she thought of him? The same as his father had thought. *Theos*, she might as well have stabbed him through his heart. The pain in his chest felt as if she had.

Sara watched Alekos stride out of her hospital room and nearly ran after him. She sank down onto the bed as the enormity of what she had done drained the little strength she had in her legs after her ordeal of the ectopic pregnancy. The sense of loss that swept over her was almost unbearable.

When she'd regained consciousness and discovered she was lying in a hospital bed she had known immediately that her baby hadn't survived. The grief she felt was greater than anything she'd experienced. It was true she had only known for a few weeks that she was pregnant but there was a hollow space inside her and she felt as though her hopes for her future as a mother had been ripped from her as savagely as her child had been ripped from her body.

Now she had lost Alekos too. She would never see him again, never feel his strong arms around her or feel him move inside her in the timeless dance of love. Because it wasn't love, she reminded herself. What she'd had with Alekos was wonderful sex that for him had been meaningless.

Much as she hated to acknowledge it, she had been just another mistress. The only difference between her and all the other countless women he'd had affairs with was that the board members of GE approved of her, which was why he had wanted to marry her despite her no longer being pregnant.

She knew she had done the right thing to turn him down. Her close brush with death when her tube had ruptured had shown her that life was too precious to waste a moment of it. There had been a moment when she'd thought Alekos was going to admit that he cared for her and she'd held her breath and hoped with all her heart, only to hear him say that he valued her in the same way that he might have said he valued a priceless painting or one of the flash superyachts his company was famous for building.

Once she would have been grateful for any crumb he offered her. She had been so lacking in self-confidence that she would have married him because she had adored him and didn't believe that a handsome, charismatic and sophisticated man such as Alekos could fall in love with his plain, frumpy secretary.

Meeting her father had made her feel like a whole person. Casting her mind back over the past months, she could see that she had taken more interest in her appearance because she felt more worthwhile, and maybe it was her new confidence that had attracted Alekos as much as her new, sexier clothes and hairstyle. But crucially she had forgotten that he'd once said love was simply a word used by poets and romantics to describe lust.

The sound of a deep male voice outside the door made her heart leap into her throat. But when she

stepped into the corridor it was not Alekos standing in front of the nurses' station, arguing with a
nurse and drawing attention from a crowd of curious onlookers.

'I don't care if my name is not on the visitor list,'
Lionel Kingsley said loudly. 'Sara Lovejoy is my
daughter and I have come to visit her.' He glanced
round and his expression became concerned when
he saw her. 'Sara, my dear, you should be resting.'
He spoke briefly on his mobile phone as he walked
over to her and Sara hurriedly pulled him into her
room and shut the door.

'What are you doing here? There must be a dozen
people who heard you say that I am your daughter.' She bit her lip. 'It's probably already on social
media and once the press get hold of the story it will
be headline news, especially as there is speculation
that you will be the new Home Secretary in the Cabinet reshuffle.'

'None of that is important.' Lionel swept her into
a bear hug. 'What matters is that you are safe and
as well as can be expected after you nearly lost your
life. Alekos phoned and told me what had happened,
and how you lost your baby.' He squeezed her so hard
that she felt breathless. 'I'm so sorry, Sara. For your
loss, and also for my behaviour. Alekos used some
very colourful language when he pointed out that I
had failed you as a father twice. The first time by not
being around when you were a child, and the second
by not publicly acknowledging you as my daughter.'

'He told you that?' she said faintly.

'And a lot more. He reminded me I was lucky to have a beautiful, compassionate and loyal daughter. When he told me how you had almost died I realised how stupid and selfish I had been. I should have welcomed you unreservedly, and I'm sorry I didn't before now.'

'But what about Charlotte and Freddie?' Sara was reeling from hearing how Alekos had stood up for her to her father. 'How do you think they will take the news that I am their sister?'

'Why don't you ask them? Or one of them, at least,' Charlotte Kingsley said as she walked into the room. 'Freddie is in America, but he said to tell you that he knows who you remind him of now.' She smiled at Sara's startled expression. 'You and I do look remarkably alike and not only because we both have green eyes. All three of dad's offspring take after his side of the family, and Freddie agrees with me that we can't think of a nicer person to have as our sister.'

'I thought you would hate me,' Sara said unsteadily.

Charlotte clasped her hand. 'Why would we hate you? Nothing that happened in the past is your fault. I'm sad that I didn't know about you for twenty-five years, but now I hope you will be part of our family for ever…if you want to be.'

Sara glanced at her father. 'Aren't you worried that the scandal will affect your political career?'

Lionel shrugged. 'These things often blow over.

I behaved badly towards your mother and my wife many years ago and the person who suffered most was you. Far more important than my career is my determination to try and make amends and be the father I should have been to you when you were growing up. And I'd like to start by taking you to my home in Berkshire so that you can recuperate, but of course I'll understand if you want to go home with Alekos.'

Her father looked puzzled. 'Actually, I assumed Alekos would be here. I know he refused to leave your bedside while you were in intensive care. And when he came to see me yesterday to tell me what he thought of me for treating you badly, he looked like he'd been to hell and back. But it's not surprising after he lost his child and could have lost you too. It's obvious how much he cares for you.'

Sara sat down heavily on the chair and buried her face in her hands. She felt as if she was on an emotional roller coaster from her intense sadness at losing her baby and the shock of realising how close she had come to losing her own life. She had rejected Alekos without considering his feelings about the loss of their child. Although her pregnancy had been in the early stages, it was likely that the trauma had reminded him of losing his brother when he was a teenager.

A sob escaped her and she felt a hand patting her shoulder. Charlotte—her sister—she thought emotively, pushed some tissues into her hand. 'Cry it out,

Sara. You've been through a terrible experience and you need time to grieve for the baby.'

As Alekos did. But she knew he would bottle up his feelings like he had when Dimitri died. 'I think I've made a terrible mistake,' she choked. Alekos needed her but she had sent him away and her tears were for the baby, for her, but mainly for the man she would always love.

CHAPTER ELEVEN

ALEKOS HAD SPENT his childhood at his parents' house just outside Athens. As a boy he had spent hours playing on the private beach but after Dimitri died he had stopped going there.

He moved away from the window, where he had been watching huge waves crash onto the shore. The recent storm had made the sea angry and the heavy sky echoed his mood. He picked up his brother's death certificate from the desk in his father's study and read it once more before he looked at his mother.

'Why didn't you tell me Dimitri suffered a heart attack when he went swimming and that was why he drowned?'

'You never wanted to talk about him. If his name was mentioned by anyone you would leave the room. Your father and I were advised not to push you to discuss the accident but to wait for you to bring up the subject.'

She sighed. 'Dimitri was born with a small hole in his heart but later tests showed that the defect had healed by itself and it was not expected to cause problems as he grew up. Your brother was such a strong, athletic boy and your father and I more or less forgot that there had been the early problem. When we learned that Dimitri had suffered heart failure we felt guilty that we should have persuaded him to have more health checks. The reason why Dimitri drowned was something we could not bear to discuss with you and your sisters. Why does your brother's cause of death matter now, so many years later?'

Alekos swallowed hard. 'I believed for all those years that Dimitri took his own life. He was heartbroken when he found out his girlfriend had cheated on him and he told me he did not want to live without Nia.'

His mother frowned. 'I remember he was upset over a girl. Your father had arranged for him to go and work in the Miami office for a few months to help him get over her. You were not at home on that last evening and so you did not see how excited Dimitri was about the trip to America.' She looked intently at her youngest son. 'I'm quite certain your brother knew he had everything to live for. He often went swimming at night and told me I worried too much when I asked him not to go into the sea alone.'

'I blamed myself for not getting help for Dimitri after he told me he felt depressed,' Alekos said gruffly. 'I felt guilty that I hadn't saved him. I missed him so much but I didn't want to cry in front of anyone because I was fourteen, not a baby. The only way I could cope was by not talking about him.'

'Dimitri's death was fate,' his mother said gently. 'I wish I had known how you felt, but I'm afraid you take after your father in the respect of not discussing your feelings. Kostas believed he must be strong for the rest of the family, but losing Dimitri made him withdraw emotionally. I think he found it hard to show how much he loved you because he was afraid of losing another child and suffering the same pain and grief he'd felt when Dimitri died.' She wiped away a tear. 'Your father was very proud of you, you know. He admired your drive and determination to take GE forward.'

'I wish I had known that Bampás approved of my ideas. I regret I didn't talk about Dimitri with him. It might have helped both of us.'

His mother nodded. 'Honesty and openness are important in a relationship and you should remember that when you marry Sara.'

Alekos's jaw clenched. 'Sara ended our engagement because I can't give her what she wants.'

'Sara does not strike me as someone who craves material possessions.'

'She says she will only marry for love.'

'Well, what other reason is there for marriage?'

He frowned. 'I thought that you and Bampás had an arranged marriage?'

His mother laughed. 'Our parents thought so too. But Kostas and I had met secretly and fallen in love, and we engineered our so-called arranged marriage. Love is the only reason to marry. Why is it a problem? You love Sara, don't you?'

Alekos could not reply to his mother's question, although he suspected the answer was somewhere in the mess of emotions that had replaced the cool logic which had served him perfectly well for two decades.

'I understand why my father was scared to love after he lost a son,' he said. His voice sounded as if it had scraped over rusty metal. He had a flashback to when he had been in the hospital waiting room, praying harder than he'd prayed in his life that Sara's life would be saved. 'Love can hurt,' he said roughly.

'But it can also bring the greatest joy,' his mother said softly. 'I am glad I was blessed with Dimitri and it was better to have him for twenty-one years than not to have known him and loved him. The pain I felt when he died was terrible, but the happiness he gave me in his short life was far greater.'

It was a wonderful party, and she was absolutely having a brilliant time, Sara told herself firmly. She looked around the ballroom of the five-star hotel in Mayfair and recognised numerous celebrities who, like her, had been invited to the birthday celebrations of a famous music producer.

Since the news that she was the daughter of Lionel Kingsley, MP, had made the headlines a month ago, she had been on the guest list at many top so-

cial events with her half-brother and half-sister. She
loved being part of a family and while she was staying at her father's beautiful house in Berkshire she'd
grown close to Lionel, Charlotte and Freddie. They
and her father had encouraged her to follow a different career path after she'd resigned from her position
as Alekos's PA. She had started an art foundation
course at college and her plan to go to university to
study for an art degree helped to take her mind off
the trauma of the ectopic pregnancy.

Long walks in the countryside and the compan-
ionship of family mealtimes had gradually enabled
her to come to terms with the loss of her baby, although there would always be a little ache in her
heart for the child she would never know. Getting
over Alekos had so far proved more difficult, especially when she had told her father and siblings
that she had broken off her relationship with him
and they had asked if she was sure she had done the
right thing.

Well, she was sure now, she thought dismally.
Photos of Alekos at a film premiere with a busty
blonde wrapped around him had featured on the front
pages of all the tabloids. She was furious with herself that she'd wasted time worrying about him. Why,
she'd even phoned him to check if he was okay because it had been his baby too. He hadn't answered
her call or replied to the message she'd left him, and
seeing the picture of him with his latest bimbo had

forced her to accept that he had moved on with his life and she should do the same.

She was jolted from her thoughts by a sharp pain in her foot. 'Sorry—again,' the man she was dancing with said ruefully when she winced. 'That must be the third time I've trodden on your toes.'

'Fourth, actually.'

She hid her irritation with a smile. He had introduced himself as Daniel, 'I'm doing a bit of modelling but I really want to be an actor,' and he was very good-looking, although it was lucky he wasn't hoping for a career as a dancer, she mused. Unfortunately, his good looks were wasted on her. She wished her heart did skip a beat when he pulled her closer, but she felt nothing. Although she managed to put on a cheerful front, she missed Alekos terribly and couldn't stop thinking about him.

'Is there a reason why the tall guy over there is staring at me as if he's planning to murder me?' Daniel murmured. 'He's coming this way and I get the feeling it's time I made myself scarce.'

'Which guy...?' Sara felt her heart slam into her ribs when Alekos materialised at her side.

'I advise you to find another woman to dance with,' he growled to Daniel, who immediately dropped his hands from Sara as if she were highly contagious. But her attention wasn't on Daniel. Alekos swamped all of her senses and he was the only man in the ballroom.

He looked utterly gorgeous dressed in slim black

trousers and a black shirt open at the throat to reveal a sprinkling of curling chest hairs. His hair was ruffled as if he'd been running his fingers through it—or someone else had, Sara thought darkly, remembering the photos of him with the blonde who'd been stuck to him with superglue. Temper rescued her from the ignominy of drooling over him.

'How dare you barge in and spoil my evening?' she snapped.

'I dare, Sara *mou*, because if I hadn't persuaded your pretty boy dance partner to back off I would have throttled him with my bare hands.' His dark eyes burned like hot embers and the tight grip of his hands on her waist warned her that he was furious. Well, that made two of them, she thought, glaring at him when she tried to pull away and he jerked her against his body. The feel of his hard thighs pressed close to hers was almost enough to make her melt.

'I am definitely not *your* Sara. Will you let go of me? You're making an exhibition of us.'

'I haven't even started,' he warned. 'You can walk out of the ballroom with me or I'll carry you out.'

She snapped her teeth together as if she would like to bite him, but to safeguard her dignity she allowed him to steer her out of the ballroom and across the hotel foyer to the lifts. 'Won't your girlfriend mind? Don't pretend you don't know who I mean. You must have seen the picture on the front page of this morning's papers of you and Miss Breast Implants.'

His puzzled expression cleared. 'Oh, you mean Charlene.'

'I don't read gossip columns so I don't know her name.'

'Charlene McCuskey is the wife of Warren Mc-Cuskey, who I'm sure you recall is buying *Artemis*. They are in London so that Warren can finalise the purchase, but he has come down with a virus and so he asked me to escort Charlene to a film premiere, which I dutifully did before I took her back to their hotel. Unsurprisingly, she is devoted to her billionaire husband,' he said sardonically.

'Oh, I see,' Sara muttered. Without fully realising what she was doing she'd followed Alekos into a lift, and as the doors closed and she was alone with him in the small space she had a horrible feeling that he saw way too much of her thoughts. 'Where are you taking me?'

'I'm staying at the hotel and we are going to my suite.'

'I don't want...'

'We need to talk.' Something in his expression made her heart give another painful jolt. The lift had mirrored walls, and her reflection showed her breasts rising and falling jerkily beneath her scarlet silk dress that she'd worn thinking the bright colour might lift her spirits. 'You look beautiful,' Alekos told her brusquely.

Her eyes flew to his face and after weeks of feeling nothing every nerve ending on her body was suddenly fiercely alive. The lift stopped, and as she followed him along the corridor and into his suite she wondered why she was putting herself through this. Seeing him again was going to make it so much harder to get over him.

'Would you like a drink?'

It would give her something to do with her hands. When she nodded he walked over to the bar, poured a measure of cassis into two tall glasses and topped them up with champagne. Sara remembered they had drunk Kir Royale the night they had become lovers on the yacht in Monaco. It seemed a lifetime ago.

'How are you?'

'Good,' she said huskily. It wasn't true, but she was working on it. 'It's been great getting to know Charlotte and Freddie. I feel very lucky that they and my father are part of my life.'

'I'm sure they feel lucky to have found you.' There was an odd note in his voice and, like in the lift, the indefinable expression in his eyes stirred feelings inside her that she told herself she must not feel.

'How about you?' She hesitated. 'I phoned you... but you didn't call back.'

'I was in Greece. I visited my mother and we talked about my brother.' He indicated for Sara to sit down on a sofa but she felt too edgy to sit, and he remained standing too. 'Dimitri died of a heart attack while he was swimming,' he told her abruptly. 'I finally read the coroner's report. My parents had their reasons for not talking about the cause of his

death and I never spoke about Dimitri because I tried
to block out my grief.'

'I'm glad you found out the truth at last and can
stop blaming yourself,' she said softly. 'I hope you can
put the past behind you and move on with your life.'

'Do you include yourself in my past and hope I
will forget about you?'

She swallowed. Alekos had moved without her
being aware of him doing so and he was standing so
close that she could see the tiny lines around his eyes
that suggested he hadn't been sleeping well. There
were deeper grooves on either side of his mouth and
she sensed he was as tense as she felt.

'I guess we both need to move forwards,' she said,
aiming for a light tone. 'Make a fresh start.'

'What if I asked you to come back to me?'

Her heart missed a beat, but she shook her head.
'I couldn't be your PA now that we…' she coloured
'…now that we have had a personal association.'

'A *personal association*?' he said savagely. '*Theos*,
Sara, we created a child together.'

'*A child you didn't want.* Any more than you
wanted to marry me.' She spun away from him, determined not to break down in front of him.

'That's not true on both counts. I did want to
marry you. I didn't respond to your phone call because when you went to stay with your father after
you left hospital, I agreed with Lionel to give you
some space. You needed to recover from the ectopic
and spend time with your new family.'

Sara shrugged to show she didn't care, even though she did desperately. Alekos frowned but continued, 'I also did what every bridegroom is expected to do and asked your father if he would allow me to marry you.'

Sara choked on her mouthful of champagne. *'You did what?'* She was so angry she wanted to hit him and for about twenty seconds she forgot that she wanted to kiss him. 'There is no way I would agree to marry you to keep the board members of GE happy.'

'Good, because that's a terrible reason for us to marry,' he said calmly, although his eyes blazed with a fierce heat that melded Sara to the floor and stopped her rushing towards the door.

'I'm being serious.' She put her hands flat on his chest to stop him coming closer but he clasped her wrists and pulled her arms down, at the same time as he tugged her against him with a force that expelled the air from her lungs.

'So am I.' He stared at her intently and his jaw clenched when he saw the tears she was struggling to hold back. 'Why were you jealous when you saw the photo of me with Charlene?'

She flushed. 'I wasn't jealous.'

'Did you feel like I did tonight when I saw you dancing with that guy and I wanted to tear his head off?'

'Definitely not.' She didn't know what game of refined torture Alekos was playing but it had to stop before the intoxicating warmth of his body pressed up against hers and ruined her for ever.

'Liar,' he taunted. 'Were you jealous because you love me?'

She could deny it but what would be the point? She couldn't fight him or herself any more, and Sara knew she would be his mistress if he asked her because she'd learned that life was too short to turn down the chance to be with him, even though he would break her heart when he ended their affair.

But she still had her pride and her eyes flashed with green fire. '*Yes*, I love you. I've loved you for ever, even though you are the most arrogant man I've ever known.'

'But I am the only man you have ever known intimately, arrogant or not,' he said softly, his mouth curving in a crooked smile that tugged on Sara's heart. He sounded strange, as if his throat was constricted, and her eyes widened in disbelief when she saw that his lashes were wet.

'Alekos?' she whispered.

'Sara *mou*…' He held her so tight that she felt the thunder of his heart. '*S'agapo*. I love you so much.' He framed her face with his hands that were shaking. 'When I watched your life ebbing away in the ambulance on the way to hospital I was terrified I would lose you. And I realised then that I had tried hard *not* to fall in love with you because of fear. I associated love with the loss and pain that I felt after Dimitri died.'

'That's not surprising,' she said shakily. 'You were at an impressionable age when he died, and your brother was your best friend.'

'We became friends when you worked for me, didn't we, Sara? I liked you and I respected you when you put me in my place. I felt closer to you than I'd ever felt with any of my mistresses. But one day I walked into my office and I was blown away by a gorgeous sexy brunette. You can imagine my shock when I discovered it was you.'

She flushed. 'Before that day you didn't notice your frumpy PA.'

'I did notice you. Often I would find myself thinking about a funny remark you'd made, and I appreciated your fierce intelligence and your advice on how to handle work issues. I almost resented you when you made me desire you too. I knew I was in danger of falling in love with you and I told myself that once we were lovers my interest in you would fade. Instead, it grew stronger every day and night that we were together. When you told me you were pregnant I seized the excuse to marry you without having to admit how I felt about you.'

How he felt about her. Sara bit her lip and told herself it was too good to be true. 'You said love is a word that poets use to describe lust. Are you sure you haven't got the two mixed up?'

'I don't blame you for doubting me, *kardia mou*. That means my heart, and I love you with all my heart.'

Sara's head advised caution but her heart was desperate to believe that, incredible as it seemed, Alekos was looking at her with adoration in his eyes. She caught her breath when he stroked his finger gently down her cheek.

'Will you marry me, my Sara, for no other reason than you are the love of my life?'

That was the moment she knew she should have listened to the warning that it was all too good to be true. Carefully she eased out of his arms and closed her eyes to blot out the sudden haggard look on his face. 'I can't.'

'*Theos*, Sara, I will do whatever it takes to prove to you that I love you.' His voice cracked. 'Please believe me.'

'I do. And I love you. But you need an heir to one day run GE, and there is a strong chance I won't be able to give you a child because I lost one tube and there is a higher risk I could have another ectopic pregnancy.'

He caught her to him and buried his face in her hair. 'Then we won't have children. There's no way I will risk your life. I need *you*,' he told her fiercely. 'Nothing else is important. Whatever the future holds, I want us to share it together, the ups and the downs, for the rest of our lives.'

He tightened his arms around her so that she was aware of his hard thigh muscles pressed against her. 'My body knew the truth before I was ready to accept it,' he said roughly. 'When we made love it was so much more than great sex.'

Joy fizzed inside Sara like champagne bubbles exploding. Hearing Alekos say he loved her wiped away the pain and misery of the past weeks and the future shimmered on the horizon like a golden sun. 'Mmm, but it was great sex, wasn't it?' Her smile was wicked and adoring. 'I think you should remind me.'

His laughter rumbled through her and the unguarded expression in his eyes stole her breath even before his mouth did the same as he claimed her lips and kissed her so thoroughly, so *lovingly*, that she was trembling when he finally lifted his head.

'I'd better warn you that this is the honeymoon suite and the staff have really gone to town,' he murmured. 'There are rose petals everywhere in the bedroom.'

Alekos had been right about the rose petals, Sara discovered when he carried her into the bedroom and laid her on the bed, adorned with fragrant red petals. He undressed her slowly, kissing each part of her body that he revealed, and when he removed her knickers and pressed his mouth to her feminine heat she told him she loved him, loved him. She repeated the words when he thrust into her so deeply that he filled her and he made love to her with all the love in his heart.

It was as wonderful as she remembered and more beautiful than she could ever have dreamed because this time Alekos didn't just show her he loved her; he told her in a mixture of English and Greek.

'Will you let me love you for ever, and will you love me?' he murmured as he drew her close and they relaxed in the sweet aftermath of loving.

'I will,' Sara promised him and she meant the words with her heart and soul.

They were married three months later on Christmas Eve, in a church decorated with holly and ivy and fragrant red roses, and filled with their families and friends. Sara wore a white satin and lace gown and carried a bouquet of white lilies. Alekos looked stunning in a dark grey suit, but it was the look in his eyes as he watched his bride walk down the aisle towards him that made his mother and sisters wipe away tears. Sara's father walked proudly beside her to meet her husband-to-be, and her half-sister was her maid of honour.

After the reception at Lionel Kingsley's home in Berkshire, the happy couple flew to South Africa for their honeymoon. 'Somewhere hot where you can wear less clothes,' Alekos had stated when Sara had asked him where he wanted to go.

As it turned out, neither of them got dressed very often during the three weeks they stayed in a private bungalow at a luxury beach resort, a fact that Sara later accounted for her pregnancy that was confirmed a month after they returned to London. It was an anxious time until an early scan showed that her pregnancy was normal and they watched the tiny beating heart of their baby with hope in their hearts.

Theodore Dimitri Gionakis, to be known as Theo, arrived in the world two weeks early with a minimum of fuss and instantly became the centre of his parents' world.

'Love changes everything,' Alekos said one evening as he held his son in the crook of one arm and slid his other arm around his wife's waist. 'You changed me, Sara *mou*. You showed me how to let love into my heart and now it's there to stay for ever.'

'For ever sounds wonderful,' she told him, and then she kissed him and no further words were necessary.

* * * * *

Claimed For The De Carrillo Twins

Abby Green

MILLS & BOON

Visit the Author Profile page at
millsandboon.com.au for more titles.

Irish author **Abby Green** threw in a very glamorous career in film and TV—which really consisted of a lot of standing in the rain outside actors' trailers—to pursue her love of romance. After she'd bombarded Harlequin with manuscripts they kindly accepted one, and an author was born. She lives in Dublin, Ireland, and loves any excuse for distraction. Visit abby-green.com or email abbygreenauthor@gmail.com.

DEDICATION

I'd like to thank Heidi Rice, Sharon Kendrick and Iona Grey for all their cheerleading; Kate Meader, who provided counsel over cocktails in the Shelbourne; and Annie West, who always provides serene and insightful advice. And of course my editor, Sheila, who has proved beyond doubt that she believes me capable of anything, apart from perhaps AWAVMOT!

Thank you, all!

PROLOGUE

CRUZ DE CARRILLO SURVEYED the thronged reception room in his London home, filled with a veritable who's who of London's most powerful players and beautiful people, all there to celebrate his return to Europe.

He felt no sense of accomplishment, though, to be riding high on the crest of his stratospheric success in North America, having tripled his eponymous bank's fortunes in less than a year, because he knew his zealous focus on work had more to do with avoiding *this* than the burning ambition he'd harboured for years to turn his family bank's fortune and reputation around.

And it killed him to admit it.

This was standing just feet away from him now—tall and slender, yet with generous curves. Pale skin. Too much pale skin. Exposed in a dress that left far too little to the imagination. Cruz's mouth compressed with distaste even as his blood ran hot, mocking him for the desire which time hadn't diminished—much to his intense irritation. It was unwelcome and completely inappropriate. Now more than ever. She was his sister-in-law.

Her blonde hair was up in a sleek chignon and a chain

of glittering gold trailed tantalisingly down her naked back, bared in a daring royal blue backless dress. She turned slightly in Cruz's direction and he had to tense every muscle to stave off the surge of fresh desire when he saw the provocative curves of her high full breasts, barely disguised by the thin draped satin.

She looked almost vulnerable, set apart from the crowd slightly, but he knew that was just a mirage.

He cursed her. And he cursed himself. If he hadn't been so weak he wouldn't know how incendiary it felt to have those curves pressed against his body. He wouldn't remember the way her eyes had turned a stormy dark blue as he'd plundered the sweetness she'd offered up to him that fateful night almost eighteen months ago, in this very house, when she'd worked for him as a housemaid.

He wouldn't still hear her soft, breathy moans in his dreams, forcing him awake, sweating, with his hand wrapped around himself and every part of him straining for release…aching to know the intimate clasp of her body, milking him into sweet oblivion.

Sweet. That was just it. There was nothing sweet about this woman. He might have thought so at one time—she'd used to blush if he so much as glanced at her—but it had all been an elaborate artifice. Because his younger half-brother, Rio, had told him the truth about what she really was, and she was no innocent.

Her seduction of Cruz had obviously been far more calculated than he'd believed, and when that hadn't worked she'd diverted her sights onto Rio, his illegitimate half-brother, with whom Cruz had a complicated relationship—to put it mildly.

A chasm had been forged between the brothers when they were children—when Cruz had been afforded every privilege as the legitimate heir to the De Carrillo fortune, and Rio, who had been born to a housemaid of the family *castillo*, had been afforded nothing. Not even the De Carrillo name.

But Cruz had never felt that Rio should be punished for their charismatic and far too handsome father's inability to control his base appetites. So he had done everything in his power after their father had died some ten years previously to make amends—going against their father's will, which had left Rio nothing, by becoming his guardian, giving him his rightful paternalistic name and paying for him to complete his education.

Then, when he had come of age, Cruz had given him a fair share of his inheritance *and* a job—first in the De Carrillo bank in Madrid, and now in London, much to the conservative board's displeasure.

At the age of twenty-one Rio had become one of Europe's newest millionaires, the centre of feverish media attention with his dark good looks and mysterious past. And he had lapped it up, displaying an appetite for the kind of playboy lifestyle Cruz had never indulged in, quickly marrying one of the world's top supermodels in a lavish wedding that had gone on for days—only for it to end in tragedy nearly a year later, when she'd died in an accident shortly after giving birth to twin boys.

And yet, much as Rio's full-throttle existence had unnerved Cruz, could he begrudge him that after being denied his heritage?

Cruz's conscience pricked. By giving Rio his due inheritance and his rightful name perhaps he'd made his brother a target for gold-diggers? Rio's first wife had certainly revelled in her husband's luxurious lifestyle, and it would appear as if nothing had changed with his second wife.

As if sensing his intense regard, his sister-in-law turned now and saw him. Her eyes widened and her cheeks flushed. Cruz's anger spiked. She could still turn it on. Even now. When he knew her real capabilities.

She faced him in that provocative dress and her luscious body filled his vision and made his blood thrum with need. He hated her for it. She moved towards him almost hesitantly, the slippery satin material moving sinuously around her long legs.

He called on every atom of control he had and schooled his body not to respond to her proximity even as her tantalising scent tickled his nostrils, threatening to weaken him all over again. It was all at once innocent, yet seductive. As if he needed reminding that she presented one face to the world while hiding another, far more mercenary one.

'Trinity.' His voice sounded unbearably curt to his ears, and he tried to ignore the striking light blue eyes. To ignore how lush her mouth was, adding a distinctly sensual edge to her pale blonde innocence.

An innocence that was skin-deep.

'Cruz…it's nice to see you again.'

Her voice was husky, reminding him vividly of how it had sounded in his ear that night. *'Please...'*

His dry tone disguised his banked rage. 'You've come up in the world since we last met.'

She swallowed, the long, delicate column of her pale throat moving. 'Wh-what do you mean?'

Cruz's jaw tightened at the faux innocence. 'I'm talking about your rapid ascent from the position of nanny to wife and stepmother to my nephews.'

That brought back the unwelcome reminder that he'd only been informed about the low-key wedding in a text from Rio.

I have you to thank for sending this beautiful woman into my life. I hope you'll be very happy for us, brother.

The news had precipitated shock, and something much darker into Cruz's gut. And yet he hadn't had any reason at that point not to believe it was a good idea—in spite of his own previous experience with Trinity, which he'd blamed himself for. Rio had been a widower, and he and Trinity had obviously forged a bond based on caring for his nephews. Cruz had believed that she was a million light years away from Rio's glamorous hedonistic first wife. *Then.*

The fact that he'd had dreams for weeks afterwards, of being held back and forced to watch a faceless blonde woman making love to countless men, was something that made him burn inwardly with shame even now.

Trinity looked pale. Hesitant. 'I was looking for you, actually. Could we have a private word?'

Cruz crushed the unwelcome memory and arched a brow. 'A private word?'

He flicked a glance at the crowd behind her and then looked back to her, wondering what the hell she was up to. Surely she wouldn't have the gall to try and seduce him under the same roof she had before, with her husband just feet away?

'We're private enough here. No one is listening.'

She flushed and then glanced behind her and back, clearly reluctant. 'Perhaps this isn't the best time or place...'

So he'd been right. Disgust settled in his belly. 'Spit it out, Trinity. Unless it's not *talking* you're interested in.'

She blanched, and that delicate flush disappeared. Once her ability to display emotions had intrigued him. Now it incensed him.

'What do you mean?'

'You know very well what I mean. You tried to seduce me in this very house, and when it didn't work you transferred your attentions to my brother. He obviously proved to be more susceptible to your wiles.'

She shook her head and frowned, a visibly trembling hand coming up to her chest as if to contain shock, disbelief. 'I don't know what you're talking about...'

Disgust filled Cruz that she could stand here and so blatantly lie while her enormous rock of an engagement ring glinted at him mockingly. All he could see was her and her treachery. But he had to crush the recriminations that rose up inside him—it was too late for them now.

Rio had revealed to Cruz on his return to the UK a

few days before that he was on the verge of bankruptcy—his huge inheritance all but wiped out. And Trinity De Carrillo's name was all over nearly every receipt and docket that had led his brother further and further into the mire. The extent of how badly Cruz had misread her was galling.

An insidious thought occurred to him and it made his blood boil. 'Your innocent act is past its sell-by date. I might not have realised what you were up to—more fool me—but I know now. Rio has told me how you've single-handedly run through almost every cent he has to his name in a bid to satisfy your greedy nature. Now you're realising his fortune isn't a bottomless pit, perhaps you're looking for a way out, or even a new benefactor?'

Before she could respond he continued in a low, bitter voice.

'I underestimated your capacity to play the long game, Trinity. You lulled Rio into a false sense of trust by manipulating his biggest vulnerability—his sons. I'm very well aware of how my actions pushed you in the direction of my brother, and that is not something I will ever forgive myself for. Needless to say if he requires financial help he will receive it, but your days of bankrupting him are over. If you're hoping to bargain your way out of this predicament then think again. You'll get no sympathy from me.'

Trinity was so white now Cruz fancied he could see the blood vessels under her skin. A part of him wished she would break out of character and get angry with him for confronting her with who she really was.

Her hand dropped back to her side and she shook her head. 'You have it all wrong.'

'That's the best you can come up with?' he sneered. 'I have it *all wrong*? If I "have it all wrong" then, please, tell me what you want to discuss.'

Cruz could see the pulse at the base of her neck beating hectically. His own pulse-rate doubled.

'I wanted to talk to you about Rio…about his behaviour. It's been growing more and more erratic… I'm worried about the boys.'

Cruz let out a short, incredulous laugh. 'Worried about the boys? You're really trying to play the concerned stepmother card in a bid to deflect attention from the fact that you're more concerned about your lavish lifestyle coming to an end?'

Bitterness filled Cruz. He knew better than most how the biological bond of a parent and child didn't guarantee love and security. Far from it.

'You're not even related to them—you've just used them as pawns to manipulate your way into my brother's bed and get a ring on your finger.'

Trinity took a step back, her eyes wide with feigned shock. He had to hand it to her. She was a good actress.

Almost as if she was talking to herself now, she said, 'I should have known he'd protect himself somehow… of course you'd believe him over me.'

A sliver of unease pierced Cruz's anger but he pushed it aside. 'I've known Rio all of his twenty-five years. I think it's safe to say I'd trust my own flesh and blood over a conniving gold-digger any day of the week.'

Heated colour came back into Trinity's cheeks. She

looked at him, big blue eyes beseeching him with commendable authenticity.

'I'm not a gold-digger. You don't understand. Everything you're saying is all wrong—my marriage with Rio is not what you—'

'*There* you are, darling. I've been looking for you. Charlotte Lacey wants to talk to you about next week's charity function.'

Cruz blanched. He hadn't even noticed Rio joining them. He'd been consumed with the woman in front of him, whose arm was now being taken firmly in her husband's hand. Rio's dark brown eyes met Cruz's over Trinity's head. They were hard. Trinity had gone even paler, if that was possible.

'If you don't mind, brother, I need to steal my wife away.'

Cruz could see it in Rio's eyes then—a familiar resentment. And shame and anger. Futility choked him. There was nothing he could do. He knew Rio would already be despising the fact that he'd allowed Cruz to see him brought so low at this woman's greedy hands.

He watched as they walked back into the crowd, and it wasn't long before they left for the evening—without saying goodbye. Rio might have shown Cruz a chink of vulnerability by revealing his financial problems, but if anything that only demonstrated how much Trinity had got to him—because he'd never before allowed his brother to see a moment's weakness. Cruz's sense that his determination to see Rio treated fairly had been futile rose up again—he had never truly bridged the gap between them.

Cruz stood at the window in his drawing room and watched his brother handing Trinity into the passenger seat of a dark Jeep in the forecourt outside the house, before he got into the driver's seat himself.

He felt grim. All he could do now was be there to pick up the pieces of Rio's financial meltdown and do his best to ensure that Rio got a chance to start again—and that his wife didn't get her grasping hands on another cent.

At the last second, as if hearing his thoughts, Trinity turned her head to look at Cruz through the ground-floor window. For a fleeting moment their eyes met, and he could have sworn he saw hers shimmer with moisture, even from this distance.

He told himself they had to be tears of anger now that she knew she'd been found out. She was trapped in a situation of her own making. It should have filled Cruz with a sense of satisfaction, but instead all he felt was a heavy weight in his chest.

Rio's Jeep took off with a spurt of gravel.

Cruz didn't realise it then, but it would be the last time he saw his brother alive.

CHAPTER ONE

Three months later. Solicitor's office.

TRINITY'S HEART STOPPED and her mouth dried. 'Mr De Carrillo is joining us?'

The solicitor glanced at her distractedly, looking for a paper on his overcrowded desktop. 'Yes—he is the executor of his brother's will, and we *are* in his building,' he pointed out redundantly.

She'd been acutely aware that she was in the impressive De Carrillo building in London's bustling financial zone, but it hadn't actually occurred to her that Cruz himself would be here.

To her shame, her first instinct was to check her appearance—which of course she couldn't do, but she was glad of the choice of clothing she'd made: dark loose trousers and a grey silk shirt. She'd tied her long hair back in a braid, as much out of habit when dealing with small energetic boys than for any other reason. She hadn't put on any make-up and regretted that now, fearing she must look about eighteen.

Just then there was a light knock on the door and

it opened. She heard Mr Drew's assistant saying in a suspiciously breathless and awestruck voice, 'Mr De Carrillo, sir.'

The solicitor stood up, immediately obsequious, greeting Cruz De Carrillo effusively and leading him to a seat beside Trinity's on the other side of his desk.

Every nerve came to immediate and tingling life. The tiny hairs on her arms stood up, quivering. She lamented her uncontrollable reaction—would she ever *not* react to him?

She sensed him come to stand near her, tall and effortlessly intimidating. Childishly, she wanted to avoid looking at him. His scent was a tantalising mix of musk and something earthy and masculine. It was his scent now that sent her hurtling back to that cataclysmic evening in his house three months ago, when she'd realised just how badly Rio had betrayed her.

The shock of knowing that Rio obviously hadn't told him the truth about their marriage was still palpable, even now. And the fact that Cruz had so readily believed the worst of her hurt far worse than it should.

It had hurt almost as much as when he'd looked at her with dawning horror and self-disgust after kissing her to within an inch of her life. It was an experience still seared onto her brain, so deeply embedded inside her that she sometimes woke from X-rated dreams, tangled amongst her sheets and sweating. Almost two years later it was beyond humiliating.

Trinity dragged her mind away from that disturbing labyrinth of memories. She had more important things to deal with now. Because three months ago, while she and Rio had been driving home from Cruz's house, they'd been involved in a car crash and Rio had tragically died.

Since that day she'd become lone step-parent to Mateo and Sancho, Rio's two-and-a-half-year-old twins. Miraculously, she'd escaped from the accident with only cuts and bruises and a badly sprained ankle. She had no memory of the actual accident—only recalled waking in the hospital feeling battered all over and learning of her husband's death from a grim and ashen-faced Cruz.

Gathering her composure, she stood up to face him, steeling herself against his effect. Which was useless. As soon as she looked at him it was like a blow to her solar plexus.

She'd seen him since the night of the accident—at the funeral, of course, and then when he'd called at the house for brief perfunctory visits to check that she and his nephews had everything they needed. He hadn't engaged with her beyond that. Her skin prickled now with foreboding. She had a sense that he'd merely been biding his time.

She forced herself to say, as calmly as she could, 'Cruz.'

'Trinity.'

His voice reverberated deep inside her, even as he oozed his habitual icy control.

The solicitor had gone back around his desk and said now, 'Espresso, wasn't it, Mr De Carrillo?'

Trinity blinked and looked to see the older gentleman holding out a small cup and saucer. Instinctively, because she was closer and because it was good manners, she reached for it to hand it to Cruz, only belatedly realising that her hand was trembling.

She prayed he wouldn't notice the tremor as she held out the delicate china to him. His hand was masculine and square. Strong. Long fingers...short, functional nails. At that moment she had a flash of remembering how his hand had felt between her legs, stroking her intimately...

Just before he took the cup and saucer there was a tiny clatter of porcelain on porcelain, evidence of her frayed nerves. *Damn.*

When he had the cup she sat down again quickly, before she made a complete fool of herself, and took a quick fortifying sip of her own cup of tea. He sat down too, and she was aware of his powerful body taking up a lot of space.

While Mr. Drew engaged Cruz De Carrillo in light conversation, before they started discussing the terms of Rio's will, Trinity risked another glance at the man just a couple of feet to her left.

Short dark blond hair gave more than a hint of his supremely controlled nature. Controlled except for that momentary lapse...an undoubtedly rare moment of heated insanity with someone he'd seen as far beneath him.

Trinity crushed the spike of emotion. She couldn't afford it.

Despite the urbane uniform of a three-piece suit, his impressive build was apparent. Muscles pushed at the fabric in a way that said he couldn't be contained, no matter how civilised he might look.

His face was a stunning portrait of masculine beauty, all hard lines and an aquiline profile that spoke of a pure and powerful bloodline. He had deep-set eyes and a mouth that on anyone else would have looked ridiculously sensual. Right now though, it looked stern. Disapproving.

Trinity realised that she was staring at him, and when he turned to look at her she went puce. She quickly turned back to the solicitor, who had stopped talking and was now looking from her to Cruz nervously, as if he could sense the tension in the room.

He cleared his throat. 'As you're both here now, I see no reason not to start.'

'If you would be so kind.'

Trinity shivered at the barely veiled impatience in Cruz's voice. She could recall only too well how this man had reduced grown men and women to quivering wrecks with just a disdainful look from those glittering dark amber eyes.

The half-brothers hadn't been very alike—where Rio had been dark, with obsidian eyes and dark hair, Cruz possessed a cold, tawny beauty that had always made Trinity think of dark ice over simmering heat. She shivered...she'd felt that heat.

'Mrs De Carrillo...?'

Trinity blinked and flushed at being caught out again. The solicitor's impatient expression came into focus. He was holding out a sheaf of papers and she reached for them.

'I'm sorry.' It still felt weird to be called Mrs De Carrillo—it wasn't as if she'd ever *really* been Rio's wife.

She quickly read the heading: *Last will and testament of Rio De Carrillo*. Her heart squeezed as she thought of the fact that Mateo and Sancho had now lost both their parents, too prematurely.

As bitter as her experience had been with Rio in the end, after Trinity had been sickened to realise just how manipulative he'd been, and how naive she'd been, she'd never in a million years have wished him gone.

She'd felt a level of grief that had surprised her, considering the fact that their marriage had been in name only—for the convenience of having a steady mother figure for the boys and because Rio had wanted to promote a more settled image to further his own ambitions.

Trinity had agreed to the union for those and myriad other reasons—the most compelling of which had to do with her bond with the twins, which had been forged almost as soon as she'd seen them. Two one-year-old cherubs, with dark hair, dark mischievous eyes and heart-stopping smiles.

Her heart had gone out to them because they were motherless, as she had been since she was a baby, and they'd latched on to her with a ferocity that she hadn't been able to resist, even though she'd known it would be more professional to try and keep some distance.

She'd also agreed because Rio's sad personal story—he had been all but abandoned by his own parents—had again chimed with echoes of her own. And because he'd agreed to help her fulfil her deepest ambitions—to go to university and get a degree, thereby putting her in a position to forge her own future, free of the stain of her ignominious past.

Rio hadn't revealed the full extent of *his* ambitions until shortly before the accident—and that was when she'd realised why he'd taken such perverse pleasure in marrying her. It had had far more to do with his long-held simmering resentment towards his older half-brother than any real desire to forge a sense of security for his sons, or to shake off his playboy moniker...

The solicitor was speaking. 'As you'll see, it's a relatively short document. There's really no need to read through it all now. Suffice to say that Mr De Carrillo bequeathed everything to his sons, Mateo and Sancho, and he named you their legal guardian, Trinity.'

She looked up. She'd known that Rio had named her guardian. Any concerns she'd had at the time, contemplating such a huge responsibility had been eclipsed by the overwhelmingly protective instinct she'd felt for the twins. And in all honesty the prospect of one day becoming their guardian hadn't felt remotely possible.

She realised that she hadn't really considered what this meant for her own future now. It was something she'd been good at blocking out in the last three months, after the shock of the accident and Rio's death, not to mention getting over her own injuries and caring for two highly precocious and energetic boys. It was as if she was afraid to let the enormity of it all sink in.

The solicitor looked at Cruz for a moment, and then he looked back to Trinity with something distinctly *uncomfortable* in his expression. She tensed.

'I'm not sure how aware you are of the state of Mr De Carrillo's finances when he died?'

Trinity immediately felt the scrutiny of the man to

her left, as if his gaze was boring into her. His accusatory words came back to her: *'You've single-handedly run through almost every cent my brother has to his name in a bid to satisfy your greedy nature. Now you're realising Rio's fortune isn't a bottomless pit...'*

She felt breathless, as if a vice was squeezing her chest. Until the evening of Cruz's party she hadn't been aware of any such financial difficulty. She'd only been aware that Rio was growing more and more irrational and erratic. When she'd confronted him about his behviour, they'd had a huge argument, in which the truth of exactly why he'd married her had been made very apparent. Along with his *real* agenda.

That was why Trinity had wanted to talk to Cruz—to share her concerns. However, he'd comprehensively shut that down.

She said carefully now, 'I was aware that things weren't...good. But I didn't know that it was linked to his financial situation.'

Mr. Drew looked grim. 'Well, it most probably was. The truth is that Rio was bankrupt. In these last three months the sheer extent and scale of his financial collapse has become evident, and it's comprehensive. I'm afraid that all he left behind him are debts. There is nothing to bequeath to his children. Or you.'

Trinity hadn't married Rio for his money, so this news didn't have any great impact on her. What did impact her, though, was the realisation that Cruz must have been putting money into the account that she used for day-to-day necessities for her and the boys and Mrs Jordan—the nanny Rio had hired once Trinity had married him, when her job had changed and she'd been expected to accompany him to social functions. Something she'd never felt comfortable doing...

The solicitor said, 'I'm sorry to deliver this news, Mrs De Carrillo, but even the house will have to be sold to cover his debts.'

Before she could absorb that, Cruz was standing up and saying, in a coolly authoritative tone, 'If you could leave us now, Mr. Drew, I'll go over the rest with my sister-in-law.'

The solicitor clearly had no issue with being summarily dismissed from his own office. He gathered some papers and left, shutting the door softly behind him.

Trinity's mind was reeling, as she tried to take everything in, and revolving with a sickening sense of growing panic as to how she was going to manage caring for the boys when she didn't have a job. How could she afford to keep Mrs Jordan on?

Cruz walked over to the floor-to-ceiling windows behind the large desk, showcasing an impressive view of London's skyline.

For a long moment he said nothing, and she could only look helplessly at his broad shoulders and back. Then he turned around and a sense of déjà-vu nearly knocked her off her chair. It was so reminiscent of when she'd first met him—when she'd gone to his house in Holland Park for an interview, applying for the position of maid in his household.

She'd never met such an intimidating man in her life. Nor such a blatantly masculine man. Based on his reputation as one of the world's wealthiest bankers, she had assumed him to be older, somewhat soft... But he'd been young. And gorgeous. His tall, powerful body had looked as if it was hewn from pure granite and steel. His eyes had been disconcertingly unreadable...

'Miss Adams...did you hear my question?'

She was back in time, caught in the glare of those mesmerising eyes, his brows drawn into a frown of impatience. His Spanish accent had been barely noticeable, just the slightest intriguing inflection. She'd felt light-headed, even though she was sitting down.

'I'm sorry...what?'

Those eyes had flashed with irritation. 'I asked how old you are?'

She'd swallowed. 'I'm twenty-two. Since last week.'

Then she'd felt silly for mentioning that detail—as if one of the richest men in the world cared when her birthday was! Not that she even knew when her birthday was for sure...

But she'd survived four rounds of intense interviews to be there to meet the man himself—evidence of how he oversaw every tiny detail of his life—so Trinity had gathered her fraying wits, drawn her shoulders back and reminded herself that she had hopes and dreams, and that if she got this job she'd be well on her way to achieving a life for herself...

'I have to hand it to you—you're as good an actress as you were three months ago when you first feigned ignorance of Rio's financial situation. But you must have known what was coming down the tracks. After all, you helped divest my brother of a small fortune.'

The past and present meshed for a moment, and then Trinity realised what Cruz had just said.

She clasped her hands tight together on her lap. 'But I didn't know.'

'Did the accident affect your memory, Trinity?' His voice held more than a note of disdain. 'Do you not recall that illuminating conversation we had before you left my house on that fateful night?'

She flushed, remembering it all too well. 'I don't have any memory of the accident, but, yes, I do recall what you said to me. You're referring to your accusation that I was responsible for Rio's financial problems.'

Cruz's mouth compressed. 'I think *ruin* would be a more accurate word.'

Trinity stood up, too agitated to stay seated. 'You're wrong. It's true that Rio spent money on me, yes, but it was for the purposes of—'

Cruz held up a hand, a distinct sneer on his face now. 'Spare me the details. I looked into Rio's accounts after he died. I know all about the personal stylist, the VIP seats to every fashion show, the haute couture dresses, private jet travel, the best hotels in the world... The list is endless. I curse the day that I hired you to work for me—because, believe me, I blame myself as much as you for ruining my brother.'

At that damning pronouncement Trinity felt something deep inside her shrivel up to protect itself. She had not been prepared for Cruz's vitriolic attack.

But then, this was the man who had wiped her taste off his mouth and looked at her with disgust when he'd realised that he'd lowered himself to the level of kissing his own maid.

Trinity bitterly recalled the intimate dinner party he'd hosted the following evening—when the gaping chasm between them had been all too apparent.

Cruz had welcomed a tall and stunningly beautiful brunette, kissing her warmly on both cheeks. As the woman had passed her fur coat to Trinity, not even glancing in her direction, Trinity had caught an expressive look from Cruz that had spoken volumes—telling her to forget what had happened. Telling her that this woman was the kind of woman he consorted with, and whatever had happened between them must be consigned to some sordid memory box, never to be taken out and examined again.

That was when she'd been unable to hold her emotions in, utterly ashamed that she'd let her crush grow to such gargantuan proportions that she'd let him actually *hurt* her. And that was when Rio, Cruz's halfbrother, who had also been a guest that night, had found her outside, in a hidden corner of the garden, weeping pathetically.

He'd come outside to smoke and had sat down beside her, telling her to relax when she'd tried to rush back inside, mortified. And somehow…she still wasn't sure how…he'd managed to get her to open up, to reveal what had happened. She hadn't told him of her burgeoning feelings for Cruz, but she probably hadn't had to. It must have been emblazoned all over her tearstained face.

'Tell me what your price is for signing away your guardianship of my nephews?'

Trinity blinked and the painful memory faded.

As she focused on his words she went cold all over. 'What did you just say?'

Cruz snapped his fingers, displeasure oozing from his tall, hard body. 'You heard me—how much will it take, Trinity, for you to get out of my nephews' lives, because I don't doubt you have a price.'

Horror curdled her insides at the thought of being removed from Mateo and Sancho. Only that morning Sancho had thrown his arms around her and said, *'I love you, Mummy...'*

She shook her head now, something much hotter replacing the horror. 'There is no price you could pay me to leave the boys.'

'I am their blood relation.'

'You've only met them a handful of times!'

Cruz snorted. 'Are you trying to tell me that you could care for them more than their own flesh and blood? You've just been using them as a meal ticket. And now that Rio's left nothing behind they're your only hope of keeping your nest feathered—presumably by extorting money out of me.'

Trinity gasped. 'I would never—'

Cruz lifted a hand. 'Spare me.'

Trinity's mouth closed as she struggled to process this. All her protective hackles were raised high now, at the suggestion that she would use her stepchildren for her own ends. She would never leave them at the mercy of a cold-hearted billionaire who didn't even really know them, in spite of that flesh and blood relationship.

Impulsively she asked, 'What qualifications could you possibly have for taking on two toddlers? Have you ever even held a baby? Changed a nappy?'

Cruz's jaw clenched. 'I do not need qualifications. I'm their uncle. I will hire the best possible staff to attend to their every need.'

His gaze narrowed on her so intently she fought against squirming under it.

'What possible qualifications could *you* have? When you came to work for me you'd left school after your A-levels with not much work experience.'

His remark went right to the heart of her and stung—badly. It stung because of the way she'd longed to impress this man at one time, and had yearned to catch his attention. It stung because of the very private dreams she'd harboured to further her education. And it stung because in all the foster homes where she'd lived through her formative years she'd instinctively found herself mothering any younger foster children, as if drawn to create what she didn't have: a family.

She pushed down the hurt at Cruz's sneering disdain now, cursing her naivety, and lifted her chin. 'I've been caring for them since they were a year old. No one is qualified to be a parent until they become one. From the moment I married Rio I became their step-parent, and I would never turn my back on them.'

'Very noble indeed. But forgive me if I don't believe you. Now, we can continue to go around in these tiresome circles, or you can just tell me how much it'll take.'

He gestured to the table and she looked down to see a chequebook.

'I will write a cheque for whatever you want, Trinity, so let's stop playing games. You've done it. Your impressive act of caring for children that aren't your own is over. You can get on with your life.'

The sheer ease with which Cruz revealed his astounding cynicism angered Trinity as much as it shocked her.

She balled her hands into fists by her sides. 'I am not playing games. And those boys are as much mine as if I'd given birth to them myself.' It hit her then— the enormity of the love she felt for them. She'd always known she loved them, but right now she'd lay her life down for them.

The thought of Cruz taking the boys and washing his hands of them the way Rio had done—abdicating all responsibility to some faceless nanny—made her feel desperate. She had to try and make him believe her.

She took a deep breath. 'Please listen to me, Cruz. The marriage wasn't what you think... The truth is that it was a marriage of convenience. The twins were primarily the reason I agreed to it. I wanted to protect them.'

Trinity could feel her heart thumping. Tension snapped between them.

Then, showing not a hint of expression, Cruz said, 'Oh, I can imagine that it was very convenient. For you. And I have no doubt that my nephews were front and centre of your machinations. I know my brother was no saint—believe me, I'm under no illusions about that. But, based on his first choice of wife, it stretches the bounds of my credulity that he would turn around and marry a mere nanny, for convenience's sake. He was a passionate man, Trinity. You are a beautiful woman. I can only imagine that you used every trick in the book to take it beyond an affair between boss and employee. After all, I have personal experience of your methods. But, believe me, the only "convenience" I see here is the way you so *conveniently* seduced your way into his bed and then into a registry office, making sure you'd be set for life.'

Trinity ignored Cruz's *'you're a beautiful woman'* because it hadn't sounded remotely complimentary. She longed to reveal that no such affair had taken place, but she felt suddenly vulnerable under that blistering gaze, all her anger draining away to be replaced with the humiliation she'd felt after that *'personal experience'* he'd spoken of.

She found the words to inform him that Rio hadn't been remotely interested in her lodging in her throat. The reality was that one brother had rejected her and another had used her for his own ends. And the fact that she was letting this get to her now was even more galling. She should be thinking of Mateo and Sancho, not her own deep insecurities.

She stood tall against the biggest threat she'd ever faced. 'I'm not going anywhere. I am their legal guardian.'

Cruz folded his arms. 'I won't hesitate to take you to court to fight for their custody if I have to. Do you really want that to happen? Who do you think the courts will favour? Their flesh-and-blood uncle, who has nothing but their best interests at heart and the means to set them up for life, or their opportunistic stepmother who systematically spent her way through her husband's wealth? Needless to say if you force this route then you will receive nothing.'

Trinity felt her blood rush south so quickly that she swayed on her feet, but she sucked in a quick breath to regain her composure before he could see it. 'You can't threaten me like this,' she said, as firmly as she could. 'I'm their legal guardian, as per Rio's wishes.'

Cruz bit out, 'I told you before—I'm not interested in playing games.'

'Neither am I!' Trinity almost wailed. 'But I'm not letting you bully me into handing over custody of Matty and Sancho.'

Cruz looked disgusted. '*Matty?* What on earth is that?'

Trinity put her hands on her hips. 'It's what Sancho has called him ever since he started talking.'

Cruz waved a hand dismissively. 'It's a ridiculous name for an heir to the De Carrillo fortune.'

Trinity went still. 'What do you mean, heir? Surely any children *you* have will be the heirs...'

Cruz was close to reaching boiling point—which wasn't helped by the fact that his libido seemed to be reaching boiling point too. He was uncomfortably aware of how Trinity's breasts pushed against the fabric of her seemingly demure silk shirt. It was buttoned to her neck, but it was the most provocative thing he'd ever seen. It made him want to push aside the desk and rip it open so he could feast his gaze on those firm swells...

Which was an unwelcome reminder of how he'd reacted that night when he'd found her in his study—
supposedly looking for a book—testing the very limits
of his control in not much more than a vest and sleep
shorts, with a flimsy robe belted around her tiny waist.

It *had* broken the limits of his control, proving that
he wasn't so far removed from his father after all, in
spite of his best efforts.

Cruz had had her backed up against the wall of
shelves, grinding his achingly hard arousal into her
quivering body, his fingers buried deep in slick heat
and his mouth latched around a hard nipple, before he'd
come to his senses...

Cursing her silently, and reining in his thundering
arousal, Cruz said, with a coolness that belied the heat
under the surface, '*Mateo* and Sancho will be my heirs,
as I have no intention of having any children.'

Trinity shook her head. 'Why would you say such
a thing?'

Already aware that he'd said too much, Cruz clamped
down on the curious urge to explain that as soon as he'd
heard Rio was having children he'd felt a weight lift off
his shoulders, not having been really aware until then
that he'd never relished the burden of producing an heir
for the sake of the family business.

He'd learnt from a young age what it was to have to
to stand by helplessly and watch his own half-brother
being treated as nothing just because he was the result
of an affair. He'd experienced the way parents—the
people who were meant to love you the most—sometimes had scant regard for their offspring. Cruz might

have been the privileged legitimate heir, but he'd been treated more like an employee than a loved son.

He'd never felt that he had the necessary skills to be a father, and he'd never felt a desire to test that assertion. However, his nephews had changed things. And the fact that Rio was no longer alive *really* changed things now. And the fact that this woman believed she could control their fate was abominable.

Cruz was aware that he barely knew his nephews—every time he saw them they hid behind Trinity's legs, or their nanny's skirts. And until Rio had died he hadn't felt any great desire to connect with them...not knowing *how* to, in all honesty. But now an overwhelming instinct to protect them rose up in him and surprised him with its force. It reminded him of when he'd felt so protective of Rio when he'd been much smaller, and the reminder was poignant. And pertinent. He hadn't been able to protect Rio, but he could protect his nephews.

Perhaps Trinity thought she'd get more out of him like this. He rued the day she'd ever appeared in his life.

Curtly he said, 'I'll give you tonight to think it over. Tomorrow, midday, I'll come to the house—and trust me when I say that if you don't have your price ready by then, you'll have to prepare yourself for a legal battle after which you'll wish that you'd taken what I'm offering.'

CHAPTER TWO

ON THE BUS back to Rio's house near Regent's Park—Trinity had never considered it hers—she was still reeling. She felt as if someone had physically punched her. Cruz had...except without using fists...and the reminder that she'd once fancied herself almost in love with him was utterly mortifying now.

The full enormity of his distrust in her was shocking—as was his threat that he would take her to court to get the boys if he had to.

She didn't need Cruz to tell her that she wouldn't fare well up against one of the world's wealthiest and most powerful men. As soon as his lawyers looked into her background and saw that she'd grown up in foster homes, with no family stability to her name, she'd be out of Matty and Sancho's lives.

It didn't even occur to her to consider Cruz's offer—the thought of leaving the twins in his cold and autocratic care was anathema to her.

Being in such close proximity to him again had left her feeling on edge and jittery. Too aware of her body. Sometimes the memory of that cataclysmic night in

Cruz's study came back like a taunt. And, no matter how much she tried to resist it, it was too powerful for her to push down. It was as vivid as if it had just happened. The scene of her spectacular humiliation.

The fact that Cruz obviously hated himself for what had happened was like the lash of a whip every time she saw him. As if she needed to be reminded of his disgust! As if he needed another reason to hate her now! Because that much was crystal-clear. He'd judged her and condemned her—he hadn't even wanted to hear her defence.

Trinity tried to resist thinking about the past, but the rain beating relentlessly against the bus windows didn't help. She felt as if she was in a cocoon...

She'd been working as Cruz's housemaid for approximately six months, and one night, unable to sleep, she'd gone down to the study to find a new book. Cruz had told her to feel welcome to read his books after he'd found her curled up in a chair reading one day.

Trinity had been very aware that she was developing a monumentally pathetic crush on her enigmatic boss—she'd even read about him in one of his discarded copies of the *Financial Times*.

She'd loved to read the papers, even though she hadn't understood half of what they talked about, and it had been her ambition to understand it all some day. She'd finally felt as if she was breaking away from her past, and that she could possibly prove that she didn't have to be limited by the fact that her own parents had abandoned her.

Cruz had epitomised success and keen intelligence,

and Trinity had been helplessly impressed and inspired. Needless to say he was the kind of man who would never notice someone like her in a million years, no matter how polite to her he was. Except sometimes she'd look up and find him watching her with a curious expression on his face, and it would make her feel hot and flustered. Self-conscious…

When she'd entered the study that night, she'd done so cautiously, even though she'd known Cruz was out at a function. She'd turned on a dim light and gone straight to the bookshelves, and had spent a happy few minutes looking for something to read among the very broad range he had. She'd been intrigued by the fact that alongside serious tomes on economics there were battered copies of John Le Carré and Agatha Christie. They humanised a very intimidating man.

She'd almost jumped out of her skin when a deep voice had said, with a touch of humour, 'Good to know it's not a burglar rifling through my desk.'

Trinity had immediately dropped the book she was looking at and turned to see Cruz in the doorway, breath-takingly gorgeous in a classic tuxedo, his bow tie rakishly undone. And her brain had just…melted.

Eventually, when her wits had returned, she'd bent down to pick up the book, acutely aware of her state of undress, and started gabbling. 'I'm sorry… I just wanted to get a book…couldn't sleep…'

She'd held the book in front of her like a shield. As if it might hide her braless breasts, covered only by the flimsiest material. But something in Cruz's lazy stance changed as his eyes had raked over her, and the air had suddenly been charged. Electric.

Her eyes had widened as he'd closed the distance between them. She'd been mesmerised. Glued to the spot. Glued to his face as it was revealed in the shadows of the room, all stark lines and angles. He'd taken the book she was holding out of her hand and looked at it, before putting it back on the shelf. He'd been so close she'd been able to smell his scent, and had wanted to close her eyes to breathe it in even deeper. She'd felt dizzy.

Then he'd reached out and touched her hair, taking a strand between two fingers and letting it run between them. The fact that he'd come so close…was touching her…had been so unlikely that she hadn't been able to move.

Her lower body had tightened with a kind of need she'd never felt before. She'd cursed her inexperience in that moment—cursed the fact that living in foster homes all her life had made her put up high walls of defence because she'd never been settled anywhere long enough to forge any kind of meaningful relationship.

She'd known she should have moved…that this was ridiculous. That the longer she stood there, in thrall to her gorgeous boss, the sooner he'd step back and she'd be totally exposed. She'd never let anyone affect her like this before, but somehow, without even trying, he'd just slipped under her skin…

But then he'd looked at her with a molten light in his eyes and said, 'I want you, Trinity Adams. I know I shouldn't, but I do.'

He'd let her hair go.

His words had shocked her so much that even though she'd known that was the moment to turn and walk out, her bare feet had stayed glued to the floor.

A reckless desire had rushed through her, heady and dangerous, borne out of the impossible reality that Cruz De Carrillo was looking at her like this...saying he wanted her. She was a nobody. She came from nothing. And yet at that moment she'd felt seen in a way she'd never experienced before.

It had come out of her, unbidden, from the deepest part of her. One word. *'Please...'*

Cruz had looked at her for a long moment, and then he'd muttered something in Spanish as he'd taken her arms in his hands and walked her backwards until she'd hit the bookshelves with a soft *thunk*.

And then he'd kissed her.

But it had been more like a beautifully brutal awakening than a kiss. She'd gone on fire in seconds, and discovered that she was capable of sudden voracious desires and needs.

His kiss had drugged her, taking her deep into herself and a world of new and amazing sensations. The feel of his rough tongue stroking hers had been so intimate and wicked, and yet more addictive than anything she'd ever known. She'd understood it in that moment—what the power of a drug might be.

Then his big hands had touched her waist, belly, breasts, cupping their full weight. They'd been a little rough, unsteady, and she hadn't expected that of someone who was always so cool. In control.

The thought that she might be doing this to him had been unbelievable.

He'd pulled open her robe so that he could pull down her vest top and take her nipple into his mouth, making Trinity moan and writhe like a wanton under his hands. She remembered panting, opening her legs, sighing with ecstasy when he'd found the naked moist heat of her body and touched her there, rubbing back and forth, exploring with his fingers, making her gasp and twist higher and higher in an inexorable climb as he'd spoken low Spanish words into her ear until she'd broken apart, into a million shards of pleasure so intense that she'd felt emotion leak out of her eyes.

And that was when a cold breeze had skated over her skin. Some foreboding. Cruz had pulled back, but he'd still had one hand between her legs and the other on her bared breast. He'd been breathing as harshly as her, and they'd looked at each other for a long moment.

He'd blinked, as if waking from the sensual spell that had come over them, and at the same time he'd taken his hands off her and said, 'What the hell…?'

He'd stepped away from her so fast she'd lurched forward and had to steady herself, acutely aware of her clothes in disarray. She'd pulled her robe around herself with shaking hands.

Cruz had wiped the back of his hand across his mouth and Trinity had wanted to disappear—to curl up in a ball and hide away from the dawning realisation and horror on his face.

'I'm sorry… I—' Her voice had felt scratchy. She hadn't even been sure why she was apologising.

He'd cut her off. '*No*. This was *my* fault. It should never have happened.'

He'd turned icy and distant so quickly that if her body hadn't still been throbbing with the after-effects of her first orgasm she might have doubted it had even happened—that he'd lost his control for a brief moment and shown her the fire burning under that cool surface.

'It was an unforgivable breach of trust.'

Miserable, Trinity had said, 'It was my fault too.'

He'd said nothing, and then, slightly accusingly, 'Do you usually walk around the house dressed like that?'

Trinity had gone cold again. 'What exactly are you saying?'

Cruz had dragged his gaze back up. His cheeks had been flushed, hair a little mussed. She'd never seen anyone sexier or more undone and not happy about it.

'Nothing,' he'd bitten out. 'Just…get out of here and forget this ever happened. It was completely inappropriate. I *never* mix business with pleasure, and I'm not about to start.' He'd looked away from her, a muscle pulsing in his jaw.

Right then Trinity had never felt so cheap in her life. He obviously couldn't bear to look at her a moment longer. She'd felt herself closing inwards, aghast that she'd let herself fall into a dream of feeling special so easily. She should have known better. Cruz De Carrillo took beautiful, sophisticated and intelligent women to his bed. He didn't have sordid fumbles with staff in his library.

The divide between them had yawned open like a

huge dark chasm. Her naivety had slapped her across the face.

Without saying another word, she'd fled from the room.

Trinity forcibly pushed the memory back down deep, where it belonged. Her stop came into view and she got up and waited for the bus to come to a halt.

As she walked back to the huge and ostentatious house by Regent's Park she spied Mrs Jordan in the distance with the double buggy.

Her heart lifted and she half ran, half walked to meet them. The boys jumped up and down in their seats with arms outstretched when they spotted her. She hugged each of them close, revelling in their unique babyish smell, which was already changing as they grew more quickly than she knew how to keep up with them.

Something fierce gripped her inside as she held them tight. She was the only mother they'd ever really known, and she would not abandon them for anything.

When she stood up, Mrs Jordan looked at her with concern. 'Are you all right, dear? You look very pale.'

Trinity forced a brittle smile. She couldn't really answer—because what could she say? That Cruz was going to come the next day and turn their world upside down? That lovely Mrs Jordan might be out of a job? That Trinity would be consigned to a scrap heap somewhere?

The boys would be upset and bewildered, facing a whole new world...

A sob made its way up her throat, but she forced it down and said the only thing she could. 'We need to talk.'

* * *

The following day, at midday on the dot, the doorbell rang. Trinity looked nervously at Mrs Jordan, who was as pale as she had been yesterday. They each held a twin in their arms, and Matty and Sancho were unusually quiet, as if sensing the tension in the air. Trinity had hated worrying the older woman, but it wouldn't have been fair not to warn her about what Cruz had said...

Mrs Jordan went to open the door, and even though Trinity had steeled herself she still wasn't prepared to see Cruz's broad, tall frame filling the doorway, a sleek black chauffeur-driven car just visible in the background. He wore a three-piece suit and an overcoat against the English spring chill. He looked vital and intimidating and gorgeous.

He stepped inside and the boys curled into Trinity and Mrs Jordan. They were always shy around their uncle, whom Matty called *'the big man'*.

'Mr De Carrillo, how nice to see you,' Mrs Jordan said, ever the diplomat.

Cruz looked away from Trinity to the older woman. There was only the slightest softening on his face. 'You too, Mrs Jordan.'

They exchanged pleasantries, and Mrs Jordan asked if he wanted tea or coffee before bustling off to the kitchen with Sancho. Trinity noticed that he'd looked at his nephews warily.

Then he looked at her with narrowed eyes. 'I presume we can talk alone?'

She wanted to say no, and run with the boys and Mrs Jordan somewhere safe. But she couldn't.

She nodded jerkily and said, 'Just let me get the boys set up for lunch and then I'll be with you.'

Cruz just inclined his head slightly, but he said *sotto voce*, as she passed him to follow Mrs Jordan to the kitchen, 'Don't make me wait, Trinity.'

Once they were out of earshot, Matty said in an awe-struck voice. 'Tha's the big man!'

Trinity replied as butterflies jumped around her belly. 'Yes, sweetie. He's your uncle, remember...?'

'Unk-*el*...' Matty repeated carefully, as if testing out the word.

Trinity delayed as much as she dared, making sure the boys were strapped securely into their high chairs, but then she had to leave.

Mrs Jordan handed her a tray containing the tea and coffee, and looked at her expressively. 'I'm sure he'll do what's right for the boys and you, dear. Don't worry.'

Trinity felt shame curl through her as she walked to the drawing room with the tray. She'd been too cowardly to tell Mrs Jordan the truth of Cruz's opinion of her. The woman believed that he only wanted custody of his nephews because he was their last remaining blood relative.

Stopping at the door for a second, she took a breath and wondered if she should have worn something smarter than jeans and a plain long-sleeved jumper. But it was too late. She balanced the tray on her raised knee, then opened the door and went in. Her heart thumped as she saw Cruz, with his overcoat off, standing at the main window that looked out over the opulent gardens at the back of the house.

She avoided looking at him and went over to where a low table sat between two couches. She put the tray down and glanced up. 'Coffee, wasn't it?'

Cruz came and sat down on the couch opposite hers. 'Yes.'

No *please*. No niceties.

Trinity was very aware of how the fabric of his trousers pulled taut over his powerful thighs. She handed over the coffee in a cup, grateful that this time her hands were fairly steady. She sipped at her own tea, as if that might fortify her, and wished it was something slightly stronger.

After a strained moment Trinity knew she couldn't avoid him for ever. She looked at him and blurted out, 'Why are you doing this now? If you're so sure I'm… what you say I am…why didn't you just step in after Rio's death?'

Cruz took a lazy sip of his coffee and put the cup down, for all the world as if this was a cordial visit. He looked at her. 'I, unlike you, grieved my brother's death—'

'That's not fair,' Trinity breathed.

Okay, so Rio had made her angry—especially at the end—and theirs hadn't been a real marriage, but she had felt a certain kinship with him. They hadn't been so different, as he'd told her—both abandoned by their parents. But then he'd betrayed her trust and her loyalty.

Cruz continued as if she'd said nothing. 'Once the state of Rio's finances became apparent, there was a lot of fire-fighting to be done. Deals he'd been involved in had to be tied up. I had to search for his mother to let her know what had happened—'

'Did you find her?' Trinity's heart squeezed as she thought of the impossible dream she never let herself indulge in: that some day she'd find *her* mother.

Cruz shook his head. 'No—and yes. She died some years ago, of a drug overdose.'

'Oh,' she said, feeling sad.

'I knew when the reading of the will would be taking place, and I wanted to see your face when you realised that there was nothing for you. And I'd been keeping an eye on you, so I knew what you were up to and how my nephews were.'

Trinity gasped. 'You had us followed?'

Cruz shrugged minutely. 'I couldn't be sure you wouldn't try to disappear. And you're the very public widow of a man most people still believe was a millionaire, with two small vulnerable children in your care. It was for your protection as much as my surveillance.'

Before she could fully absorb that, he went on, with palpable impatience.

'Look, I really don't have time for small talk, Trinity. Tell me how much you want so that I can get on with making the necessary arrangements to have my custody of my nephews legalised.'

His words were like a red rag to a bull—having it confirmed that he'd just been biding his time. That she'd never really registered on his radar as anyone worth giving the benefit of the doubt to.

She put her cup down with a clatter on the tray and glared at him. 'How dare you? Do you really think it's that simple? They are not pawns, Cruz. They are two small human beings who depend on structure and routine, who have lost both their parents at a very vulnerable age. Mrs Jordan and I are the most consistent people in their lives and you want to rip them away from that?'

She stood up then, too agitated to keep sitting down. Cruz stood too, and Trinity immediately felt intimidated.

He bit out, 'I want to take them away from a malignant influence. *You*. Are you seriously telling me you're prepared to go up against me? You know what'll happen if you do. You'll lose.'

'*No!*' Trinity cried passionately. 'The twins will lose. Do you know they've only just stopped asking for their *papa* every night? Because that's usually when he came to see them, to say goodnight. Their world has been turned upside down and you want to do it again. Who will be their primary carer? Don't tell me it's going to be *you*.' Trinity would never normally be so blunt or so cruel, but she felt desperate. 'Have you noticed how they look at you? They're intimidated by you. They hardly know who you are.'

Clearly unaccustomed to having anyone speak to him like this, Cruz flashed his eyes in disapproval. 'If anyone has been these boys' primary carer, I'd wager it's been Mrs Jordan. There's no reason why she can't remain as their nanny. But you have no claim on these boys beyond the legal guardianship you seduced out of Rio in a bid to protect your own future.'

Trinity's hands balled into fists. Her nails cut into her palms but she barely noticed. She wondered how she'd ever felt remotely tender about this man. 'That is *not* true. I love these boys as if they were my own.'

Cruz let out a curt laugh. 'I *know* that's not true.'

His smile faded, and his face became sterner than she'd ever seen it.

'And do you know why? Because Rio and I both learned that the people who are meant to love you the most *don't*. There's no such thing as an unbreakable bond.'

The fire left Trinity's belly. She felt shaky after the rush of adrenalin. Rio had told her about the way he'd been treated like an unwelcome guest in his own father's home. How his mother had abandoned him. It had played on all her sympathies. Now she wondered about Cruz's experience, and hated herself for this evidence that he still got to her.

'Not all parents were like yours or Rio's.'

Cruz arched a brow. 'And you know this from personal experience, when you grew up in a series of foster homes? Your experience wasn't too far removed from ours, was it, Trinity? So tell me how you know something I don't.'

Trinity went very still. 'How do you know that?'

He watched her assessingly. 'I run background checks on all my staff.' His lip curled. 'To think I actually felt some admiration for you—abandoned by your parents, brought up in care, but clearly ambitious and determined to make something of yourself. I seriously underestimated how little you were actually prepared to work to that end.'

The unfairness of his assessment winded her when

she thought of the back-breaking work she'd done, first as a chambermaid in a hotel, then as a maid in his house, before becoming nanny to two demanding babies. And then Rio's *wife*.

Feeling seriously vulnerable upon finding out that Cruz had known about her past all this time and had mentioned it so casually, she said, 'My experience has nothing to do with this.'

Liar, said a voice. It did, but not in the way Cruz believed.

'I love Matty and Sancho and I will do anything to protect them.'

Cruz was like an immovable force. 'You have some nerve to mention love. Are you seriously trying to tell me you loved Rio?'

Feeling desperate, she said, 'I told you—it wasn't like that.'

He glared at her. 'No, it wasn't. At least you're being honest about that.'

Trinity shivered under his look. His anger was palpable now. She said then, 'I did care for him.'

Before Cruz could respond to that there was a commotion outside, and Mrs Jordan appeared in the doorway with a wailing Sancho, who was leaning out of her arms towards Trinity, saying pitifully, *'Mummy...'*

Everything suddenly forgotten, she rushed forward and took him into her arms, rubbing his back and soothing him.

Mrs Jordan said apologetically, 'Matty hit him over the head with his plastic cup. It's nothing serious, but he's fractious after not sleeping well again last night.'

Trinity nodded and Mrs Jordan left to go back to Matty. She was walking up and down, soothing a now hiccupping Sancho, when she realised Cruz was staring at her with an angry look on his face.

He said almost accusingly, 'What's wrong with him?'

Suddenly Trinity was incredibly weary. 'Nothing much. He had a bug and he hasn't been sleeping, so he's in bad form. Matty just wound him up.' When Cruz didn't look appeased she said, 'Really, it's nothing.' She felt exposed under Cruz's judgemental look. 'Let me settle him down for a nap. That's all he needs.'

Cruz watched Trinity walk out of the room with Sancho in her arms, his nephew's small, chubby ones wrapped tight around her neck, his flushed face buried in her neck as if it was a habitual reflex for seeking comfort. He had stopped crying almost as soon as he'd gone into her arms.

Cruz had felt a totally uncharacteristic sense of helplessness seeing his nephew like that. It reminded him uncomfortably of his own childhood, hearing Rio cry but being unable to do anything to help him—either because Rio would glare at him with simmering resentment or his father would hold him back with a cruel hand.

Sancho's cries hadn't fazed Trinity, though. In fact she'd looked remarkably capable.

Feeling angry all over again, and this time for a reason he couldn't really pinpoint, Cruz turned back to the window. He ran a hand through his hair and then loosened his tie, feeling constricted. And he felt even more constricted in another area of his anatomy when he re-called how his gaze had immediately dropped to take in the provocative swell of Trinity's bottom as she'd walked away, her long legs encased in those faded jeans that clung like a second skin.

Damn her.

Witnessing this little incident was forcing Cruz to stop and think about what he was doing here. It was obvious that not only had Trinity seduced Rio for her own ends, she'd also ensured that the boys would depend on her…in case of this very scenario?

Cruz thought of pursuing his plans to take Trinity to court to fight her for custody, but he'd already seen what a good actress she was. If someone were to come to the house and see her interacting with his nephews they wouldn't be able to help being swayed by her *apparent* love and concern. As he had just been.

And did he really want to court a PR frenzy by pitting himself against the grieving widow of his brother? He knew she wasn't grieving—she wasn't even pretending. But no one else would see that. They'd only see him, a ruthless billionaire, protecting his family fortune.

It had taken him since his father's death to change the perception his father had left behind of a failing and archaic bank, blighted by his father's numerous high-profile affairs. Did he really want to jeopardise all that hard work?

Something hardened inside him as he had to acknowledge how neatly Trinity had protected herself. She was potentially even worse than he'd thought—using his nephews like this, manipulating them to need her.

She'd lived a quiet life since Rio's death—she'd only moved between the house, the local shops and the nearby park. No shopping on Bond Street or high-profile social events.

When she'd been with Rio, Cruz had seen countless pictures of them at parties and premieres, so she had to be approaching the end of her boredom threshold.

He thought again of her assertion that she loved the boys... He couldn't countenance for a second that she loved these children who weren't even her own flesh and blood.

A memory of his own mother came back with startling clarity—he'd been a young teenager and he'd confronted her one day, incensed on her behalf that his father had been photographed in the papers with his latest mistress.

She'd just looked at him and said witheringly, 'The only mistake he made, Cruz, was getting caught. This is how our world works.' She'd laughed then—nastily. '*Dios mio*, please tell me you're not so naive as to believe we married because we actually had *feelings* for one another?'

He'd looked at his mother in shock. No, he'd never laboured under the misapprehension that any such thing as *affection* existed between his parents, but he'd realised in that moment that some tiny part of him that hadn't been obliterated after years of only the most perfunctory parenting had still harboured a kernel of hope that something meaningful existed... Shame had engulfed him for being so naive.

She'd said then, with evident bitterness, 'I was all but

packaged up and sent to your father, because our two families belong to great dynasties and it was a strategic match. I did my duty and bore him a son, and I put up with his bastard son living under this very roof, and his mistresses—because, no matter what he does, this family's legacy is safe with you, and *I* have ensured that. That is all that matters in this life Cruz. Cultivating our great name and protecting it. One of these days your father will die, and as far as I'm concerned it can't come soon enough. Because then *you* will restore this family's reputation and fortune. That is your duty and your destiny, above all else.'

She'd died not long after that speech. The memory of her had faded but her words hadn't. *Duty and destiny.* There was no room for emotion, and he'd had to acknowledge the enormity of what he stood to inherit. He'd become a man that day, in more ways than one, leaving behind any childish vulnerabilities and misconceptions.

And because he'd stepped up to that responsibility he now had something solid to pass on to his nephews. They aroused something in him that he'd only felt before for Rio—an urge to protect and forge a bond. He'd become Rio's guardian while he'd still been underage, and he wanted to do the same for his vulnerable nephews. He vowed now that they would not go the way of their father. By the time they came of age they would know how to handle their legacy...he would make sure of it.

When Cruz had realised that he hadn't been named as guardian after Rio's death he'd felt inexplicably hurt, even though he'd known that he was hardly in a position to take on two small children he barely knew. It had been like a slap from beyond the grave, and he'd had to wonder if the rapprochement he'd believed to be present in his relationship with Rio had actually been real.

Or, as he'd come to suspect, was it more likely to have been someone else's influence?

Cruz had looked at Trinity, dressed in black on the other side of Rio's grave at the funeral, as his brother had been lowered into the ground. Her face had been covered in a gauzy veil, her body encased in a snug-fitting black suit. And that was when he'd vowed to do whatever it took to make sure her influence over his nephews was thwarted. He wanted them under his protection—away from a gold-digging manipulator.

Suddenly an audacious idea occurred to him. He immediately thrust it aside—appalled that he'd even thought it. But it wouldn't go away. It took root, and as he looked at it analytically it held a kind of horrific appeal.

He stared out over the gardens without really seeing them, and finally had to acknowledge grimly that there was really only one option where Trinity was concerned—but was he prepared to go to those lengths?

His gut answered him. *Yes*.

As if fate was contriving to make sure he didn't have time to change his mind he heard a noise and turned around to see Trinity coming back into the room. Her hair was pulled back into a low ponytail, but loose tendrils curled around her face. He noticed for the first time that there were delicate smudges of colour under her cornflower-blue eyes. Evidence of fatigue.

He ruthlessly pushed down a very curious sensation he'd never felt in relation to a woman before—and certainly not one he welcomed for this one: *concern*.

He faced her and saw how she tensed as she came towards him, folding her arms in a defensive gesture. Her chin tilting towards him mutinously.

With not a little relish, Cruz said, 'I have a solution which I think will work for both of us, my nephews and Mrs Jordan.'

He could see Trinity's arms tighten fractionally over her chest and he focused on her treacherously beautiful face. Even now she looked as innocent as the naive twenty-two-year-old who had come to work for him. Except, of course, she hadn't been naive. Or innocent. And she was about to face the repercussions of her actions.

'What solution?'

Cruz waited a beat and then said, very deliberately, 'Marriage, Trinity. You're going to marry me.'

CHAPTER THREE

FOR A MOMENT all Trinity heard was a roaring in her ears. She shook her head but Cruz was still looking at her with that expression on his face. Determined.

She asked weakly, 'Did you just say marriage?'

'Yes, I did.'

Trinity's arms were so tight across her chest she was almost cutting off her air supply. 'That is the most ridiculous thing I've ever heard.' And yet why was there an illicit shiver deep in her belly at the thought of being married to this man?

Cruz started to stroll towards her and Trinity had a very keen sense that he was a predator, closing in on his prey.

'Even though I know I'd win in a courtroom battle for the twins, I don't really have the inclination to invite unnecessarily adverse PR in my direction by pitting myself against my brother's widow. And from what I've seen it's evident to me that Mateo and Sancho are clearly attached to you.'

'Of course they are,' she said shakily. 'I'm all they've known as a mother since they were one.'

He stopped within touching distance and Trinity's breath hitched at his sheer charisma. She forced herself to fill her lungs. She couldn't afford to let him distract her.

'Why on earth would you suggest marriage?'

He grimaced, 'You are legally my nephews' guardian, and I don't trust you not to exert your right to do something drastic. Marriage will make me their legal guardian too, and I'm not prepared to settle for anything less to ensure their protection.'

Trinity shook her head and took a step back, hating herself for it but needing some space. 'You're crazy if you think I'll agree.'

With lethal softness he said now, 'Who do you think has been funding your existence these past few months?'

'You,' she said miserably.

'If you were to walk out of this house with my two nephews that allowance would be stopped immediately. How on earth do you think you would cope without a nanny?'

Desperation clawed upwards. 'I could get a job.'

Cruz was scathing. 'You'd be happy to lower yourself to Mrs Jordan's status again? Because that's all you're qualified for—either working as a maid or as a nanny.'

Trinity refused to let him intimidate her. 'Of course— if I had to.' A voice screamed at her—how on earth could she work with two small children in tow?

Cruz was obdurate, and Trinity knew with a sinking feeling that one way or the other he wasn't leaving until he'd got what he wanted. Her. And his nephews.

'It's very simple. I don't trust you not to take advantage of your position. And you seem to be forgetting a very pertinent fact.' He looked at her.

Eventually, with extreme reluctance and the sensation of a net closing around her, she said, 'What fact?'

'Since Rio's death those boys have had nothing but their name. The only way they will receive their inheritance now is through me, and I'm not going to let that happen unless you marry me.'

The net closed around Trinity as the full significance of that sank in. She would be responsible for not letting Matty and Sancho receive their inheritance?

'That's blackmail,' she breathed, astounded at his ruthlessness.

Cruz all but shrugged, supremely unperturbed. 'Their legacy is considerable, and as such I have a responsibility to see that it, and they, are protected.'

Affront coursed through her. 'I would never touch what's theirs.'

Cruz's lip curled. 'And yet you managed to divest Rio of a small fortune within less than a year of marriage?'

Trinity opened her mouth to defend herself again but from the look on Cruz's face she knew it would be pointless to say anything. Not in this emotive atmosphere.

She whirled away from that mocking look in his eyes and took refuge by a solid object—the couch. When she felt relatively composed again, she turned back to face him.

'There has to be some other way.' She seized on an

idea. 'I can sign something. A contract that says I have no claim to their inheritance.'

Cruz shook his head and moved, coming closer. 'No. Marriage is the only option I'm prepared to consider. I've decided to move back to the De Carrillo ancestral home in Spain, near Seville. The bank is flourishing here in the UK, and in America. Its reputation has been restored. It's time to build on that, and presenting a united family front will only strengthen the business and in turn my nephews' legacy.'

Rendered speechless, Trinity could only listen as Cruz went on.

'Locking you into a marriage with me is the only way they'll get their inheritance and I'll be satisfied that you're not going to prove to be a threat to my nephews. And as it happens a convenient wife will suit my needs very well. But I'm afraid I can't offer you the bling of married life with Rio. You might have been keeping a low profile since my brother died, but I would estimate that once the reality of living in a remote *castillo* hits you'll be climbing the walls and looking for a divorce before the year is out…which I'll be only too happy to grant once I've got full custody of my nephews.'

The extent of his cynicism shocked her anew. She'd surmised from Rio's account of his early life that things probably hadn't been idyllic for Cruz either, but she'd never imagined that he carried such a deep-rooted seam of distrust.

Trinity hated it that it aroused her empathy and curiosity—again. She cursed herself. She'd felt empathy for

Rio and she'd let him manipulate her. If it hadn't been for Mateo and Sancho she'd tell Cruz where to shove his autocratic orders and storm out.

But how could she? He was threatening to withhold their very legacy if she didn't comply. And there was no way she was leaving her boys in his cold and cynical care alone. She was all they had now.

Surely, she thought quickly, if she said yes he'd realise what he was doing—marrying someone he hated himself for kissing—and agree to make some kind of compromise? Trinity shoved down the betraying hurt that Cruz would never even be suggesting such a thing if she didn't have something he wanted. His nephews.

She called his bluff. 'You leave me no choice. Yes, I'll marry you.'

She waited for Cruz to blanch, or for realisation to hit and for him to tell her that he'd only been testing her commitment, but he showed no emotion. Nor triumph. After a beat he just looked at his watch, and then back at her, as cold as ice.

'Good. I'll have my team draw up a pre-nuptial agreement and organise a fast and discreet civil wedding within the next few weeks, after which we'll leave directly for Spain.'

He had turned and was walking out of the room before the shock reverberating through Trinity subsided enough for her to scramble after him—clearly he was not a man who was easily bluffed. He was deadly serious about this.

His hand was on the doorknob when she came to a stumbling halt behind him, breathless. 'Wait a minute—

you don't really want to marry me. What about falling in love?'

Cruz turned around with an incredulous look on his face, and then threw his head back and laughed so abruptly that Trinity flinched. When he looked at her again his eyes glittered like dark golden sapphires.

'*Love?* Now you really are over-acting. Choice in marriage and falling in love are best left to the deluded. Look where infatuation got my brother—driven to fatal destruction. I have no time for such emotions or weaknesses. This marriage will be one in name only, purely to protect my nephews from your grasping hands, and you will fulfil your role as my wife to the best of your ability.'

Trinity tried one more time. 'You don't have to do this. I would never harm my stepsons, or take their inheritance from them.'

Cruz's eyes gleamed with stark intent. 'I don't believe you, and I don't trust you. So, yes, we *are* doing this. You'll need to see if Mrs Jordan is happy to stay in my employment and come to Spain. If not, we'll have to hire another nanny. The sooner you come to terms with this new reality and start preparing the boys for the move the easier it will be for me to make the necessary arrangements.'

For long minutes after he'd walked out Trinity stood there in shock. What had she just done?

True to his word, just over two weeks later Trinity stood beside Cruz De Carrillo in a register office. He was dressed in a sleek dark grey suit, white shirt and matching tie. She wore an understated cream silk knee-length sheath dress with matching jacket. Her hair was up in a smooth chignon, her make-up light.

In the end resistance had been futile. No matter which way she'd looked at it, she'd kept coming back to the fact that she wasn't prepared to walk away from Mateo and Sancho after all they'd been through—as well as the fact that the thought of leaving them made her feel as if someone was carving her heart out of her chest.

By agreeing to marry Rio she'd at least felt that she could offer them some permanence, which she'd never had. She hadn't wanted them to go through the same insecurity…and now she was in exactly the same position. So it had come down to this: she had nowhere to go, and no one to turn to.

When she'd put Cruz's plan to Mrs Jordan, the woman had thought about it, consulted with her son who was at university in Scotland, and then agreed to stay with them as long as she could be guaranteed regular visits home. Trinity had felt emotional, knowing that at least she'd have Mrs Jordan's quiet and calm support.

She was acutely conscious now of Cruz's tall, hard body beside her as the registrar spoke the closing words of the ceremony. She was all but a prisoner to this man now. The perfect chattel. She looked at the simple gold band on her finger that marked her as married for the second time in her life. This time, though, she thought a little hysterically, at least she wasn't remotely deluded about her husband's intentions.

'I now pronounce you husband and wife. Congratulations. You may kiss your wife, Mr De Carrillo.'

Slowly, reluctantly, Trinity turned to face Cruz. She looked up. Even though she wore high heels, he still towered over her.

Cruz just looked at her for a long moment. Trinity's breath was trapped in her throat like a bird. Was he going to humiliate her in front of their small crowd of witnesses—largely made up of his legal team—by refusing to kiss her?

But then, just when she expected him to turn away dismissively, he lowered his head and his mouth touched hers. Firm. Cool. His lips weren't tightly shut, and neither were hers, so for a second their breaths mingled, and in that moment a flame of pure heat licked through her with such force that she was hurled back in time to that incendiary kiss in his study.

Before she could control her reaction, though, Cruz was pulling back to look down at her again with those hard, glittering eyes. They transmitted a silent but unmistakable message: he would do the bare minimum in public to promote an image of unity, but that was as far as it would go.

Trinity was humiliated by her reaction, by the fact that he still had such a devastating effect on her. And terrified at the prospect of him realising it. She tried to pull her hand free of his but he only tightened his grip, reminding her of how trapped she was.

She glared up at him.

'Smile for the photos, *querida*.'

Trinity followed Cruz's look to see a photographer waiting. Of course. This was all part of his plan, wasn't it? To send out a message of a family united.

Aware that she must look more like someone about to be tipped over the edge of a plank than a besotted bride, Trinity forced a smile and flinched only slightly when the flash went off.

Cruz could hear his nephews chattering happily as they were fed at the back of the plane. Then he heard softer, lower tones… Trinity's… He tensed. Any sense of satisfaction at the fact that he'd achieved what he'd set out to achieve was gone. He cursed silently. Who was he kidding? He'd been tense since he'd left her standing in that room in Rio's house, with her eyes like two huge pools of blue, and a face leached of all colour.

It should have given him an immense sense of accomplishment to know he'd pulled the rug from under her feet, but he'd walked away that day with far more complicated emotions in his gut—and a very unwelcome reminder of when he'd seen a similar look of stunned shock on her face…the night he'd kissed her.

She'd been the last person he'd expected to see when he'd walked into his study that night, weary from a round of engaging in mind-numbingly boring small-talk. And fending off women who, up until a few months before, would have tempted him. His mind had been full of…*her*. And then to find her there, stretching up, long legs bare and exposed, the lush curve of her bottom visible under the short robe and the even more provocative curve of her unbound breasts… It was as if she'd walked straight out of his deepest fantasy…

He could still recall the second he'd come to his senses, when he'd realised he was moments away from lifting her up against his shelves and finding explosive release in her willing body, all soft and hot and *wet*. No other woman had ever caused him to lose it like that. But she'd been his *employee*. Someone he'd been in a position of power over.

The stark realisation that he was following in his father's footsteps in spite of every effort he'd made to remove the shadow of that man's reputation had been sickening. He was no better after all.

He'd been harsh afterwards…angry at his reaction… demanding to know what she was doing there as if it had been her fault. He'd felt like a boor. Little had he known then that she'd obviously been waiting until he got home and had made sure he found her…

It was galling. A sign of weakness. Cruz scowled. Trinity had no power over his emotions. She represented a very fleeting moment in time when he'd forgotten who he was.

The reality of his situation hit him then—in marrying Trinity he was consigning himself to a life with a woman he would never trust. But the sacrifice would be worth it for his nephews' sake.

At least now she was under his control and his watchful eye.

He'd felt anything *but* watchful earlier, though, when she'd turned to face him in that sterile register office and everyone had waited for their kiss. He'd had no intention of kissing her—it would show her how it would be between them. And prove that he could control himself around her… But for a split second his gaze had dropped to that lush mouth and every cool, logical intention had scattered, to be replaced with an all too familiar desire just to take one sip, one taste…

So he'd bent his head, seeing the flash of surprise in her eyes, and touched his mouth to hers. And he'd felt her breath whisper over his mouth. It had taken more effort than he liked to admit to pull back and deny himself the need he'd had to take her face in his hands, angle her mouth for better access so he could explore her with a thoroughness that would have made him look a complete fool…

Cruz only became aware that he was being watched when the hairs went up on the back of his neck, and he turned his head from brooding out of the small window. He had to adjust his gaze down to see that one of his nephews—he couldn't tell which—was standing by his chair with small pudgy hands clutching the armrest.

For a second time was suspended, and his mind went blank. Two huge dark eyes stared up at him guilelessly. Thick, dark tousled hair fell onto a smooth forehead and the child's cheeks were flushed. Something that looked like mashed carrot was smeared around his mouth. And then he smiled, showing a neat row of baby teeth. Something gripped Cruz tight in his chest, throwing him back in time to when he'd looked at an almost identical child, six years his junior.

'*Matty*, don't disturb your uncle.'

That low, husky voice. Gently chiding. Two slender pale hands came around his nephew to lift him up and away. Trinity held him easily with one arm, against her body. The small face showed surprise, and then started to contort alarmingly just before an ear-splitting screech emerged.

Cruz noted that she looked slightly frayed at the edges. Her hair was coming loose and she had smears of food on her jacket. He looked down and saw pale bare feet, nails painted a delicate shade of coral, and he felt a surge of blood to his groin. Immediately he scowled at his rampant reaction and Trinity backed away.

'Sorry, I didn't realise he'd slipped out of his chair.'

She was turning to walk back down the plane when Cruz heard himself calling out, 'Wait.'

She stopped in her tracks and Cruz saw Mrs Jordan hurrying up the aisle, reaching for Mateo to take him from Trinity. The indignant shouting stopped as the older woman hushed him with soothing tones.

Trinity turned around and Cruz felt something pierce him as he acknowledged that, *in*convenient wedding or not, most brides were at least given a meal before being whisked away after their nuptials.

They'd gone straight from his solicitor's office, where Trinity had signed the pre-nuptial agreement, to the register office and then to the plane. He'd expected her to pore over the pre-nuptial agreement, but she'd just glanced through it and then looked at him and said, 'If we divorce then I lose all custody of the boys, is that it?'

He'd nodded. Aware of his body humming for her even while they were surrounded by his legal team. She'd just muttered something under her breath like, *Never going to happen,* and signed. Cruz had had to include some kind of a severance deal for her if they divorced, so Trinity would always be a wealthy woman, but he knew she could have fought him for a better deal.

So why hadn't she? asked a voice, and Cruz didn't like the way his conscience smarted. He wasn't used to being aware of his conscience, never doubting himself in anything—and he wasn't about to start, he told himself ruthlessly. For all he knew Trinity's actions thus far were all an act to lull him into a false sense of security.

'Have you eaten yet?' he asked abruptly, irritated that she was making him doubt himself.

She looked at him warily and shook her head as she tucked some hair behind her ear. 'I'll eat when the boys have eaten.'

Cruz gestured to the seat across the aisle from him. 'Sit down. I'll get one of the staff to take your order.' He pressed the call button.

Trinity looked towards the back of the plane for a moment. Her visible reluctance was not a reaction he was used to where women were concerned.

'Sit before you fall. They're fine. And we have some things to discuss.'

She finally sat down, just as an attentive air steward appeared and handed her a menu. Trinity's head was downbent for a moment as she read, and Cruz found it hard to look away from that bright silky hair.

When the air steward had left Trinity felt uncomfortable under Cruz's intense gaze. It was as if he was trying to get into her head and read her every thought. Just the prospect of that made her go clammy—that he might see the effect his very chaste kiss had had on her.

In a bid to defuse the strange tension, she prompted, 'You said we have things to discuss…?'

Cruz blinked and the intensity diminished. Trinity sucked in a breath to acknowledge how attuned she felt to this man. It was disconcerting—and unwelcome.

'As soon as you're settled at the *castillo* I'll organise interviews for another nanny to help Mrs Jordan. You're going to be busy as my wife.'

The castillo. It even sounded intimidating. She said, as coolly as she could, as if this was all completely normal, 'Maybe this would be a good time for you to let me know exactly what you expect of me as your wife.'

Maybe, crowed a snide voice, *it would have been a good idea for you not to get so attached to two babies that aren't yours in a bid to create the family you never had.*

Trinity gritted her jaw.

Cruz said, 'My calendar is already full for the next three months, and I should warn you that my social events are more corporate-orientated than celebrity-based… I'll expect you on my arm, looking the part, and not scowling because you're bored.'

Trinity boiled inside. Clearly he was expecting her to last for about two weeks before she ran for the hills. And he was obviously referring to Rio's predilection for film premieres or events like the Monte Carlo Grand Prix, which Trinity had found excruciating—all she could remember of that particular event was the overwhelming diesel fumes and the constant seasickness she'd felt while on some Russian oligarch's yacht.

Rio had invariably paraded her in public and then

promptly dropped her once the paparazzi had left—which had suited her fine. She'd usually been in her own bed, in her own separate room, by the time he'd finished partying around dawn. But she could just imagine telling Cruz that, and how he'd merely shut her down again.

Then she thought of something. 'What do you mean, "looking the part"?'

He swept an expressive look over her, and at that moment she was aware of every second of sleep she hadn't got in the past couple of years. *And* the fact that today was probably the first day she'd worn smart clothes and actually put on make-up in months.

Compounding her insecurity, Cruz said, 'As *my* wife you'll need to project a more...classic image. I've already arranged for you to be taken shopping to buy new clothes.'

Trinity tensed at the barb. 'But I have clothes.'

His lip curled. 'The kind of clothes you wore around my brother will not be suitable and they've been donated to charity.'

Her face grew hot when she recalled seeing Cruz again, for the first time since her marriage to Rio, three months ago. His effect on her had been instantaneous—a rush of liquid heat. And then he'd looked at her as if she was a call girl. How could she blame him? She'd felt like one.

Rio's sense of style for women had definitely favoured the 'less is more' variety. He'd handed her a dress to wear for that party that had been little more than a piece of silk. Skimpier than anything she'd ever worn.

She'd protested, but he'd said curtly, 'You're working for me, Trinity. Consider this your uniform.'

It hadn't been long after their row and her finding out exactly why he'd married her. Rio had been acting more edgily than usual, so Trinity hadn't fought him on the dress and had assured herself that she'd talk to Cruz that night—seek his help. Except it hadn't turned out as she'd expected. She'd been a fool to think she could turn to him.

The memory left her feeling raw. She averted her eyes from Cruz's now and said stiffly, 'It's your money—you can spend it as you wish.'

The air steward came back with Trinity's lunch, and she focused on the food to try and distract herself from a feeling of mounting futile anger and impotence. But the fact that she was destined to dance to the tune of another autocratic De Carrillo man left the food in her mouth tasting of dust.

She gave up trying to pretend she had an appetite and pushed her plate away. Cruz looked up from the small laptop he'd switched his attention to. He frowned with disapproval at how little she'd eaten—it was an expression that was becoming very familiar to Trinity, and one she guessed was likely to become even more familiar.

Her anger rose. 'Was this marriage really necessary?' she blurted out, before she could censor her tongue.

A bit late now, whispered that annoying voice.

As if privy to that voice, Cruz mocked, 'It really is futile to discuss something that's already done. But by all means, Trinity, feel free to seek a divorce whenever you want.'

And leave Matty and Sancho at this man's mercy? Never, vowed Trinity.

Just then a plaintive wail came from the back of the plane.

'Mummy!'

She recognised the overtired tone. Seizing her opportunity to escape, Trinity stood up and tried not to feel self-conscious in her creased dress and bare feet.

'Excuse me. I should help Mrs Jordan.'

She walked away with as much grace as she could muster and tried her best not to feel as though her whole world was shrinking down to the size of a prison cell— even if it was to be the most luxurious prison cell in the world.

A few hours later Trinity shivered, in spite of the warm Spanish breeze. They'd driven into a massive circular courtyard and she was holding a silent and wide-eyed Sancho in her arms, thumb stuck firmly in his mouth. Mrs Jordan was holding a similarly quiet Matty. They were still a little groggy after the naps they'd had on the plane.

Her instinct about the *castillo* being intimidating had been right. It was massive and imposing. A mixture of architecture, with the most dominant influence being distinctly Moorish. Cruz had explained that they were about midway between Seville and a small historic town called El Rocio, which sat on the edge of a national park. But there was nothing around them now except for rolling countryside; he hadn't been lying about that.

Cruz was greeting some staff who had appeared in

the imposing porch area. They were all dressed in black. Trinity caught Mrs Jordan's eye and was relieved to see that the older woman looked as intimidated as she felt.

Mrs Jordan said brightly, 'Well, my word, I don't think I've ever seen anything so grand. I'm sure it's bright and airy on the inside.'

But when they went in, after a whirlwind of introductions to several staff whose complicated names Trinity struggled to imprint on her brain, it wasn't bright and airy. It was dark and cool—and not in a refreshing way.

The stone walls were covered with ancient tapestries that all seemed to depict different gruesome battles. Then there were portraits of what had to be Cruz's ancestors. She could see where he got his austere expression. They all looked fearsome. There was one in particular whose resemblance to Cruz was uncanny.

She hadn't even noticed that she'd stopped to stare at it for so long until a cool voice from behind her said, 'That's Juan Sanchez De Carrillo—my great-great-grandfather.'

Unnerved, in case he might guess why she'd been momentarily captivated by the huge portrait, Trinity desisted from saying that she thought it looked like him. Instead she asked, 'So is this where you and Rio grew up?'

For a moment he said nothing, and Trinity looked at him. She caught a fleeting expression on his face that she couldn't read, but then it was gone.

He led her forward, away from the portrait, as he said smoothly, 'Yes, we were both born in this *castillo*. But our circumstances couldn't have been more different.'

'I know,' Trinity said cautiously. 'Rio told me that his mother was a maid here, and that she blackmailed your father for money after their affair and then left Rio behind.'

In spite of everything that had happened, she *still* felt sympathy. These dark corridors and austere pictures only confirmed that Cruz's experience couldn't have been much happier here. That treacherous curiosity to know more rose up again, much to her disgust. She was a soft touch.

But Cruz was clearly not up for conversation. He was moving again, leaving the long corridor, and she had to follow or be left behind. He opened a door to reveal an enclosed open-air courtyard and Trinity automatically sucked in a deep breath, only realising then how truly oppressive the *castillo* had felt.

They'd lost Mrs Jordan and the other staff somewhere along the way. Afraid that Cruz suspected she was angling for a personal tour, she shifted Sancho's heavy and now sleeping weight on her shoulder and hurried after his long strides.

'You don't have to show me around—there'll be plenty of time for that.'

A whole lifetime, whispered that wicked voice.

Cruz just said brusquely, 'This isn't a tour. We're just taking another route to your quarters.'

Trinity felt a childish urge to poke her tongue out at his back. *Your quarters.* She shivered a little.

He led them back into the *castillo* on the other side of the surprisingly pretty courtyard. The sensation of the walls closing around her again made her realise that this was *it*. Hers and the boys' home for the foreseeable future. The prospect was intimidating, to say the least.

Trinity vowed then and there to do everything she could to ensure Matty and Sancho's happiness and security in such a dark and oppressive atmosphere. After all, she'd chosen to be their protector and she had no regrets.

Cruz helped himself to a shot of whisky from the sideboard in his study on the other side of the *castillo*. He took a healthy sip, relishing the burn which distracted him from the uncomfortable feeling that lingered after walking away from Trinity, Mrs Jordan and the boys, all looking at him with wide eyes, as if they'd just been transported to Outer Mongolia.

He didn't like the way his nephews fell silent whenever he approached them, looking at him so warily, clinging on to Trinity. His urge to protect them had grown exponentially since he'd decided marriage was the only option—thanks to which he was now their legal guardian too.

While the jury was still very much out on Trinity—her easy signing of the pre-nup had thrown up questions he wasn't eager to investigate—he had to admit grudgingly that so far it didn't look as if his nephews were being adversely affected by her.

Cruz had been surprised to discover that Rio had told her the full extent of his mother's treachery.

When he and Rio had been younger they'd never been allowed to play together, and on the few occasions Cruz had managed to sneak away from his nanny to find Rio his younger half-brother had always looked at him suspiciously.

One day they had been found together. Cruz's father had taken Rio into his study, and he could still remember the shouts of humiliation as his father had beaten him. Rio had eventually emerged with tears streaking his red face, holding his behind, glaring at Cruz with a hatred that had been vivid.

Their father had appeared in the doorway and said to Cruz, 'That's what'll happen if you seek him out again. His is *not* your real brother.'

Cruz had felt so angry, and yet so impotent. That was the moment he'd vowed to ensure that Rio was never denied what was rightfully his…much good it had done his brother in the end.

He realised now for the first time that the knowledge that he was his nephews' legal guardian had soothed something inside him. Something he never could have acknowledged before, while Rio had held him at arm's length. It was the part of him that had failed in being able to protect his brother when they were younger. He was able to do this now for his nephews in the most profound way. It made emotion rise up, and with it futile anger at Rio's death.

Cruz's mind deviated then, with irritating predictability, back to his new wife. He'd expected something more from her by now—some show or hint of defiance that would reveal her irritation at having her wings clipped. But there was nothing. Just those big blue eyes, looking at him suspiciously. As if he might take a bite out of her... That thought immediately made him think of sinking his teeth into soft pale flesh.

What the hell was wrong with him? He would not fall into that pit of fire again. She disgusted him.

A little voice jeered at him. *She disgusts you so much that your blood simmers every time she's close?*

Cruz shut it down ruthlessly.

Trinity would not tempt him again. This situation was all about containment and control and ensuring his nephews were in his care and safe. That was all that mattered—their legacy. As soon as she realised how limited her life would be she'd be begging for a divorce, and that day couldn't come soon enough.

CHAPTER FOUR

A WEEK LATER Trinity felt as if she were on a slightly more even keel. She and the boys and Mrs Jordan had finally settled, somewhat, into their palatial rooms. Decorated in light greys and soft pinks and blues, with contemporary furniture and a modern media centre, they made for a more soothing environment than the rest of the dark and brooding *castillo*, which was not unlike its owner.

Mrs Jordan had an entire apartment to herself, as did Trinity, and they were both connected by the boys' room, which was light and bright but other than that showed no indication that it was home to two small boys with more energy than a bag of long-life batteries.

They took their meals in a large sunny dining room, not far from their rooms, that led out to a landscaped garden. Trinity and Mrs Jordan spent most of their time running after Matty and Sancho, trying to stop them pulling the very exotic-looking flowers out of the pristine beds.

Trinity sighed now, and pushed some hair behind her ear as she contemplated the two napping toddlers who looked as exhausted as she felt. She'd have to talk to Cruz about modifying their bedroom and installing something more practical outside that would occupy their vast energy and satisfy their need to be stimulated. Otherwise the head gardener was going to be very upset, and the boys were going to grow more and more frustrated.

The staff they'd seen so far—a taciturn housekeeper who spoke no English and a young girl who looked terrified—hardly inspired confidence in it being a happy household where she could get to know people and let the boys run free. It was very obvious that Cruz believed he had corralled them exactly where he wanted them and had now all but washed his hands of her, in spite of his decree that she be available as his social escort.

Mrs Jordan had had the morning off, and was going to keep an eye on the boys this afternoon when they woke, so Trinity took the opportunity to go and see if Cruz had returned from his trip to Madrid yet—she'd managed to ascertain that he'd gone from the shy maid.

She refused to give in to a growing feeling of helplessness but while making her way from their wing of the *castillo*, back through the pretty courtyard, she could feel her heart-rate increasing. She told herself it was not in anticipation of seeing Cruz after a few days. What was wrong with her? Was she a complete masochist?

As she walked past the stern portraits of the ancestors she didn't look up, not wanting to see if their eyes would be following her censoriously, judging her silently.

Just at that moment a door opened and a tall hard

body stepped out—right in front of Trinity. She found herself slamming straight into the man who so easily dominated her thoughts.

Big hands caught her upper arms to stop her lurching backwards. All her breath seemed to have left her lungs with the impact as she stared up into those tawny eyes.

Somehow she managed to get out the words, 'You're back.'

Cruz's hands tightened almost painfully on Trinity's arms. 'I got back late last night.'

Tension was instant between them, and something else much more ambiguous and electric. She tried to move back but she couldn't.

Panic that he might see her reaction to him spiked. 'You can let me go.'

Cruz's eyes widened a fraction, as if he'd been unaware he was holding her, and then suddenly he dropped his hands as if burnt. Trinity stepped back, feeling sick at the expression crossing his face—something between disgust and horror. She'd seen that look before, after he'd kissed her.

She said quickly, 'I was looking for you, actually.'

After a silent moment Cruz stepped aside and gestured for her to go into the room he'd just left. She stepped inside, still feeling shaky after that sudden physical impact.

Cruz closed the door and walked to his desk, turning around to face her. 'I'll call for some coffee—or would you prefer tea?'

'Tea would be lovely, thank you.'

So polite. As if he *hadn't* just dumped her and her

stepsons in his remote intimidating home and left them to their own devices. Maybe he thought she would have run screaming by now?

When Cruz turned away to lean over his desk and pick up the phone Trinity had to consciously drag her gaze away from where his thin shirt stretched enticingly over flexed and taut muscles. She looked around the room, which was huge and obviously his home office.

Dark wood panelling and big antique furniture gave it a serious air. Floor-to-ceiling shelves dominated one whole wall, and Trinity felt a wave of heat scorch her from the inside out as the memory of another wall of shelves flashed back, of how it had felt to have Cruz press her against it so passionately.

'Do you still read?'

Trinity's head snapped back to Cruz. She hadn't even noticed that he'd finished the call. She was mortified, and crushed the memory, hoping her cheeks weren't flaming.

She shook her head, saying with a slightly strangled voice, 'I haven't had much time lately.' She was usually so exhausted when she went to bed now that her love of reading was a thing of the past. A rare luxury.

'Well? You said you were looking for me?'

He was looking at her expectantly, one hip resting on his desk, arms folded. Formidable. Remote. Her ex-employer, now her husband, but a stranger. It struck her then that even though they'd shared that brief intimacy, and she'd had a glimpse of what lay under the surface, he was still a total enigma.

She shoved down her trepidation. 'Yes. I wanted to talk to you about the boys.'

A light knock came on the door, and he called for whoever it was to come in as he frowned and said, 'What's wrong? Are they okay?'

The maid, Julia, appeared with a tray of tea and coffee, distracting Trinity. She noticed how the girl blushed when Cruz bestowed a polite smile on her and said thank you. Trinity felt humiliation curl inside her. She'd used to blush like that when she'd worked for him. It felt like a lifetime ago.

When the girl had left Cruz was still looking at Trinity, waiting for her answer. Feeling exposed under that laser-like intensity, she said, 'Nothing is wrong with them—they're fine. Settling in better than I'd expected, actually.'

Some of the tension left Cruz's shoulders and she felt a dart of unexpected emotion—what if he really did care about the boys?

He deftly poured tea for her and coffee for him and handed her a cup. 'Sit down.'

She chose a chair near the desk and cradled her cup, watching warily as he took a seat on the other side of his desk. He took a sip of his coffee and arched one dark golden brow, clearly waiting for her to elaborate.

She put the cup down on the table in front of her and sat up straight. 'The rooms...our rooms...are lovely. And very comfortable. But the boys' room isn't exactly tailored for children their age. It could do with brightening up, being made more cheerful—somewhere they can play and where they'll want to go to sleep. Also, they've been playing in the gardens—which they love—but again it's not exactly suitable for them. Your head gardener has already had to replant some of his flowerbeds.'

Cruz's conscience pricked as he acknowledged that he'd not even had the courtesy to stick around for one day and make sure that Trinity and his nephews and their nanny were comfortable.

He knew that the *castillo* was dated in parts, but the rooms he'd given to them had been those used by his mother before her death, so they were the most up-to-date. But evidently not up-to-date enough.

It hadn't even occurred to him to make the space child-friendly, and that stung now. What also stung was the fact that he had to acknowledge that his trip to Madrid had been less about business and more about putting some space between him and this new domestic world he'd brought back to Spain with him.

He was distracted by Trinity's very earthy clean-faced appeal. A look he had thought she'd eschewed as soon as she'd married Rio. Certainly any pictures he'd seen of them together had shown her to have morphed into someone who favoured heavy make-up and skimpy clothes.

And yet where was the evidence of that now? Her hair was pulled back into a low, messy bun. She was wearing soft jeans and a loose shirt, with a stain that looked suspiciously like dried food on her shoulder—as unalluring as any woman who had ever appeared in front of him, and yet it didn't matter. Cruz's blood sizzled over a low-banked fire of lust.

'So, what are you suggesting?' he asked, irritated at this reminder of how much she affected him.

Trinity swallowed, making Cruz notice the long slim column of her throat. Even that had an effect on him. *Damn it.*

'I'd like to make the boy's room more colourful and fun. And with regards to the garden… I'm not saying that that's not enough for them—your grounds are stunning—but they're bright, inquisitive boys and they're already becoming frustrated with being told they can't roam freely and touch what they want. Perhaps if they had something that would occupy their energy, like swings… They loved the children's playground in Regent's Park.'

All of what she'd just said was eminently reasonable, yet Cruz felt a tide of tension rising up through his body.

'Anything else?'

As if she could sense his tension, something flashed in her eyes. Fire. It sent a jolt of adrenalin through Cruz. She certainly wasn't the shy girl who'd come for that job interview a couple of years ago. More evidence of her duality, if he'd needed it.

She lifted her chin. 'Yes, actually. I don't know how the school systems work here, but if it's anything like in the UK I'll—' She stopped herself and flushed slightly. 'That is, *we'll* have to think about enrolling them in a local school. Also, I'd like to investigate playschools in the area—they should be around other children their own age. Surely you weren't expecting to them to never go beyond the *castillo* gates?'

He'd never been allowed beyond the *castillo* gates until he'd gone to boarding school in England.

He reacted testily to the fact that she was showing a level of consideration for his nephews that he'd never expected to see. 'Are you sure you're not just looking for opportunities to spread your own wings beyond these walls? You're not a prisoner, Trinity, you can leave any time you want. But if you do the boys remain here.'

She paled dramatically, any bravado gone, but seconds later a wash of bright pink came into her cheeks. Cruz was momentarily mesmerised by this display of emotion—he was used to people disguising their natural reactions around him. It had intrigued him before and he was surprised that she still had the ability.

She stood up. 'I'm well aware that I am here because I have little or no choice—not if I want to see my stepsons flourish and be secure—but I will never walk away from them. Not while they need me. I will do whatever it takes to ensure their happiness and wellbeing.'

Her blue eyes blazed. *Dios*, but she was stunning.

'So if you're hoping to see the back of me it won't be any time soon, I can assure you.'

With that, she turned on her heel and stalked out of the room, the heavy door closing with a solid *thunk* behind her. Cruz cursed volubly and stood up, muscles poised to go after her. But then he stopped.

He turned to face the window, which took in the breathtaking vista of the expanse of his estate. He couldn't allow Trinity to distract him by fooling him into thinking she'd changed. Because the moment he dropped his guard she'd have won.

'What on earth did you say to him?'

Trinity was too shocked to respond to Mrs Jordan's question as she took in the scene before her. Building was underway on a playground for the boys...an exact replica of the playground in Regent's Park.

At that moment the atmosphere became charged with a kind of awareness that only happened around one person. *Cruz.*

Mrs Jordan reacted to his presence before Trinity did. 'Mr De Carrillo, this really is spectacular—the boys will love it.'

He came to stand beside Trinity and his scent tickled her nostrils, earthy and masculine. Her belly tightened and she flushed. Superstitiously she didn't want to look at him, as if that might make his impact less.

He answered smoothly, 'Please, Mrs Jordan, call me Cruz... Trinity was right—the boys need somewhere they can expend their energy safely.'

Matty and Sancho were currently playing with big toy building bricks in an area that had been cordoned off for them by the builders. They were wearing small hard hats and jeans and T-shirts and they looked adorable, faces intent, trying to keep up with the real builders just a few feet away.

Mrs Jordan turned to Cruz more directly and said, with an innocent tone in her voice, 'We were just about to bring the boys in for lunch—won't you join us?'

Trinity glanced at the woman, aghast, but Mrs Jordan was ignoring her. Fully expecting Cruz to refuse, she couldn't believe it when, after a long moment, he said consideringly, 'Thank you. That would be lovely.'

Mrs Jordan smiled. 'I'll ask Julia to add another place.'

She disappeared with a suspicious twinkle in her eye before Trinity could say anything. She supposed she couldn't really blame the woman for taking the opportunity to meddle gently when it arose.

When Trinity glanced up at Cruz she almost expected him to look irritated at the thought of spending lunch with them, but he was staring at the boys with an enigmatic expression on his face. Uncertainty?

Then, as if he sensed her watching him, the expression was gone and he looked down at her. 'You haven't said anything—are the plans all right?'

Against her best intentions to remain impervious to this man's pull, something inside her melted a little at his thoughtfulness. She forced a smile. 'They're perfect. I didn't expect you to take my words so literally.'

He frowned. 'But you said they loved that playground, so naturally I would try to recreate it for them.'

Trinity desisted from pointing out that only a billionaire would think along such lavish lines and just said dryly, 'It's extremely generous, and they will love it. Thank you.'

Cruz looked away from her to the boys and another curious expression crossed his face. She'd seen it before when he looked at them: something between fear and longing. Trinity cursed herself for not reading it properly till now. This man scrambled her brain cells too easily.

She said, 'They won't bite, you know. They're as curious about you as you are about them.'

Without taking his eyes off them Cruz said gruffly, 'They always seem to look at me as if they don't know what I am.'

Trinity felt something weaken inside her at this evidence of rare vulnerability. 'They don't really know you yet, that's all. Once they become more used to you they'll relax. Why don't you help me get them in for lunch?'

She moved forward before he could see how easily he affected her.

'Matty! Sancho!' she called out when she came near to where they were playing so happily. 'Time to go in for lunch.'

Two identical faces looked up with predictable mulishness—and then they spied Cruz and immediately put down what they were playing with to come to Trinity. She bent down to their level and took their hats off, ruffling their heads, feeling the heat from their small, sturdy bodies. Even though they were in the shade the Spanish spring was getting warmer every day.

Cruz was towering over them in one of his trademark pristine suits. No wonder he intimidated the boys. He intimidated her. Softly she said, 'It might help if you come down to their level.'

He squatted down beside her and the movement made her uncomfortably aware of his very potent masculinity. She closed her eyes for a second. What was wrong with her? Until she'd shared that incendiary moment with him in his study she'd had no great interest in sex. And yet a couple of days in Cruz's company again and all her hormones seemed to have come back to life.

She focused her attention on her boys, who were huddled close, brown eyes huge. 'Matty, Sancho…you know this is your Uncle Cruz's house, where we're going to live from now on?' She ignored the pang inside her when she said that, and the thought of a life stretching ahead of her as a wife of inconvenience.

'Man. The big man,' Matty observed.

Trinity bit back a smile at the innocent nickname. 'Yes, sweetie—but he's also your uncle and he wants to get to know you better.'

Sancho said nothing, just regarded his uncle. Then he said imperiously, 'Play with us.'

Matty jumped up and down. 'Yes! Play!'

Sensing things starting to unravel, Trinity said firmly, 'First lunch, and then you can play again for a little while.'

She scooped up Matty and handed him to Cruz, who took him awkwardly and rose to his feet. She then picked up Sancho and started to walk inside, almost afraid to look behind her and see how Matty must be tarnishing Cruz's sartorial perfection.

He was saying excitedly, 'Higher, Unkel Cooz… higher!'

Seeing his brother in the arms of the tall, scary man who now wasn't so scary was making Sancho squirm to get free from Trinity's arms. 'I want higher too!'

They walked into the bright dining room where Mrs Jordan was waiting for them. Trinity didn't miss the gleam of approval in the woman's eyes when she saw Cruz carrying one of his nephews.

Trinity thought again of that rare chink of vulnerability Cruz had revealed outside. She realised belatedly that this had to be hard for him—coming from such a dark and dour place with only a half-brother he'd never been allowed to connect with properly. And yet he was making a real effort.

A rush of tenderness flooded her before she could stop it.

She tried to hide her tumultuous emotions as she strapped Sancho into his high seat. When she felt composed again she looked up to see Mrs Jordan showing Cruz how to strap Mateo into his. He looked flummoxed by such engineering, and it should have emasculated the man but it didn't. It only made that tenderness surge again. Pathetic.

Cruz sat down at the head of the table. The boys were seated one on each side beside Trinity and Mrs Jordan. Staff scurried in and out, presenting a buffet of salads and cold meats, cheese and bread. The boys were having chopped up pasta and meatballs. They ate with their habitual gusto, insisting on feeding themselves and invariably spraying anyone in close proximity with tiny bits of pasta and meat.

Trinity sneaked another glance at Cruz to see if this domestic milieu was boring him, but he was watching his nephews, fascinated.

'How do you tell them apart?' he asked, during a lull when small mouths were full.

Trinity nodded her head towards Mateo on the other side of the table. 'Matty is a tiny bit taller and leaner. He's also a little more gregarious than Sancho. Where he leads, Sancho follows. She scooped some of Sancho's food back onto his plate and said with a fond smile, 'Sancho is more watchful and quiet. He's also got a slightly different coloured right eye—a tiny discolouration.'

Cruz leaned forward to look and Sancho grinned at the attention, showing tiny teeth and a mouth full of masticated food.

When he pulled back, Cruz said a little faintly, 'Rio had the same thing...one eye was slightly lighter in colour.'

'He did...?' Trinity had never noticed that detail.

Cruz sent her a sharp glance and she coloured and busied herself cleaning up Sancho's tray, feeling absurdly guilty when she had no reason to. It wasn't as if she'd spent any time looking deep into Rio's eyes. Not that Cruz would believe that. She wondered if he ever would.

It didn't escape her notice that Mrs Jordan had excused herself on some flimsy pretext. Trinity sighed inwardly. She wouldn't put it past the woman, who subsisted on a diet of romance novels, to try and matchmake her and Cruz into a real marriage.

The thought of that was so absurd that she coloured even more for a moment, as if Cruz might see inside her head.

The very notion of this man looking at her with anything other than suspicious disdain was utterly inconceivable.

But he looked at you differently once before, said a little voice.

Trinity blocked it out. Cruz wouldn't touch her again if his life depended on it—of that she was sure. And that suited her just fine. If he ever discovered how susceptible she still was—*and* how innocent she still was, in spite of his belief that her marriage to Rio had been a real one... The thought sent a wave of acute vulnerability through her.

Cruz's comprehensive rejection of her had left a wound in a deeply private feminine space. The thought of opening herself up to that rejection again was terrifying.

Cruz cleared his throat then, and said, 'I've arranged for you to be taken to a local boutique tomorrow morning, where a stylist will help you choose a wardrobe of clothes. Think of it as a trousseau.'

Trinity put down the napkin and looked at him. She felt raw after her recent line of thinking. She hated to be so beholden to him. It made her feel helpless and she didn't like that. She saw the look in his eye, as if he was just waiting for her to show her true avaricious nature.

'There's not just me to think of,' she said testily. 'I need to get the boys some new clothes too, more suitable for this warmer climate. They're growing so fast at the moment that they've almost outgrown everything.'

Cruz inclined his head, only the merest glint in his eye showing any reaction to her spiky response. 'Of course. I should have thought of that. I'll see to it that the stylist takes you to a suitable establishment for children also.'

The boys were starting to get bored now, having eaten enough and grown tired of the lack of attention and activity. Sancho was already manoeuvring himself to try and slip out of his chair and Trinity caught him deftly.

She took advantage of the distraction. 'I'll let them play some more while their lunch digests and then it'll be time for their afternoon nap.'

Without asking for help, Cruz stood and plucked a clearly delighted Matty, little arms outstretched, out of his seat. It irked her no end that Cruz was already holding him with an ease that belied the fact that it was only the second time he'd held one of his nephews in his arms.

It suited him. Matty looked incredibly protected in those strong arms and a sharp poignancy gripped her for a moment as she realised that he was already charming them. They'd gone from looking at him as if he was about to devour them whole, to looking at him with something close to awe and adoration. Their tiny minds were obviously cottoning onto the fact that this tall person might become an important ally and be able to do things that Trinity and Mrs Jordan couldn't.

Sancho was whingeing—he wanted to be in the big man's arms too.

Cruz held out his other arm, 'I can take him.'

After a moment's hesitation Trinity handed him over, to see Cruz expertly balance Sancho in his other arm. And then he walked out of the room, two glossy brown heads lifted high against his chest. The twins were delighted with themselves, grinning at her over those broad shoulders.

And just like that Trinity knew she'd started to lose them to Cruz… And, as wrong as it was, she couldn't but help feel a tiny bit jealous at how easily he accepted the innocence of his nephews when he would never ever accept the possibility of Trinity's. Not while he was so blinded by his loyalty to his deceased brother.

The next few days passed in a blur for Trinity. She was taken to cosmopolitan and beautiful Seville by Cruz's driver, to a scarily exclusive boutique where she lost track of the outfits she tried on. Then she was taken to a department store that stocked children's clothes, where she picked up everything she needed for the boys.

Their bedroom had been refurbished, and once again Cruz's efficiency had been impressive. An interior designer had taken her ideas on board and now, with murals of animals and tractors and trains on the walls, it was a bright and inviting space for two small boys. And they each had a bed, built in the shape of a car.

For a moment, when she'd seen it transformed and the way the boys had stood there in wide-eyed awe, she'd felt ridiculously emotional. They would have so much more than she'd ever had…or even their father.

She would have thanked Cruz, but he hadn't been around much in the last few days. He hadn't joined them for lunch again, and the boys had been asking for him plaintively.

Trinity folded up the last of Sancho and Matty's new clothes and put them in the colourful set of drawers, chastising herself for the constant loop in her head that seemed to veer back to Cruz no matter how hard she tried to change it.

She was about to push the drawer closed when a deep voice came from behind her. 'Where are the boys?'

She jumped and whirled around to see Cruz filling the doorway, dressed in jeans and a shirt open at the neck. Irritation at the way she'd just been wondering about him, and the effortless effect he had on her, made her say waspishly, 'They're outside, playing with Mrs Jordan.'

Her irritation only increased when she found herself noticing how gorgeous he looked.

'They've been asking for you, you know. If you're going to be in their lives you need to be more consistent. They don't understand why you're there one day but not the next...it confuses them.'

Her conscience pricked. What she really meant was that it put *her* on edge, not knowing where or when he was likely to turn up...

His gaze narrowed on her and he slowly raised one brow. Clearly the man wasn't used to having anyone speak to him like this. Well, tough, she told herself stoutly. She was no longer in awe of her scarily sexy stern boss. She folded her arms.

'I understand that you've had your wardrobe replenished, as well as my nephews'?' Cruz drawled.

Trinity flushed. She immediately felt churlish and unfolded her arms. 'I wanted to say thank you for the bedroom—it worked out beautifully, and the boys love it. And, yes, we got clothes… But more clothes were delivered from the boutique than I ever looked at or tried on…it's too much.'

Cruz shook his head slowly, a hard light in his eye. 'Still with the act? I'm impressed. I thought you would have cracked by now and shown your true colours— but perhaps you're saving yourself for a more appreciative audience.'

She just looked at him. This evidence of his continued mistrust hurt her and, terrified to look at why that was, and not wanting him to see her emotions, she focused on the last thing he'd said. 'What do you mean, *audience?*'

'I have a function to attend in Seville tomorrow night. It'll be our first public outing as husband and wife.'

Panic gripped her. 'But Mrs Jordan—'

Cruz cut her off. 'Has already agreed to babysit. And we're rectifying that situation next week. I've organised with a local recruitment agency for them to send us their best candidates for another nanny. It'll free you up to spend more time with me, and Mrs Jordan will have more of her own free time.'

'Is that really necessary?' she asked, feeling weak at the thought of more time with him.

'Yes.' Cruz sounded impatient now. 'I'll have social functions to attend and I expect you to be by my side. As discussed.'

Trinity's irritation flared again. and she welcomed it. 'As I recall it was more of a decree than a discussion.'

Cruz's jaw clenched. 'You can call it what you want. We both know that, thanks to Rio's dire financial state when he died, you had no way of offering independent support to my nephews without me. The sooner you accept this as your new reality, the easier it will be for all of us.'

And evidently Cruz still believed that state of financial affairs to be *her* fault, based on her alleged profligate spending of her husband's money.

For a moment Trinity wanted to blurt out the truth— that Rio had hated Cruz so much he'd wanted to ruin him—but Cruz wouldn't believe her, and she found that the impulse faded quickly. First of all, it wasn't in her to lash out like that, just to score a point. And she also realised she didn't want to see the effect that truth would have on him, when he clearly believed that his brother had been flawed, yes, but inherently decent.

And that shook her to the core—knowing that she resisted wanting to hurt him. Even as he hurt her.

She had to take responsibility for the fact that she'd agreed to the marriage of convenience with Rio. She really had no one to blame but herself.

And, as much as she hated this situation and being financially dependent, she couldn't deny the immutable fact that Matty and Sancho were in the privileged position of being heirs to this great family legacy and fortune. She didn't have the right to decide on their behalf, even as their legal guardian, that she was going to fight to take them away from all this and turn their lives into something it didn't have to be.

The silence grew between them almost to breaking

point, a battle of wills, until eventually Trinity said, 'Fine. What time do I need to be ready?'

There was an unmistakable gleam of triumph in Cruz's eyes now and he said, 'We'll leave at six. It's a formal event, so wear a long gown. I'll have Julia show you to the vaults so you can pick out some jewellery.'

Jewellery...vaults... Not wanting him to see how intimidated she was, or how easily he affected her emotions, she just said coolly, 'Fine. I'll be ready by six.'

CHAPTER FIVE

THE FOLLOWING EVENING Cruz paced back and forth in the entrance hall of the *castillo* and looked at his watch again impatiently. He forced himself to take a breath. It was only just six o'clock so Trinity wasn't actually late *yet*. Just then he heard a sound and looked to where she stood at the top of the main stairs.

For a long second he could only stare, struck dumb by the glittering beauty of the woman in front of him. She was refined…elegant. Classic. Stunning.

Her dress was long—as he'd instructed—and a deep blue almost navy colour. It shone and glistened and clung to those impossibly long legs, curving out to her hips and back in to a small waist. It shimmered as she came down the stairs. It clung everywhere—up over her torso to where the material lovingly cupped full, perfectly shaped breasts. All the way to the tantalising hollow at the base of her throat.

Cruz was dimly aware that he'd possibly never seen less flesh revealed on a woman, and yet this dress was sexier than anything he'd ever seen in his life. Her hair was pulled back at the nape of her neck, highlighting the delicate slim column of her throat and her bone structure.

She gestured to herself and he could see that she was nervous.

'What is it? Is the dress not suitable?'

Cruz realised he was ogling. He felt a very uncharacteristic urge to snap, *No, the dress is entirely unsuitable.* And yet that would be ridiculous. The dress effectively covered her from head to toe and he was reacting like an animal in heat—how the hell would he react when he saw some flesh? As it was, all the blood in his body was migrating from his brain to between his legs with alarming speed.

Any delusion he'd been under that he could successfully block out his awareness of this woman was laughable. She was under his skin, in his blood, and he couldn't deny it. His intellect hated this desire for her but his body thrummed with need.

Calling on all the control and civility he possessed, Cruz locked eyes with Trinity's—not that that helped. The colour of the dress only made her bright blue eyes stand out even more. They were like light sapphires, stunning and unusual.

'It's fine,' he said tightly. And then, goaded by thoughts of how she'd dressed for Rio, he said provocatively, 'Or perhaps you'd feel more comfortable in less material?'

To his surprise he saw the faintest shudder pass through her body. 'No. I never felt comfortable in the clothes Rio wanted me to wear.'

He looked at her. For some reason that admission only made him feel more conflicted.

Tersely he said, 'The driver is waiting—we should go.'

He indicated for her to precede him out of the *castillo* and his gaze tracked down her back and snagged on the enticing curves of her buttocks. He cursed himself. He was behaving as if he'd never seen a beautiful woman before in his life.

The driver helped her into the back of the luxury Jeep and Cruz got in the other side. As they were pulling out of the *castillo* courtyard his gaze swept over her again and he noticed something. 'You're not wearing any jewellery. Didn't you go to the vaults?'

She looked at him and Cruz saw a flush stain her cheeks. 'I did, but everything was so valuable-looking I was afraid to take anything.'

Something dark pierced him—was this finally evidence of her avaricious methods? Was this how she angled for more?

'Perhaps you'd have preferred something from Cartier or Tiffany's?'

She shook her head, eyes flashing. 'No, I wouldn't prefer that.' She held out her hand. 'I'm wearing the wedding band—isn't that enough? Or maybe you'd prefer if I wore a diamond-studded collar with a lead attached so no one is mistaken as to whom I belong?'

Irritation vied with frustration that she was so consistently refusing to conform to what he expected. He curtly instructed his driver to turn around and go back to the *castillo*.

'Why are we going back?' Trinity asked.

Cruz looked straight ahead. 'We're going back to get you an engagement ring.'

'I don't need one,' she said stubbornly.

He looked at her. 'It's not a choice. People will expect you to have a ring.'

She rounded on him, tense and visibly angry. 'Oh, and we can't have anyone suspecting that this isn't a real marriage, can we? Do you really think an engagement ring will convince people that you fell in love with your brother's widow?'

Cruz wanted to laugh at her suggestion of anyone in his circle ever being convinced that people married for love, but for some reason the laugh snagged in his chest.

'Don't be ridiculous,' he breathed, his awareness of her rising in an unstoppable wave in the confined space. 'No one would expect that. They'll know I'm protecting what's mine—my heirs.'

'And I'm just the unlucky pawn who got in your way.'

The bitterness in Tiffany's voice surprised him. Anger spiked at the way his control was starting seriously to fray at the edges. 'You put yourself in the way—by seducing my brother. By inserting yourself into my nephews' lives so they'd come to depend on you.'

She went pale and looked impossibly wounded. 'I've told you—that's not—'

Before she could issue another lie Cruz's control snapped and he acted on blind instinct and need. He reached for Trinity, clamping his hands around her waist, and pulled her towards him, vaguely registering how slender and light she felt under his hands.

He only had a second of seeing her eyes widen with shock before his mouth crashed down onto hers, and for a long second nothing existed except this pure, spiking shard of lust, so strong that he had no option but to move his mouth and haul Trinity even closer, until he could feel every luscious curve pressed against him.

And it was only in that moment, when their mouths were fused and he could feel her heart clamouring against his chest, that he could finally recognise the truth: he'd been aching for this since the night he'd kissed her for the first time.

Trinity wasn't even sure what had happened. A minute ago she'd been blisteringly angry with Cruz and now she was drowning and burning up at the same time. The desire she'd hoped she could keep buried deep inside her was shaming her with its instant resurrection. Brought back to life by a white-hot inferno scorching along every artery and vein in her body.

Cruz's mouth was hot and hard, moving over hers with such precision that Trinity couldn't deny him access, and when his tongue stroked hers with an explicitness that made heat rush between her legs her hands tightened around his arms, where they'd gone instinctively to hang on to something…anything…so she wouldn't float away.

His hands were still on her waist and one started moving up her torso, until it came tantalisingly close to the side of her breast, where her nipple peaked with need, stiffening against the sheer material of her underwear and her dress. She remembered what it was like

to have his mouth on her there…the hot sucking heat…
the excruciating pleasure of his touch.

A voice from the past whispered through the clamour
of her blood—his voice. *'It should never have happened.'* It was like a slap across the face.

Trinity jerked backwards away from Cruz. She was
panting as if she'd just run a race. Mortification was
swift and all-consuming. He'd barely had to touch her
before she'd gone up in flames. Any hope of convincing him she didn't want him was comprehensively an-
nihilated. It wasn't even a comfort to see that his hair
was dishevelled and his cheeks were flushed.

Those amber eyes glittered darkly. He muttered, 'I
told myself I wouldn't touch you ever again, but I can't
not touch you.'

She took her hands off him, but he caught them and
held them tightly. The recrimination on his face was far
too painfully familiar. She was angry and hurt.

'So now it's justifiable for you to kiss me, even if you
still hate yourself for it? Because I'm your wife and not
just a lowly maid?'

She pulled her hands free and balled them into fists
in her lap.

Cruz frowned, 'What the hell are you talking about—
justifiable?'

Trinity tried not to sound as emotional as she felt.
'You rejected me that night because you couldn't bear
the thought that you'd kissed your maid. I saw the kind
of women you took as lovers, and you don't need to tell
me that I was nowhere near their level—socially, eco-
nomically or intellectually.'

Cruz clamped his hands around her arms, his face flushing. He was livid. 'You think I stopped making love to you because I was a snob? *Dios* Trinity, that was *not* the case. I had to stop because you were my employee and I had a duty of care towards you. I put you in a compromising situation where you might have felt too scared to say no.'

His mouth twisted.

'My father was renowned for his affairs—some of which were with willing and impressionable staff members at the *castillo*. I vowed that I would never follow his footsteps—not least because I'd seen the destruction one of his affairs cost us all. He slept with Rio's mother, who took advantage of the situation, only to then abandon her son.'

Trinity was speechless for a moment as she absorbed this. 'You think,' she framed shakily, 'that I'm like Rio's mother, then? That I'm no better...?'

Cruz's wide, sensual mouth compressed. 'I didn't think so at first—not that night. I hated myself for losing control like that, but I didn't blame you. Since then...let's just say any illusions about your innocence I may have had have been well and truly shattered.'

An awful poignancy gripped Trinity at the thought that for a short while Cruz *had* seen the real her...and respected her. But even the memory of her naivety and humiliation couldn't stop her saying bitterly, 'It would only have ever been a mistake, though, wouldn't it? I mean, let's not fool ourselves that it would have developed into anything...more...'

More. Like the kind of more that Cruz had once

hoped existed until any such notion was drummed out of him by his mother and her bitter words? Since then he'd never been proved wrong—any woman he'd been with had only confirmed his cynicism. Not least this one. And yet...when he'd first laid eyes on her he'd never seen anyone who looked so untouched and innocent.

And she was looking at him now with those huge eyes, taunting him for his flight of fancy. It was as if she was reaching inside him to touch a raw wound.

He was unaware of his hands tightening on her arms, knew only that he needed to push her back.

'More...like what?' he all but sneered. 'Hearts and flowers? Tender lovemaking and declarations of undying love? I don't *do* tender lovemaking, Trinity, I would have taken you until we were both sated and then moved on. I have no time for relationships—my life isn't about that. It never was and it never will be. I have a duty of care to my nephews now, and you're here only because I'm legally bound to have you here.' His mouth twisted. 'The fact that I want you is a weakness I'm apparently not capable of overcoming.'

A veritable cavalcade of emotions crossed Trinity's face, and then a look of almost unbelievable hurt—it had to be unbelievable—superseded them all. She shrank back, pulling herself free, and he only realised then how hard he'd been holding her. He curled his hands into fists and cursed himself. What was it about this woman that made his brain fuse and cease functioning?

In a low voice that scraped along all of Cruz's raw

edges she said, 'I wasn't looking for anything more than a book that night, no matter what you choose to believe.'

Cruz still felt volatile, and even more so now at this protestation of innocence and her stubborn refusal to reveal her true nature. He ground out, 'Maybe if I'd taken you as I'd wanted to, there against the bookshelves, we wouldn't be here now and Rio would still be alive.'

Trinity had thought he couldn't hurt her much more than he already had, but he just had—even as a lurid image blasted into her head of exactly the scenario he mentioned...his powerful body holding her captive against a wall of books while he thrust up, deep into her body.

She held herself rigid, denying that hurt, and blasted back, 'So you would have thrown over that elegant brunette beauty for me? Am I supposed to be flattered that you would have been happy to conduct an affair on your terms, only to discard me by the wayside when you were done with me?'

A muscle ticked in Cruz's jaw but he just said tersely, 'We're back at the *castillo*, we should get the ring. We've wasted enough time.'

Wasted enough time.

Trinity was still reeling as she followed Cruz's broad tuxedoed form down stone steps to the vaults, holding her dress up in one hand. The depth of his cynicism astounded her all over again, and she hated it that he'd hurt her so easily.

She blamed his interaction with Matty and Sancho. It had made her lower her guard against him and he'd punished her for it, reminding her that he was not remotely someone to pin her hopes and dreams on... She scowled at herself. Since when had she ever entertained those notions herself? It wasn't as if she'd ever been under any delusions of *more*.

More existed for people who weren't her or Cruz. Who had grown up with normal, functioning, loving families. And yet she couldn't deny that when she'd worked for him for a brief moment she'd entertained daydreams of him noticing her...wanting her...smiling at her—

Trinity slammed a lid on that humiliating Pandora's box.

She wasn't sure what was worse—finding out that Cruz hadn't dismissed her because she was a nobody all those years ago, or believing that if he'd taken her *until they were both sated* he could have averted Rio's destruction. Right now, she hated Cruz with a passion that scared her.

But not far under her hatred was something much more treacherous. A very illicit racing excitement at the knowledge that he still wanted her. And that he'd rejected her because he'd felt he'd taken advantage of his position, not because he'd been horrified to find himself attracted to her...

Once in the vault, Trinity welcomed the change of scenery from the heightened and heated intensity of the back of the Jeep even as she shivered in the cold, dank air.

She hated herself for it, but found herself instinctively moving closer to Cruz's tall, lean form because the place gave her the creeps. She could imagine it being used as a location for the Spanish Inquisition, with its dark stone walls and shadowy cavernous corridors.

She thought, not a little hysterically, that if they'd been back in medieval times Cruz might have just incarcerated her down here in a cell.

He had pulled out a velvet tray of rings from a box in the wall and stood back. 'Choose one.'

Trinity reluctantly stepped forward. Almost immediately one ring in the centre of the tray caught her eye. It was one of the smallest rings, with an ornate gold setting and a small square ruby in the middle.

Cruz followed her gaze and picked it up. 'This one?'

She nodded. He took her hand and held it up and slid the ring onto her finger. It was a perfunctory gesture, so it shouldn't feel in any way momentous but it did. The ring fitted like a glove and, bizarrely, Trinity felt emotion rising when emotion had no place there—especially not after what had just passed between them.

Swallowing the emotion with effort, Trinity was unprepared when Cruz took her chin in his thumb and forefinger, tipping it up. The look in his eyes burned.

'As much as I'd like to be able to resist you, I don't think I can.'

Her heart thumped—hard. The thought of Cruz touching her again and seeing right through to where she was most vulnerable was anathema.

She jerked her chin out of his hand. 'Well, I can resist you enough for both of us.'

He smiled urbanely and stood back, putting out a hand to let her go ahead of him up the stairs and out of the vaults. 'We'll see,' he said with infuriating arrogance as she passed him, and she had to stop herself from running up the stairs, away from his silky threat.

This was Cruz's first social appearance back in Seville. His return was triumphant, now he had tripled his family's fortune and restored the reputation of the once great bank. Now no one would dare say to his face or behind his back the things they'd used to say when his father had been alive.

And yet he could not indulge in a sense of satisfaction. He was too keyed-up after that white-hot explosion of lust in the back of the Jeep, which had proved to him that where Trinity was concerned he had no control over his desires.

His body still throbbed with sexual frustration. And he was distracted by their exchange, and how it had felt to see her with that ring on her finger down in the vaults. It had affected him in a place he hadn't welcomed. As if it was somehow *right* that she should wear one of his family's heirlooms.

Down in that vault it had suddenly been very clear to him that he couldn't fight his desire for her—so why should he? He might not like himself for his weakness but she was his wife, and the prospect of trying to resist her for the duration of their marriage was patently ridiculous.

But something niggled at him—why wasn't she using his desire for her as a means to negotiate or manipulate? Instead she'd looked almost haunted when she'd fled up the steps from the vault. She was still pale now, her eyes huge. Irritation prickled across Cruz's skin. Maybe now that she knew he wanted her she was going to play him in a different way, drive him mad...

'What is it?' he asked abruptly. 'You look paler than a wraith.'

She swallowed, the movement drawing Cruz's gaze to that long, slender column. Delicate. Vulnerable. Damn her. She *was* just playing him. He was giving in to his base desires again and—

'I'm fine. I just... Events like this are intimidating. I never get used to it. I don't know what to say to these people.'

Cruz's recriminations stopped dead. If she was acting then she was worthy of an award. He had a vivid flashback to seeing her standing alone in the crowd at that party in his house, the night of the accident, her stunning body barely decent in that scrap of a dress.

Cruz had been too distracted by the rush of blood to his extremities to notice properly. He'd hated her for making him feel as if he was betraying his brother by still feeling attracted to her. But the memory jarred now. Not sitting so well with what he knew of her.

Almost without registering the urge, Cruz took his hand off her elbow and snaked it around her waist, tugging her into his side. It had the effect of muting his desire to a dull roar. She looked up at him, tense under his arm. Something feral within him longed for her to admit to this attraction between them.

'What are you doing?'

'We're married, *querida*, we need to look it. Just follow my lead. most of the people here are committed egotists, so once you satisfy their urge to talk about themselves they're happy.'

'You don't count yourself in that category?'

Her quick comeback caused Cruz's mouth to tip up. Suddenly the dry, sterile event wasn't so…boring. And she had a flush in her face now, which aroused him as much as it sent a tendril of relief to somewhere she shouldn't be affecting him.

He replied dryly, 'I find it far more fruitful to allow others to run their mouths off.'

Cruz's hand rested low on Trinity's hip and he squeezed it gently.

She tensed again, as someone approached them, and he said, 'Relax.'

Relax…

It had been the easiest thing and the hardest thing in the world to melt into his side, as if she was meant to be there. It was a cruel irony that she seemed to fit there so well, her softer body curving into his harder form as if especially made for that purpose.

Cruz hadn't let her out of his orbit all night. Even when she'd gone to the bathroom as soon as she'd walked back in to the function room his eyes had been the first thing she'd seen, compelling her back to his side like burning beacons.

It had been both disconcerting and exhilarating. In social situations before she'd invariably been left to fend for herself, Rio being done with her once their initial entrance had been made.

Trinity sighed now and finished tucking Matty and

Sancho into their beds—she'd come straight here upon their return from the function, all but running away from Cruz, who had been lazily undoing his bow tie and looking utterly sinful.

The boys were spreadeagled, covers askew, pyjamas twisted around their bodies. Overcome with tenderness for these two small orphaned boys, she smoothed back a lock of Sancho's hair and sat on the side of Matty's bed, careful not to disturb him. Resolve filled her anew not to bow under Cruz's increasingly down-and-dirty methods to disturb her—that incendiary kiss in the back of his Jeep, his words of silky promise in the vault...

After this evening things had changed. Cruz had obviously given himself licence to seduce her. And she knew if he touched her again her ability to resist would be shamefully weak.

She looked at the ring on her finger—heavy, golden. A brand. And an unwelcome reminder of the emotion she'd felt when Cruz had pushed it onto her finger.

She hated it that he believed whatever lies Rio had told him about her so easily. She wasn't remotely mercenary or avaricious. She had remonstrated with Rio countless times over the amounts of money he was spending on her. But he hadn't wanted to know. He'd told her that they had a certain standard to maintain, and that she needed to educate herself about fashion, art, et cetera.

The prospect of a future in which Cruz refused to listen to her and wore down her defences until he found out about her innocence in the most exposing way possible filled Trinity with horror.

She stood up and left the room decisively. She had

to at least try to make Cruz see that she wasn't who he thought she was. She would appeal to him rationally, without emotion and physical desire blurring the lines between them.

Above all, she had to make him see that the twins were and always had been her priority.

It was time to talk to her husband and make him listen to her.

'Come in.'

Trinity nearly lost her nerve at the sound of that deeply authoritative voice, but she refused to give in to it and pushed the door open. Cruz was sitting behind his desk, jacket off, shirtsleeves rolled up and the top of his shirt undone. There was a glass of something in his hand. He epitomised louche masculine sensuality.

He looked up from the papers he'd been perusing and immediately sat up straight and frowned when he saw it was her. 'What's wrong? Is it the boys?'

His instant concern for his nephews heartened something inside her. Some fledgling and delicate hope that perhaps she *could* appeal to him. In spite of all the evidence so far to the contrary.

She shook her head. 'No, they're fine. I just checked on them.'

'Well, is it something else?'

Trinity came further into the room, suddenly aware that Cruz was looking at her with a very narrow-eyed assessing gaze and that she was still in the dress. She cursed herself for not having changed into something less…dramatic.

Cruz stood up. 'Would you like a drink?'

She shook her head, thinking that the last thing she needed was to cloud her brain. 'No, thank you.'

He gestured to a seat on the other side of the table and as she sat down he said, 'I noticed you didn't drink much earlier—you don't like it?'

She shook her head. 'Not really. I never acquired the taste.' As soon as she said that, though, she regretted not asking for some brandy—she could do with the Dutch courage.

'So? To what do I owe the pleasure of this late-night visit?'

Trinity looked at Cruz suspiciously. Something about the tone of his voice scraped across her jumping nerves. Was he mocking her for having exposed herself so easily earlier, when he'd kissed her? His expression was unreadable, though, and she told herself she was imagining things.

She took a breath. 'I just...wanted to talk to you about this arrangement. About going forward, making a practical life together.'

Cruz took a sip of his drink and lowered the glass slowly again. 'Practical? I seem to recall events earlier which would turn the "practical" aspects of this relationship into far more pleasurable ones.'

Trinity immediately stood up, agitated. He *was* mocking her. 'I did not come here to talk about that.'

Totally unperturbed, and like a lazy jungle cat eyeing its prey, Cruz just sat back and said, 'Pity. What did you want to talk about, then?'

She ploughed on before this far more disturbing and *flirty* Cruz could make her lose her nerve.

'I know that I won't be able to continue with this sham marriage while you believe the worst of me and don't trust me. It'll start to affect the boys. They're too young to pick up on the tension now, but they're intelligent and inquisitive and it'll soon become apparent. That kiss earlier…it was unacceptable and disrespectful of my boundaries. This is meant to be a marriage in name only. You will either need to learn to deal with your antipathy for me or…' she took a breath '…we can move on from the past.'

Cruz went very still and then he put his glass down. He stood up and put his hands on the table, his eyes intense. A muscle ticked in his jaw. 'You think that kiss was a demonstration of my antipathy? That kiss was the inevitable result of our explosive mutual desire and proof that you want me as much as I want you.'

Trinity sucked in a breath, mortification rushing through her, and in a desperate bid to deny such a thing she blurted out, 'You gave me no time to respond. I was in shock.'

He arched a brow. 'So your response was down to shock?'

He stood up straight and started to move towards her. Trinity panicked, stepping away from the chair. She should never have come in here. This had been a terrible idea.

'Yes,' she said desperately. 'Of course it was shock. And you can't do that… Just…manhandle me when you feel like it.'

* * *

Cruz stopped in his tracks. Trinity's words hung starkly in the air between them. Anger raced up his spine. No, *fury*. He had to control himself, because he was very close to *manhandling* her into admitting that their kiss had been very mutual.

But she was looking at him with wide eyes, as if he was some kind of wild mountain lion. He felt wild, and he was *not* wild. He was civilised.

He bit out, 'For someone being *manhandled* your response was very passionate.'

He saw her throat move as she swallowed and the pulse beating frantically at the base of her neck. Right now he knew with every cell in his body that if he was to touch her they would combust. But something held him back—some sense of self-preservation. He couldn't trust that she wasn't just baiting him on purpose.

When they did come together it would be on his terms, and he wouldn't be feeling these raw, uncontrolled urges pushing him to the limits of his control.

'Look,' she said, 'I'm here because there are things I want to talk to you about. Important things.'

Cruz kept his gaze up, away from her tantalising curves in that amazing dress. He would put nothing past her. One thing was for sure, though. She wasn't going to see how his blood throbbed just under the surface of his skin. He wouldn't lose it twice in one evening.

He leant back against his desk and folded his arms, as if that might stop him from reaching for her. 'Well, no one is stopping you from talking now, Trinity. I'm all ears.'

She swallowed visibly, and Cruz saw that she was nervous. Once again she could be taking advantage of this situation, seducing him, but she wasn't. It irritated him.

'All that stuff Rio told you about me being a gold-digger...none of it is true. He lied to you.'

Cruz went cold. She didn't have to come here and seduce him—she was smarter than that. She just had to come and mess with his head.

He stood and closed the distance between them and her eyes widened. He stopped just short of touching her. 'How dare you use the fact that my brother is silenced for ever as an excuse to further your own cause?'

'I'm not,' she said fiercely, tipping up her chin. 'You need to listen to me. You need to know the real truth of my marriage to Rio...'

A dark emotion was snapping and boiling inside Cruz at the thought of *the truth* of her marriage to Rio. Sharing his bed. The thought that his brother had got to fully taste what she'd offered up to Cruz so enticingly before he'd stopped her.

Did he want to hear about that? *No.* He wished that thoughts of her with Rio would make him turn from her in disgust, but the fire inside him only burnt brighter as he battled a primal urge to stake a claim that reduced him to an animal state.

He caught her arms in his hands and hauled her into his body, so he could remind her of where she was and with whom. *Him.*

He ground out, 'When will you get it that I will never trust a word you say? From now on if you want to try to manipulate me I'd prefer if you used the currency you use best…your body. At least that way we'll both get pleasure out of the interaction and it'll be a lot more honest.'

'*Cruz…*'

That was all he heard before he stopped Trinity's poisonous words with his mouth.

The kiss was an intense battle of wills. Cruz's anger was red-hot, thundering in his veins. But then she managed to break free, pulling back, her hands on his chest, breathing heavily. If Cruz had been able to call on any rationality he would have been horrified. No woman had ever driven him to such base urges. To want to stamp his brand on her.

They stared at each other, tension crackling. But then, as he looked down into those blue eyes, swirling with something he couldn't fathom, the intense anger dissipated to be replaced by something far less angry and more carnal.

He curled an arm around her waist, drawing her right in, close to his body, until he saw her cheeks flush with the awareness of his erection against her soft flesh. It was torture and pleasure all at once. With his other hand he reached around to the back of her head and undid her hair, so that it fell around her shoulders in a golden cloud.

He could feel her resistance melting. Even though she said, 'Cruz…don't…'

'Don't what?' he asked silkily. 'Do this?' And he touched her jaw, tracing its delicate line, then cupped her cheek, angling her head up.

She spread her hands on his chest and he thought she was going to push him away, but she didn't. Something inside him exulted. This time when he bent his head and kissed her there was an infinitesimal moment of hesitation and then her mouth opened to him and his blood roared. There was just *this,* and this was all that mattered right now.

CHAPTER SIX

TRINITY WAS RUNNING down the long, dark corridors of the *Castillo*. The stern faces of all those ancestors were staring down at her, each one silently judging her. The footsteps behind her were getting closer…her heart was in her throat, thumping so hard she could hardly breathe…

There was an open door on the left. She ducked in and slammed the door shut, chest heaving, sweat prickling on her skin. And then she heard it. The sound of breathing in the room…

Terror kept her frozen in place, her back to the door as the breathing got closer and closer. And then out of the gloom appeared a face. A very familiar, starkly beautiful face. Amber eyes hard. Stern. Angry. *Hot.*

Hands reached for her and Trinity knew she should try to escape. But suddenly she wasn't scared any more. She was excited… And instead of running she threw herself into Cruz's arms…

The disturbing dream still lingered, and Trinity shivered in the bright morning sunlight of another beautiful day. She didn't have to be a psychologist to figure out where it had come from. When Cruz had kissed her after that angry exchange in his study at first she'd resisted, but then something had changed...and when he'd touched her again she'd responded against her best intentions.

All the man had to do was touch her, look at her, and she wanted him. And with each touch and kiss it was getting harder to resist... She'd finally had the sense to pull back and step away last night, but it had taken every last shred of control she had.

Shakily she'd said, 'I didn't come here for this.'

'So you say,' Cruz had answered, with infuriating insouciance, looking as if he hadn't just kissed her so hard she could barely see straight. It had been particularly galling, because just moments before he'd demonstrated that once again any attempt to defend herself or tell the truth would be met with stubborn resistance.

A sense of futility made her ache inside. How could she continue like this? With Cruz blatantly refusing to listen to her? Maybe this was how he'd drive her away... by stonewalling her at every turn...

Matty shouted, 'Mummy, look! Unkel Cooz!'

Sancho jumped up, clapping his hands. 'Play, play!'

Trinity tensed all over as a long shadow fell over where she was sitting cross-legged in the grass; the boys were playing nearby. With the utmost reluctance she looked up, shading her eyes against Cruz's sheer masculine beauty as much as against the sun. Matty and Sancho—not scared of him at all any more—had grabbed a leg each, looking up at their new hero.

He lifted both boys up into his arms with an easy

grace that annoyed her intensely. The fact that he was dressed down, in faded jeans and a dark polo shirt that strained across his chest muscles, was something she tried desperately not to notice. But it was hard when his biceps were bulging enticingly, reminding her of how it felt when they were wrapped around her.

She stood up, feeling at a disadvantage.

Cruz said, 'I came to tell you that I've been invited to another function this evening. We'll leave at seven.'

His autocratic tone sliced right into her, as did the scary prospect of countless more evenings like the previous one, when she'd reveal herself more and more. When he might *touch* her again.

She folded her arms and said coolly, 'I'm not going out this evening.'

The boys were squirming in Cruz's arms, growing bored already, and when he put them down they scampered off to the nearby sandpit. Trinity saw how his eyes followed them for a moment, making sure they were all right, and his concern made her feel warm inside until she clamped down on the sensation. This man evoked too much within her.

He looked back at her. 'I don't recall you being offered a choice.'

Irritation spiked at her reaction as much as to his tone. 'I'm not just some employee you can order around. It would be nice if you could pretend you're polite enough to *ask* if I'd like to come.'

'You're my wife,' Cruz offered tersely.

Something poignant gripped Trinity—if she was his wife for *real* then presumably they'd have a discussion about this sort of thing… She might agree to go because he'd tell her he'd be bored, or that he'd miss her if she didn't. The thought of that kind of domesticity made a treacherous shard of longing go through her before she could stop it.

Where had that illicit fantasy come from? One of the reasons she'd agreed to marry Rio—apart from her concern for the boys—was because after years of being an outsider in other people's homes as a foster child it had been easier to contemplate a marriage of convenience than to dare dream that she might one day have a real family of her own…

The prospect of Cruz ever seeing that deeply inside her made her go clammy all over.

Her arms tightened. 'I'm not going out this evening because I think the boys are coming down with something and I want to observe them for twenty-four hours to make sure they're okay. Sancho still isn't over his bug completely.'

Cruz glanced at the boys and back to her. 'They look fine to me.'

'They were off their food at breakfast, which isn't like them.'

'Mrs Jordan can watch them, and call us if she's worried.'

Exasperated, Trinity unfolded her arms and put her hands on her hips. 'You don't get it, do you? I'm worried about them, and even if it's only a niggle then I will put them first. *I* am the one they need if they're not feeling well.'

Scathingly, Cruz said, 'So you're not above using my nephews as an excuse?'

Hurt that he should think her capable of such a thing she said, 'Their welfare comes first, so I don't really care what you think.'

Cruz's jaw clenched, and then he just said, 'Seven p.m., Trinity. Be ready.' And then he turned and walked away.

To her shame she couldn't stop her gaze from dropping down his broad back to where his worn jeans showed off his powerful buttocks. Disgusted with herself, she whirled around and went over to the boys who, she had to admit, would look fine to most observers but not to her, who knew all their little habits and foibles.

Something wasn't quite right and she wasn't going to let Cruz bully her.

Later that evening Cruz's blood was boiling. No one had ever stood him up. Certainly not a woman. But Trinity had. Julia, looking terrified—*was he really that scary?*—had come with a note when he'd been waiting for Trinity in the hall.

Sorry, Cruz, but I'm just not certain the boys aren't coming down with something. I'm not coming. T.

The note was crumpled in his palm now, as he strode along the dark corridors to the wing Trinity and the boys occupied. Something about the oppressiveness of the *castillo* scraped along his nerves, when it never really had before. It was as if having Trinity and the boys here was throwing everything into sharp relief...

When he was near the boys' bedroom he could hear fractious cries and Trinity's tones, soothing. He stopped in the doorway to see her changing a clearly cranky Sancho into his pyjamas.

Mateo was running around in his nappy. As soon as he saw Cruz he sped over. 'Come play, Unkel Cooz!'

Cruz's chest felt tight. He bent down. 'Not now, *chiquito*. Tomorrow.'

He put his hand to Mateo's head and it felt warm. He looked up to see Trinity standing in front of him, still wearing the jeans and shirt she'd had on earlier. She really wasn't coming.

He straightened up and a determined expression came over her face. 'I meant it, Cruz, I'm worried about the boys. They've been off their food all day and they're both running slight temperatures. They also didn't nap today, so they're overtired now. It's probably nothing serious, but I'm not leaving them. I've given Mrs Jordan the evening off so she can take over in the morning.'

Cruz was slightly stunned yet again to think that she wasn't even their mother. Right now, with the boys in the room behind her, he had the distinct impression of a mother bear guarding her cubs from danger. He couldn't figure out what she could possibly be gaining from this if she *was* playing some game.

To his surprise something dark gripped his gut, and it took him a moment to acknowledge uncomfortably that it was jealousy—and something else…something more ambiguous that went deeper.

Jealousy of his nephews, who were being afforded such care and protection—the kind of protection he'd vowed to give them but which now he realised he was too woefully inexperienced to give.

The something deeper was a sharp sense of poignancy that his own mother had never cared for him like this. *Dios*, even his nanny hadn't shown this much concern.

Feeling very uncharacteristically at a momentary loss, he recognised that for the first time in his life he would have to back down.

'Call me if they get worse, or if you need anything. Maria the housekeeper has the number of my doctor.'

Trinity nodded, shocked that Cruz was conceding. She'd half expected him to insist on dressing her himself and dragging her out of the *castillo*.

He stepped away and said, 'I'll check on you when I get back.'

The thought of him coming in later, with his bow tie undone and looking far too sexy, made her say quickly, 'There's no—'

He looked at her warningly. 'I'll check on you.'

'Okay.'

For a moment something seemed to shimmer between them—something fragile. Then Cruz turned and left and she breathed out an unsteady breath. She turned around to focus on the boys and told herself that she'd just been imagining that moment of softening between them. Wishful thinking.

* * *

When Cruz returned later that night he went straight to the boys' room, where a low light leaked from under the door. He ruminated that he hadn't enjoyed one minute of the function—not that he usually did, because he considered these events work—and he realised now with some irritation that he'd missed having Trinity at his side. Seeing her reaction to everything. Having her close enough to touch.

He opened the door softly and stepped in. His eyes immediately tracked to the two small figures in their beds and he went over, finding himself pulling their covers back over their bodies from where they'd kicked them off. Something turned over in his chest at seeing them sprawled across their beds, dark lashes long on plump cheeks, hair tousled. They looked so innocent, defenceless. Once again he was overcome with a sense of protectiveness.

Then he looked up and saw another figure, curled in the armchair near the beds. Trinity. She was asleep, her head resting on her shoulder. A book lay open on her thigh and he looked at it: *The A-Z of Toddlers.*

For a moment he felt blindsided at this evidence of her dedication. That sense of poignancy he'd felt earlier gripped him again, and it was deeply disturbing and exposing.

Something else prickled under his skin now. If she was playing a game then it was a very elaborate one.

He recalled her coming into his office last night and her words: *'All that stuff that Rio told you about me being a gold-digger...none of it is true.'*

Cruz's rational mind reminded him that there was evidence of her treachery. Her name on receipts. Demands she'd made. Rio's humiliation. Maybe this was her game—she was trying to convince him she was something she wasn't and would wriggle under his skin like she had with Rio until he too felt compelled to give her everything...

'Cruz?'

She was awake now, blinking up at him. She sat up, looking deliciously dishevelled, compounding the myriad conflicting emotions she evoked.

His voice was gruff when he spoke. 'Go to bed, Trinity. I'll sit up with them.'

She looked flustered. 'No!' She lowered her voice. 'You don't have to do that. It's fine... I think they're okay now, anyway. Their temperatures were normal last time I checked.'

'Go to bed. I'll let you know if anything happens.'

She looked up at him helplessly and he offered ruefully, 'I'm going to have to get used to doing this kind of thing. I'm their uncle, and I don't intend to treat them like guests in my home.'

For the first time since Rio had died it struck Cruz forcibly that he hadn't really thought about how taking responsibility for his nephews would affect him until now. And this was what it meant, he realised with a kind of belated wonder. Being concerned. Sitting up all night to watch over them if need be.

Trinity eyes were wide, and even in this light Cruz could see the smudges of fatigue under them. From this angle he could also see down her shirt to the bountiful swells of her breasts. His body reacted.

He gritted out, 'Just go.'

She stood up jerkily, as if her muscles were protesting. 'You'll let me know if they wake?' She sounded uncertain.

Cruz nodded and took her place on the chair, stretching out his long legs and picking up the book. He gestured with it for her to go.

Feeling more than a little discombobulated at having woken to find Cruz standing over her, looking exactly like the sexy fantasy she'd envisaged earlier, Trinity eventually moved towards her own room, glancing back to see Cruz tipping his head back and closing his eyes, hands linked loosely across his flat abdomen.

Her footsteps faltered, though, as she was momentarily transfixed by the fact that he had insisted on staying. Emotion expanded in her chest at the domestic scene—dangerous emotion—as she thought how incongruous he looked here, yet how *right*.

His willingness to forge a bond with his nephews made that emotion turn awfully poignant... She had a vision of going over to him, smoothing his hair back... of him looking up at her and reaching for her, smiling sexily as he pulled her down onto his lap...

Shock at the vividness of this fantasy made her breathless. And at how much she yearned for it. When it was only his nephews he cared about. Not her.

Without opening his eyes, Cruz said softly, 'Go to bed, Trinity.'

And she fled before he might see any vestige of that momentary fantasy on her face.

When Trinity woke the following morning it was later than she'd ever slept since she'd started looking after the twins. And they were her first thought.

She shot out of bed and went into their room, to see that their beds were empty and their pyjamas were neatly folded on their pillows.

She washed quickly and got dressed in jeans and a T-shirt, pulling her hair back into a low ponytail as she went down to the dining room, where she found Mrs Jordan and the twins.

'*Mummy!*' they both screeched in unison when they saw her, and her heart swelled.

She went over and kissed them both. She looked at the older woman. 'You should have woken me.'

Mrs Jordan waved a hand. 'Cruz wouldn't hear of it. He insisted that you sleep in and I agreed. You've been looking tired lately.'

Trinity's heart skipped. She still felt raw after that moment of insanity when she'd wished for a domestic idyll that would never exist.

'He was still there this morning?'

She sat down and helped herself to coffee, noting with relief that the boys seemed to be making up for their lack of appetite the previous day, with their mouths full of mushy cereal.

Mrs Jordan nodded and a look of unmistakable awe came over her face. 'He was changing them when I went in this morning, and apart from putting Sancho's nappy on back to front he didn't do a bad job at all...'

Trinity choked on her coffee, spraying some out of her mouth inelegantly, and the boys went into paroxysms of giggles.

'Funny, Mummy...do it again!'

She distracted them for a minute, playing aeroplanes with their spoons as she fed them, and avoided Mrs Jordan's far too shrewd gaze. She almost felt angry with Cruz for blurring the boundaries like this and inducing disturbing fantasies. And then she felt awful—she should be happy that he was intent on connecting with his nephews in a real and meaningful way.

After the boys had finished their breakfast, and Mrs Jordan had taken them outside to play, Trinity sipped her coffee, recalling again how dangerously intimate it had felt to share that space with Cruz last night. And how seductive.

Just then a sound made her look up and her heart stopped at the sight of the object of her thoughts standing in the doorway, dressed in a three-piece suit, looking so gorgeous it hurt.

He came in and Trinity still felt a little raw, unprepared to see him. It made her voice stiff. 'Thank you for watching the boys last night.'

Cruz poured himself a cup of coffee and took a seat opposite her. He shook his head minutely. 'Like I said, I'm going to be in their lives in a meaningful way.'

Feeling absurdly shy, she said, 'Mrs Jordan told me you changed them.'

Cruz's eyes gleamed with wry humour and it took

Trinity's breath away. 'I won't ever again underestimate the ability of a two-and-a-half-year-old to create a toxic smell to rival the effluent of a chemical plant. Or the skill it takes to change one of those things.'

Cruz took a sip of his coffee and put down the cup. 'I've arranged for some potential nannies to come later today, for you and Mrs Jordan to interview.'

'Do you really think that's necessary?'

'Yes.' The wry gleam was gone from his eyes now. 'I've been invited to an event at the newly refurbished opera house in Madrid this Friday night, and I have meetings to attend in the afternoon. Barring any unforeseen events, I am asking you to attend the function with me in Madrid. We'll be gone until Saturday. It'll be a good opportunity for the new nanny to start and get used to the boys under Mrs Jordan's supervision.'

Two things were bombarding Trinity at once. Namely he fact that he was *asking* her, even if it was slightly mocking, and that she'd be away for a whole night with Cruz.

'But I've never left the boys for that long before.'

His tone was dry. 'I think they'll survive less than twenty-four hours without you, and with two nannies in attendance. I spoke with Mrs Jordan about it earlier—she's fine.'

Of course she was, thought Trinity churlishly. Mrs Jordan was his number one fan.

'Tell me, Trinity,' Cruz asked silkily, 'is the reason you're reluctant because you fear maintaining the lie that you don't want me? Are you afraid that you won't be able to control your urges if we're alone? I don't think it's out of concern for the boys at all—I think it's much more personal.'

She felt shamed. He was right. She *was* scared—scared of her reactions around this man. Scared of what might happen if he touched her again. Scared to have him see underneath to where her real vulnerabilities lay. Scared of what he would do if he were faced with the ultimate truth of just how deeply Rio had loathed him. Her guts twisted at the thought in a way that told her she was far more invested in this man than she liked to admit.

But as Cruz looked at her, waiting for her response, she knew she couldn't keep running. She could resist him. She had to.

Coolly she ignored what he'd said and replied, 'Friday should be fine. What time do we leave?'

A few days later Trinity risked looking at Cruz from where she sat in the back of the chauffeur-driven limousine that had picked them up at Madrid airport, but he was engrossed in his palm tablet on the other side of the car, seemingly oblivious to her. She'd just had a conversation on her mobile phone with Mrs Jordan, to check on her and the boys and the new nanny, who were all fine.

As if reading her mind, Cruz put down his tablet and looked at her, that golden amber gaze sweeping down her body and taking in the very elegant and classic sheath dress and matching jacket she'd put on that day in a bid to look presentable.

His gaze narrowed on her assessingly, and she had to fight not to squirm self-consciously. 'What is it?'

She was half raising a hand to check her hair when Cruz answered simply, 'You're a good mother to them.'

If there'd been a grudging tone in his voice Trinity would have hated him, but there hadn't. He'd sounded... reluctantly impressed. She desperately tried to ignore the rush of warmth inside her that signified how much she wanted his approval.

'I love them, Cruz, even though they're not mine.' Impulsively she asked, 'Why is that so hard for you to believe? Is it because of your upbringing?'

He smiled, but it wasn't a nice smile. 'You could say that. Rio wasn't the only one neglected in the *castillo*. Once she'd had me, my mother considered her maternal duty taken care of. She didn't love me, and she didn't love my father either. Their marriage was a purely strategic one, bringing two powerful families together as was the tradition in my family for centuries.'

Cruz's eyeline shifted over Trinity's shoulder just as the car came to a smooth halt on a wide tree-lined street.

'We're here,' he said, leaving Trinity's brain buzzing with what he'd just shared.

She looked out of the window on her side, saw a scrum of men with cameras waiting for them and instantly felt nervous. She'd always hated the way Rio had wanted to court as much media attention as possible.

Cruz said tersely, 'Wait in the car. I'll come round to get you.'

Trinity would have been quite happy if the car had turned around and taken them straight back to the airport.

When Cruz appeared outside the car the scrum had

become a sea of flashing lights and shouting. Her door was opened and his hand reached in for her. She took it like a lifeline. He hustled her into the foyer of the gleaming building and within seconds they were in the elevator and ascending with a soft *whoosh*.

It was the hushed silence after the cacophony of sound that registered first, and then Trinity became burningly aware that she was pressed from thigh to breast into Cruz's body. His free arm was around her shoulder and her other hand was still in his, held over his taut belly.

She couldn't be any closer to him if she climbed into his very skin.

She scrambled apart from him, dislodging his arm and taking her hand from his. She couldn't look at him. For a split second before she'd come to her senses she'd loved the sensation of his strength surrounding her, and for someone who'd long ago learnt to depend on herself it was scary how easy it had felt just to…give in.

Thankfully the lift doors opened at that moment, and the sight that greeted Trinity took her breath away. She stepped out into a huge open space dominated on all sides by massive glass windows which showcased the breathtaking view of one of Europe's most beautiful and stately cities.

She walked over to one of the windows and could see a huge cathedral soaring into the blue sky.

'That's the Almudena Cathedral, infamous for taking five hundred years to complete.'

Cruz's voice was far too close, but Trinity fought the urge to move away and instead turned around to take in the penthouse apartment. It was unmistakably a bachelor pad, every inch of every surface gleaming and pristine. But it was also cultured—low tables held massive coffee table books on photography and art. Bookshelves lined one entire interior wall. Huge modern art canvases sat in the centre of the few walls not showcasing the view.

'Let me show you around.'

Trinity followed Cruz as he guided her through a stunning modern kitchen that led into a formal dining room, and then to where a series of rooms off a long corridor revealed themselves to be sumptuous en-suite bedrooms and an office.

When they were back in the main open-plan living and dining area, she felt a little dazed. 'Your apartment is stunning.'

'But not exactly toddler-proof.'

She looked at Cruz, surprised that he'd articulated the very thing she'd just been thinking in her head: it was beautiful apartment but a potential death trap for small energetic boys.

He glanced at her and she quickly closed her open mouth, looking around again. 'No. Not exactly.'

'I will ensure this place is made child-friendly for when the boys come to visit. I intend on my nephews becoming familiar with their capital city. This is where the seat of the main De Carrillo bank has been since the Middle Ages. This is where their legacy resides, as much as it does in Seville.'

Their capital city. It had been said with such effortless arrogance. But the truth was that Cruz was right—

he was undoubtedly a titan of this city. Probably owned a huge swathe of it. And the twins would one day inherit all this.

It was mind-boggling to contemplate, and for the first time Trinity felt a sense of fear for the boys and this huge responsibility they'd have one day.

She rounded on Cruz. 'What happens if Matty and Sancho don't want any of this?'

His gaze narrowed on her and something flashed across his face before she could decipher it. Something almost pained.

'Believe me, I will do what's best for my nephews. They will not be forced to take on anything they can't handle or don't want. I won't let that happen to them.'

Trinity's anger deflated. She'd heard the emotion in Cruz's voice. Almost as if he was referring to someone who *had* taken on something they couldn't handle. Was he thinking of Rio and the irresponsible and lavish way he'd lived?

Cruz looked at his watch. 'I have to go to meetings now, but I'll be back to get ready for the function this evening. We'll leave at six p.m.'

Before he left he took something out of his inner pocket. He handed her a black credit card.

She took it warily. 'What is this? A test?'

His face was unreadable, but she wasn't fooled. She knew he'd be assessing her every reaction.

'You'll need access to funds. Do what you want for the afternoon—a driver will be at your disposal downstairs.'

He left then, and for a long minute Trinity found

herself wondering if he *had* been talking about Rio not being able to handle things…

Then, disgusted with herself for obsessing like this, she threw the credit card down on a nearby table and paced over to a window. When she looked down to the street far below she could see Cruz disappearing into the back of another sleek Jeep.

It pulled into the flow of traffic and she shivered slightly, as if he could somehow still see her. He was so all-encompassing that it was hard to believe he wasn't omnipresent.

She sighed and leaned forward, placing her hot forehead against the cool glass. It felt as if every time they took a step forward they then took three backwards. Clearly the credit card was some kind of a test, and he expected her to revert to type when given half a chance.

Cruz was standing with his back to the recently emptied boardroom on the top floor of the De Carrillo bank, loosening his tie and opening a top button on his shirt. Madrid was laid out before him, with the lowering sun leaving long shadows over the streets below where people were leaving their offices.

He hated himself for it, but as soon as the last person had left the room he'd pulled out his phone to make a call, too impatient to wait.

'*Where* did she go?' he asked incredulously, his hand dropping from his shirt.

His driver answered. 'She went to the Plaza Mayor, where she had a coffee, and then she spent the afternoon in the Museo Del Prado. She's just returned to the apartment.'

'And she walked,' Cruz repeated flatly, not liking the way the thought of her sightseeing around Madrid on her own made him feel a twinge of conscience. As if he'd neglected her. 'No shopping?'

'No, sir, apart from two cuddly toys in the museum shop.'

Cruz terminated the call. So Trinity hadn't spent the day shopping in Calle de Serrano, home to the most lavish boutiques. He had to admit that the credit card *had* been a test, and a pretty crude one at that. But once again either she was playing a longer game than he'd given her credit for...or he had to acknowledge that she had changed. Fundamentally. And in Cruz's experience of human nature that just wasn't possible.

Cruz didn't deal in unknowns. It was one of the driving motives behind his marrying Trinity—to make sure she was kept very much within his sphere of *knowns*.

Suddenly he wasn't so sure of anything any more.

But *how* could he trust her over his own brother?

He could still see the humiliation on Rio's face when he'd had to explain to Cruz that that his own wife had tipped him over the edge. Cruz knew that Rio's lavish lifestyle and his first wife had undoubtedly started the process of his ultimate destruction, but Trinity had finished it off. And, worse, used his nephews to gain privileged access.

But then he thought of her, standing between him and his nephews the other night, so adamant that they came first. And he thought of how he'd found her, curled up asleep in the chair... He shook his head angrily and turned away from the window. *Merda*, she was messing with his head.

Cruz blocked out the niggles of his conscience. He would be the biggest fool on earth if he was to believe in this newly minted Trinity De Carrillo without further evidence. She was playing a game—she had to be. It was that simple. And he had no choice but to go along with it for now...

Because eventually she would reveal her true self, and when she did Cruz would be waiting.

CHAPTER SEVEN

A COUPLE OF hours later Cruz's mind was no less tangled. The woman beside him was drawing every single eye in the extravagantly designed and decorated open-air court-yard of the new opera house. When he'd arrived back at the apartment she'd been in her room getting ready, so he'd been showered and changed before he'd seen her, waiting for him in the living area of the apartment.

The shock of that first glimpse of her still ran through his system, constricting his breath and pumping blood to tender places. She wore a strapless black dress that was moulded to every curve. Over one shoulder was a sliver of chiffon tied in a bow.

She wore no jewellery apart from the engagement ring and her wedding band. Her nails were unpainted. Minimal make-up. And yet people couldn't stop look-ing at her. *He* couldn't stop looking at her.

Very uncharacteristically, Cruz wanted to snarl at them all to look at their own partners. But he couldn't, because he could see what they saw—a glowing dia-mond amidst the dross. She appealed to this jaded crowd because she had an unfashionable air of wonder about her as she looked around, which only reinforced the shadow of doubt in his mind...

Just then her arm tightened in his and he looked down to see a flush on her cheeks. She was biting her lip. Irritated at the effect she had on him, he said more curtly than he'd intended, 'What is it?'

She sounded hesitant. 'I shouldn't have put my hair up like this. I look ridiculous.'

Cruz looked at her hair, which was in a sleek high ponytail. He didn't consider himself an expert on women's hairstyles, but he could see that the other women had more complicated things going on. Another reason why Trinity stood out so effortlessly. She looked unfussy—simple and yet sexy as sin all at once.

'Someone left a fashion magazine on the table in the café earlier and I saw pictures of models with their hair up like this. I thought it was a thing...'

The shadow of doubt loomed larger. He thought of how she'd shrunk back from the paparazzi earlier. She certainly hadn't been flaunting herself, looking for attention. Anything but. She'd clung to him as if terrified.

He took her arm above the elbow and she looked up at him. He could see the uncertainty and embarrassment in her eyes. It was getting harder and harder to see her as the cold-hearted mercenary gold-digger who had willingly fleeced his brother.

His voice was gruff. 'Your hair is absolutely fine. They're looking because you're the most beautiful woman here.'

Trinity was disorientated by Cruz's compliment. He'd barely said two words to her since he'd got back to the apartment and they'd left to go out again, and he'd just looked at her suspiciously when he'd asked her what she'd done for the afternoon.

Cruz was staring at her now, in a way that made her heart thump unevenly. But then a low, melodic gong sounded, breaking the weird moment.

He looked away from her and up. 'It's time for the banquet.'

Breathing a sigh of relief at being released from that intensity, and not really sure what it meant, she followed Cruz into a huge ballroom that had the longest dining table she'd ever seen in her life. Opulent flowers overflowed from vases and twined all along the table in artful disarray. A thousand candles flickered, and low lights glinted off the solid gold cutlery. She sighed in pure wonder at the scene—it was like a movie set.

And then she spotted Lexie Anderson, the famous actress, and her gorgeous husband, Cesar Da Silva, and felt as if she'd really been transported into a movie. The stunning petite blonde and her tall husband were completely engrossed in each other, and it made something poignant ache inside her.

'Trinity?'

She blushed, hating it that Cruz might have caught her staring at the other couple, and sat down in the chair he was holding out for her.

When she was seated, Trinity saw Cruz walking away and she whispered after him. 'Wait, where are you going?'

He stopped. 'I've been seated opposite you—beside the president of the Spanish Central Bank.'

'Oh, okay.' Trinity feigned nonchalance, even though

she was taking in the vast size of the table and realising he might as well be sitting in another room.

Of course he couldn't resist the opportunity to mock her. He came back and bent down, saying close to her ear, 'Don't tell me you'll miss me, *querida*?'

'Don't be ridiculous,' she snapped, angry that she'd shown how gauche she was. She turned away, but hated it that her stomach lurched at the thought of being left alone to fend for herself in an environment where she'd never felt comfortable.

She couldn't take her eyes off him as he walked around to the other side of the table, being stopped and adored by several people on his way. One of them was Cesar Da Silva, who got up to shake Cruz's hand, and the two tall and ridiculously handsome men drew lots of lingering looks. He even bent down to kiss Lexie Anderson on both cheeks, and it caused a funny twisting sensation in Trinity's stomach, seeing him bestow affection so easily on anyone but her.

No, what he'd bestow on *her* was much darker and full of anger and mistrust.

Determined not to be intimidated, Trinity tried talking to the person on her left, but he couldn't speak English and she had no Spanish so that went nowhere. She had more luck with an attractive older gentleman on her right, who turned out to be a diplomat and did speak English, and who put her at ease as only a diplomat could.

Finally she felt herself relax for the first time in weeks, chuckling at her companion's funny stories of various diplomatic disasters. With Cruz on the other side of the very large and lavishly decorated table she relished a reprieve from the constant tension she felt around him, even if she fancied she could feel his golden gaze boring into her through the elaborate foliage. She resisted the urge to look in his direction. She'd already given far too much away.

After the coffee cups had been cleared away her dinner partner's attention was taken by the person on his other side. Trinity risked a look across the table and saw that Cruz's seat was empty. And then she spotted him—because it would be impossible to miss him. He was walking towards her with that lean animal grace, eyes narrowed on her, this time oblivious to people's attempts to get his attention.

The tension was back instantly. Making her feel tingly and alive as much as wary. When he reached her he didn't even have to touch her for a shiver to run through her body.

'Cold?' The tone of his voice was innocuous, but the expression on his face was hard.

Trinity shook her head, feeling a sense of vertigo as she looked up, even though she was sitting down. 'No, not cold.'

'Enjoying yourself?'

Now his words had definite bite in them, and she saw his eyeline shift over her head. 'Nice to see you, Lopez,' he drawled. 'Thank you for keeping my wife amused.'

The man's smoothly cultured voice floated over Trinity's shoulder.

'The pleasure was all mine, De Carrillo. Trinity is a charming, beautiful woman. A breath of fresh air.'

Trinity watched, fascinated, as Cruz's face darkened and a muscle ticked in his jaw. 'Then I'm sorry that I must deprive you of her presence. I believe the dancing has started.'

She barely had time to get a word out to say goodbye to the other man before Cruz was all but hauling her out of her chair and onto the dance floor, where a band was playing slow, sexy jazz songs. His arm was like steel around her back and her other hand was clasped in his, high against his chest.

He moved around the floor with such effortless expertise that Trinity didn't have time to worry about her two left feet. To her horror, though, she felt absurdly vulnerable, reminded of how lonely she'd felt during the day even while she'd appreciated the beautiful majesty of Madrid.

She'd missed Matty and Sancho and she'd felt a very rare surge of self-pity, wondering if this would be her life now—forever on the periphery of Cruz's antipathy.

It was a long time since she'd indulged in such a weak emotion and it made her voice sharp. 'What do you think you're doing?'

Cruz's mouth was a thin line. 'I'm not sure. Maybe you want to tell me? Sebastian Lopez is a millionaire and renowned for his penchant for beautiful young women—maybe you knew that and saw an opportunity to seek a more benevolent benefactor?'

Trinity fought to control her breathing and her temper, and hated it that she was so aware of every inch of her body, which seemed to be welded against his.

'Don't be ridiculous,' she hissed. 'He's old enough to

be my father and there was nothing remotely flirtatious about our conversation.' She tilted her head back as much as she could so she could look Cruz dead in the eye. 'But do you know what? It was nice to talk to someone who doesn't think I'm one step above a common thief.'

Terrified that Cruz would see emotion she shouldn't be feeling, she managed to pull herself out of his embrace and stalked off the dance floor, apologising as she bumped into another couple. She walked blindly, half expecting a heavy hand on her shoulder at any moment, but of course Cruz wouldn't appreciate that public display of discord.

She made it out to the marbled foyer area, where a few people milled around, and walked out to the entrance. She sucked in a breath to try and steady her heart. Night was enfolding Madrid in a glorious velvet glow but it couldn't soothe her ragged nerves.

It wasn't long before she felt Cruz's presence. The little hairs all over her body seemed to stand up and quiver in his direction. She refused to feel foolish for storming off. He'd insulted her.

He came to stand beside her, but said nothing as his car arrived at the front of the building with a soft sleek purr. Trinity cursed the fact that she hadn't been quicker to call a cab. Cruz held open the back door and she avoided his eye as she got in, not wanting to see the undoubtedly volcanic expression on his face.

As the driver pulled into the light evening traffic Trinity said frigidly, 'You don't have to leave. You should stay. Your brother soon learned that it made more sense to let me leave early.'

* * *

Cruz was in the act of yanking at his bow tie and opening his top button, wanting to feel less constricted. But now his hand stilled and the red haze of anger that had descended over his vision during the course of the evening as he'd watched Trinity talking and laughing with that man finally started to dissipate.

'What did you just say?' he asked.

Trinity was staring straight ahead, her profile perfect. But she was tense—her full lips pursed, jaw rigid.

It slammed into him then—the truth he'd been trying to deny. He was insanely jealous. He'd been jealous since the day she'd walked out of his house and got into Rio's car to go and work for him.

At that moment she looked at him, and he could feel himself tipping over the edge of an abyss. Those huge blue eyes were full of such...*injury.*

Her voice was tight. 'I said that your brother soon learned that I don't fit into those events well. I'm not from that world, and I don't know what to do or say.'

She clamped her mouth shut then, as if she'd said enough already.

Cruz reeled. His impression had been that Rio had taken her everywhere and that she'd loved it and milked it, but something in the tightness of her voice told him she wasn't lying, and that revelation only added to the doubts clamouring for attention in his head.

He tried and failed to block out the fact that when she'd pulled free of his arms on the dance floor and stalked away he'd thought he'd seen the glitter of tears in her eyes.

She turned her head away again and he saw the column of her throat working. His gaze took in an expanse of pale skin, slim shoulders, delicate clavicle, the enticing curve of her breasts under the material of the dress, and heat engulfed him along with something much more nebulous: an urge to comfort, which was as bewildering as it was impossible to resist.

He reached across and touched Trinity's chin, turning her face towards him again. 'I'm sorry,' he said. 'You didn't deserve that. The truth is that I didn't like seeing you with that man.'

The shock on her face might have insulted Cruz if he hadn't been so distracted by those huge eyes.

Her mouth opened and the tense line of her jaw relaxed slightly. 'I...okay. Apology accepted.'

That simple. Another woman would have made the most of Cruz's uncharacteristic apology.

His thumb moved back and forth across Trinity's jaw, the softness of her delicate skin an enticement to touch and keep touching.

'What are you doing?'

He dragged his gaze up over high cheekbones, perfect bone structure. 'I can't *not* touch you.' The admission seemed to fall out of him before he could stop it.

Trinity put a hand up over his. The car came to a smooth stop. Cruz knew that he had to keep touching her or die. And he assured himself that it had nothing to do with the emotion that had clouded his judgement and his vision as he'd watched her at ease with another man, and everything to do with pure, unadulterated lust.

* * *

Trinity was locked into Cruz's eyes and the intensity of his gaze. One minute she'd been hurt and angry, and then he'd apologised…once again demonstrating a level of humility that she just wouldn't have expected from him. And now… Now she was burning up under his explicit look that told her that whatever they'd just been talking about was forgotten, that things had taken a far more carnal turn.

She felt a breeze touch her back. She blinked and looked around to see the driver standing at the door, waiting for her to get out. They'd arrived back at the apartment building and she hadn't even noticed.

She scrambled out inelegantly, feeling seriously jittery. It was as if some kind of silent communication had passed between them, and she wasn't sure what she'd agreed to.

The journey up to the apartment passed in a blur. The lift doors opened and they stepped into the hushed interior of Cruz's apartment. He threw off his jacket and Trinity's mouth dried as she watched the play of muscles under the thin silk of his shirt.

He glanced back at her over his shoulder. 'I know you don't really drink, but would you like something?'

Trinity was about to refuse, but something in the air made her feel uncharacteristically reckless. She moved forward. 'Okay.'

'What would you like?'

She stopped, her mind a blank. Embarrassment engulfed her—she was no sophisticate.

Cruz looked at her. 'I've got all the spirits. What do you like?'

Trinity shrugged one shoulder. 'I'm not sure…'

He looked at her for a long moment and then turned back to the drinks table, doing something she couldn't see. Then he turned and came towards her with two glasses. One was large and bulbous, filled with what looked like brandy or whisky. The other glass was smaller, with an orange liquid over a couple of ice cubes.

He handed her the second glass. 'Try this—see what you think.'

After a moment's hesitation she reached for the glass and bent her head, taking a sniff. Cruz was waiting for her reaction, so she took a sip of the cool liquid and it slid down her throat, leaving a sweet aftertaste. She wrinkled her nose, because she'd been expecting something tart or strong.

She looked at him. 'It's sweet. I like it—what is it?'

A small smile played around the corner of Cruz's mouth. 'It's Pacharán—a Spanish liqueur from Navarre. Very distinctive. It tastes sweet, but it packs quite the alcoholic punch. Hence the small amount.'

Before he could suck her under and scramble her brain cells with just a look Trinity went and sat down at the end of one couch, bemused by this very fragile cessation in hostilities. Cruz sat too, choosing the end of a couch at right angles to hers. He effortlessly filled the space with his muscled bulk, long legs stretched out, almost touching hers.

Trinity felt unaccountably nervous, and a little bewildered. She was so used to Cruz coming at her with his judgement and mistrust that she wasn't sure how to navigate these waters. He sat forward, hands loose around his glass, drawing her attention to long fingers.

'Tell me something about yourself—like your name. How did you get it?'

She tensed all over. Every instinct within her was screaming to resist this far more dangerous Cruz. 'What are you doing? You're not interested in who I am…you don't have to ask me these things.'

'You were the one,' he pointed out reasonably, 'who said we need to learn to get along.'

And look how that had ended up—with him kissing her and demonstrating just how weak she was. What could she say, though? He was right.

Hating it that she was exposing her agitation, but needing space from his focus on her, Trinity stood up and walked over to one of the windows, holding her glass to her chest like some kind of ineffectual armour.

Looking out at the view, she said as lightly as she could, 'I was called Trinity after the church where I was found abandoned on the steps. The Holy Trinity Church in Islington.'

She heard movement and sensed Cruz coming to stand near her. She could feel his eyes on her.

'Go on,' he said.

Night had descended over Madrid, and the skyline was lit up spectacularly against the inky blackness.

'They think I was just a few hours old, but they can't be sure, and it wasn't long after midnight, so they nominated that date as my birthday. I was wrapped in a blanket. The priest found me.'

'What happened then?'

Trinity swallowed. 'The authorities waited as long as they could for my biological parent, or parents, to come and claim me. By the time I was a toddler I was in foster care, and there was still no sign of anyone claiming me, so they put me forward for adoption.'

'But your file said you grew up in foster homes.'

Trinity was still astounded that he'd looked into her past. She glanced at him, but looked away again quickly. 'I did grow up in foster homes. But I was adopted for about a year, until the couple's marriage broke up and they decided they didn't want to keep me if they weren't staying together.'

She shouldn't be feeling emotion—not after all these years. But it was still there…the raw, jagged edges of hurt at the knowledge that she'd been abandoned by her own mother and then hadn't even managed to persuade her adoptive parents to keep her.

'Apparently,' she said, as dispassionately as she could, 'I was traumatised, so they decided it might be best not to put me through that experience again. That's how I ended up in the foster home system.'

'Were you moved around much?'

'Not at the start. But when I came into my teens, yes. I was in about six different foster homes before I turned eighteen.'

'Your affinity with Mateo and Sancho… You have no qualification in childcare, and yet you obviously know what to do with small children.'

Trinity felt as if Cruz was peeling back layers of skin. It was almost physically painful to talk about this. 'For some reason the small children in the foster homes used to latch on to me… I felt protective, and I liked mothering them, watching over them…'

But then the inevitable always happened—the babies and toddlers would be taken away to another home, or put up for adoption, and Trinity would be bereft. And yet each time it had happened she'd been helpless to resist the instinct to nurture. Of course, she surmised grimly now, a psychologist would undoubtedly tell her she'd been desperately trying to fulfil the need in herself to be loved and cared for.

And the twins were evidence that she hadn't learned to fill that gap on her own yet.

'Did you ever go looking for your parents?'

Trinity fought to control her emotions. 'Where would I start? It wasn't as if they'd logged their names anywhere. I could have investigated pregnant women on record in the local area, who had never returned to give birth, but to be honest I decided a long time ago that perhaps it was best to just leave it alone.'

The truth was that she didn't think she could survive the inevitable rejection of her parents if she ever found either one of them.

She felt her glass being lifted out of her hands, and looked to see Cruz putting it down on a side table beside his. He turned back and took her hand in his, turning it over, looking at it as if it held some answer he was looking for. The air between them was charged.

'What are you doing?' Trinity asked shakily.

Their eyes met and she desperately wanted to move back, out of Cruz's magnetic orbit, but she couldn't.

'You're an enigma,' he said, meeting her eyes. 'I can't figure you out and it bothers me.'

Feeling even shakier now, she said, 'There's nothing to figure out. What you see is what you get.'

Cruz gripped her hand tighter and pulled her closer, saying gruffly, 'I'm beginning to wonder if that isn't the case.'

It took a second for his words to sink in, and when they did Trinity's belly went into freefall. Was he… could he really listen to her now? And believe her?

But Cruz didn't seem to be interested in talking. His hand was trailing up her arm now, all the way to where the chiffon was tied at her shoulder.

With slow, sure movements, and not taking his eyes off hers, Cruz undid the bow, letting the material fall down. He caressed her shoulder, moving his hand around to the back of her neck and then up, finding the band in her hair and tugging it free so that her hair fell down around her shoulders.

Trinity was feeling incredibly vulnerable after revealing far more than she'd intended, but Cruz was looking at her and touching her as if he was burning up inside, just as she was, making her forget everything. Almost.

She couldn't let him expose her even more…

It was the hardest thing in the world, but she caught his hand, pulling it away. 'We shouldn't do this…'

He turned her hand in his, so he was holding it again, pulling her even closer so she could feel every inch of her body against his much harder one.

'Oh, yes, we should, *querida*. It's inevitable. The truth is that it's been inevitable since we first kissed.'

Cruz wrapped both hands around her upper arms. Trinity's world was reduced down to the beats of her heart and the heat prickling all over her skin. Surely his mention of that cataclysmic night should be breaking them out of this spell? But it wasn't...

A dangerous lassitude seeped into her blood, draining her will to resist. Cruz bent his head close to hers, his breath feathering over her mouth.

'Tell me you want this, Trinity. At least this is true between us—you can't deny it.'

She was in a very dangerous place—feeling exposed after her confession and the tantalising suggestion that Cruz might be prepared to admit that he was wrong about her... All her defences were snapping and falling to pieces.

As if sensing her inner vacillation, Cruz touched her bare shoulder with his mouth and moved up to where her neck met her shoulder. He whispered against her skin. 'Tell me...'

Unable to stop herself, she heard the words falling out of her mouth. 'I want you...'

He pulled back, a fierce expression on his face. Triumph. It made her dizzy. She didn't even have time to think of the repercussions before Cruz's mouth was on hers and suddenly everything was slotting into place. She didn't have to think...she only had to feel. It was heady, and too seductive to resist.

The intimacy of his tongue stroking roughly along hers made blood pool between her legs, hot and urgent. Pulsing in time with her heart.

Time slowed down as Cruz stole her very soul right

out from inside her. A fire was taking root and incinerating everything in its path.

His hands landed on her waist, hauling her right into him, where she could feel the solid thrust of his arousal just above the juncture of her legs. Any warning bells were lost in the rush of blood as her own hands went to Cruz's wide chest and then higher, until she was arching into him and winding her arms around his neck.

When his mouth left hers she gasped for air, lightheaded, shivering as he transferred his attention to her neck, tugging at her skin gently with his teeth before soothing with his tongue.

Air touched her back as the zip of her dress was lowered. The bodice loosened around her breasts and she finally managed to open her eyes. Cruz's short hair was dishevelled, his eyes burning, as he pulled the top of her dress down, exposing her bare breasts to his gaze. The cut of the dress hadn't allowed for a bra.

'So beautiful,' he said thickly, bringing a hand up to cup the weight of one breast in his palm.

Trinity felt drunk…dazed. She looked down and saw her own pale flesh surrounded by his much darker hand. Her nipple jutted out, hard and stark, as if begging for his touch. When he brushed it with his thumb she let out a low moan and her head fell back.

Her arms were weakening around his neck and her legs were shaking. There was so much sensation on top of sensation. It was almost painful. And then suddenly the ground beneath her feet disappeared altogether and she gasped when she realised that Cruz had picked her up and was now laying her down on the nearby couch.

Her dress was gaping open and she felt disorientated yet hyper-alert. Cruz came down on his knees beside her supine body and pulled her dress all the way down to her waist, baring her completely.

She couldn't suck in enough air, and when he lowered that dark golden head and surrounded the taut peak of her breast with sucking heat her back arched and she gasped out loud, funnelling her hands through his hair…

She ignored the part of her whispering to stop this *now*…she couldn't stop. She wasn't strong enough. She'd never felt so wanted and connected as she did right in that moment, and for Trinity that was where her darkest weakness lay. Still…

Cruz was drowning…in the sweetest, softest skin he'd ever felt or tasted in his life. The blood thundering through his veins and arteries made what he'd felt for any other woman a total mockery. It was as if he'd been existing in limbo and now he was alive again.

One hand was filled with the flesh of Trinity's breast, the hard nipple stabbing his palm, and he tugged the sharp point of her other breast into his mouth, his tongue laving the hard flesh, making it even harder. She tasted of sweet musky female and roses, and she felt like silk.

He wasn't even aware of her fingers clawing into his head so painfully. He was only aware of this pure decadent heaven, and the way she was arching her body at him so needily.

He finally let go of the fleshy mound of her breast and found her dress, pulling it up over her legs. He needed to feel her now, feel how ready for him she was. He wanted to taste her... His erection hardened even more at that thought.

He found her heat, palpable through the thin silk of her panties, and lifted his head, feeling animalistic at way she throbbed so hotly into his palm.

Trinity stopped moving. Her eyes opened and Cruz wanted to groan when he saw how sensually slumberous she looked, golden hair spread around her, breasts moving up and down, nipples moist from his touch. Mouth swollen from his kisses.

Giving in to his base needs, he moved down, pulling her dress up higher. Her panties were white and lacy and he pulled them off, heedless of the ripping sound, dropping them to the floor.

'Cruz...what are you doing...?'

She sounded breathless, rough. Needy. And there was some other quality to her voice that Cruz didn't want to investigate. Something like uncertainty.

'I need to taste you, *querida.*'

Her eyes widened. 'Taste me...? You mean like...?'

Cruz touched her with his finger, sliding it between soft silken folds. She gasped and tried to put her hand down, but he caught it and stopped her. He explored the hot damp seam of her body, pressing into the fevered channel of her body and exerting pressure against her clitoris.

He took his finger away, even though he wanted to thrust it all the way inside, and brought it to his mouth, taking the wet tip into his mouth. His eyes closed... his erection jumped. For the first time since he was a teenager Cruz was afraid he'd spill before he even got inside her.

The taste of her musky heat on his tongue...

He opened his eyes and she was looking at him, shocked. Two spots of red in her cheeks. A thought drifted across the heat haze in his brain... Why was she looking so shocked? Surely she'd...? But he batted the thought away, not wanting images of what she'd done with previous lovers—*his brother*—to intrude.

There would only be one lover now. Him. She was here and she was *his*.

He said in a rough voice, 'I need to taste you...like that.'

She said nothing. He saw her bite her lip. She looked feverish, and then she gave an almost imperceptible nod. Cruz pushed her legs apart, exposing the blonde curls covering her slick pink folds...slick for him.

There was none of his usual finesse when he touched her. He licked her, sucked and tasted, until he was dizzy and drunk. He thrust two fingers inside her heat, moving them in and out. He felt her hips jerk, her back arch. Heard soft moans and gasps, felt hands in his hair.

Her thighs drew up beside his head and her whole body tensed like a taut bow, just seconds before powerful muscles clamped down tight on his fingers and her body shuddered against his mouth.

She was *his*.

CHAPTER EIGHT

TRINITY WAS BARELY CONSCIOUS, floating on an ocean of such satisfaction that she wondered if she might be dead. Surely this wasn't even possible? This much pleasure? For her body to feel so weighted down and yet light as a feather? She could feel the minor contractions of her deepest muscles, still pulsing like little quivering heartbeats...

She finally came back to some level of consciousness when she felt a soft surface under her back and opened her eyes. She was on a bed, and Cruz was standing before her, pulling off his shirt and putting his hands on his trousers, undoing them, taking them down.

She saw the way his erection tented his underwear, and watched with avid fascination as he pulled that off too, exposing the thick stiff column of flesh, moisture beading at the tip.

'If you keep looking at me like that—' He broke off with a curse and bent down, hands on the sides of her dress, tugging it free of her body.

Trinity was naked now, and yet she felt no sense of self-consciousness. She was so wrapped in lingering pleasure and so caught up in this bubble of sensuality that she ignored the persistent but faint knocking of something trying to get through to her…

Cruz reached beside the bed for a condom and rolled it onto his erection, the latex stretched taut. Incredibly, as he came down onto the bed and moved over her, she felt her flesh quiver back to life. Her pulse picked up again and she no longer felt like floating…she wanted to fly again.

Cruz's hips pushed her legs apart and he took himself in his own hand, touching the head of his sex against hers, teasing her by pushing it in slightly before drawing it out again, her juices making them both slick. She felt as if she should be embarrassed, but she wasn't.

Between her legs she could feel her flesh aching for Cruz, aching for more than his mouth and tongue and fingers…aching for more.

She arched up. 'Please, Cruz…'

Was that ragged voice hers? She didn't have time to wonder, because with one feral growl and a sinuous move of his lean hips he thrust deep inside her. His whole body went taut over hers, and the expression on his face was one of pure masculine appreciation.

But Trinity wasn't seeing that. It had taken only a second for the intense need and pleasure to transform into blinding hot pain. She couldn't breathe, couldn't make sense of what she was feeling, when seconds ago she'd craved for him to do exactly this…

'*Dios,* Trinity…' he breathed. 'You're so tight…'

Cruz started to pull back, and Trinity's muscles protested. She put her hands on his hips and said, as panic mounted through her body along with the pain, 'Get off me! I can't...breathe...'

Cruz stopped moving instantly, shock in his voice. 'I'm hurting you?'

Her eyes were stinging now, as she sobbed while trying to push him off, '*Yes*, it hurts!'

He pulled away and Trinity let out a sound of pain. Cruz reared back, staring at her, and then down at something on the bed between them.

'What the hell—?'

She was starting to shiver in reaction and she looked down. The cover on the bed was cream, but even in the dim light she could see the spots of red—blood.

Her head started to whirl sickeningly as what had just happened sank in and she scrambled to move, almost falling off the bed in her bid to escape. She got to the bathroom and slammed the door behind her.

Cruz paced up and down after pulling on his trousers. There was nothing but ominous silence from the bathroom. His mind was fused with recrimination. He simply could not believe what her tight body and the evidence of blood told him. That she was innocent. That she was a virgin. It was like trying to compute the reality of seeing a unicorn, or a pig flying across the sky.

It simply wasn't possible. But then his conscience blasted him... He'd never been so lost in a haze of lust—he'd thought she was there with him, as ready as he was.

He wanted to go after her, but the sick realisation hit

him that he was probably the last person she wanted to see right now. Nevertheless, he went and knocked softly on the door. 'Trinity?'

Silence.

Just when Cruz was about to try and open the door she said, 'I'm fine. I just need a minute.'

Cruz's hand clenched into a fist at the way her voice sounded so rough. He took a step back from the door and then he heard the sound of the shower being turned on. His guts curdled. Was she trying to wash him off her?

He'd never been in this situation before. He'd never slept with a virgin before...

And then his mind went on that disbelieving loop again—how was it even possible? She'd been his brother's *wife*!

Cruz sat down on the end of the bed and a grim expression settled over his features as he waited for Trinity to come out of the bathroom and explain what the hell was going on.

Trinity sat on the floor of the shower stall, knees pulled into her chest, arms wrapped around them and her head resting on the wall behind her, eyes closed as the hot water sluiced down over her skin. She couldn't stop shivering, and all she could see was the shock on Cruz's face.

Between her legs it still stung slightly, but the red-hot pain had gone. And yet along with that pain Trinity had felt something else—something on the edges of the pain, promising more—but the shock of realising that Cruz was witnessing her ultimate exposure had eclipsed any desire to keep going.

She opened her eyes and saw nothing but steam. In the heated rush of more pleasure and sensations than she'd ever known, maybe she'd hoped that Cruz wouldn't realise...

But he had. And what she'd experienced before when he'd rejected her was nothing compared to the prospect of how he would look at her now.

When Trinity emerged a short time later, wrapped in a thick towelling robe, Cruz stood up from where he'd been sitting on the end of the bed. He looked as pale as she felt, and something quivered inside her.

His chest was bare, and it was if she hadn't really seen it the first time he'd bared it. She'd been so consumed with desire. It was wide, with defined musculature and dark golden hair covering his pectorals, leading down in a line between an impressive six-pack to arrow under his trousers. A glorious example of a masculine male in his prime.

'Trinity...?'

She looked at his face and saw an expression she'd never seen before—something between contrition and bewilderment.

'I'm sorry,' she said, her voice husky.

Now something more familiar crossed his face—irritation. 'Why the hell didn't you tell me that you were still a virgin?'

She wanted to curl up in a corner, but she stood tall. 'I didn't think you'd notice.'

He frowned. 'How could I not have noticed?'

He seemed to go even paler for a second, as if he was remembering what it had been like to breach that secret and intimate defence. And that only made Trinity remember it too—the pain and then that other tantalising promise of pleasure...hovering on the edges. How amazing it had felt up to that point. How lost she'd been, dizzy with need and lust. Forgetting everything. Forgetting that she needed to protect herself from this...

She went to move past him. 'I don't really want to talk about this now.'

He caught her arm as she was passing. 'Wait just a second—'

'Look, I *really* don't want to talk about this right now.' She felt flayed all over, and way too vulnerable.

Cruz's hand tightened on her arm. 'I deserve an explanation. *Dios*, Trinity, I *hurt* you. And you were married to my brother—how the hell are you still a virgin?'

Her heart slammed against her ribs. This was it. The moment when Cruz would *have* to listen to her. Because of the irrefutable physical humiliation she'd just handed him on a plate.

She turned to face him and looked up. Her voice was husky with emotion. 'I've been trying to explain to you all along that it wasn't a real marriage, Cruz, but you didn't want to hear it. It was a marriage of convenience.'

There was silence for a long moment. The lines of Cruz's face were incredibly stark and grim. He said, 'I'm listening now.'

Trinity's legs felt wobbly and she sat down on the

edge of the bed, seeing the stain of her innocence on the sheets in her peripheral vision.

Her cheeks burning, she gestured with her hand. 'I should do something with the sheet—the stain—'

'Can wait,' Cruz said with steel in his tone. 'Talk, Trinity, you owe me an explanation.'

Anger surged up, because if he'd been prepared to listen to her weeks ago they could have avoided this scene, but it dissipated under his stern look. In truth, how hard had she really tried to talk to him? Had she been happy just to let him think the worst so she could avoid him seeing how pathetic she really was? Contriving to make a home out of a fake marriage with children who weren't even her own?

'Okay,' Cruz said, when the words still wouldn't come. 'Why don't we start with this: why did you go to work for Rio? I hadn't fired you.'

She looked up at him. 'How could I have stayed working for you after what had happened? I was embarrassed.' Realising that she'd reached peak humiliation, she said bitterly, 'I had a crush on you, Cruz. I was the worst kind of cliché. A lowly maid lusting after her gorgeous and unattainable boss. When you rejected me that night—'

'I told you,' he interrupted. 'I did not reject you. I hated myself for crossing a line and taking advantage of you.'

Trinity stood up, incensed. 'You asked me if I regularly walked around the house in my nightclothes, as if I'd done it on purpose!'

A dull flush scored along Cruz's cheekbones. 'I

didn't handle the situation well. I was angry... But it was with myself. Not you—no matter how it sounded.'

Refusing to be mollified, Trinity said, 'The following night you gave me that look as you greeted the beautiful brunette... You were sending me a message not to get any ideas. Not to forget that what had happened was a huge mistake.'

Cruz ran his hands through his hair impatiently, all his muscles taut. 'I don't even remember who that was. All I could see was you and that hurt look on your face.'

Trinity's cheeks burned even hotter. She'd been so obvious.

She continued, 'At one point during the evening I went outside. Rio was there, smoking a cigarette. He saw that I was upset and he asked me why...so I told him. He seemed nice. Kind. And then...then he told me that he was looking for a new nanny. He asked me if I'd be interested...and I said yes. I couldn't imagine staying in your house knowing that every time you looked at me it would be with pity and regret.'

Cruz's eyes burned. 'And yet after six months you were his wife?'

Trinity sat down again on the bed. 'Yes.'

Cruz was pacing back and forth now, sleek muscles moving sinuously under olive skin. Distracting.

He stopped. 'So do you want to tell me how you went from nanny to convenient wife?'

She'd wanted this moment to come, hadn't she? And yet she felt reluctant. Because she knew she'd be revealing something of Rio to Cruz that would tarnish him in his eyes, and even after everything she was loath to do that.

But she didn't have a choice now.

She took a breath. 'I'd gone out to the cinema one night. Rio had assured me he had no plans and that he'd be home all evening. When I got back the twins were awake in their room and hysterical. Their nappies were soaking and I don't think they'd been fed. It took me a couple of hours to calm them down, feed them and put them down again. Frankly, it terrified me that they'd been in that state. I went downstairs and found Rio passed out over his desk, drunk. I managed to wake him up and get some coffee into him...but it was clear then that he was in no fit shape to be left alone with his sons—ever.'

Cruz looked shocked. 'I know Rio liked to indulge, but I never would have thought he'd do it while looking after his sons.'

Trinity sucked in a breath. 'I threatened to tell the police...even call you...but Rio begged me not to. He said it was a one-off. I told him I couldn't stand by and let him neglect his children and he begged me to listen to him before I did anything. He told me what had happened to him as a child. He told me he wasn't a perfect father but that he didn't want his boys to be taken into care.'

Trinity looked at Cruz.

'He knew about my past...where I'd come from. I'd told him not long after I started working for him.' Her mouth compressed at the memory of her naivety. 'He seemed to have an ability to unearth people's secrets.

And he used that to make me feel guilty for even suggesting that I'd report him. That I would risk subjecting his sons to the same experience I'd had.'

Cruz interjected. 'I would never have let that happen.'

'You were on the other side of the world,' Trinity pointed out. 'And Rio didn't want me to tell you what had happened. I knew you weren't close, so how could I go behind his back?'

She stood up, feeling agitated. Pacing back and forth, aware of Cruz's preternatural stillness.

'But then suddenly he was offering me a solution—to marry him. It was crazy, ridiculous, but somehow he made it seem...logical.'

She stopped and faced Cruz.

'He promised that it would be strictly in name only. He told me he'd hire a nanny to help. He said he wanted to appear more settled, to prove to people that he wasn't just a useless playboy. He said that in return for taking care of the boys and going to some social functions with him I could name my price. Whatever I wanted...'

Something gleamed in Cruz's eyes. 'What was it, Trinity? What did you want?'

She hated it that even now Cruz seemed to be waiting for her to expose herself. She lifted her chin. 'I told him I'd always wanted to go to college. To get a degree. And so he promised to fund my course once the boys were a little older and in a more settled routine.'

Cruz looked at her for a long moment and then shook his head. 'I don't get it. Even with the promise of fulfilling your college dream, why would you agree to a marriage like that unless you were going to get a lot more out of it? Evidently you didn't sleep with Rio, but did you want to? Did you plan on seducing him? Making the marriage real?'

Disappointment vied with anger. 'You will never believe me, will you? Even when you have to admit that I'm not a gold-digger, your cynicism just won't let you...'

She went to walk out of the room, but Cruz caught her arm. She stopped and gritted her jaw against the reaction in her body.

Cruz pulled her around to face him, but before he could say anything, she inserted defensively, 'Of course I wasn't planning on seducing Rio. I had no interest in him like that, and he had no interest in me.'

She looked down for a moment, her damp hair slipping over one shoulder, but Cruz caught her chin between his thumb and forefinger, tipping it back up. Not letting her escape. There was something different in his eyes now—something that made her heart flip-flop.

He just said, '*Why*, Trinity?'

She felt as if he could see right down into the deepest part of her, where she had nothing left to hide.

She pulled her chin away from his hand and said, 'I felt a sense of affinity with him...with the fact that in spite of our differences we had a lot in common.' Her voice turned husky. 'But the largest part of why I agreed was because I'd come to love Matty and Sancho. They needed me.' Afraid that the next thing she'd see on Cruz's face would be pity, Trinity said, 'I'm well aware that my motivations had a lot to do with my own experiences, but I'm not afraid to admit that. They had no one else to look out for them, and I believed I was doing the right thing by them.'

She tried to pull her arm free of Cruz's grip but it only tightened.

She glared at him, hating him for making her reveal so much. 'Just let me go, Cruz. Now you know everything...and I know that after what just happened you won't want a repeat performance...so can we just put it behind us? *Please?*'

He frowned. 'Won't want a repeat performance?'

He pulled her closer. Her breath hitched and her heart started pounding.

'I hurt you, Trinity. If I'd known it was your first time I would have been much more gentle.'

She looked away, humiliation curdling her insides. 'You really don't have to pity me, Cruz. You came to your senses after kissing me that first time. I was unsuitable before and now I'm *really* unsuitable.'

Trinity had managed to pull her arm free and take a couple of steps towards the door when Cruz acted on blind instinct and grabbed her waist and hauled her back, trapping her against him with his arms around her body.

He was reeling from everything that had just transpired—the sheer fact of Trinity's physical innocence was like a bomb whose aftershocks were still being felt. He didn't like to admit it, but the knowledge that her marriage to Rio hadn't been real... It eclipsed everything else at that moment, making a ragged and torn part of him feel whole again.

Trinity put her hands on his arms and tried to push, but he wouldn't let her go. *Not now. Not ever*, whispered a voice. Base desires were overwhelming his need to analyse everything she'd just said. *Later.* When his brain had cleared.

She said in a frigid voice, 'Let me go, Cruz.'

He turned her so she was facing him. Her face was flushed, eyes huge. He felt feral as he said, 'Believe me when I say that the last thing I feel for you is pity, Trinity. Or that you're unsuitable. And you're wrong, you know...'

'Wrong about what?' She sounded shaky.

Looking down at her now, some of the cravening need Cruz was feeling dissipated as his chest tightened with an emotion he'd never expected, nor welcomed. But this woman evoked it effortlessly, especially after the shattering revelations of her innocence, and in more ways than one.

He shook his head, honesty compelling him to say, 'I haven't come to my senses since that night. You've bewitched me, Trinity.'

'What do you mean?'

Cruz knew that he'd never before willingly stepped into a moment of emotional intimacy like this. No other woman had ever come close enough to precipitate it. After everything that had just happened he felt exposed and raw, in a way that should have been making him feel seriously claustrophobic, but what he *was* feeling was...a kind of liberation.

'What I mean is that I haven't looked at another woman since that night.' His voice turned rough as he admitted, 'I haven't *wanted* another woman since I touched you.'

Her eyes widened. Her mouth closed and then opened again. Finally she said, 'You're not just saying this?'

Her vulnerability was laid bare, and Cruz wondered bleakly how he'd blocked it out before now.

Because he'd wanted to. Because it had been easier to believe the worst rather than let himself think for a second that she could possibly be as pure as he'd believed from the start. Because then he'd have had to acknowledge how she made him feel.

He shook his head. 'No, I'm not just saying this. You're all I want, Trinity. I hated thinking of you and Rio together... I was jealous of my own brother.'

Trinity felt breathless at Cruz's admission. She could see how hard it was for him to open up like this, even as it soothed a raw hurt inside her. And with that came the heavy knowledge that he was beating himself up now over feeling jealous of Rio—and that was exactly the result Rio had wanted to achieve. To mess with Cruz's head.

Loath to shatter this fragile moment, Trinity pushed that knowledge down deep, like a coward, and said, 'We were never together...not like that.' Feeling absurdly shy, she said, 'No other man has ever made me feel like you did. After...that night... I couldn't stop thinking about you...about how it would have been...'

'If we hadn't stopped?'

She nodded jerkily.

He gathered her closer and a tremor ran through her

body. The air shifted around them, tension tightening again. 'We don't have to stop now...'

Trinity couldn't battle the desire rising inside her—not after what he'd just told her. She was already laid bare. Nowhere to hide any more. And she wanted this—wanted to fulfil this fantasy more than she wanted to take her next breath.

She looked up at him and fell into molten amber heat. 'Then don't stop, Cruz. Please.'

He waited for an infinitesimal moment and then lowered his head, touching his firm mouth to her softer one with a kind of reverence that made emotion bloom in her chest. To counteract it, because she wasn't remotely ready to deal with what it meant, she reached up and twined her arms around his neck, pressing closer, telling him with her body what she wanted...

He deepened the kiss, stroking into her mouth with an explicitness that made her groan softly, excitement mounting again. His hands moved around to her front, unknotting her robe. He pushed it apart and spread his hands on her hips, tracing her curves, before she broke away from the kiss, breathing raggedly.

He pulled back and looked at her, before pushing her robe off completely. Without looking away, he opened his trousers and pushed them down, kicking them off. Now they were both naked. Trinity looked down and her eyes widened. That stiff column of flesh jerked under her look, and a sense of very feminine wonder and sensuality filled her at the thought that she could have an effect on him like this.

He took her hand and brought it to his hard flesh,

wrapping her fingers around him. Slowly, gently, he guided her, moving her hand up and down... It was heady, the way her skin glided over steely strength...

Cruz felt beads of perspiration pop out on his forehead as Trinity's untutored touch drove him to the edge of any reason he had left. It was a special kind of torture... and before she could reduce him to rubble he took her hand from him and led her to the bed.

He wanted to consume her until she was boneless and pliant and *his*.

When he laid her down on the bed and came down alongside her she reached out a tentative hand and touched his chest.

He sucked in a breath. 'Yes...touch me.'

His eyes devoured her perfect curves, slender and yet lush all at once. An intoxicating mix. Innocent and siren.

Innocent.

She laid her hand flat on his pectoral, and then bent her head and put her tongue to the blunt nub of his nipple. Cruz tensed. He'd never even known he was sensitive there. Small teeth nibbled gently at his flesh and his erection grew even harder at the certainty that she would be a quick study...that she would send him to orbit and back all too easily.

A fleeting moment of vulnerability was gone as she explored further and took him in her hand again, moving over his flesh with more confidence.

He groaned and put his hand over hers. She looked at him—suddenly unsure—and it made his chest squeeze.

'If you keep touching me like that I won't last...and I need to.'

'Oh,' she said, a blush staining her cheeks.

Cruz cupped her chin and said roughly, 'Come here.'

She moved up and his arm came around her. He hauled her into him so that she half lay on him, breasts pressed against his side. Her nipples scraped against his chest. Cruz pressed a hot kiss to her mouth, his tongue tangling lazily with hers, revelling in the lush feel of her body against his and the taste of her.

When he could feel her moving against him subtly, he gently pushed her back so that he was looking down at her. Her sheer beauty reached out and grabbed him deep inside, transcending the physical for a moment. Her eyes were wide and her pupils dilated. Her cheeks were flushed and her hair was spread around her head like a golden halo.

She was perfection. And everything she'd told him, if it was true— Cruz shut his mind down. He couldn't go there now.

He explored her body with a thoroughness that made her writhe against him, begging and pleading. But there was no way he wasn't going to make sure she was so ready for him that when they came together there would be no pain. Only pleasure.

He smoothed his hand over her belly, down to where her legs were shut tight. He bent his head again, kissing her deeply, and as he did so he gently pushed them apart and felt her moist heat against his palm.

He cupped her sex, letting her get used to him touching her there, and explored along the seam of her body, releasing her heat, opening her to him with his fingers. He moved his fingers in and out. He could feel her body grow taut, and then he lifted his head to look down at her.

'Come for me, Trinity...'

And as if primed to do his bidding, she did, tipping over the edge with a low, keening cry. He had to exert extreme control to stop himself from spilling at the stunning beauty of her response.

Her hand was gripping his arm, and he could feel her body pulsating around his fingers. He looked at her for a long moment and said, 'If you don't want to go any further now, that's okay.'

Her eyes opened and it seemed to take her a second to focus on him. She shook her head. 'No, I'm okay. Keep going...'

Cruz sent up a prayer of thanks to some god he'd never consulted before. He reached over her to get protection from the drawer. When he was sheathed, he came up on his knees between her legs, pushing them apart, hands huge on her thighs.

Cruz came forward, bracing himself on one hand on the bed beside her, and with his other hand notched the head of his erection against her body, using her arousal to ease his passage into her. He teased her like this until she started panting a little, and arching herself towards him.

Unable to wait a second longer, slowly, inch by inch, he sank into her body, watching her face. She stared up at him, focused, and something inside him turned over even as all he could think about was how perfect it felt to have his body filling hers.

And then, when Cruz was so deep inside her that he could barely breathe, he started to move in and out, with achingly slow precision. She wrapped one of her legs around his waist and he had to clench his jaw as it deepened his penetration.

'I'm okay...' she breathed. 'It feels...good.'

He couldn't hold back. The movements of his body became faster, more urgent. Trinity was biting her lip, her pale skin dewed with perspiration. Cruz reached under her and hitched her hips up towards him, deepening his thrusts even more. Trinity groaned.

'That's it, *querida*, come with me.'

When she shattered this time it was so powerful that he shattered with her, deep inside her, his whole body curving over hers as they rode out the storm together.

Trinity woke slowly from a delicious dream, in which she had arms wrapped tight around her and she was imbued with an incredible sense of acceptance, belonging, safety, home.

Trust.

As soon as that little word reverberated in her head, though, she woke up. She was in Cruz's bedroom, amongst tangled sheets, and her whole body was one big pleasurable ache.

And she was alone.

When that registered it *all* came back.

Trinity's sense of euphoria and well-being faded as she recalled telling Cruz *everything*.

She'd trusted him with her deepest vulnerabilities.

Trust. Trinity went even colder as the magnitude of that sank in. She'd let Cruz into a space inside her that had been locked up for as long as she could remember.

Trust was not her friend. Trust had got her where she was today. First of all she'd trusted herself to follow her instincts and allow Cruz to kiss her that night. Then she'd trusted Rio, believing his motives for hiring her and marrying her were transparent and benign. Instead he'd manipulated her into becoming a tool of destruction against Cruz.

And now that urge was whispering to her again...to trust Cruz just because he'd made her body weep with more pleasure than she'd ever known could be possible. And because he'd admitted that he hadn't been with another woman since that night in his study. Since he'd kissed her.

Just remembering that now made her chest grow tight all over again. She'd never expected him to say that. What if it had just been a line, though? To get her back into bed? And she, like the fool, had believed him...

Feeling panicky now, at the thought of Cruz suddenly appearing and finding her when she felt so raw, she got out of bed and slipped on a robe. She picked up her severely crumpled dress, her face burning.

There was no sign of him as she went back to her room, and after a quick shower and changing into clean clothes she went into the main part of the apartment. She was very conscious of her body—still tender in private places—and it only made her feel more vulnerable. As if Cruz had branded her.

She knew he wasn't there even before she saw that it was empty and an acute sense of disappointment vied with relief. What had she wanted? To wake up with his arms around her? *Yes*, whispered a voice, and Trinity castigated herself. Men like Cruz didn't indulge in such displays of affection.

Her phone pinged from her bag nearby just then, and Trinity took it out to see a text from Cruz. Instantly her heart skipped a beat. Scowling at herself she read it.

I had an early-morning meeting and some things have come up so I'm going to stay in Madrid for another day/night. My driver is downstairs and he will take you to the airport where the plane is waiting whenever you are ready. Cruz.

Trinity dithered for a few minutes before writing back.

Okay.

She almost put an automatic *x* in the text, but stopped herself just in time.

A couple of minutes later there was another ping from her phone. She put down the coffee she'd just poured to read the text.

Just okay?

Feeling irritated at the mocking tone she could almost hear, she wrote back.

Okay. Fine.

Ping.

How are you feeling this morning?

Trinity's face was burning now. She would bet that Cruz didn't text his other lovers like this. They'd know how to play the game and be cool.

She wrote back.

Totally fine. Same as yesterday.

Ping.

Liar.

She responded.

I thought you had meetings to go to?

Ping.

I'm in one. It's boring.

Trinity was smiling before she stopped herself and wrote back.

Okay, if you must know I'm a little tender, but it feels nice.

She sent it before she had time to change her mind, feeling giddy.

Ping.

Good.

Not knowing how to respond to that smug response, Trinity put the phone down and took a deep breath. Her phone pinged again and she jumped.

Cursing Cruz, she picked it up.

We'll talk when I get back to the castillo.

The giddiness Trinity had been feeling dissipated like a burst balloon. She went cold. Of course they would talk. He'd had a chance to process what she'd told him now, and she could imagine that he didn't appreciate her telling him those less than savoury things about Rio.

That wasn't even the half of it. He didn't know the full extent of just how much Rio had despised him.

Trinity wrote back.

Okay.

Cruz didn't respond. She left the coffee untouched and put her arms around herself as the full enormity of what had happened the previous night sank in. She walked to the huge window in the living room and stared out, unseeing.

The prospect of Cruz going over what she'd told him

and digging any deeper than he'd already done, finding out the true depth of hatred that Rio had harboured for him, made her go icy all over. She couldn't do that to him.

And that was the scariest revelation of all. The intensity of the emotion swelling in her chest told her she was in deep trouble. The walls she'd erected around herself from a young age to protect herself in uncaring environments were no longer standing—they were dust.

First two small brown-eyed imps had burrowed their way in, stealing her heart, and now—

She put a hand to her chest and sucked in a pained breath. She could no longer claim to hate Cruz for what he'd done in forcing her into this marriage—if she ever truly had.

From the start she'd been infatuated with him, even after what she'd perceived to be his rejection of her. And then she'd seen a side to him that had mocked her for feeling tender towards him. But hadn't he shown her last night that he could be tender? Achingly so.

And, as much as she was scared that he'd just spun her a line about there being no women since he'd kissed her, just to get her into bed, she realised that she *did* trust him. He was too full of integrity to lie about something like that. He didn't need to.

And that left her teetering on the edge of a very scary precipice—although if she was brutally honest with herself she'd fallen over the edge a long time ago. Right about the time when Cruz had insisted on her going to bed so that he could sit up with the twins and she'd found herself yearning to be part of that tableau. *A family...*

She whirled away from the window, suddenly needing to leave and get back to the *castillo*—put some physical space between her and Cruz. One thing was uppermost in her mind—there couldn't be a repeat of last night. She wasn't strong enough to withstand Cruz's singular devastating focus and then survive when he got bored or decided to move on—which he would undoubtedly do.

For the first time, shamefully, Trinity had to admit to feeling unsure of her ability to sacrifice her own desires for the sake of Matty and Sancho. And she hated Cruz for doing this to her. Except...she didn't.

She loved them all and it might just kill her.

CHAPTER NINE

TRINITY HATED FEELING so nervous. She smoothed her hand down over the linen material of her buttoned shirt-dress. She'd changed after Julia had come to tell her that Cruz was back and wanted to see her.

She hated that she wondered if it was a bad omen that Cruz hadn't come looking for her himself. If not for her, then for the boys, who'd been asking for him constantly.

Cursing her vacillation, she lifted her hand and knocked on his study door, feeling a sense of déjà-vu when she heard him say, 'Come in.'

She went in and saw Cruz was behind the desk. He stood up, his gaze raking her up and down, making her skin tingle. She was conscious of her bare legs. Plain sandals. Hair tied back.

She closed the door behind her.

Cruz gestured to a chair. 'Come in…sit down.'

His voice sounded rough and it impacted on her.

She walked over and took the seat, feeling awkward. Not knowing where to look but unable to look away from those spectacular eyes and that tall, broad body.

Remembering how it had felt when he'd surged between her legs, filling her—

Cruz sat down too. 'How are the boys?'

Trinity fought against the blush she could feel spreading across her chest and up into her face. Sometimes she really hated her colouring.

'They're fine... They were asking for you, wondering where you were.'

An expression that was curiously vulnerable flashed across Cruz's face. 'I'll go and see them later,' he said. 'How are you?' he asked then.

Trinity fought not to squirm. 'I'm fine.'

An altogether more carnal look came across his face now. 'No...soreness?'

Trinity couldn't stop the blush this time. 'No.'

The carnal look faded and suddenly Cruz stood up again, running a hand through his hair. Trinity's gaze drank him in, registering that he must have changed when he got back as he was wearing soft jeans and a polo shirt.

When he didn't say anything for a moment she dragged her gaze up to his face and went still. He looked tortured.

She stood up, immediately concerned. 'What is it?'

He looked at her. 'I owe you an apology...on behalf of me *and* my brother.'

She went very still, almost afraid to say the words. 'You believe me, then...?'

Cruz paced for a moment, and then stopped and faced her again. He looked angry, but she could recognise that it wasn't with her.

'Of course I do.'

She sat down again on the chair behind her, her legs suddenly feeling weak. She waited for a feeling of vindication but it didn't come. She just felt a little numb.

Cruz shook his head. 'After Rio died I took everything his solicitor told me for granted. The truth was that I was in shock...grieving. Based on what he'd told me, I believed you deserved to be the focus of my anger and resentment, so I didn't do what I should have done—which was to investigate his finances with a fine-tooth comb. I've started to do that now,' he said heavily, 'and I had my own legal team haul in his solicitor for questioning yesterday. That's why I stayed behind in Madrid.'

Trinity's throat moved as she swallowed. 'What did you find?'

'Did you know he was a chronic gambler?'

She shook her head, shocked. 'No, of course not... He was away a lot. And worked odd hours. He never really explained himself.'

Cruz was grim. 'He hid it very well. It seems that as soon as he knew what was happening he spent even more money, and he started putting your name on things— like authorising the redecoration of the house, ordering credit cards in your name but using them himself...'

Trinity breathed in, feeling sick. 'So *that* was the trail directly back to me?'

Cruz nodded. 'He made sure you were seen out and about, at fashion shows and events, so if anyone ever questioned him he could point to you and say that you'd been instrumental in his downfall.' Cruz continued,

'You shouldn't feel like he duped you too easily—he did it to countless others along the way. Including me. If I hadn't been so blinkered where Rio was concerned, and had looked into his affairs before now—'

'Then you wouldn't have felt obliged to marry me because you'd have known I wasn't a threat,' Trinity said quickly.

She was avoiding his eye now and Cruz came over.

'Look at me,' he commanded.

After an infinitesimal moment she did, hoping her emotions weren't showing.

'I'm Matty and Sancho's uncle, and I'm going to be in their lives. You are the only mother my nephews have known and I was always going to come back here. Marriage was the best option.'

Trinity felt herself flinch minutely. *Marriage was the best option.* Suddenly feeling exposed under that amber gaze, she stood up and stepped around the chair in a bid to put some space between them. He was too close.

'We haven't finished this conversation,' he said warningly.

Her need to self-protect was huge. 'I think we have. You've said sorry and I accept your apology.'

'There's more, though, isn't there?' he asked now, folding his arms. 'That night—the night of the party at my house—you wanted to tell me something but I shut you down. What was it, exactly?'

Trinity felt panicky and took a step back towards the door. 'It was just my concerns about Rio—he'd been acting irrationally and I was worried, and we'd had that row—' She stopped suddenly and Cruz seized on it.

'You had a row? What about?'

She cursed her mouth and recognised the intractability in Cruz. He wouldn't let this go. He'd physically stopped her leaving before, and if he touched her now…

Reluctantly she said, 'I'd confronted him about being so…erratic. He was spending no time with the boys. He was drinking. And I'm sure he was doing drugs. I threatened to call you and tell you I was worried.'

Rio had sneered at her. *Go on, run to lover boy and cry on his shoulder and you'll see how interested he still is. Cruz doesn't care about you, or me. He only cares about the precious De Carrillo legacy. The legacy that's mine!'*

'What did he say?'

Trinity forced herself out of the past. 'He said that if I did anything of the sort he'd divorce me and never let me see Matty or Sancho again, and that he'd ruin any chances for my future employment, not to mention my chances of going to college.'

Cruz said, 'That must have been just after I'd returned to London. I'd asked to meet him—I'd been alerted by our accountants that he was haemorrhaging money. That's when he told me those lies about you and blamed you for pretty much everything. I had no reason not to believe him when there were all those receipts and the evidence of your social lifestyle…'

Trinity felt unaccountably bitter to hear Cruz confirming all this. She was also shocked at one person's ability to be so cruel. Without thinking, she said, 'He used me because he wanted to get back at you. He wanted to make you jealous because he—' She stopped suddenly, eyes fixed guiltily on Cruz.

What was wrong with her? It was as if she physically couldn't keep the truth back.

'Because he *what*?' Cruz asked, eyes narrowed on her flaming face.

She backed away, feeling sick. 'Nothing.'

Cruz was grim as he effortlessly reached for her, caught her by the hands and pulled her back, forcing her back down into the chair and keeping her hands in one of his.

'Tell me, Trinity. I know there's more to it than just the fact that Rio was going off the rails. He'd been going off the rails ever since he got his inheritance and, believe me, I know that's my fault.'

She looked up at him, momentarily distracted. Anger rushed through her because Cruz felt such irrational guilt over someone who didn't deserve it. Especially when that guilt had blinkered him to Rio's true nature and crimes.

She pulled her hands back, resting them on her lap. 'That wasn't your fault, Cruz. I lived with him for a year and a half, so I should know. Rio was selfish and self-absorbed, and all that inheritance did was highlight his flaws.'

Cruz looked at her carefully. 'There's still more.'

She shook her head, desperately wishing he'd drop it. 'No, there's not.'

He grabbed a nearby chair and pulled it over to sit down right in front of her, all but trapping her. Their knees were touching and she was very conscious of her bare legs under the dress. It didn't help when his gaze dropped momentarily to her chest.

He looked up again and arched a brow. She scowled at him. 'You can't force me to talk.'

'You'll talk, Trinity, and if you don't want to talk then we'll find other ways to occupy our time until you do.'

He put a hand on her bare knee, sliding it up her thigh until she slapped her hand down on his. He gripped her thigh and she felt a betraying pulse throb between her legs.

'Your choice. Either way, you're talking.'

She was between a rock and a hard place. If Cruz touched her she'd go up in flames and might not be able to hold back her emotions. But if she told him the truth about Rio, and he realised why she'd been so reluctant to tell him...

But he deserved to know—however hard it was. However much she wished she didn't have to.

She blurted out, 'I don't want to tell you because I don't want to hurt you.'

Cruz looked at her. Trinity couldn't have said anything more shocking. No one had ever said such a thing to him because no one had ever cared about hurting him before. Certainly not a lover, because he was always very careful not to give them that power.

But right now he could feel his insides contracting, as if to ward off a blow. Instinctively he wanted to move back, but he didn't. 'What are you talking about?'

Her eyes were like two blue bruises.

'Rio set me up way before he needed to use me to blame for his money problems.' She felt her face grow hot as she admitted, 'He offered me the job because he saw an opportunity to distract you, to make you jealous. He told me when we had the row that he'd hated you for as long as he could remember, but that he'd managed to make you believe he was grateful for the hand-outs he said you gave him.'

Cruz forced himself to say, 'Go on.'

'His ultimate ambition was to take you over—to use the marriage and his sons as evidence that he was the more stable heir. That he could be trusted. He wanted to see you humiliated, punished for being the legitimate heir. He never got over his resentment of you, Cruz.'

He realised dimly that he should be feeling hurt, exactly as Trinity had said. But it wasn't hurt he was feeling. It was a sense of loss—the loss of something he'd never had. And that realisation was stark and painful.

Trinity was looking at him and he couldn't breathe. He took his hand off her thigh and moved back, standing up. A sense of inarticulate anger rushed up...that awful futility.

Trinity stood too, and she was pale, and it made his anger snap even more. An irrational urge to lash out gripped him. A need to push her back to a safe distance, where it wouldn't feel as if her eyes could see right down to the depths of his very soul.

'You have to admit,' he said now, 'things worked out for you remarkably well, considering. You still managed to elevate yourself from humble maid to nanny to wife. You may have proved your physical innocence, but can

I really trust that you weren't the one who saw your opportunity that night when you spoke to Rio? Maybe you followed him into the garden?'

'No!'

She shook her head, and now there was fire in her eyes as well as something far more disturbing. Something that twisted Cruz's guts.

'*No.* I was hurt, and I was naive enough to let him see it...and he took advantage of that.'

All Cruz could see was her. Beautiful. Injured. *His fault.* The desire to push her back faded as quickly as it had come on.

Acting on instinct, he went over to her, chest tight. The desk was behind her—she couldn't move. Cruz took her face in his hands, lifting it up. 'Who are you, Trinity Adams? Is it really possible that you're that wide-eyed naive girl who turned up in my office looking for a chance? Full of zeal and a kind of innocence I've never seen before?'

Cruz's character assessment of her chafed unbearably, and Trinity balled her hands into fists at her sides.

'Yes,' she said, in a low voice throbbing with pain. 'I was that stupidly naive girl who was so starved for a sense of belonging that at the first sign of it she toppled right over the edge.'

She hated it that his proximity was making her melt even as hurt and anger twisted and roiled in her gut.

She took his hands down off her face. 'Just let me go, Cruz... There's nothing more to discuss. There's nothing between us.'

She felt his body go rigid and saw his eyes burn.

'You're wrong. There isn't nothing—there's this.'

His mouth was over hers before she could take another breath and Trinity went up in flames. Panic surged. She couldn't let this happen.

She tore her mouth away. 'Stop, Cruz, this isn't enough.'

'It's more than enough, *querida,* and it's enough for now.'

He started undoing the buttons of her shirt-dress, exposing her breasts in her lacy bra, dragging one cup down and thumbing her nipple. She wanted to tell him to *stop* again, but it was too late. She was tipping over the edge of not caring and into wanting this more. Anything to assuage the ache in her heart.

He lifted her with awesome ease onto the side of his desk. She heard something fall to the floor and smash, but it was lost in the inferno consuming them. He was yanking open her dress completely now...buttons were popping and landing on the floor.

He captured her mouth again as he pushed the dress off her shoulders and down her arms, pulling her bra down completely so her breasts were upthrust by the wire and exposed. The belt was still around her waist— the only thing keeping her dress attached to her body.

He palmed her breast as he stroked his tongue along hers, thrusting, mimicking a more intimate form of penetration. Trinity groaned into his mouth, instinctively arching her back to push her breast into his palm more fully, gasping when he trapped a hard nipple between his fingers before squeezing tightly.

She blindly felt for his T-shirt, pushing it up until

they had to break apart so he could lift it off. He dropped it to the floor and Trinity reached for his jeans, snapping open the top button, aware of the bulge pressing against the zip. Heat flooded her—and urgency.

She was hampered when Cruz bent down and tongued a nipple, his hand going between her legs, spreading her thighs and pushing aside her panties to explore along her cleft. He pulled her forward slightly, so that she was on the edge of the desk, feet just touching the ground.

He slowly thrust one finger in and out, while torturing her breasts with his mouth and tongue. She was throbbing all over, slick and ready. The previous emotional whirlwind was blissfully forgotten in this moment of heated insanity.

'Please, Cruz...'

He looked up, his face stark with need. He undid his jeans and pushed them down and his erection sprang fee. Trinity took it in her hand, the moisture at the tip wetting her palm.

Cruz settled himself between her legs, the head of his erection sliding against her sex, and it was too much. She was ready to beg when he tipped her back and notched himself into her heat. They both groaned, and he rested his forehead on hers for a moment.

Then he said, 'Wrap your legs around my waist.'

She did, barely aware that her sandals had fallen off. Cruz pulled her panties to one side and with one earthshattering movement thrust into her, deep enough to steal her breath and her soul for ever.

He put an arm around her and hauled her even closer

as he slowly thrust in and out, each glide of his body inside hers driving them higher and higher to the peak. She wrapped one arm around his neck, the other around his waist, struggling to stay rooted.

'Look at me,' he commanded roughly.

She opened her eyes and tipped back her head. The look on his face made a spasm of pure lust rush through her. It was feral. Desperate. Hungry. *Raw.*

Their movements became rougher…something else fell to the floor.

Cruz pushed her back onto the table, lying her flat, and took her hands in one of his, holding them above her head as he kept up the relentless rhythm of their bodies. She dug her heels into his buttocks, biting her lip to stop from screaming as the coil of tension wound so tight she thought she couldn't bear it any longer. But just at that moment he drew her nipple into his mouth, sucking fiercely, and the tension shattered to pieces and Trinity soared free of the bond that had been holding her so tight.

Cruz's body tensed over hers and she felt the hot burst of his release inside her.

Cruz took her to his room in his arms, because her legs were too wobbly to hold her up. She'd buried her face in his shoulder, eyes closed, weakly trying to block out the storm that had just passed but had left her reeling and trembling.

Her head hurt after too many confessions and an overload of pleasure. And too many questions that she didn't want to answer now. Or ever, maybe.

His room was dark and austere. There was a four-poster bed with elaborate drapes. This was very evidently the old part of the *castillo*.

He put her down on the side of his bed and she felt shell-shocked when he disappeared into what she presumed to be the bathroom. She heard the sound of running water and a few minutes later he appeared again and took her into the en-suite.

The bath smelled amazing. Like Cruz. Musky and exotic. He helped her out of her dishevelled clothes and into the hot water. She sank down and looked at him warily. He wore nothing but his jeans, slung low on his hips. She wished she had the nerve to ask him to join her, but she also wanted time to herself, to try and take in everything without him scrambling her brain to pieces.

As if reading her mind, he said, 'I'll be waiting outside,' and walked out, leaving her alone with thoughts she suddenly didn't want to think about.

Coward. She wanted to sink down under the water and block everything out, but she couldn't.

She let out a long, shuddering breath. It really was as if a storm had taken place down in Cruz's study, whipping everything up and then incinerating it in the fire that had blown up between them, white-hot and devastating. But a very fragile sense of peace stole over her as she lay there, even as she had to acknowledge that she wasn't sure where she stood now. And wasn't sure if she wanted to find out.

Aware that the water was cooling rapidly, and Cruz was waiting, she washed perfunctorily, stiffening as a jolt of sensation went through her when she touched the tenderness between her legs.

When she finally emerged, in a voluminous towelling robe with the sleeves rolled up her arms, Cruz was standing at the window. He turned around and she could see that he'd changed into dark trousers and a long-sleeved top and his hair was damp. So he'd gone to another room to shower. Because he'd wanted to give her space, or because he couldn't bear to spend more time with her?

Trinity gritted her jaw against the sudden onset of paranoia.

He came forward. 'How are you?'

She nodded. 'I'm okay.'

He was looking at her with a strange expression on his face, as if he'd never seen her before. In spite of the explosive intimacies they'd just shared Trinity felt as if a chasm yawned between them now.

'I'm sorry,' she said impulsively, thinking of the look on his face when she'd revealed the depth of Rio's hatred.

A muscle ticked in Cruz's jaw. 'You're sorry? For what? It's me who should be apologising to you for all but forcing you into this marriage, and for what my brother put you through to get back at me.'

His belief in her innocence didn't make her feel peaceful now—it made her feel sick. If he really believed that she had just been a pawn in Rio's game what future was there for them? Her heart lurched. *None.* Because he had to be regretting this marriage, which had been born out of an erroneous belief that he couldn't trust her and that he needed to protect his nephews.

It was the last question she wanted to ask, but she had to. 'What happens now?'

He smiled, but it was mirthless. 'What happens now? What happens now is that you could be pregnant. We didn't use protection.' He cursed volubly. 'I didn't even think of it.'

Trinity sank down onto the side of the bed nearest to her as her legs gave way. 'Neither did I,' she said faintly. She'd felt it...the hot rush of his release inside her...and she'd conveniently blocked it out.

She stared at Cruz's grim countenance as the significance of this sank in. The full, horrifying significance.

If she was pregnant then he wouldn't be able to disentangle himself from this marriage—and she didn't need to be psychic to intuit that that was exactly what he wanted. He was angry.

'There was two of us there,' she pointed out, feeling sick. 'It wasn't just your oversight.'

His mouth twisted. 'As much as I appreciate your sentiment, I was the one who should have protected you.'

You. Not *us.*

Panic galvanised Trinity at the prospect of Cruz resenting her for ever for a moment of weakness.

She calculated swiftly and stood up. 'I'm sure I'm not pregnant. It's a safe time for me. And even if it happened, by some miracle, it doesn't mean anything. We don't have to stay married—we could work something out.'

'That,' Cruz said coolly, fixing his amber gaze on her, 'would never be an option in a million years. If you are pregnant then we stay married.'

'But if I'm not...?'

'Then we will discuss what happens. But for now we wait. I have to go to Madrid again in two weeks. I'll set up an appointment with my doctor and we'll go together. That should be enough time for a pregnancy test to show up positive or negative...'

Feeling numb, Trinity said, 'We could just wait. I'll know for sure in about three weeks.'

Cruz shook his head. 'No, we'll find out as soon as possible.'

Trinity really hated the deeply secret part of her that hoped that she might be pregnant, because that was the only way she knew she'd get to stay in Cruz's life. But if she wasn't... The sense of desolation that swept over her was so acute that she gabbled something incoherent and all but ran out of the room to return to hers.

Cruz didn't come after her, or try to stop her, which told her more eloquently than words ever could how he really felt about her.

Cruz stood in the same spot for a long time, looking at the door. He'd had to let Trinity go, even though it had taken nearly everything he possessed not to grab her back. But he couldn't—not now. Not after the most monumental lapse in control he'd ever experienced.

He started to pace back and forth. He'd fallen on her in his study like a caveman. Wild. Insatiable. Filled with such a maelstrom of emotions that the only way he'd known how to avoid analysing them was to sink inside her and let oblivion sweep them away. But he couldn't avoid it now.

He'd been angry with her for revealing the extent of Rio's antipathy—but hadn't he known all along, really? And she'd just been the reluctant messenger.

He'd felt anger at himself for indulging in that delusion in a bid to forge some meagre connection with his only family. And he'd felt anger that Trinity had been so abused by Rio *and* him. He hadn't deserved her purity and innocence after all he'd put her through, and yet she'd given it to him with a sensuality and abandon that still took his breath away.

He stopped. Went cold. He'd actually had a tiny moment of awareness just before he'd come that there was no protection. But he'd been so far gone by then that to have pulled away from Trinity's clasping heat would have killed him… Cruz knew that there was no other woman on this earth who would have had that effect on him.

The insidious suspicion took root… Had he subconsciously wanted to risk getting her pregnant? Because he was aware that after what she'd told him he could no longer insist they stay married if she was innocent of everything he'd thrown at her?

Cruz sank down heavily on the end of the bed. If that was what had happened then he was an even sicker bastard than Rio.

When he thought of how he'd treated Trinity…how he'd shoved the past down her throat at every opportunity without giving her a chance to defend herself or explain…he deserved for her to walk away without a second glance.

But if she was pregnant then she would stay. And Cruz would be aware every day of his life that he had trapped her for ever.

That moment when she'd said so emotionally, *'I don't want to tell you because I don't want to hurt you,'* came back to him. Its full impact.

The fact that she'd actually been willing to keep it from him—the full extent of Rio's ambition and hatred—made him feel even worse. At best she pitied him. At worst she would come to resent him, just as Rio had, if she was pregnant and had no choice but to stay…

By the time Trinity came down for breakfast with the boys the following morning, feeling hollow and tired, she knew that Cruz was no longer in the *castillo*. And sure enough Julia appeared with a note for her.

I have to go to Madrid for a couple of days and then New York. I'll return in time for the doctor's appointment. Cruz.

It couldn't be more obvious that he didn't want to have anything to do with her until they knew if she was pregnant and then he would *deal* with it.

Even Mrs Jordan seemed to sense that something was going on, because she kept shooting Trinity concerned looks. She did her best to project as happy a façade as possible, and suggested that Mrs Jordan take the opportunity to go to Scotland for a few days to see her son, telling her that she'd just need her back for when she would be going to Madrid.

She also, if she was honest, wanted time alone with the boys to lick her wounds.

She filled their days with activities, wearing herself and the boys out so comprehensively that she could sleep. But that didn't stop the dreams, which now featured her running through the *castillo*, going into every room, endlessly searching for Cruz.

And each night before she went to sleep she forced herself to remember what he'd said in London, when she'd asked him about marrying for love: *'I have no time for such emotions or weaknesses...'*

Two weeks later...

Trinity was standing on Harley Street, having just come out of the doctor's office, in the bright spring sunshine. Cruz had brought her to London instead of Madrid at the last minute, because there had been something urgent he had to attend to at the UK bank.

She felt raw now, being back here. Where it had all started. And she felt even more raw after her appointment with the doctor...

A sleek car pulled up just then, and stopped. Trinity saw a tall figure uncoil from the driver's seat. *Cruz.* He'd timed his meeting so that he could meet her after the doctor's appointment.

He held the passenger door open for her to get in, saying nothing as she did so, just looking at her carefully. When he was behind the wheel he looked at her again.

Feeling too brittle at that moment, Trinity said, 'I'll tell you when we get to the house.'

They were staying overnight.

A muscle pulsed in Cruz's jaw, but he said nothing and just drove off. Trinity felt a little numb as she watched the streets go by outside, teeming with people engrossed in their daily lives.

When they got to the Holland Park house her sense of déjà-vu was overwhelming. The door closed behind them, echoing in the cavernous hall. Trinity's heart was thumping and she could feel clammy sweat breaking out on her skin. She sensed Cruz behind her, watching her, waiting, and slowly turned around.

She knew she had to say the words. She opened her mouth and prayed to sound cool and in control. Not as if she was breaking apart inside. She looked at him.

'I'm not pregnant, Cruz.'

He said nothing for a long moment. Trinity was expecting to see relaxation in the tense lines of his body. Eventually he said, 'We should talk, then.'

She recoiled at the thought of doing it right now. 'Can we do it later, please? I'm quite tired.'

Cruz nodded once. 'Of course. Whenever you're ready. I'll be in my study.'

'Okay,' Trinity said faintly, and turned to go up the stairs to the bedrooms. Calling herself a coward as she did so. She was just staying the execution. That was all.

CHAPTER TEN

AFTERNOON PASSED INTO dusk and evening outside Cruz's study, but he was oblivious. Two words echoed in his head: *not pregnant...not pregnant.* He'd felt an unaccountably shocking sense of loss. When he had no right.

Trinity would get pregnant one day, and create the family she'd always wanted. And she deserved that. There was no reason for him not to let her go now. If anything, *he had to.* It was time for him to make reparation.

It had come far too belatedly—the realisation that Rio's deep hatred of Cruz hadn't irreparably damaged his ability to care. That his mother's even deeper cynicism hadn't decimated the tiny seed of hope he'd believed to have been crushed long ago—hope for a different kind of life, one of emotional fulfilment and happiness. One not bound by duty and destiny and a desire to protect himself from emotional vulnerability at all costs.

He'd never wanted more because he'd never really known what that was. Until he'd seen Trinity interact so lovingly and selflessly with his nephews and had found himself sitting up in their room all night, watching them sleep and vowing to slay dragons if he had to, to keep them safe.

The thought of family had always been anathema to him, but now—

He heard a sound and looked up to see his door open. *Trinity.* She'd changed and was wearing soft faded jeans and a long cardigan, which she'd pulled around herself. Her hair was down and a little mussed, and her face was bare of make-up. Her feet were bare too.

For a second Cruz thought he might be hallucinating…even though she wasn't wearing the same clothes as that night… Past and present were meshing painfully right now. Mocking him with the brief illusory fantasy that perhaps there could be such a thing as a second chance.

He stood up as she came in and shut the door behind her.

Her voice was husky. 'I'm sorry. I slept far later than I wanted to.'

On automatic pilot, Cruz asked, 'Are you hungry? Do you want to eat?'

She shook her head and smiled, but it was tight. 'No, thanks—no appetite.'

A bleakness filled Cruz. No doubt she just wanted to sort this out and be gone. Back to the life he'd snatched out of her hands.

'Please, sit down.'

Again, so polite. Trinity came in and sat down. The weight of their history in this room was oppressive.

She'd told a white lie about sleeping—she hadn't slept a wink all afternoon, was too churned up. She'd spent most of her time pacing up and down.

After an initial acute sense of loss that she wasn't pregnant she'd felt a sense of resolve fill her. She wasn't going to give up without a fight. She knew Cruz had an innate sense of honour and decency, so even if that was all she had to work with she would.

Cruz sat down. His shirt was open at the top and his shirtsleeves were rolled up.

'You said that part of the deal with Rio was that he would pay for you to do a degree?'

Trinity blinked, taken by surprise that he'd remembered that. 'Yes, he did.'

'Do you still want to do it?'

She felt as if she was in an interview. 'Well, I haven't had much time to think about it lately, but yes…at some point I think I'd like to.'

Cruz nodded. 'I'll make sure you get a chance to do your degree, Trinity, wherever you want to do it.'

'Cruz…' She trailed off, bewildered. 'I presumed we were going to talk about what happens next—not my further education and career options.'

His voice was harsh. 'That is what happens next. You get to get on with your life—the life you would have had if you hadn't had the misfortune to meet me and my brother.'

He stood up then, and walked to the window which overlooked the park. It was still light outside—just.

Trinity stood up too, anger starting to sizzle. 'You do not get to do this, Cruz—blame yourself for what happened. Even Rio can't be apportioned blame either... not really.'

She came around the desk and stood a few feet away from him.

'I was just as much to blame. I shouldn't have been so hurt after what had happened between us that I spilled my guts to Rio with the slightest encouragement. You might not have handled it very well, but you didn't take any liberty I wasn't willing to give. It was the most thrilling moment of my life up to that point.'

Cruz turned around. Trinity saw his gaze drop and widen, and colour darken his cheeks. She didn't have to look down to know that her cardigan had fallen open, revealing her flimsy vest top and braless breasts underneath. She could feel her nipples peak under his gaze, and her heart thumped hard. She couldn't deny that she'd hoped to provoke a reaction from him.

'And there's this, Cruz.' She gestured between them, where tension crackled. 'This hasn't gone away...has it?'

His gaze rose and his jaw clenched. 'It's not about that any more. It's about you getting a divorce and moving on.'

Divorce.

Trinity's heart started thumping. She pulled the cardigan around herself again, feeling exposed. 'I told you before that I won't abandon Matty and Sancho—that hasn't changed.'

Cruz's voice was tight. 'The fact that you stepped in and protected and nurtured my nephews went above and beyond the call of duty.'

Trinity felt even more exposed now. 'I told you—I explained why—'

'I know,' Cruz said, and the sudden softness in his voice nearly killed her. 'But they're not really your responsibility. You have a life to live. And I won't be responsible for stopping you. We can work out a custody arrangement. I wouldn't stop you from being in their lives. But they're in good hands now.'

For a second Trinity wondered how she was still standing…how she wasn't in a broken heap at Cruz's feet. Whatever pain she'd experienced in her life didn't come close to the excruciating agony she felt right now.

Yet something dogged deep within her forced her to ask hoarsely, 'Do *you* want a divorce, Cruz?'

His eyes were burning. 'I want you to have your life back, Trinity. And I will support you and your relationship with the boys however you want.'

She folded her arms across her chest and Cruz's gaze dropped again to where the swells of her breasts were pushed up. Something came to life in her blood and belly. The tiniest kernel of *hope*.

'You didn't answer me. Do *you* want a divorce?'

His eyes met hers and she saw something spark deep in their golden depths before it faded. Something cold skated across her skin. A sense of foreboding.

'What I want,' Cruz bit out, 'is for my life to return to where it was before I ever met you.'

Trinity looked at him blankly for a long moment. And then, as his words impacted like physical blows, she sucked in a pained breath. Her fight drained away and her arms dropped heavily to her sides.

She might have fought Cruz if she'd thought there was half a chance. But there wasn't. He wanted her to have her life back. But he wanted his back too. She'd been a fool to think they had a chance. To think that she could persuade him by seducing him...

She whirled around to leave, terrified he'd see how badly he'd hurt her. The door was a blur in her vision as she reached for the knob, just wanting to escape.

She heard a movement behind her and then Cruz said hoarsely, 'Stop. Do not walk out through that door, Trinity.'

Her hand was on the knob. Her throat was tight, her vision blurring. She wouldn't turn around. 'Why?' she asked rawly.

His voice came from much closer. He sounded broken. 'Because I let you go through it once before and it was the worst mistake of my life.'

He put his hands on her shoulders and turned her around. She didn't want him to see the emotion on her face. But this was Cruz, who demanded and took, so he tipped her face up and cursed.

She looked at him and her heart flip-flopped. The stark mask was gone and he was all emotion. Raw emotion. And it awed her—because she realised now how adept he'd been at holding it all back for so long.

He'd been so controlled. But no more.

'I'm sorry,' he said, cupping her face, thumbs wiping at tears she hadn't even realised were falling. 'I didn't mean what I just said. It was cruel and unforgivable. I only said it because in that split second I thought going back to the life I had before I knew you was preferable to the pain of opening up. I thought I was doing the right thing…forcing you out of my life…'

Trinity whispered brokenly, 'I don't want you to force me out of your life.'

Cruz's whole body tensed. 'Do you mean that?'

She nodded, heart thumping. She put her hands on his and repeated her question. 'What do you want, Cruz?'

His eyes glowed with a new light. He said roughly, 'I want you. For ever. Because I know there can never be anyone else for me. I want to stay married to you and I want a chance to show you how sorry I am—for everything.'

Trinity just stared at him. Wondering if she was hallucinating.

He went on. 'I want to create a family with you— the kind of family neither of us had. Nor Rio. Maybe through his sons we can give him that finally. But,' he said, 'if you want a divorce…if you want to walk away… then I won't stop you. As much as I wanted you to be pregnant, I'm happy you aren't because I couldn't have borne knowing that you'd never had a choice… Now you do have a choice.'

Trinity's vision blurred again. 'I choose you, Cruz. I would always choose you.'

'I love you,' Cruz said fervently.

Trinity blinked back her tears and sucked in a shuddering breath. 'I came down here this evening prepared to fight and make you see, and then you said—'

Cruz stopped her mouth with his in a long soulful kiss. When they broke apart they were both breathing heavily, and Trinity realised that her back was against the wall of shelves. Cruz's body was pressed against hers, the unmistakable thrust of his arousal turning her limbs to jelly and her blood into fire. With an intent look on his starkly beautiful face he pushed her cardigan off her shoulders and pulled it off.

Euphoria made Trinity's heart soar. 'What are you doing?'

But Cruz was busy pulling down the straps of her vest top and exposing her breasts to his hungry gaze. Hoarsely he said, 'I'm taking care of unfinished business—if that's all right?'

As he made short work of undoing her jeans and pulling them down excitement mounted, and she said breathily, 'I have no objections.' She kicked her jeans off completely.

Cruz stopped for a moment and looked at her, all teasing and sexy seductiveness gone as the significance of the moment impacted on them. 'I love you.'

Trinity nodded, biting her lip to stave off more emotion. 'I love you too...'

But then their urgency to connect on a deeper level took over again.

Cruz stepped out of his clothes. She reached up and wound her arms around his neck, revelling in the friction of her body against his, and when Cruz picked her up she wrapped her legs tight around his hips and together they finished what they'd started, soaring high enough to finally leave the past behind and start again.

EPILOGUE

'CAREFUL, BOYS, YOUR little sister is not a doll,' Cruz admonished Matty and Sancho, who were tickling their four-month-old sister where she lay in her pram in the shade. The fact that she was their cousin and not really their sister was something they could wrap their heads around when they were older.

The boys giggled and ran away, chasing each other down the lawn, dark heads gleaming in the sunlight.

Cruz watched them go. They'd grown so much in the two years since he and Trinity had officially adopted them—turning their legal guardianship into something much more permanent and binding.

One day, not long after the adoption had come through, they'd both suddenly started calling him Papa. As if they'd taken a private mutual consultation to do so. The day it had happened he'd looked at Trinity, unable to keep the emotion from filling his eyes and chest. She'd reached out and taken his hand, her eyes welling up too as they'd realised what had just happened.

They were a family.

He shook his head now, marvelling that he couldn't

even remember a time before these two small boys existed. He would die for them. It was that simple. It was bittersweet to know that he was finally able to show his love for Rio by protecting and nurturing his nephews like this.

A happy gurgle made Cruz look down again to see his daughter, Olivia—who was already being called Livvy—smiling gummily and waving her arms and legs. She had the bright blue eyes of her mother and a tuft of golden curls on her head, and she had Cruz so wrapped around her tiny finger that he could only grin like a loon and bend down to pick her up.

'Hey,' protested a sleepy voice, 'you're meant to be getting her to sleep.'

Cruz looked to where Trinity was lying in a gently rocking hammock between two trees. Her hair was loose and long around her shoulders and she was wearing short shorts and a halterneck top that showed off her lightly golden skin and luscious curves. An indulgent smile made her mouth curve up, telling Cruz that he was *so* busted where his baby daughter was concerned.

Whatever he felt for his children expanded tenfold every time he looked at this woman, who filled his heart and soul with such profound grace and love he was constantly awed by it.

In spite of their busy lives she was already one year into a three-year degree in business and economics at the University of Seville, and loving it.

The *castillo* was almost unrecognisable too, having undergone a massive renovation and redecoration. Now it was bright and airy, with none of the darkness of its tainted past left behind.

Cruz devoured her with his eyes as he walked over, holding his precious bundle close. Trinity's cheeks flushed as their eyes met and desire zinged between them. Ever-present. Everlasting.

She made room for him on the family-sized hammock and then settled under the arm he put behind her, her hand over Livvy where she was now sleeping on his chest, legs and arms sprawled in happy abandon.

The boys were shouting in the distance—happy sounds. Cruz could hear Mrs Jordan's voice, so he knew they were being watched. He took advantage of the brief respite and tugged Trinity closer into his chest. She looked up at him, her mouth still turned up in a smile that was halfway between innocent and devilishly sexy.

Emotion gripped him, as it so often did now, but instead of avoiding it he dived in. 'Thank you,' he said, with a wealth of meaning in his words.

Thank you for giving him back his heart and an emotional satisfaction he would never have known if he hadn't met her and fallen in love.

And even though he didn't say those words he didn't have to, because he could see from the sudden brightness in her eyes that she knew exactly what he meant.

She reached up and touched her lips to his—a chaste kiss, but with a promise of so much more. And she whispered emotionally against his mouth, 'I love you, Cruz. Always.'

'Always,' he whispered back, twining his fingers with hers where they rested over their daughter.

Trinity rested her head in the spot made for her, between his chin and his shoulder, and the future stretched out before them, full of love and endless days just like this one.

* * * * *

Kidnapped For The Tycoon's Baby
Louise Fuller

MILLS & BOON

Books by Louise Fuller

Harlequin Modern

Blackmailed Down the Aisle
Claiming His Wedding Night
A Deal Sealed by Passion
Vows Made in Secret

Visit the Author Profile page at
millsandboon.com.au for more titles.

Louise Fuller was a tomboy who hated pink and always wanted to be the prince—not the princess! Now she enjoys creating heroines who aren't pretty pushovers but are strong, believable women. Before writing for Harlequin she studied literature and philosophy at university, and then worked as a reporter for her local newspaper. She lives in Tunbridge Wells with her impossibly handsome husband, Patrick, and their six children.

DEDICATION

For Adrian. My brother, and one of the good guys.

CHAPTER ONE

'I'M SORRY ABOUT THIS, Ms Mason. But don't worry. I'll get you there on time, just like always.'

Feeling the car slow, Nola Mason looked up from her laptop and frowned, her denim-blue eyes almost black within the dark interior of the sleek executive saloon.

Glancing out of the window, she watched a flatbed truck loaded with cones lumber slowly through the traffic lights. There had been some kind of parade in Sydney over the weekend, and the police and street cleaners were still dealing with the aftermath.

Thankfully, though, at five o'clock on Monday morning the traffic was limited to just a few buses and a handful of cars and, closing her laptop, she leaned towards her driver.

'I know you will, John. And please don't worry. I'm just relieved to have you.'

Relieved, and grateful, for not only was John punctual and polite, he also had near photographic recall of Sydney's daunting grid of streets.

As the car began to move again she shifted in her seat. Even after two months of working for the global tech giant RWI it still felt strange—fraudulent, even—having a chauffeur-driven limo at her disposal. She was a cyber architect, not a celebrity! But Ramsay Walker, the company's demanding and maddeningly autocratic CEO, had insisted on it.

Her mouth twisted. It had been the first time she'd objected to something, only to have Ramsay overrule her, but it hadn't been the last. His dictatorial behaviour and her stubborn determination to make a stand had ensured that they clashed fiercely at every subsequent meeting.

But now it was nearly over. Tomorrow was her last day in Sydney and, although, she and her partner Anna were still under contract to troubleshoot any problems in the RWI cyber security framework, they would do so from their office in Edinburgh.

She breathed out softly. And what a relief to finally be free of that intense grey gaze! Only, why then did what she was feeling seem more like regret than relief?

Glancing up at the imposing RWI building, she felt her heart begin beating hard and high in her chest. But right now was *not* the time to indulge in amateur psychology. She was here to work—and, if she was lucky, at this time of the morning she could expect a good two to three hours of uninterrupted access to the security system.

But as she walked past the empty bays in the visitor parking area some of her optimism wilted as she spotted a familiar black Bentley idling in front of the main entrance.

Damn it! She was in no mood for small talk—particularly with the owner of that car—and, ducking her chin, she began to walk faster. But she was not fast enough. Almost as she drew level with the car, the door opened and a man slid out. A woman's voice followed him into the early-morning light, together with the faintest hint of his cologne.

'But, baby, why can't it wait?' she wheedled. 'Come on—we can go back to mine. I'll make it worth your while…'

Unable to stop herself, Nola stole a glance at the man. Predictably, her breath stumbled in her throat and, gritting her teeth, she began to walk faster. She couldn't see his face, but she didn't need to. She would recognise that profile, that languid yet predatory manner anywhere. It was her boss—Ramsay Walker. In that car, at this time of the morning, it was always her boss.

Only the women were different each time.

Ignoring the sudden slick of heat on her skin, she stalked into the foyer. She felt clumsy and stupid, a mix of fear and restlessness and longing churning inside of her. But longing for what?

Working fourteen-hour days, and most weekends, she had no time for romance. And besides, she knew nobody in Sydney except the people in this building, and there was no way she would *ever* have a relationship with a colleague again. Not after what had happened with Connor.

Remembering all the snide glances, and the way people would stop talking when she walked by, she winced inwardly. It had been bad enough that everyone had believed the gossip. What had been so hurtful—so hurtful that she'd still never told anyone, not even her best friend and business partner, Anna—was that it had been Connor who'd betrayed her. Betrayed her and then abandoned her—just like her father had.

It had been humiliating, debilitating, but finally she had understood that love and trust were not necessarily symbiotic or two-way. She'd learnt her lesson, and she certainly wasn't about to forget it for an office fling.

She glanced back to where the woman was still pleading with Ramsay. Gazing at the broad shoulders beneath the crumpled shirt and the tousled surfer hair, Nola felt her heart thudding so loudly she thought one of the huge windows might shatter.

Workplace flings were trouble. But with a man like him it would be trouble squared. Cubed, even.

And anyway her life was too complicated right now for romance. This was the biggest job Cyber Angels had ever taken on, and with Anna away on her honeymoon she was having to manage alone, and do so with a brain and a body that were still struggling to get over three long-haul flights in as many weeks.

Trying to ignore the swell of panic rising inside her, she smiled mechanically at the security guard as he checked her security card. Reaching inside her bag, she pulled out her lift pass—and felt her stomach plummet as it slipped from her fingers and landed on the floor beside a pair of handmade Italian leather loafers.

'Allow me.'

The deep, masculine voice made her scalp freeze. Half turning, she forced a smile onto her face as she took the card from the man's outstretched hand.

'Thank you.'

'My pleasure.'

Turning, she walked quickly towards the lift, her skin tightening with irritation and a sort of feverish apprehension, as Ramsay Walker strolled alongside her, his long strides making it easy for him to keep pace.

As the lift doors opened it was on the tip of her tongue to tell him that she would use the stairs. But, given that her office was on the twenty-first floor, she knew it would simply make her look churlish or—worse—as though she cared about sharing the lift with him.

'Early start!'

Her skin twitched in an involuntary response to his languid East Coast accent, and she allowed herself a brief glance at his face. Instantly she regretted it. His dark grey eyes were watching her casually...a lazy smile tugged at his beautiful mouth. A mouth that had been kissing her all over every night since she'd first met him—but only in her dreams.

Trying to subdue the heat of her thoughts, praying that her face showed nothing of their content, she shrugged stiffly. 'I'm a morning person.'

'Is that right?' he drawled. 'I like the night-time myself.'

Night-time. The words whispered inside her head and she felt her body react to the darkness and danger it implied, her pulse slowing, goosebumps prickling over her skin. Only how was it possible to create such havoc with just a handful of syllables? she thought frantically.

'Really?' Trying her hardest to ignore the strange tension throbbing between them, she forced her expression into what she hoped looked like boredom and, glancing away, stared straight ahead. 'And yet here you are.'

She felt his gaze on the side of her face.

'Well, I got waylaid at a party...'

Remembering the redhead in the car, she felt a sharp nip of jealousy as stifling a yawn, he stretched his arms back behind his shoulders, the gesture somehow implying more clearly than words exactly what form that waylaying had taken.

'It seemed simpler to come straight to work. I take it you weren't out partying?'

His voice was soft, and yet it seemed to hook beneath her skin so that suddenly she had no option but to look up at him.

'Not my scene. I need my sleep,' she said crisply.

She knew she sounded prudish. But better that than to give this man even a hint of encouragement. Not that he needed any—he clearly believed himself to be irresistible. And, judging by his hit rate with women, he was right.

He laughed softly. 'You need to relax. Clio has a party most weekends. You should come along next time.'

'Surely that would be up to Clio?' she said primly, and he smiled—a curling, mocking smile that made the hairs on the back of her neck stand up.

His eyes glittered. 'If I'm happy, she's happy.'

She gritted her teeth. Judging by the photos of supermodels with tear-stained faces, papped leaving his apartment, that clearly wasn't true. Not that it was any of her business, she thought quickly as the lift stopped.

There was a short hiss as the doors opened, and then, turning to face him, Nola lifted her chin. 'Thank you, but no. I never socialise with people at work. In my opinion, the disadvantages outweigh the benefits.'

His eyes inspected her lazily. 'Then maybe you should let me change your opinion. I can be very persuasive.'

Her stomach dipped, and something treacherously soft and warm slipped over her skin as his grey gaze rested on her face. When he looked at her like that it was hard not to feel persuaded.

She drew a breath. Hard, but not impossible.

'I don't doubt that. Unfortunately, though, I always put workplace considerations above everything else.'

And before he had a chance to respond she slipped through the doors, just before they slid shut.

Her heart was racing. Her legs felt weak. Any woman would have been tempted by such an invitation. But she had been telling the truth.

Since her disastrous relationship with Connor, she had made a decision and stuck to it. Her work life and her personal life were two separate, concurrent strands, and she never mixed the two. She would certainly never date anyone from work. Or go to a party with them.

Particularly if the invitation came from her boss.

Remembering the way his eyes had drifted appraisingly over her face, she shivered.

And most especially not if that boss was Ramsay Walker.

In business, he was heralded as a genius, and he was undeniably handsome and sexy. But Ramsay Walker was the definition of trouble.

Okay, she knew with absolute certainty that sex with him would be mind-blowing. How could it not be? The man was a force of nature made flesh and blood—the human personification of a hurricane or a tsunami. But that was why he was so dangerous. He might be powerful, intense, unstoppable, but he also left chaos and destruction behind him.

Even if she didn't believe all the stories in the media about his womanising, she had witnessed it with her own eyes. Ramsay clearly valued novelty and variety above all else. And, if that wasn't enough of a warning to stay well away, he'd also publicly and repeatedly stated his desire never to marry or have children.

Not that she was planning on doing either any time soon. She and her mother had done fine on their own, but getting involved on any level with a man who seemed so determinedly opposed to such basic human connections just wasn't an option. It had taken too long to restore her pride and build up a good reputation, to throw either away for a heartbreaking smile.

Three hours later, though, she was struggling to defend both.

In the RWI boardroom silence had fallen as the man at the head of the table leaned back in his chair, his casual stance at odds with the dark intensity of his gaze. A gaze that was currently locked on Nola's face.

'So let me get this right,' he observed softly. 'What

you're trying to say is that I'm being naive. Or complacent.'

A pulse of anger leapfrogged over his skin.

Did she *really* think she was going to get away with insulting him in his own boardroom? Ram thought, watching Nola blink, seeing anger, confusion and frustration colliding in those blue, blue eyes.

Eyes that made a man want to quench his thirst—and not for water. The same blue eyes that should have warned him to ignore her CV and glowing references and stick with men in grey suits who talked about algorithms and crypto-ransomware. But Nola Mason was not the kind of woman it was easy to ignore.

Refusing his invitation to meet at the office, she had insisted instead that they meet in some grimy café in downtown Sydney.

There, surrounded by surly teenagers in hoodies and bearded geeks, she had shown him just how easy it was to breach RWI's security. It had been an impressive display—unorthodox, but credible and provocative.

Only not as provocative as the sight of her long slim legs and rounded bottom in tight black jeans, or the strip of smooth bare stomach beneath her T-shirt that he'd glimpsed when she reached over to the next table for a napkin.

It wasn't love at first sight.

For starters, he didn't believe in love.

Only, watching her talk, he had been knocked sideways by lust, by curiosity, by the challenge in those blue eyes. By whatever it was that triggered sexual attraction between two people. It had been beyond his conscious control, and he'd had to struggle not to pull her across the table by the long dark hair spilling onto the shoulders of her battered leather jacket.

But it was the dark blue velvet ribbon tied around her throat that had goaded his senses to the point where he had thought he was going to black out.

Those eyes, that choker, had made up his mind. In other words, he'd let his libido hire her.

It was the first time he'd ever allowed lust to dictate a business decision. And it would be the last, he thought grimly, glancing once again at the tersely written email she had sent him that morning. He gritted his teeth. If Ms Nola Mason was expecting him to pay more, she could damn well sing for it.

Nola swallowed, shifting in her seat. Her heart was pounding, and she was struggling to stay calm beneath the battleship-grey of Ram's scrutiny. Most CEOs were exacting and autocratic, but cyber security was typically an area in which the boss was almost always willing to hand over leadership to an expert.

Only Ram was not a typical boss.

Right from that first interview it had been clear that not only was his reputation as the *enfant terrible* of the tech industry fully justified, but that, unusually, he could also demonstrate considerably more than a working knowledge of the latest big data technologies.

Truthfully, however, Ram's intelligence wasn't the only reason she found it so hard to confront him. His beauty, his innate self-confidence, and that still focus— the sense that he was watching her and only her—made her heart flip-flop against her ribs.

Her blue eyes flickered across the boardroom table to where he sat, lounging opposite her. It might be shallow, but who wouldn't be affected by such blatant perfection? And it didn't help that he appealed on so many different levels.

With grey eyes that seemed to lighten and darken in harmony with his moods, messy black hair, a straight nose, and a jaw permanently darkened with stubble, he might just as easily be a poet or a revolutionary as a CEO. And the hard definition of muscle beneath his gleaming white shirt only seemed to emphasise that contradiction even more.

Dragging her gaze back up to his face, Nola felt her nerves ball painfully. The tension in his jaw told her that she was balancing on eggshells. *Concentrate*, she told herself—surely she hadn't meant to imply that he was naive or complacent?

'No, that's not what I'm saying,' she said quickly, ignoring the faint sigh of relief that echoed round the table as she did so. She drew in a deep breath. 'What you're actually being is arrogant, and unreasonable.'

Somebody—she wasn't sure who—gave a small whimper.

For a fraction of a second Ram thought he might have misheard her. Nobody called him arrogant or unreasonable. But, glancing across at Nola, he knew immediately that he'd heard her correctly.

Her cheeks were flushed, but she was eyeing him steadily, and he felt a flicker of anger and something like admiration. She was brave—he'd give her that. And determined. He knew his reputation, and it had been well and truly earned. His negotiating skills were legendary, and his single-minded ruthlessness had turned a loan from his grandfather into a global brand.

A pulse began to beat in his groin. Normally she would be emptying her desk by now. Only the humming in his blood seemed to block out all rational thought so that he felt dazed, disorientated by her accusation. But why? What was it about this woman that made it so difficult for him to stay focused?

He didn't know. But whatever it was it had been instant and undeniable. When he'd walked into that coffee shop she had stood up, shaken his hand, and his body had reacted automatically—not just a spark but a fire starting in his blood and burning through his veins.

It had been devastating, unprecedented. At the time he'd assumed it was because she was so unlike any of the other women of his acquaintance. Women who would sacrifice anything and *anyone* to fit in, to make their lives smooth. Women who chose conformity and comfort over risk.

Nola took risks. That was obvious from the way she had dressed and behaved at her interview. He liked it that she broke the rules. Every single time he came into contact with her he liked it more—liked *her* more.

And she liked him too.

Only every single time she came into contact with him she gave him the brush-off. Or at least she tried too. But her eyes gave her away.

As though sensing his thoughts, Nola glanced up and looked away, her hand rising protectively to touch her throat. Instantly the pulse in his groin began to beat harder and faster.

He had never had to chase a woman before—let alone coax her into his bed. It was both maddening and unbelievably erotic.

At the thought of Nola in his bed, wearing nothing but that velvet choker, he felt a stab of sexual frustration so painful that he had to grip the arms of his chair to stop himself from groaning out loud.

'That's a pretty damning assessment, Ms Mason,' he said softly. 'Obviously if I thought you were being serious we'd be having a very different conversation. So I'm going to assume you're trying to shock me into changing my mind.'

Nola took a breath. Her insides felt tight and a prickling heat was spreading up her spine. Could everyone else in the room feel the tension between her and Ram? Or was it all in her head?

Stupid question. She knew it was real—and not just real. It was dangerous. Whatever this thing was between them, it was clearly hazardous—not only to her reason but to her instinct for self-preservation. Why else was she picking a fight with the boss in public?

Abruptly he leaned forward, and as their eyes met she shivered. His gaze was so intent that suddenly it felt as though they were alone, facing each other like two Western gunslingers in a saloon bar.

'Nice try! But I'm not that sensitive.'

Without warning the intensity faded from his handsome features and, glancing swiftly round the room, she knew her anger must look out of place—petulant, even. No doubt that had been his intention all along: to make her look emotional and unprofessional.

Gritting her teeth, she leaned back in her chair, trying to match his nonchalance.

Watching her fingers curl into a fist around her pen, Ram smiled slowly. 'I don't know whether to be disappointed or impressed by you, Ms Mason. It usually takes people a lot less than two months to realise I'm arrogant and unreasonable. However, they don't tend to say it to my face. Either way, though, I'm not inclined to change my mind. Or permit you to change yours. You see, I only have one thousand four hundred and forty minutes in any day, and I don't like to waste them on ill-thought-out negotiations like this one.'

Watching the flush of colour spread over her pale skin, he felt a stab of satisfaction. She had got under his skin; now he had not got under hers, And he was going to make sure it stung.

'I gave you a budget—a very generous budget—and I see no reason to increase it on the basis of some whim.'

Nola glared at him. 'This is not a whim, Mr Walker. It is a response to your email informing me that the software launch date has been brought forward by six weeks.'

Had he stuck to the original deadline, the new system would have been up and running for several months prior to the launch, giving her ample time to iron out any glitches. Now, though, the team she'd hired and trained for RWI would have to work longer hours to run all the necessary checks, and overtime meant more money.

Ram leaned forward. 'I run a business—a very successful one—that is currently paying your salary, and part of that success comes from knowing my market inside out. And this software needs to be on sale as soon as possible. And by "as soon as possible" I mean *now*.'

She blinked trying to break the spell of his eyes on hers and the small taunting smile on his lips.

Taking a breath, she steadied herself. 'I understand that. But *now* changes things. *Now* is expensive. But not nearly as expensive as it will be when your system gets hacked.'

'That sounds awfully like a threat, Ms Mason.'

She took another quick breath, her hand lifting instinctively to her throat. Feeling the blood pulsing beneath her fingertips, she straightened her spine.

'That's because it is. But better that it comes from me than them. Hackers break the rules, which means *I* have to break the rules. The difference is that I'm not about to steal or destroy or publicise your data. Nor am I going to extort money from you.'

'Not true.' The corner of his mouth lifted, as though she had made a joke, but there was no laughter in his eyes. 'Okay, you don't sneak in through the back door. You just give me one of those butter-wouldn't-melt-in-your-mouth smiles and put an invoice on my desk!'

'I can protect your company, Mr Walker. But I can't do that if my hands are tied behind my back.'

He tilted his head, his expression shifting, his dark gaze locking onto her face. 'Of course not. But, personally, I never let anyone tie me up unless we've decided on a safe word beforehand. Maybe you should do the same.'

There was some nervous laughter around the table. But before she could respond, he twisted in his seat and gestured vaguely towards the door.

'I need to have a private conversation with Ms Mason.'

Stomach churning, Nola watched as the men and women filed silently out of the room. Finally the door closed with a quiet click and she felt a ripple of apprehension slither over her skin as she waited for him to speak.

But he didn't say anything. Instead he simply stared out of the window at the blue sky, his face calm and untroubled.

Her heartbeat accelerated. *Damn him!* She knew he was making her wait, proving his power. If only she could tell him where to put his job. But this contract was not only paying her and Anna's wages, RWI was a global brand—a household name—and getting a good reference would propel their company, Cyber Angels, into the big time.

So, willing herself to stay cool-headed, she sat as the silence spread to the four corners of the room. Finally he pushed back his seat and stood up. Her pulse twitched in her throat as she watched him walk slowly around the table and come to a halt in front of her.

'You're costing me a great deal of money already. And now you're about to cost me a whole lot more.' He stared at her coolly. 'Are you sure there's nothing else you'd like, Nola? This table, perhaps? My car? Maybe the shirt off my back?'

He was looking for her to react. Which meant she should stay silent and seated. But it was the first time he had said her name, and hearing it spoken in that soft, sexy drawl caught her off guard.

She jerked to her feet, her body acting independently, tasting the sharp tang of adrenaline in her mouth.

Instantly she knew she'd made a mistake. She was close enough to reach out and touch that beautifully shaped mouth. In other words, too close. *Walk away*, she shouted silently. *Better still, run!* But for some reason her legs wouldn't do what her brain was suggesting.

Instead, she glowered at him, her blue eyes darkening with anger. 'Yes, that's right, Mr Walker. That's exactly what I want. The shirt off your back.'

But it wasn't. What she really wanted was to turn the tables. Goad him into losing control. Make him feel this same conflicted, confusing mass of fear and frustration and desire.

His fingers were hovering over the top button of his shirt, his eyes holding hers. 'You're sure about that?' he said softly.

The menacing undertone beneath the softness cut through her emotion and brought her to her senses.

At the other end of a table, surrounded by people, Ram Walker was disturbing, distracting. But up close and unchaperoned he was formidable.

And she was out of her depth.

Breathing in sharply, she shook her head, her pulse quickening with helpless anger as he gave her a small satisfied smile.

'And I thought you liked breaking the rules.'

His eyes gleamed and she knew he was goading her again, but she didn't care. Right now all she wanted was to be somewhere far away from this man who seemed to have the power to turn her inside out and off balance.

'Is there anything else you'd like to discuss?' he asked with an exaggerated politeness that seemed designed to test her self-control.

He waited until she shook her head, and then, turning, he walked towards the door.

'I'll speak to the accountants today.'

It was with relief bordering on delirium that she watched him leave the room.

Back in her office, she sat down behind her desk and let out a jagged breath.

Her hands were trembling and she felt hot and dizzy.

Leaning back in her chair, she picked up her notebook and a pencil. She knew it was anachronistic for a techie like herself to use pen and paper, but her mother had always used a notebook. Besides, it helped her clear her mind and unwind—and right now, with Ram Walker's goading words running on a loop round her head, she needed all the help she could get.

But she had barely flipped open her notebook when her phone buzzed. She hesitated before picking it up. If it was Ram, she was going to let it ring out. Her nerves were still jangling from their last encounter, and she couldn't face another head-to-head right now. But glancing at the screen, she felt a warm rush of happiness.

It was Anna.

A chat with her best friend would be the perfect antidote to that showdown with Ram.

'Hey, I wasn't expecting to hear from you. Why are you calling me? This is your honeymoon. Shouldn't you be gazing into Robbie's eyes, or writhing about with him on some idyllic beach?'

Hearing Anna's snort of laughter, she realised just how much she was missing her easy-going friend and business partner.

'I promise you, sex on the beach is overrated! Sand gets everywhere. And I mean *everywhere*.'

'Okay, too much information, Mrs Harris.' She began to doodle at the edges of the paper.

'Oh, Noles, you have no idea how weird it is to be Mrs Somebody, let alone Mrs Harris.'

'No idea at all! And planning to stay that way,' she said lightly.

Marriage had never been high on her to-do list. She was happy for Anna, of course. But her parents' divorce had left her wary of making vows and promises. And her disastrous relationship with Connor had only reinforced her instinctive distrust of the sort of trust and intimacy that marriage required.

Anna giggled. 'Every time anyone calls me that I keep thinking my mother-in-law's here. It's terrifying!'

She and Nola both burst out laughing.

'So why are you ringing me?' Nola said finally, when she could speak again.

'Well, we were at the pool, and Robbie got talking to this guy, and guess what? He's a neurosurgeon too. So you can imagine what happened next.'

Nola nodded. Anna's husband had recently been appointed as a consultant at one of Edinburgh's top teaching hospitals. He was as passionate about his work as he was about his new wife.

'Anyway, I left them yapping on about central core function and some new scanner, and that made me think of you, slogging away in Sydney all on your own. So I thought I'd give you a call and see how everything's going…'

Tucking the phone against her shoulder, Nola rolled her eyes. 'Everything's fine. There was a bit of a problem this morning, but nothing I couldn't handle.'

She paused, felt a betraying flush of colour spreading over her cheeks, and was grateful that Anna was on the end of a phone and not in the same room.

There was a short silence. Then, 'So, you and Ramsay Walker are getting on okay?'

Nola frowned.

'Yes…' She hesitated. 'Well, no. Not really. It's complicated. But it's okay,' she said quickly, as Anna made a noise somewhere between a wail and groan.

'I knew I should have postponed the honeymoon! Please tell me you haven't done anything stupid.'

Nola swallowed. She had—but thankfully only in the safe zone of her imagination.

'We had a few words about the budget, but I handled it and it's fine. I promise.'

'That's good.' She heard Anna breathe out. 'Look, Noles, I know you think he's arrogant and demanding—'

'It's not a matter of opinion, Anna. It's a fact. He *is* arrogant and demanding.'

And spoiled. How could he not be? He was the only son and heir to a fortune; his every whim had probably been indulged from birth. He might like to boast that he said no to almost everything, but she was willing to bet an entire year's salary that nobody had ever said no to him.

'I know,' her friend said soothingly. 'But for the next twenty-four hours he's still the boss. And if we get a good reference from him we'll basically be able to print money. We might even be able to pay off our loan.' She giggled. 'Besides, you have to admit that there are *some* perks working for him.'

'Anna Harris, you're a married woman. You shouldn't be having thoughts like that.'

'Why not? I love my Robbie, but Ram Walker is *gorgeous*.'

Laughing reluctantly, Nola shook her head. 'He is so not your type, Anna.'

'If you believe that you must have been looking too long into that big old Australian sun! He's *every* woman's type. As long as they're breathing.'

Opening her mouth, wanting to disagree, to deny what she knew to be true, Nola glanced down at her notepad, at the sketch she had made of Ram.

Who was she trying to kid?

'Fine. He's gorgeous. Happy now?'

But as she swung round in her seat her words froze on her lips, and Anna's response was lost beneath the sudden deafening beat of her heart.

Lounging in the open doorway, his muscular body draped against the frame, Ram Walker was watching her with a mocking gaze that told her he had clearly heard her last remark.

There was no choice but to front it out. Acknowledging his presence with a small, tight smile, she closed her notebook carefully and, as casually as she could manage, said, 'Okay, that all sounds fine. Send the data over as soon as possible and I'll take a look at it.'

Ignoring Anna's confused reply, she hung up.

Her heart was ricocheting against her ribs.

'Mr Walker. How can I help you?'

He stared at her calmly, his grey eyes holding her captive.

'Let's not worry about that now,' he said easily. 'Why don't we talk about how I can help *you*?'

She stared at him in silence. Where was this conversation going?

'I don't understand—*you* want to help *me*?'

'Of course. You're only with us one more day, and I want to make that time as productive as possible. Which is why I want you to have dinner with me this evening.'

'You mean tonight?'

Her voice sounded too high, and she felt her cheeks grow hot as he raised an eyebrow.

'Well, it can't be any other night,' he said slowly. 'You're flying home tomorrow, aren't you?'

Nola licked her lips nervously, a dizzying heat sliding over her skin. Dinner with her billionaire boss might sound like a dream date, but frankly it was a risk she wasn't prepared to take.

'That would be lovely. Obviously,' she lied. 'But I've

got a couple of meetings, and the one with the tactical team at five will probably overrun.'

He locked eyes with her.

'Oh, don't worry. I cancelled it.'

She gazed at him in disbelief, and then a ripple of anger flickered over her skin.

'You cancelled it?'

He nodded. 'It seemed easier. So is seven-thirty okay?'

'Okay?' she spluttered. 'No, it's *not* okay. You can't just march in and cancel my meetings for a dinner date.'

He raised an eyebrow and took a step backwards. 'Date? Is that why you're so flustered? I'm sorry to disappoint you, Ms Mason, but I'm afraid we won't be alone.'

His words made her heart hammer against her chest, and a hot flush of embarrassment swept across her face. She was suddenly so angry she wanted to scream.

'I don't want to be alone with you,' she snapped, her hands curling into fists. 'Why would I want that?'

He smiled at her mockingly. 'I suppose for the same reason as any other woman in your position. Sadly, though, I've invited some people I think you should meet. They'll be good for your business.'

She stared at him mutely, unable to think of anything to say that wouldn't result in her being fired on the spot.

His gaze shifted from her face to her fists, grey eyes gleaming like polished pewter.

'Nothing else to say? You disappoint me, Ms Mason! I was hoping for at least one devastating comeback. Okay, I'll pick you up from your hotel later. Be ready.

And don't worry about thanking me now. You can do that later too.'

'But I've got to pack!' she called after him, the bottleneck of words in her throat finally bursting.

But it was too late. He'd gone.

Staring after him, Nola felt a trickle of fury run down her spine. *Any other woman in your position.* How dared he lump her in with all his other wannabe conquests? He was impossible, overbearing and conceited.

But as a hot, swift shiver ran through her body she swore under her breath, for if that was true then why did he still affect her in this way?

Well, it was going to stop now.

Standing up, she stormed across her office and slammed the door.

Breathing out hard, she stared at her shaking hands. It felt good to give way to frustration and anger. But closing a door was easy. She had a horrible feeling that keeping Ram Walker out of her head, even when she was back in Scotland, was going to be a whole lot harder.

CHAPTER TWO

FROM HIS OFFICE on the twenty-second floor, Ram stared steadily out of the window at the Pacific Ocean. The calm expression on his face in no way reflected the turmoil inside his head.

Something was wrong. He looked down at the file he was supposed to be reading and frowned. For starters, he was sleeping badly, and he had a near permanent headache. But worst of all he was suffering from a frustrating and completely uncharacteristic inability to focus on what was important to him. His business.

Or it had been important to him right up until the moment he'd walked into that backstreet café and met Nola Mason.

A prickling tension slid down his spine and his chest squeezed tighter.

Down in the bay, a yacht cut smoothly through the waves. But for once his eyes didn't follow its progress. Instead it was the clear, sparkling blue of the water that drew his gaze.

His jaw tightened, pulling the skin across the high curves of his cheekbones.

Two months ago his life had been perfect. But one particular woman, whose eyes were the exact shade as the ocean, had turned that life upside down.

Nola.

He ran the syllables slowly over his tongue. Before he'd met her the name had simply been an acronym for New Orleans—or the Big Easy, as it was also known. His eyes narrowed. But any connection between Nola Mason and the city straddling the Mississippi ended there. Nola might be many things—sexy, smart and seriously good at her job. But she wasn't easy. In fact she was unique among women in that she seemed utterly impervious to his charms.

Thinking back to their conversation in the boardroom, remembering the way she had stood up to him in front of the directors, he felt the same mix of frustration, admiration and desire that seemed to define every single contact he had with her.

It was a mix of feelings that was entirely new to him.

Normally women tripped over themselves to please him. They certainly never kept him at arm's length, or spouted 'workplace considerations' as a reason for turning him down.

Turning him down! Even just thinking the words inside his head made him see every shade of red. Nobody had ever turned him down—in the boardroom *or* the bedroom.

He glanced down at the unread report, but there was no place to hide from the truth: despite the fact that his instincts were screaming at him to keep his distance, he couldn't stop thinking about Nola and her refusal to sleep with him. Her stupid, logical, perfectly justified refusal to break the rules. *Her* rules.

He closed the file with a snap. His rules too.

And that was what was really driving him crazy. The fact that up until a couple of months ago he would have agreed with her. Workplace relationships were a poisoned chalice. They caused tension and upset. And not once had he ever been tempted to break those rules and sleep with an employee.

Only Nola Mason was not just a temptation.

She was a virus in his blood.

No. His mouth twisted. She was more like malware in his system, stealthily undermining his strength, his stability, his sanity.

But there was a cure.

His groin hardened.

He knew what it was, and so did she.

He'd seen it in the antagonism flickering in those blue eyes, heard it in the huskiness of her voice. And her resistance, her refusal to acknowledge it was merely fuelling his desire. His anticipation of the moment when finally she surrendered to him.

He tossed the file onto his desk, feeling a pulsing, breathless excitement scrabbling up inside him.

Of course, being Nola, she would offer a truce, not a surrender. Those eyes, that mouth, might suggest an uninhibited sensuality, but he sensed that the determined slant of her chin was not just a pose adopted for business but a reflection of how she behaved out of work and in bed.

Picturing Nola, her blue eyes narrowing into fierce

slits as she straddled his naked body, he felt his spine melt into his chair. But truces could only happen if both parties came to the table—which was why he'd invited her to dinner. Not an intimate, candlelit tryst. He knew Nola, and she would have instantly rejected anything so blatant. But now she knew it was to be a business dinner at a crowded restaurant, she would relax—hell, they might even end up sharing a dessert.

His mouth curved up into a satisfied smile. Or, better still, they could save dessert until they got back to his penthouse.

So this was what it felt like to be famous, Nola thought as she walked self-consciously between the tables in the exclusive restaurant Ram had chosen. It was certainly an experience, although she wasn't sure it was one she'd ever want to repeat.

The Wool Shed was the hottest dining ticket in town, but even though it was midweek, and the award-winning restaurant was packed, to her astonishment Ram hadn't bothered to book. For any normal person that would have meant looking for somewhere else to eat. Clearly those rules didn't apply to Ram Walker, for now, within seconds of his arrival, the maître d' was leading them to a table with a view across the bay to the Opera House.

'I think I may have told our guests that dinner was at eight, so it's going to be just the two of us for a bit. Sorry about that.'

Nola stared at him warily. He didn't sound sorry; he sounded completely unrepentant. Meeting his gaze, she saw that he didn't look sorry either. In fact, he seemed to be enjoying the uneasiness that was clearly written all over her face.

Sliding into the seat he'd pulled out, Nola breathed out carefully. 'That's fine. It'll give you a chance to brief me on our mystery guests.'

She felt him smile behind her. 'Of course—and don't worry, your chaperones will arrive very soon. I promise.'

Gritting her teeth, she watched him drop gracefully into the chair beside her. At work it had been easy to tell herself that the tension between them was just some kind of personality clash or a battle of wills. Now, though, she could see that ever since she'd met Ram that first time, the battle had been raging inside her.

A battle between her brain and her body...between common sense and her basest carnal urges. And, much as she would have liked to deny it, or pretend it wasn't true, the sexual pull between them was as real and tangible as the bottles of still and sparkling water on the table. So much so that only by pressing her fingers into the armrests of her chair could she stop herself from reaching out to touch the smooth curve of his jaw.

Her hand twitched. It was like trying to ignore a mosquito bite. The urge to scratch was overwhelming.

But surely walking into this restaurant with him was just what she'd needed to remind her why it was best not to give in to that urge—for Ram wasn't just her boss. He was way out of her league.

In a room filled with beautiful people, he was the unashamed focus of every eye. As he'd strolled casually to their table conversations had dwindled and even the waiters had seemed to freeze; it had been as though everyone in the restaurant had taken a sort of communal breath.

And it was easy to see why.

Glancing up, she felt a jolt of hunger spike inside her.

There was something about him that commanded attention. Of course he looked amazing—each feature, from his long dark eyelashes to the tiny scar on his cheekbone, looked as though it had been lovingly executed by an artist. But it wasn't just his dark, sculpted looks that tugged at the senses. He had a quality of certainty that was unique, compelling, irresistible.

He was the ultimate cool boy at school, she decided. And now he was sitting next to her, his arm resting casually over the back of her chair, the scent of his cologne making a dizzy heat spread over her skin.

Unable to stop herself, she glanced sideways and felt her breath catch in her throat.

He was just too ridiculously beautiful.

As though sensing her focus, he turned, and the air was punched out of her lungs as his dark grey gaze scanned her face.

'What's the matter?'

'Nothing,' she lied. 'Are you going to tell me who we're meeting?' She tried to arrange her expression into that same mix of casual and professional that he projected so effortlessly. 'Are they local?'

'They're a little bigger than just Australia. It's Craig Aldin and Will Fraser. They own—'

'A&F Freight,' she finished his sentence. 'That's the—'

'The biggest logistics company in the southern hemisphere.'

His eyes glittered as he in turn finished *her* sentence, a hint of a smile tugging at his mouth. 'Maybe we should try ordering dinner this way. It would be like a new game: gastronomic consequences.'

She tried not to respond to that smile, but it was like trying to resist gravity.

'It could be fun,' she said cautiously. 'Although we might end up with some challenging flavour combinations.'

His eyes didn't leave her face. 'Well, I've never been that vanilla in my tastes,' he said softly.

Her heart banged against her ribs like a bird hitting a window. There it was again—that spark of danger and desire, her flint striking his steel.

But as he picked up the water bottle and filled her glass she bit her lip, felt a knot forming in her stomach. Flirting with Ram in this crowded restaurant might feel safe. Playing with fire, however, was never a good idea—and especially not with a man who was as experienced and careless with women as he was.

She needed to remember that the next time he made her breath jerk in her throat, but right now she needed to dampen that flame and steer the conversation back to work.

'Is A&F looking to upgrade its system?' she asked quickly, ignoring the mocking gleam in his eyes.

Ram stared at her for a moment and then shrugged.

It was the same every time. Back and forth. Gaining her trust, then losing it again. Like trying to stroke a feral cat. Just as he thought he was close enough to touch, she'd retreat. It was driving him mad.

He shifted in his seat, wishing he could shift the ache inside his body. If he couldn't persuade her to relax soon he was going to do himself some permanent damage.

His eyes drifted lazily over her body. In that cream blouse, dark skirt and stockings, and with those blue eyes watching him warily across the table, she looked more like a sleek Siamese than the feisty street cat she'd been channelling in their meeting that morning.

'Yes—and soon. That's why I want you to meet with them today.'

As he put the bottle back on the table his hand brushed against hers, and suddenly she was struggling to remember what he'd just said, let alone figure out how to reply.

'Thank you,' she said finally.

His expression was neutral. 'Of course it might mean coming back to Australia.'

Frowning, she looked into his face. 'That won't be a problem.'

'Really? It's just that you live on the other side of the world. I thought you might have somebody missing you. Someone significant.'

Nola blinked. How had they ended up talking about this? About her private life.

Ram Walker was too damn sharp for his own good. He made connections that were barely visible while she was still struggling to join the dots.

His gaze was so intense that suddenly she wanted to lift her hand and shield her face. But instead she thought about her flat, with its high ceilings and shabby old sofas. It was her home, and she loved it, but it wasn't a *somebody*. Truthfully, there hadn't been anyone in her life since Connor.

Her throat tightened. Connor—with his sweet face and his floppy hair. And his desire to be liked. A desire that had meant betraying her trust in the most humiliating way possible. He hadn't quite matched up to her father's level of unreliability, but then, he'd only been in her life a matter of months.

Of course since their break-up she hadn't taken a vow of celibacy. She'd gone out with a couple of men on more than a couple of dates and they'd been pleasant enough. But none had been memorable, and right now the only significant living thing in her flat was a cactus called Colin.

She shook her head. 'No,' she said at last. 'Anna's the home bird. I've no desire to tie myself down any time soon. I like my independence too much.'

Ram nodded. Letting his gaze wander over her face, he took in the flushed cheeks and the dilated pupils and felt a tug down low in his stomach. A pulse of heat flickered beneath his skin.

Independence. The word tasted sweet and dark and glossy in his mouth—like a cherry bursting against his tongue. At that moment, had he believed in soulmates, he would have thought he'd found his. For here was a woman who was not afraid to be herself. To stand alone in the world.

His heart was pounding. He wanted her more than he'd ever wanted anyone—anything. If only he could reach over and pull her against him, strip her naked and take her right here, right now—

But instead a waiter brought over some bread and, grateful for the nudge back to reality, Ram leaned back in his chair, trying to school his thoughts, his breathing, his body, into some sort of order.

'She's impressive, your partner,' he said, when finally the waiter left them alone.

He watched her face soften, the blue eyes widen with affection, and suddenly he wondered how it would feel to be the object of that incredible gaze. For someone to care that much about him.

The idea made him feel strangely vulnerable and, picking up his glass, he downed his water so that it hit his stomach with a thump.

She nodded eagerly. 'She was always top of the class.'

He nodded. 'I can believe that. But I wasn't talking about her tech skills. It's her attitude that's her real strength. She's pragmatic; she understands the value of compromise. Whereas you...'

He paused, and Nola felt her skin tighten. That was Anna in a nutshell. But how could Ram know that? They'd only met once, when they'd signed the contracts.

And then her muscles tensed, her body squirming with nerves at what he might be about to reveal about her.

'You, on the other hand, are a rebel.'

Reaching out, he ran his hand lightly over her sleeve and she felt a thrill like the jolt of electricity. This wasn't like any conversation she'd ever had. It was more like a dance—a dazzling dance with quick, complicated steps that only they understood.

She swallowed. 'What kind of rebel works *for* the system?'

Beneath the lights, his eyes gleamed like brushed steel. 'You might look corporate on the outside, but if I scratched the surface I'd find a hacker beneath. Unlike your partner—unlike most people, really—you like to cross boundaries, take risks. You're not motivated by money; you like the challenge.'

The hum of chatter and laughter faded around them and a pulse began to beat loudly inside her head. Reaching forward to pick up her glass, she cleared her throat with difficulty.

'You're making me sound a lot edgier than I am,' she said quickly. 'I'm actually just a "white hat".'

'Of course you are!'

Ram shifted in his seat, his thigh brushing against her leg so that her hand twitched around the stem of the glass. It was a gambler's tell—a tiny, visible sign of the tension throbbing between them.

'It's not like I'd ever catch you hanging out in some grimy internet café with a bunch of wannabe anarchists.'

He lounged back in his seat, one eyebrow lifted, challenging her to contradict him.

Remembering their first meeting, Nola felt her heart beat faster, her stomach giving way to that familiar mix of apprehension and fascination, the sense that there was something pulling them inexorably closer.

But even as she felt her skin grow warm his teasing

words stirred something inside her. Suddenly the desire to tease him back was overwhelming—to put the heat on *him*, to watch those grey eyes turn molten.

'Actually, wannabe anarchists are usually pretty harmless—like sheep. It's the wolf in sheep's clothing you need to worry about.'

She kept her expression innocent, but heat cascaded down through her belly as his gaze locked onto hers with the intensity of a tractor beam. A small, urgent voice in the back of her head was warning her to back down, to stop playing Russian roulette with the man who'd loaded the gun she was holding to her head.

But then suddenly he smiled, and just like that nothing seemed to matter except being the focus of his undivided attention. It was easy to forget he was self-serving and arrogant...easy to believe that breaking the rules—*her* rules—wouldn't matter just this once.

Her heart began to beat faster.

Except she knew from experience that it *would* matter. And that smile wasn't a challenge. It was a warning—a red light flashing. *Danger! Keep away!*

Breathing in, she gave him a quick, neutral smile of her own. 'Now, this menu!' Holding her smile in place, she forced a casual note into her voice. 'My French is pretty non-existent, so I might need a little help ordering.'

'Don't worry. I speak it fluently.'

'You do?' She gazed at him, torn between disbelief and wonder.

He shrugged. 'My mother always wanted to live in Paris, but it didn't work out. So she sent me to school there.'

Nola frowned. 'Paris! You mean Paris in France?'

'I don't think they speak French in Paris, Texas.'

His face was expressionless. but there was a tension in his shoulders that hadn't been there before.

Her eyes met his, then bounced away. 'That's such a long way from here,' she said slowly.

'I suppose it is.'

Her pulse twitched.

It would have been easy to take his reply at face value, as just another of those glib, offhand remarks people made to keep a conversation running smoothly.

But something had shifted in his voice—or rather left it. The teasing warmth had gone, had been replaced by something cool and dismissive that pricked her skin like the sting of a wasp.

It was her cue to back off—and maybe she would have done so an hour earlier. But this was the first piece of personal information he had ever shared with her.

She cleared her throat. 'So how old were you?'

Along the back of her seat, she could feel the muscles in his arm tensing.

'Seven.' He gazed at her steadily. 'It was a good school. I had a great education there.'

She knew her face had stiffened into some kind of answering smile—she just hoped it looked more convincing than it felt. Nodding, she said quickly, 'I'm sure. And learning another language is such an opportunity.'

'It has its uses.' He spoke tonelessly. 'But I wasn't talking about speaking French. Being away taught me to rely on myself. To trust my own judgement. Great life lessons—and brilliant for business.'

Did he ever think of anything else? Nola wondered. Surely he must have been homesick or lonely? But the expression on his face made it clear that it was definitely time to change the subject.

Glancing down at her menu again, she said quickly, 'So, what do you recommend?'

'That depends on what you like to eat.'

Looking up, she saw with relief that the tightness in his face had eased.

'The fish is great here, and they do fantastic steaks.' He frowned. 'I forgot to ask. You do eat meat?'

She nodded.

'And no allergies?'

His words were innocent enough, but there was a lazy undercurrent in his voice that made the palms of her hands grow damp, and her heart gave a thump as his eyes settled on her face.

'Apart from to me, I mean...'

Her insides tightened, and a prickling heat spread over her cheeks and throat as she gave him a small, tight, polite smile.

'I'm not allergic to you, Mr Walker.' She bit her lip, her eyes meeting his. 'For a start, allergies tend to be involuntary.'

'Oh, I see. So you're *choosing* to ignore this thing between us?'

She swallowed, unable to look away from his dark, mocking gaze.

'If by "ignore" you mean not behave in an unprofessional and inappropriate manner, then, yes, I am,' she said crisply.

He studied her face in silence, and as she gazed into his flawless features a tingling heat seeped through her limbs, cocooning her body so she felt drowsy and blurred around the edges.

'So you do admit that there is something between us?'

His words sent a pulse up her spine, bringing her to her senses instantly, and she felt a rush of adrenaline. Damn him! She was in security. It was her job to keep out unwanted intruders, to keep important data secret. So why was it that she fell into each and every one of his traps with such humiliating ease?

She wasn't even sure how he did it. No one else had ever managed to get under her skin so easily. But he seemed not only able to read her mind, but to turn her inside out so that she had nowhere to hide. It made her feel raw, flayed, vulnerable.

Remembering the last time she had felt so vulnerable, she shivered. Connor's betrayal still had the power to hurt. But, even though she knew now that it was her ego not her heart that he'd damaged, no good was going to come of confessing any of that to Ram—a man who had zero interest in emotions, his own and other people's.

And that was why this conversation was going to stop.

Lifting her chin, she met his gaze with what she hoped was an expression of cool composure.

'I don't think a business meeting is really the right time to have this particular conversation,' she said coolly. 'But, as you have a girlfriend, I'm not sure when or where *would* be right.'

'Girlfriend?' He seemed genuinely surprised. 'If you mean Clio, then, yes, she's female. But "girlfriend"? That would be stretching it. And don't look so out-raged. She knows exactly what's on offer, and she's grateful to take it.'

She stared at him in disbelief. 'Grateful! For what? For being fortunate enough to have sex with the great Ramsay Walker?'

'In a nutshell.'

He seemed amused rather than annoyed.

'You surprise me, Ms Mason. Given the nature of your job, I thought you of all people would know that it pays to look beneath the surface.' His eyes gleamed. 'You really shouldn't believe everything you read on the internet.'

A quivering irritation flickered through her brain, like static on the radio.

'Is that right? So, for example, all those times you're meant to have said you don't want to get married or have children—that was all lies? You were misquoted?'

Ram stared past her, felt the breath whipping out of him. Used to women who sought to soothe and seduce, he felt her directness like a rogue wave, punching him off his feet. Who did she think she was, to question him like this? To put him, his life, under a spotlight?

But beneath his exasperation he could feel his body responding to the heat sparking in her eyes.

Ignoring his uneven heartbeat, he met her furious blue gaze. 'I'm not in the business of explaining myself, Ms Mason. But this one time I'll answer your question.

I wasn't misquoted. Everything I said was and is true. I have no desire whatsoever to marry or have children.'

That was an understatement. Marriage had never been a priority for him. Parenthood even less so. And for good reason. Both might appear to offer security and satisfaction, but it had been a long time since he'd believed in the myths they promised.

Out in the bay, the Opera House was lit up, its sails gleaming ghost-white. But it was the darkness that drew his gaze. For a moment he let it blot out the twisting mass of feelings that were rising up inside him, unbidden and unwelcome.

Commitment came at a cost, and he knew that the debt would never be paid. A wife and a child were a burden—a responsibility he simply didn't want. Had never once wanted.

And he didn't intend to start now.

Leaning back in his chair, he shrugged. 'Marriage and parenthood are just a Mobius strip of emotional scenes that quite frankly I can do without. I'm sorry if that offends your romantic sensibilities, Ms Mason, but that's how I choose to live my life.'

There was a moment of absolute silence.

Nola drew a breath. By 'romantic', he clearly meant deluded, soppy and hopelessly outdated. It was also obvious that he thought her resistance to him was driven not by logic but by a desire for something more meaningful than passion.

She felt a pulse of anger beneath her skin. Maybe it was time to disabuse him of that belief.

Eyes narrowing, she stared at him coldly. 'Sorry to

disillusion you, Mr Walker, but I don't have any "romantic sensibilities". I don't crave a white wedding. Nor am I hunting for a husband to make my life complete. So if I actually had an opinion on how you live your life it would be that I have no problem with it at all.'

His watched—no—*inspected* her in silence, so that the air seemed to swell painfully in her lungs.

'But you do have a problem...' He paused, and the intent expression on his face made her insides tighten and her throat grow dry and scratchy. 'You think I say something different in private to the women you refer to as my "girlfriends".'

He shook his head slowly. 'Then it's my turn to disillusion you. I don't make false promises. Why would I? It's not as if I need to. I always get exactly what I want in the end.'

She shook her head. 'You're so arrogant.'

'I'm being honest. Isn't that what you wanted from me?'

'I don't want anything from you,' she said hoarsely, trying to ignore the heat scalding her skin, 'except a salary and a reference. I certainly have no interest in being some accessory to your louche lifestyle.'

Watching his mouth curl into a slow, sexy smile, she felt her stomach drop as though the legs of her chair had snapped.

'So why are you blushing?' he asked softly. 'Surely not because of my "louche lifestyle". I thought you were more open-minded than that.'

She glowered at him.

'I'm as open-minded as the next woman. But not if

it means being a part of your harem. That's never been one of my fantasies.'

'Sadly, I'm going to have to put your fantasies on hold,' he said softly, raising his hand in a gesture of greeting to the two tall blond men who were weaving their way towards them. 'Our guests are here. But maybe we could discuss them after dinner?'

'I think that's the first time I've seen you relax since you arrived.'

Glancing up at Ram, Nola frowned.

Dinner was over, and his limo had dropped them back at the RWI building. Now they were standing in the lift.

Like many of his remarks, it could be read in so many ways. But she was too tired to do anything but take it at face value.

'It was fun,' she said simply. 'I enjoyed the food and the company.'

He did a mock stagger. 'I'm flattered.'

Glancing up, she saw that he was smiling, and she felt a panicky rush of nerves. In daylight, Ram Walker was flawless but unattainable. Now it was night-time, and beneath the low lighting, with his top button undone and a shadow of stubble grazing his face, he looked like the perfect after-dark female fantasy.

But the point about fantasies was that they were never supposed to become reality, she told herself quickly.

Shaking her head, she gave him a small, careful smile. 'I suppose it hasn't occurred to you that I might be talking about Craig and Will?'

His eyes gleamed. 'Nope.'

She swallowed. 'They're nice people.'

'And I'm not?'

Her throat felt as though it was closing up. And, was it her imagination, or was the lift getting smaller and hotter?

'You can be,' she said cautiously. She felt her pulse twitch beneath his gaze. 'But I don't know you very well. We don't know each other very well.'

Suddenly she was struggling to breathe, and her heart was beating very fast.

He smiled. 'Oh, I think we know each other very well, Nola!'

Her stomach dropped as though the lift cable had suddenly snapped, and somewhere at the edge of her vision stars were flickering—only that couldn't be right for they weren't outside.

'And I think you're a lot like me,' he said softly. 'You're focused, and determined, and you like breaking the rules. Even when you're scared of the consequences.'

There was a tiny shift in the air...softer than a sigh.

She watched, dry-mouthed, her stomach twisting into knots as he reached out and ran his finger along her cheekbone. She could feel her heartbeat echoing inside her head like footsteps fleeing. As she should be.

Except that she couldn't move—could hardly breathe.

He moved closer, sliding his hand through her hair.

'When I met you in that café you took my breath away. You still do.'

There was silence as she struggled to speak, struggled against the ridiculous pleasure his words provoked. Pleasure she knew she shouldn't acknowledge, let alone feel. Not for her boss anyway.

But maybe she was making too big a deal about that. He might be a CEO, but he was just a man, and as a woman she was his equal. Besides, as of tomorrow he wouldn't even be her boss.

The thought jumped inside her head like popping candy, and then somehow her hand was on his arm, the magnetic pull between them impossible to resist.

'Ram...' She whispered his name and he stared down at her mutely. His eyes were dark and fierce, and she could see that he was struggling for control.

She felt a shiver of panic tumble down her spine.

But why?

What did she care if he was struggling? So was she. Like her, he was fighting himself—fighting this desire.

Desire.

The word jangled inside her head like a warning bell, for was desire a big enough reason to play truth or dare with this man? After all, she knew the risks, knew the consequences.

Her head was spinning. Memories of that first kiss with Connor were slip-sliding into an image of his face, resentful and distant, on that last day.

But there was no reason it would be the same with Ram.

Nola knew she had been reckless with Connor—clueless, really. She'd jumped off the highest board and hoped for what? Love? A soulmate? A future? But *this* was never going to be anything but lust. There was no expectation. No need to make promises.

And, most importantly, there would be no consequences. After tomorrow they would never see one another again. It would be a perfect moment of pure passion. So why shouldn't she give in to it?

But even as the question formed in her mind she knew two things. One, it was purely rhetorical. And two, it was too late.

The warmth of his body had melted away the last of her resistance; the battle was already lost.

And, as though he could read her mind, Ram leaned forward and kissed her.

Groaning softly, he reached out blindly for the wall of the lift, trying to steady himself. He'd expected to feel something—hell, how could he not after the tension that had been building between them for weeks?—but the touch of her lips on his was like being knocked sideways by a rogue wave.

His head was spinning. Somewhere, the world was still turning, but it didn't matter. All that mattered was here and now and Nola. Her body was melting into him, moving as he moved, her breath and his breath were one and the same. He felt her lips part and, deepening the kiss, he pulled her closer.

As the doors opened he pulled her against him and out of the lift. Hands sliding over each other, they staggered backwards, drunkenly banging into walls, barely noticing the impact. Somehow they reached his office, and as he pushed open the door they stumbled into the room as one.

Nola reached out for him, her fingers clutching the front of his shirt. He could feel her heart pounding, hear her breath coming in gasps. She pulled him closer and, groaning softly, he wrapped his fingers around hers and dragged her arms behind her back, holding her captive.

Ram shuddered. His heart was pounding so hard he thought it might burst and, reaching down, he jerked her closer, crushing her body against his. But it wasn't enough. He wanted more. Breathing out shakily, he nudged her backwards, guiding her towards the sofa.

As they slid onto the cushions he dragged his mouth from hers and she gazed up at him, her eyes huge and dazed.

His breath caught in his throat. He wanted her so badly, but he needed to know that she wanted what *he* wanted—what he could give.

'I don't do for ever. Or happy-ever-after. This is about now. About you and me. If you're hoping for something more than that—'

In answer, she looped her arm about his neck, gripping him tightly. 'Stop talking and kiss me,' she whispered, her fingers tugging at his arms, his shirt, his belt.

He knew that relief must be showing on his face, but for once he didn't care that he'd shown his true feelings. She had said what he wanted to hear and, lowering his mouth, he kissed her fiercely. As her lips parted he caught hold of the front of her blouse and tugged it loose.

Instantly he felt his groin harden. For a moment his eyes fed hungrily on the soft, pale curve of her stomach, and the small rounded breasts in the black lace bra.

She was beautiful—every bit as beautiful as he'd imagined.

And he couldn't wait a moment longer.

Leaning forward, he fumbled with the fastening of her bra and it was gone. Then he lowered his mouth to her bare breast, feeling the nipple harden beneath his tongue.

Nola whimpered. His tongue was pulling her upwards. She felt as if she was floating; her blood was lighter than air.

Helplessly, she let her head fall back, arching her spine so that her hips were pressing against his thighs. Her head was spinning, her body so hot and tight with need that she hardly knew who she was. All she knew was that she wanted him—wanted to feel him on her and in her.

She couldn't fight it anymore—couldn't fight herself.

Desperately she squirmed beneath him, freeing him with her fingers. She heard him groan, then a choking sound deep in his throat as she slid her hand around his erection.

For a moment he steadied himself above her, the muscles of his arms straining to hold his weight, his beautiful clean profile tensing with the effort.

Breathing out unsteadily, he gazed down at her. 'What about—?' he began. 'Are you protected?'

Nola gazed at him feverishly. She didn't want to talk. Didn't want anything to come between them—and, besides, there was no need.

'It's fine,' she whispered.

His eyes flared, his expression shifting, his face

growing tauter as slowly he pushed the hem of her skirt up around her hips. She shivered, the sudden rush of air cooling her overheated skin, and then she breathed in sharply as he pressed the palm of his hand against the liquid ache between her thighs.

Helplessly, eagerly, she pressed back, and then suddenly he pulled her mouth up to meet his and pushed into her.

His fingers were bumping over her ribcage, his touch making her heartbeat stagger. She reached up, sliding her hand through his hair, scraping his scalp. The ache inside her was beating harder and faster and louder, the urge to pull him closer and deeper overwhelming her so that suddenly she was moving desperately, reaching for him, pressing against him.

She felt a sting of ecstasy—a white heat spreading out like a supernova—and then she arched against him, her breath shuddering in her throat. As her muscles spasmed around him he groaned her name and tensed, filling her completely.

CHAPTER THREE

Nola woke with a start.

For a moment she lay in the darkness, her brain still only on pilot light, wondering what had woken her. Almost immediately the warmth of her bed began tugging her back towards sleep and, stifling a yawn, she wriggled drowsily against the source of the heat.

And froze.

Not just her body, but her blood, her heartbeat. Even the breath in her throat hardened like ice, so that suddenly she was rigid—like a tightrope walker who'd just looked down beyond the rope.

Head spinning, she slid her hand tentatively over her thigh and touched the solid, sleeping form of Ram. As her fingers brushed against him she felt him stir and shift closer, his arm curving over her waist, and instantly she was completely, fiercely awake.

Around her the air stilled and the darkness closed in on her. Someone—Ram?—had turned off the lights in the office. Or maybe they just switched off automatically. But her eyes were adjusting now, and she could just make out the solid bulk of his desk. And strewn across the floor, distorted into strange, unfamiliar shapes, were their discarded clothes.

Picturing how they had torn them off in their hurry to feel each other's naked skin, she felt her cheeks grow hot and she blew out a breath.

Finally they'd done it. They'd had sex.

Her skin tightened in the darkness, her heartbeat fluttering, as a smile pulled at her mouth.

Sex! That made it sound so ordinary, or mechanical. But it had been anything but that.

Beside her, Ram shifted in his sleep, and the damp warmth of his body sent a tremor of hot, panicky excitement over her skin.

Remembering his fierce, hard mouth on hers, his hands roaming at will over her aching, desperate body, she pressed her hand against her lips, her stomach flip-flopping as she felt the slight puffiness where he'd kissed her again and again.

She'd expected the sex to be incredible. But now, with his hard, muscular arm curled possessively around her waist, and her body still throbbing from the frenzied release of their lovemaking, she knew that what she and Ram had shared had been more than incredible.

It had been—she searched for a word—it had been *transformative*. Beautiful and wild and breathless, flaring up like a forest fire, so hot and fast that it had consumed everything in its path straight to the sea.

And then afterwards calm, a peace such as she had never known. Just the two of them glowing in each other's arms, spent, sated, their bodies seeping into one another.

It had felt so right. *He'd* felt so right.

She shivered again. Ram had been the lover she'd imagined but never expected to meet in real life. Intuitive, generous, his touch had been a masterclass in power and precision.

He had demanded more from her than she had been willing to give, but she had yielded, for it had been impossible to resist the strength of her desire. The intensity of his.

Over and over he had pulled her against him, touching her, finding the place where liquid heat gathered, using his lips, his hands, his body to stir and torment her until the blood had beaten inside her so hard and so fast she'd thought she would pass out. She had been frantic and feverish—hadn't known who or where she was. Her entire being—every thought, every beat of her heart—had been concentrated on him, on his mouth, his body, his fingertips…

A memory of exactly what he'd done with those fingers dropped into her head and she squirmed, pressing her thighs together.

She couldn't understand why she was feeling this way. Why she had responded so strongly to a man she barely knew and didn't even really like.

She'd loved Connor—or at least she'd thought she had—yet sex with him had only ever been satisfying. Whereas with Ram it had been sublime.

It made no sense.

But then, nothing she'd thought, said or done in the last twenty-four hours had even come close to making sense. Not least sleeping with the man who, for the next twelve hours or so, was still her boss.

Her breath felt thick and scratchy in her throat.

Oh, she knew why she'd done it.

Ram Walker was not your average man. Even just being in his orbit made her feel as if someone had handed her the keys to a top-spec sports car and told her to put her foot down. He was exhilarating, irresistible.

But she knew from sleeping with Connor that giving in to temptation had consequences. Messy, unexpected and painful consequences. And so she'd waited until now, until the day before her contract ended, to give in, believing that she was being smart.

Believing it would just be one perfect night of pure pleasure.

Her skin grew hot, then cold.

She'd thought it would be so easy. Not just the sex, but the aftermath. Maybe there might be a few awkward moments. But surely nothing too dramatic or life-changing. After all, she barely knew Ram.

It had never once crossed her mind that she would feel this way—so moved, so alive.

She'd thought once would be enough. That her body would be satisfied and she could forget him and move on.

She almost laughed out loud.

Forget him!

As if she could ever forget him.

Right now, there was only him.

It was as though he'd wiped her mind—erased every memory and experience she'd ever had. And it wasn't only the past he'd obliterated. Her future would never be the same now either. How could it be after last night? She might not have a crystal ball, but she didn't need one to know that sex was never going to be as good with any other man.

But what if today was the last time she ever saw Ram?

Was she really that naive? So stupid as to imagine they were done? That she could put last night in a box, wrap it up neatly with a bow and that would be it.

Her pulse began to race.

Since breaking up with Connor she'd been so careful. She'd had a couple of short relationships, but at the first hint of anything serious she had broken them off. It had seemed safer, given her bad luck when it came to men. Or was it bad judgement?

Her father, Richard, had been charming—financially generous. But even before her parents' divorce he had been unreliable—often disappearing without explanation, and always utterly incapable of remembering anything to do with his wife and daughter, from birthdays to parents' evenings.

Then she'd met Connor—sweet, funny Connor— who had cared about everything from saving the planet to the trainers he wore. Miraculously, he had cared about her too, so she'd thought it would be different with him.

And it had been—for a time.

Until he'd betrayed her trust...shared the most private details of their life together over a pint in the pub. And then not even stepped up to defend her reputation.

She almost laughed, but felt more as if she was about to cry.

Her reputation.

It made her sound like some foolish eighteenth-century heroine who'd let the wrong man pick up her fan. But that was what she'd felt like. Foolish and powerless. And the fact that her supposed boyfriend had sacrificed her to impress his mates still had the power to make her curl up inside with misery.

Breathing out silently, she closed her eyes.

She'd vowed never again to trust her judgement. And with Ram she hadn't needed to. Her opinion of him was irrelevant; the facts spoke for themselves.

Even before they'd met in that café in Sydney she'd known his reputation as a ruthless womaniser. Yet she'd still gone ahead and slept with him.

And why?

Because she'd become complacent.

She'd assumed, like last time, that the worst-case scenario would be the two of them having to work in the same building. Now, though, she could see that geography didn't matter, and that the worst-case scenario was happening inside her head. And it was all to do with *him*, and how he'd made her feel.

But she couldn't think about this anymore. Not with his body so warm and solid beside her.

Her breathing faltered.

It was time to leave.

Moving carefully, so as not to wake him, she slid out from beneath his arm and began groping in the darkness for her discarded bra and shoes. Her bag was harder to find, but finally she located it by one of the armchairs.

Clutching her blouse in one hand, she tiptoed to the door and gently pushed down the handle. There was a tiny but unmistakable click and she held her breath. But there was no sound from within the darkened office and slowly, carefully, she pulled open the door and slid through it into the empty corridor.

As she waited for the lift her heartbeat sounded like raindrops on a tin roof. Every second felt like a day, and she couldn't shift the feeling that at any moment she would hear Ram's voice or his footsteps in the darkness.

Pressing her forehead against the wall, she breathed out slowly. She should be feeling relief, and in some ways she was, for now she wouldn't have to go through that horrific about-last-night conversation, or the alternative—the awkward let's-pretend-it-never-happened version.

But she couldn't help feeling that somehow she was making a mistake. That what had happened between them had been so rare, so right, that she shouldn't just walk away from it.

She turned and gazed hesitantly down the darkened corridor.

Was she doing the right thing?

Or was she about to do something she'd regret?

But what would happen if she stayed?

Her heart was racing like a steeplechaser. What should she do?

She needed help. Fifty/fifty? Ask the audience?

She felt a rush of relief.

Phone a friend.

Stepping into the lift, she pulled out her mobile. It was four in the morning here, which made it two in the afternoon in Barbados. She would let it ring three times and then hang up.

Anna picked up on the second ring.

'Hi, you. This is a surprise…'

She paused, and for a moment Nola could almost picture her friend's face, the slight furrow between her eyes as she mentally calculated the time difference between the Caribbean and Australia.

'Have you been pulling an all-nighter or did you just randomly get up to watch the sunrise?'

Anna's voice was as calm as ever, but there was a brightness to it that Nola recognised as concern. And, despite everything, that made her feel calmer.

She swallowed. 'Neither. Look, I'm not hurt or anything, but…' She breathed out slowly. 'I've just done something really stupid. At least I think it was really stupid.'

There was the shortest of silences, and then Anna said firmly, 'In that case I'll get Robbie to make me a Rum Punch and you can tell me all about it.'

It was not the daylight creeping into his office that woke Ram. Nor was it the faint but aggravating hum of some kind of machinery. It was Nola.

Or rather the fact—the quite incredible fact—that at some unspecified point in the night she had gone.

Left.

Done a runner.

Hightailed it.

He felt a sudden sharp, inexplicable spasm of...of what? Irritation? Outrage? Disappointment?

No. A twitch ran down his spine and, breathing out, he sat up slowly and ran his hand over the stubble already shadowing his jaw. It was shock. That was all.

Sitting up, he stared in disbelief around the empty office.

This had *never* happened. Ever. And, despite the evidence proving that it had, he still couldn't quite believe his eyes.

His heart started to beat faster. But, really, should he be that surprised? Every single time he thought he'd got Nola Mason all figured out she threw him a curveball that not only knocked him off his feet but left him wondering who she really was.

Who *he* really was.

He scowled. In this instance that should have been an easy question to answer.

He was the one who dressed and left.

He was always the one who chose the venue, and he never slept over.

Spending the night with a woman hinted too strongly at a kind of commitment he'd spent a lifetime choosing to avoid.

His face hardened. That didn't mean, though, that women upped and left him.

But, squinting into the pale grey light that was seeping into the room, he was forced to accept that on this occasion, with this woman, it did mean exactly that.

Which should be a good thing. Most women were

tedious about their need to be held, or to talk, or to plan the next date, even when he couldn't have made it any clearer that none of the above was on offer.

Only for some reason Nola's departure felt premature.

Incomprehensible.

Maybe he was just overthinking it.

But why did her leaving seem to matter so much?

Probably because, although superficially she might have seemed different, he'd assumed in the end that she would behave like every other woman he knew. Only nothing about last night had turned out as he'd imagined it would.

He'd thought he was seducing her, but he'd never lost control like that.

He certainly hadn't planned to have sex with her *here*, on the sofa in his office. But could he really be blamed for what had happened?

The tension between had been building from the moment they'd first met. In the restaurant it had been so intense, so powerful, he was surprised the other diners hadn't been sucked in by its gravitational pull.

She'd been as shaken by it as him—he was sure of it—and in the lift she had responded to his kiss so fiercely, and with such lack of inhibition, that he'd never got as far as inviting her back to his apartment.

Remembering that beat before they'd kissed, he felt his heart trip, heat and hunger tangling inside him. Watching that to-hell-with-you expression on her face grow fiercer, then soften as she melted into him, he'd wanted her so badly that he would have taken there and then in the lift if the doors hadn't opened.

Glancing round his office, his eyes homed in on his discarded shirt and he felt suddenly breathless, winded by the memory of how he'd sped her through the building with no real awareness of what he was doing, no conscious thought at all, just a need to have her in the most primitive way possible.

Reaching down, he picked his shirt up from the floor and slid his arms carelessly into the sleeves.

He hadn't hurt her. He would never do that. But he hadn't recognised himself. Hadn't recognised that fire, that urgency, that need—

The word snagged inside his head. No, not *need*.

It had been a long time since he had let himself *need* anyone. Not since he'd been a child, fighting misery and loneliness in a school on the other side of the world from his mother. Needing people, being needed, was something he'd avoided all his adult life, and whatever he might have felt for Nola he knew it couldn't have been that.

No, what he'd felt for Nola had been lust. And, like hunger and thirst, once it had been satisfied it would be forgotten. *She* would be forgotten.

And that was what mattered. After months of feeling distracted and on edge, he could finally get back to focusing on his work.

After all, that was the real reason he'd wanted to sleep with her. To soothe the burn of frustration that had not only tested his self-control but made it impossible for him to focus on the biggest product launch of his career.

Now, though, just as he had with every other female he'd bedded, he could draw a line under her and get on with the rest of his life.

Straightening his cuffs, he stood up and walked briskly towards the door.

Ten hours later he was wrapping up the last meeting of the day.

'Right, if there's nothing else then I think we'll finish up here.'

It was five o'clock.

Ram glanced casually around the boardroom, saw his heads of department were already collecting their laptops and paperwork. His loathing of meetings was legendary among his staff, as was his near fanatical insistence that they start *and* end on time.

Pulling his laptop in front of him, he flipped it open as they began to leave the room.

The day had passed with grinding slowness.

Nothing had seemed to hold his attention, or maybe he simply hadn't been able to concentrate. But, either way, his thoughts had kept drifting off from whatever spreadsheet or proposal he was supposed to be discussing, and his head had filled with memories of the night before.

More specifically, memories of Nola—her body straddling his, her face softening as his own body grew harder than it had ever been...

He gritted his teeth. For some reason she had got

under his skin in a way no woman ever had before. He'd even fallen asleep holding her in his arms. But for once intimacy had felt natural, right.

Staring down blankly at his computer screen, he felt his chest tighten. So what if it had felt right? He'd held her *in his sleep.* He hadn't even been conscious. And of course he would like to have sex with Nola again. He was a normal heterosexual man, and she was a beautiful, sexy woman.

Abruptly his muscles tensed, his eyes narrowing infinitesimally as through the open door he caught a glimpse of gleaming dark hair.

Nola! His stomach tightened involuntarily and he felt a rush of anticipation.

All day he'd been expecting to bump into her, had half imagined that she might seek him out. But now he realised that wouldn't be her way. She'd want it to play out naturally—like the tide coming in and going out again.

He breathed out sharply, his pulse zigzagging through his veins like a thread pulled through fabric, and before he even knew what he was doing he had crossed the room and yanked open the door.

But the corridor was empty.

Anger stuttered across his skin.

What the—? Why hadn't she come in to talk to him? She *must* have seen him.

Breathing out slowly, he stalked swiftly through the corridor to his office.

Jenny, his secretary, glanced up from her computer, her eyes widening at the expression on his face.

'Get Nola Mason on the phone. Tell her I want her in my office in the next five minutes.'

Slamming his office door, he strode across the room and stared furiously out of the window.

Was this some kind of a game?

Hopefully not—for *her* sake.

There was a knock at the door, and he felt a rush of satisfaction at having dragged Nola away from whatever it was she'd been doing.

'Come in,' he said curtly.

'Mr Walker—'

He turned, his face hardening as he saw Jenny, hovering in the doorway.

She smiled nervously. 'I'm sorry, Mr Walker. I was just going to tell you, but you went into your office before—'

He frowned impatiently. 'Tell me what?'

'Ms Mason can't come right now.'

'Can't or won't?' he snapped.

Jenny blinked. 'Oh, I'm sure she would if she were here, Mr Walker. But she's not here. She left about an hour ago. For the airport.'

Ram stared at her in silence, his eyes narrowing.

The airport?

'I—I thought you knew,' she stammered.

'I did.' He gave her a quick, curt smile. 'It must have slipped my mind. Thank you, Jenny.'

As the door closed his phone buzzed in his jacket and he reached for it, glancing distractedly down at the screen. And then his heart began to beat rhythmically in his chest.

It was an email.

From *Nola_Mason@CyberAngels.org*.

The corner of his mouth twisted, and then the words on the screen seemed to slip sideways as he slowly read, then reread, the email.

Dear Mr Walker

I am writing to confirm that in accordance with our agreement, today will be the last day of my employment at RWI. My colleague, Anna Harris—nee Mackenzie—and I will, of course, be in close contact with the on-site team, and remain available for any questions you may have.

I look forward to the successful completion of the project, and I wish to take this opportunity to thank you for all your personal input.

Nola Mason

Ram stared blankly at the email.

Was this some kind of a joke?

Slowly, his heart banging against his ribs like bailiffs demanding overdue rent, he reread it.

No, it wasn't a joke. It was a brush-off.

He read it again, his anger mounting with every word. Oh, it was all very polite, but there could be no mistaking the thank-you-but-I'm-done undertone. Why else would she have included that choice little remark at the bottom?

I wish to take this opportunity to thank you for all your personal input.

His fingers tightened around the phone.

Personal input!

He could barely see the screen through the veil of anger in front of his eyes, and it didn't help that he knew he was behaving irrationally—hypocritically, even. For in the past he'd ended liaisons with far less charm and courtesy.

But this was the woman he was paying to protect his business from unwanted intruders. Why, then, had he let her get past the carefully constructed emotional defences he'd built between himself and the world?

CHAPTER FOUR

Three months later

GLANCING UP AT the chalkboard above her head, Nola sighed. It was half past ten and the coffee shop was filling up, and as usual there was just too much choice. Today though, she had a rare morning off, and she wasn't about to waste the whole of it choosing a hot drink! Not even in Seattle, the coffee-drinking capital of the world.

Stepping forward, she smiled apologetically at the barista behind the counter. 'Just a green tea. Drink in. Oh, and one of those Danish, please. The cinnamon sort. Thanks.'

The sun was shining, but it was still not quite warm enough to sit outside, so she made her way to a table with a view of Elliott Bay.

Shrugging off her jacket, she leaned back in her seat, enjoying the sensation of sunlight on her face. Most of her time at work was spent alone in an office, hunched over a screen, so whenever she had any free time she liked to spend it outside. And her favourite place was right here, on the waterfront.

It was a little bit touristy. But then she *was* a tourist. And, besides, even if it did cater mainly to visitors, the restaurants still served amazingly fresh seafood and the coffee shops were a great place to relax and people-watch.

It was two weeks since she'd arrived in Seattle. And three months since she'd left Sydney. Three months of picking over the bones of her impulsive behaviour. Of wondering why she had ever thought that the consequences of sleeping with her boss would be less messy than sleeping with any other colleague?

Her pulse hopscotched forward. It was a little late to start worrying about consequences now. Particularly when one of them was a baby.

Breathing out slowly, she glanced down at her stomach and ran her hand lightly over the small rounded bump.

She had never imagined having a child. Her parents' unhappy marriage and eventual divorce had not exactly encouraged her to think of matrimony as the fairy-tale option that many of her friends, including Anna, believed it to be.

Being a mother, like being married, had always been something she thought happened to other people. Had she thought about it at all, she would probably have wanted the father of her baby to be a gentle, easy-going, thoughtful man.

She took another sip of tea.

So not Ram Walker, then.

And yet here she was, carrying his baby.

Across the café a young couple sat drinking *lattes*,

gazing dotingly at a baby in a buggy. They looked like a photoshoot for the perfect modern family, and suddenly the cup in her hand felt heavy. Almost as heavy as her heart. For it was a life her child would never enjoy.

Not least because she hadn't told Ram about the baby.

And nor would she.

Had he shown any sign, any hint that he wanted to be a father, she would have told him the moment she'd found out. But some men just weren't cut out for relationships and commitment, and Ram was one of them.

He'd said so to her face, so it had been easy at first to feel that her silence was justified—especially when she was still struggling not just with the shock of finding out she was pregnant but with nausea and an exhaustion that made getting dressed feel like a tough mission.

Only now, when finally she was in a fit enough state to think, she was almost as overwhelmed with guilt as she had been with nausea.

Evening after evening had been spent silently arguing with herself over whether or not she should tell him about the baby. But with each passing day she'd convinced herself that there really was no point in letting him know.

He'd clearly stated that he didn't want to be a father, and she knew from the way he lived his life that he wasn't capable of being one.

She didn't mean biologically. He clearly could father a child—and had. But what kind of a father would he be? His relationships with women lasted days, not years—not much use for raising a child to adulthood. Their brief affair had given her first-hand experience of his limited attention span. That night in his office she had felt as though he was floating through her veins. But afterwards he'd barely acknowledged the email she'd sent him. Just sent a single sentence thanking her for her services.

Her face felt hot. Was that the real reason why she hadn't told him about the baby? Her pride? Her ego? A yearning to keep her memories of that night intact and not made ugly by the truth? The truth that he'd never wanted anything more than a one-night stand. Never wanted her *or* this baby.

She felt the hot sting of tears behind her eyes as silently she questioned her motives again. But, no, it wasn't pride or sentimentality that was stopping her from saying anything.

It was him. It was Ram.

She didn't need to confront him to know that he wouldn't want to know about the baby, or be a father, or be in their lives. Whatever connection there had been between them had ended when she'd crept out of his office in the early hours of that morning. Nothing would change that, so why put herself through the misery of having him spell it out in black and white?

She shifted in her seat. So now she was three months pregnant, unmarried, living out of a suitcase—and happy.

It was true that she sometimes got a little freaked out at the thought of being solely responsible for the baby growing inside her. But she knew she could bring a child up on her own—better than if Ram was involved.

Her mum had done it and, besides, Anna and Robbie would be there for her—when she finally got round to telling them.

She felt a twinge of guilt.

Unlike with Ram, she didn't have any doubts about telling her friends about the baby. Quite the opposite. She wanted them to know. But by the time she'd done a test she'd been in Seattle, struggling with morning sickness. Besides, she wanted to tell her friend face-to-face, not over the—

Her phone rang and, glancing down at the screen, she frowned. It was Anna. Quickly, she answered it.

'That is so weird. I was literally just thinking about you.'

Anna snorted. 'Really? What happened? Did you eat some shortbread and finally remember your old pal in Scotland?'

'I spoke to you three days ago,' Nola protested.

'And you said you'd call back. But what happens? Nothing. No text. No email…'

'I've been busy.'

'Doing what?' Anna paused. 'No, let me guess. Drinking coffee?'

Nola smiled. Since her arrival in Seattle, it was a private joke between them that Nola was drinking coffee every time her friend called.

Tucking the phone under her chin, she smiled. 'Actually, it's green tea, and it's delicious. And the Danish isn't bad either!'

'You're eating a Danish? That's fantastic.'

The relief in Anna's voice caught Nola off guard. They might barely have seen one another over the last few months but she knew her friend had been worried about her, and if she wasn't going to tell her about the baby, the least she could do was put Anna's mind at rest.

'Yeah, you heard it here first. The appetite's back. Pizzerias across the entire state of Washington are rejoicing! In fact I might even get a national holiday named after me.'

Anna laughed. 'I always said you had Italian roots.'

'Was it my blue eyes or my pale skin that gave it away?' Nola said teasingly. 'Okay, that's enough of your amateur psychology, Dr Harris. Tell me why you've rung.'

There was a slight pause.

'You mean I need something more than just being bossy?'

Nola frowned. There was something odd about her friend's voice. She sounded nervous, hesitant. 'I don't know—do you?'

There was a short silence, then Anna sighed. 'Yes. I still can't believe it happened, but...you know how clumsy I am? Well, I was out walking yesterday with Robbie, and I tripped. Guess what? I broke my foot.'

Relief, smooth and warm, surged over Nola's skin.

'Oh, thank goodness.' She frowned. 'I don't mean thank goodness you broke your foot—I just thought it was going to be something worse.' She breathed out. 'Are you okay? Does it hurt? Have you got one of those crazy boot things?'

'I'm fine. It doesn't hurt anymore and, yeah, I've got a boot. But, Noles...'

Anna paused and Nola felt the air grow still around her.

'But, Noles, what?' she said slowly.

'I can't fly for another week. It's something to do with broken bones making you more at risk of blood clots, so—'

Nola felt her ribcage contract. Glancing down, she noticed that her hands were shaking. But she'd read the email. She knew what was coming.

'So you want me to go to Sydney?'

Nola swallowed. Even just saying the words out loud made panic grip her around the throat.

'I really didn't want to ask you, and ordinarily I'd just postpone it. But the launch is so close.' There was another infinitesimal pause. 'And we *are* under contract.'

Anna sounded so wretched that Nola was instantly furious with herself.

Of course she would go to Sydney. Her friend had been a shoulder to cry on after she'd slept with Ram and generally fallen apart. She damn well wasn't going to make her sweat and feel guilty for asking one tiny favour.

'I know, and I understand—it's fine,' she heard herself say.

'Are you sure? I thought there might be a problem—'

There definitely *would* be a problem, Nola thought dully. About six feet of problem, with tousled dark hair and cheekbones that could sharpen steel. But it would be *her* problem, not Anna's.

'There won't be!' Nola shook her head, trying to shake off the leaden feeling in her chest. 'And it's me who should be sorry. Moping around and making a huge fuss about some one-night stand.'

'You didn't make a fuss,' Anna said indignantly, sounding more like herself. 'You made a mistake. And if he wasn't paying us such a huge sum of money, I'd tell him where he could stick his global launch.'

Nola laughed. 'Let's wait until the money clears and then we can tell him together. Look, please don't worry, Anna. It'll be fine. It's not as if he's going to be making an effort to see me.'

'Oh, you don't need to worry about that,' Anna said quickly. 'I checked before I called you. He's in New York on some business trip. He won't be back for at least five days, so you definitely won't have to see him. Not that you'd have much to say to him even if he was there.'

Hanging up, Nola curled her arms around her waist protectively.

Except that she did.

She had a lot to say.

Only she had no intention of saying any of it to Ram—ever.

Glancing out of the window of his limo, Ram stared moodily up at the RWI building with none of the usual excitement and pride he felt at seeing the headquarters of his company. His trip to New York had been productive and busy—there had been the usual hectic round of meetings—but for the first time ever he had wanted to come home early.

As the car slowed he frowned. He still didn't understand why he'd decided to shorten his trip. But then, right now he didn't understand a lot of what was happening in his life, for it seemed to be changing in ways he couldn't control or predict.

Nodding at the receptionists on the front desk, he strode through the foyer and took the lift up to the twenty-second floor. Closing the door to his office, he stared disconsolately out of the window.

The launch date was rapidly approaching, but he was struggling to find any enthusiasm and energy for what amounted to the biggest day of his business career.

Nor was he even faintly excited about any of the beautiful, sexy women who were pursuing him with the determination and dedication of hungry cheetahs hunting an impala.

Why did he feel like this? And why was he feeling like it *now*?

He gritted his teeth. He knew the answer to both those questions. In fact it was the same answer. For, despite his having tried to erase her from his mind, *Nola* was the answer, the punchline, the coda to every single question and thought he'd had since she'd left Australia.

It might have been okay if it was just every now and then, but the reality was that Nola was never far from his thoughts. Even though she'd been gone for months now, every time he saw a mass of long dark hair he was still sure it was her. And each time that it wasn't he felt the same excitement, and disappointment, then fury.

There was a knock at the door, and when he was sure his face would give away nothing of what he was feeling, he said curtly. 'Come in.'

It was Jenny.

'I emailed you the data you asked for.' She handed him a folder. 'But I know you like a hard copy as well.'

He nodded. 'Anything crop up while I was away?'

'Nothing major. There were a couple of problems with some of the pre-order sites, and the live stream was only working intermittently on Tuesday. But Ms Mason sorted them out so—'

Ram stiffened. 'Ms Mason? Why didn't you tell me she called?'

Jenny's eyes widened. 'Because she didn't call. She's here.'

He stared past her, his chest tightening with shock. 'Since when?'

'Since Monday.' She smiled. 'But she's leaving tonight. Oh, and she's pr—'

He cut her off. 'And nobody thought to tell me?' he demanded.

'I thought you knew. I— Is there a problem?' Jenny stammered. 'I thought she was still under contract.'

Blood was pounding in his ears.

Glancing at his secretary's scared expression, he shook his head and softened his voice. 'There isn't, and she is.'

He could hardly believe it. Nola was in the building and yet she hadn't bothered to come and find him.

As though reading his thoughts, Jenny gave him a small, anxious smile. 'She probably thinks you're still in New York. I'm sure she'd like to see you,' she said breathlessly.

Remembering the email Nola had sent him, he felt his pulse twitch. That seemed unlikely, but it wasn't her choice.

He smiled blandly. 'I'm sure she does. Maybe you could get her on the phone, Jenny, and tell her I'd like to see her in my office. When it's convenient, of course. It's just that we have some unfinished business.'

But it wasn't going to stay unfinished for long.

Watching the door close, he leaned back in his chair, his face expressionless.

Finally she was done!

Resting her forehead against the palms of her hands, Nola stifled a yawn. It might only be four o'clock in the afternoon, but it felt as if she'd worked an all-nighter. If only she could go back to bed. Really, though, what would be the point? The fact she was sleeping badly was nothing to do with jet lag.

It was nerves.

She scowled. Not that she had any real reason to be nervous. Anna had been right—Ram was in New York on business. But that hadn't stopped the prickling sensation in the back of her neck as she'd walked into the RWI foyer, for even if the man himself wasn't in the building his presence was everywhere, making it impossible to shake off the feeling that there was still some link between them—an invisible bond that just wouldn't break.

Lowering her hands, she laid her fingers protectively over her stomach.

Not so invisible now.

For the last few weeks she'd been wearing her usual clothes, but today, for the first time, she'd struggled to get into her jeans. Fortunately she'd packed a pair of stretchy trousers that, although close-fitting, were more forgiving. She glanced down at her bump and smiled. It wasn't large, but she definitely looked pregnant now, and several people—mostly women—had noticed and congratulated her.

It was lovely, seeing their faces light up and finally being able to share this new phase of her life. But she would still be glad when it was all over and she could walk out through the huge RWI doors for the last time. And not just because of Ram's ghostly presence in the building. It felt wrong that people she barely knew—people who worked for Ram—knew that she was pregnant when he didn't.

And somehow, being here in his building, telling herself that he wouldn't want to know about the baby or be a father, didn't seem to be working anymore. He *was* the father. And being here had made that fact unavoidable.

Thankfully her train of thought was interrupted as her phone rang. Glancing at the screen, she frowned, her stomach clenching involuntarily.

It was Ram's secretary, Jenny.

'Hi, Jenny. Is everything okay?

'Yes, everything's fine, Ms Mason. I was just ringing to ask if you'd mind popping up to the office? Mr Walker would like to see you.'

Mr Walker.

She opened her mouth to say some words, but no sound came from her lips.

'I thought he was away,' she managed finally. 'On business.'

'He was.' To her shell-shocked ears Jenny's voice sounded painfully bright and happy. 'But he flew back in this afternoon. And he particularly asked to see you. Apparently you have unfinished business?'

Nola nodded, too stunned by Jenny's words even to register the fact that the other woman couldn't see her.

'Okay, well, he said to come up whenever it's convenient, so I'll see you in a bit.'

'Okay, see you then,' Nola lied.

As she hung up her heart began leaping like a salmon going upstream. For a moment she couldn't move, then slowly she closed her laptop and picked up her jacket.

Where could she go? Not her hotel. He might track her down. Nor the airport—at least not yet. No, probably it would be safest just to hide in some random café until it was time to check in.

On legs that felt like blancmange, she walked across the office and out into the corridor.

'Mr Walker? I'm just making some coffee. Can I get you anything?'

Ram looked up at Jenny.

'No, thank you, Jenny. I'm good.'

He glanced down at his phone and frowned. It was half past four. A flicker of apprehension ran down his spine.

'By the way, did you call Ms Mason?' he asked casually.

She nodded. 'Yes, and she said she'd be up in a bit.'

He nodded. 'Good. Excellent.'

He felt stupidly elated at her words, and suddenly so restless that he couldn't stay sitting at his desk a moment longer.

'Actually, I might just go and stretch my legs, Jenny. If Ms Mason turns up, ask her to wait in my office, please.'

The idea of Nola having to wait for him was strangely satisfying and, grabbing his jacket, he walked out through the door and began wandering down the corridor. Most of his staff were at their desks, but as he turned the corner into the large open-plan reception area he saw a group of people waiting for the lift.

Walking towards them, he felt a thrill of anticipation at the thought of finally seeing her again—and then abruptly he stopped dead, his eyes freezing with shock and disbelief. For there, standing slightly apart from the rest, her jacket folded over her arm, was Nola.

He watched, transfixed, as she stepped into the lift. Her long dark hair was coiled at the nape of her neck, and a tiny part of his brain registered that he'd never seen her wear it like that before.

But the bigger part was concentrating not on her hair but on the small, rounded, unmistakable bump of her stomach.

He heard his own sharp intake of breath as though from a long way away.

She was pregnant.

Pregnant.

A vice seemed to be closing around his throat. He felt like a drowning man watching his life play out in front of his eyes. A life that had just been derailed, knocked off course by a single night of passion.

And then, just as his legs overrode his brain, the lift doors closed and she was gone.

He stood gazing across the office, his head spinning, his breath scrabbling inside his chest like an animal trying to get out.

She was pregnant—several months pregnant at least—and frantically he rewound back through the calendar. But even before he reached the date when they'd slept together he knew that the baby could be his.

The blood seemed to drain from his body.

So why hadn't she said anything to him?

She'd been in the office for days. Yes, he'd been in New York when she arrived, but Jenny had spoken to her earlier. Nola knew he was in the building. Knew that he wanted to see her—

Remembering his remark about unfinished business, he almost laughed out loud.

Unfinished business.

You could say that again.

So why hadn't she said anything to him?

The question looped inside his head, each time growing louder and louder, like a car alarm. The obvious and most logical answer was that he was not the father.

Instantly he felt his chest tighten. The thought of Nola giving herself to another man made him want to smash his fists into the wall.

Surely she wouldn't—she couldn't have.

A memory rose up inside him, stark and unfiltered, of Nola, her body melting into his. She had been like fire under his skin. For that one night she had been his.

But was that baby his too?

A muscle flickered along the line of his jaw and he felt his anger curdle, swirling and separating into fury and frustration. Turning, he strode back into his office.

There was no way he could second-guess this. He had to know for certain.

'Tell Mike to bring the car round to the front of the building—*now*,' he barked at Jenny. 'I need to get to the airport.'

Ten minutes later he was slouched in the back of his limo. His head was beginning to clear finally, and now his anger was as cold and hostile as the arctic tundra.

How could she do this?

Treating him as if he didn't matter, as if he'd only had some walk-on part in her life. If he was the father, he should be centre stage.

His hands clenched in his lap. He hated the feeling of being sidelined, of being secondary to the key players in the drama, for it reminded him of his childhood, and the years he'd spent trying to fit into his parents' complex relationship.

But he wasn't a child anymore. He was man who might be about to have a child of his own.

His breath stilled in his throat.

Only *how* could he be the father? She had told him she was safe. But there was always an element of risk—particularly for a man like him, a man who would be expected to provide generous financial support for his child. Which was why he always used precautions of his own.

Except that night with Nola.

He'd wanted her so badly that he couldn't bring himself to do anything that might have risked them pausing, maybe changing their minds—like putting on a condom.

Feeling the car slow, he glanced up, his pulse starting to accelerate.

Was the baby his? He would soon find out.

Before the limo had even come to a stop, he was opening the door and stepping onto the pavement.

Dragging her suitcase through the airport, Nola frowned. She had waited as long as possible before arriving at the airport, and now she was worried she would be too late to check in her luggage.

But any worry she might be feeling now was nothing to the stress of staying at the office. Knowing he was in the building had been unsettling enough, but the fact that Ram had asked to see her—

She didn't need to worry about that now and, curving her hand protectively over her stomach, she breathed out slowly, trying to calm herself as she stopped in front of the departures board.

She was just trying to locate her flight when there was some kind of commotion behind her and, turning, she saw that there was a crowd of people pointing and milling around.

'They're shooting a commercial,' the woman standing next to her said knowledgeably. 'It was in the paper. It's for beer. Apparently it's got that rugby player in it, and a crocodile.'

'A real one?'

The woman laughed. 'Yes, but it's not here. I just meant in the advert. I don't think they'd be allowed to bring a real croc to an airport. That'd be way too dangerous.'

Nodding politely, Nola smiled—and then she caught her breath for, striding towards her, his lean, muscular body parting the crowds like a mythical wind, and looking more dangerous than any wild animal, was Ram Walker.

CHAPTER FIVE

As she watched his broad shoulders cutting through the clumps of passengers like a scythe through wheat Nola couldn't move. Or speak, or even think. Shock seemed to have robbed her of the ability to do anything but gape.

And as he made his way across the departures lounge towards her she couldn't decide if it was shock or desire that was making her heart feel as if it was about to burst.

Mind numb, she stood frozen, like a movie on pause. It was just over three months since she'd last seen him. Three months of trying and failing to forget the man who had changed her life completely.

She'd assumed she just needed more time, that eventually his memory would fade. Only now he was here, and she knew she'd been kidding herself. She would never forget Ram—and not just because she was pregnant with his baby.

Her body began to shake, and instinctively she folded her arms over her stomach.

A baby he didn't even know existed.

A baby she had deliberately chosen to conceal from him.

And just like that she knew his being here wasn't some cosmic coincidence: he was coming to find her.

Before that thought had even finished forming in her head he was there, standing in front of her, and suddenly she wished she was sitting down, for the blazing anger in his grey gaze almost knocked her off her feet.

'Going somewhere?' he asked softly.

She had forgotten his voice. Not the sound of it, but the power it had to throw her into a state of confusion, to turn her emotions into a swirling mass of chaos that made even breathing a challenge.

Looking up at him, hoping that her voice was steadier than her heartbeat, she said hoarsely, 'Mr Walker. I wasn't expecting to see you.'

He didn't reply. For a moment his narrowed gaze stayed fixed on her face, and then her skin seemed to blister and burn as slowly his eyes slid down over her throat and breast, stopping pointedly on the curve of her stomach.

'Yes, it's been a day of surprises all round.'

His heart crashing against his ribs, Ram stared at Nola in silence. He had spent the last two hours waiting at the check-in desk for her, his nerves buzzing beneath his skin at the sight of every long-haired brunette. At first when she hadn't turned up he'd been terrified that she'd caught another flight. But finally it had dawned on him that she was probably just hoping to avoid him, and therefore was going to arrive at the last minute.

Now that she was here, he was struggling to come to terms with what he could see—for seeing her in the office had been such a shock that he'd almost started to think that maybe what he'd seen might not even have been real. After all, it had only been a glimpse...

Maybe it had been another woman with dark hair, and after months of thinking and dreaming about her he'd just imagined it was Nola.

Now, though, there could be no doubt, no confusion.

It was Nola, and she was pregnant.

But that didn't mean he was the father.

He felt himself jerk forward—doubt and then certainty vibrating through his bones.

If that baby was another man's child, he knew she would have met his gaze proudly. Instead she looked hunted, cornered, like a small animal facing a predator it couldn't outrun.

In other words, guilty as hell.

With an effort he shifted his gaze from her stomach to her face. Her lips were pale, and her blue eyes were huge and uncomprehending. She looked, if possible, more stunned than he felt. But right now feelings were secondary to the truth.

'So this is why you've been giving me the runaround?' he asked slowly. 'I suppose I should offer my congratulations.' He paused, letting the silence stretch between them. *'To both of us.'*

Watching her eyes widen with guilt, he felt new shoots of anger pushing up inside him, so that suddenly his pulse was too fast and irregular.

'I wonder—when, exactly, were you going to tell me you were pregnant?'

Looking up into his face, Nola felt her breath jerk in her throat. He was angrier than she'd ever seen him.

Angrier than she'd ever seen anyone. And he had every right to be.

Had she been standing there, confronted by both this truth and the months of deception that had preceded it, she would have felt as furious and thwarted as he did. But somehow knowing that made her feel more defensive, for that was only half the story. The half that *didn't* include her reasons for acting as she had.

Lifting her chin, she met his gaze. 'Why would I tell you I'm pregnant? As of twenty minutes ago, I don't actually work for you anymore.'

Her hands curled up into fists in front of her as he took a step towards her.

'Don't play games with me, Nola.'

His eyes burned into hers, and the raw hostility in his voice suffocated her so that suddenly she could hardly breathe.

'And don't pretend this has got anything to with your employment rights. You're having a baby, and we both know it could be mine. So you should have told me.'

Around her, the air sharpened. She could feel people turning to stare at them curiously.

Forcing herself to hold his gaze, she glared at him. 'This has got nothing to do with you.'

A nerve pulsed along his jawline.

'And you want me to take your word for that, do you?' He gazed at her in naked disbelief. 'On the basis of what? Your outstanding display of honesty up until now?'

She blinked. 'You don't know for certain if you're the father,' she said quickly, failing to control the rush of colour to her face.

His eyes locked onto hers, and instantly she felt the tension in her spine tighten like a guy rope.

'No. But *you* do.'

She flinched, wrong-footed.

How was this happening?

Not him finding her. It would have been a matter of moments for his secretary to check her flight time. But why was he here? Over the last three months she'd spent hours imagining this moment, playing out every possible type of scenario. In not one of them had he pursued her to the airport and angrily demanded the truth.

Her heart began to pound fiercely.

It would be tempting to think that he cared about the baby.

Tempting, but foolish.

Ram's appearance at the airport, his frustration and anger, had nothing to do with any sudden rush of paternal feelings on his part. Understandably, he hadn't liked finding out second-hand that she was pregnant. But that didn't mean he could just turn up and start throwing his weight around.

'I don't see why you're making this into such a big deal,' she snapped. 'We both know that you have absolutely no interest in being a father anyway.'

Ram studied her face, his pulse beating slow and hard.

It was true that up until this moment, he'd believed that fatherhood was not for him. But he'd been talking about a concept, a theoretical child, and Nola knew that as well as he did.

His chest tightened with anger.

'That doesn't mean I don't want to know *when* I am going to be one. In fact, I think I have a right to know. However, if you're saying that you really don't know who the father is, then I suggest we find out for certain.' His eyes held hers. 'I believe it's a fairly simple test. Of course it would mean you'd have to miss your flight…'

Imprisoned by his dark grey gaze, Nola gritted her teeth.

He was calling her bluff, and she hated him for it.

But what she hated more was the fact that in spite of her anger and resentment she could feel her body unfurling inside, as though it was waking from a long hibernation. And even though he was causing mayhem in her life, her longing for him still sucked the breath from her lungs.

Glancing at his profile, she felt a pulse of heat that had nothing to do with anger skim over her skin. But right now the stupid, senseless way she reacted to Ram didn't matter. All she cared about was catching that plane—and that was clearly not going to happen unless Ram found out, one way or another, if this baby was his.

So why not just tell him the truth?

Squaring her shoulders, she met his gaze. 'Fine,' she said slowly. 'You're the father.'

She didn't really know how she'd expected him to react, but he didn't say or do anything. He just continued to stare at her impassively, his grey eyes dark and unblinking.

'I know you don't want to be involved, and that's fine. I'm not expecting you to be,' she said quickly. 'That's one of the reasons I didn't tell you.'

'So you had more than one reason, then?' he said quietly.

She frowned, unsure of how she should respond. But she didn't get a chance to reply, for as though he had suddenly become conscious of the sidelong glances and the sudden stillness surrounding them, he reached down and picked up her suitcase.

'I suggest we finish this in private.'

Turning, Ram walked purposefully across the departures lounge. Inside his head, though, he had no idea where he was going. Or what to do when he got there.

You're the father!

Three words he'd never expected or wanted to hear.

Then—*boom!*—there they were, blowing apart his carefully ordered world.

His chest grew tight. Only this wasn't just about his life anymore; there was a new life to consider now.

Through the haze of his confused thoughts he noticed two empty chairs in the corner, next to a vending machine, and gratefully sat down in one.

His head was spinning. Seeing Nola pregnant at the office, he'd guessed that he might be the father. But it had been just that. A guess. It hadn't felt real—not least because he'd spent all his life believing that this moment would never happen.

Only now it had, and he would have expected his response to be a mix of resentment and regret.

But, incredibly, what he was actually feeling was resolve. A determination to be part of his child's life.

Now all he needed to do was persuade Nola of that fact.

Glancing over to where Ram now sat, with that familiar shuttered look on his handsome face, Nola felt resentment surge through her. How could he do this? Just stroll back into her life and take over, expecting her to follow him across the room like some puppy he was training?

He had said he wanted to know the truth and so she'd told him, hoping that would be the end of their conversation. Why, then, did they need to speak in private? What else was there to say?

Her eyes narrowed. Maybe she should just leave him sitting there. Leave the airport, catch a train, or just go and hide in some nameless hotel. Show Ram that she wasn't going to be pushed around by him.

But clearly he was determined to have the last word, and trying to stop him doing so would be like trying to defy gravity: exhausting, exasperating, and ultimately futile.

The fact was that he was just so much more relentless than she could ever be, and whatever it was that drove his desire—no, his determination to win, she couldn't compete with it. Whether she liked it or not, this conversation was going to have to happen, so she might as well get on with it or she would never get on that plane.

Mutinously, she walked over to him and, ignoring the small satisfied smile on his face, sat down next to him.

Around her people were moving, picking up luggage and chatting, happy to be going home or going on holiday, and for a split second she wished with an intensity that almost doubled her over that it was her and Ram going away together. That she could rewind time, meet him in some other way, under different circumstances, and—

Her lip curled.

And what?

She and Ram might share a dizzying sexual chemistry, but there was no trust, no honesty and no harmony. Most of their conversations ended up in an argument, and the only time they'd managed to stay on speaking terms was when they hadn't needed to speak.

Remembering the silence between them in the lift, the words left unspoken on her lips as he'd covered her mouth with his, she felt heat break out on her skin.

That night had been different. That night all the tension and antagonism between them had melted into the darkness and they had melted into one another, their quickening bodies hot and liquid...

She swallowed.

But sex wasn't enough to sustain a relationship. And one night of passion, however incredible, wasn't going to make her change her mind. It had been a hard decision to make, but it was the right one. A two-parent set-up might be traditional—desirable, even—but not if one of those parents was always halfway out through the door, literally and emotionally.

Breathing out slowly, she turned her head and stared into his eyes. 'Look, what happened three months ago has got nothing to do with now...' She paused. 'It wasn't planned—we just made a mistake.'

For a moment, his gaze held hers, and then slowly he shook his head.

'We didn't make a mistake, Nola.'

'I wasn't talking about the baby,' she said quickly.

His eyes rested intently on her face.

'Neither was I.'

And just like that she felt her stomach flip over, images from the night they'd spent together exploding inside her head like popping corn. Suddenly her whole body was quivering, and it was all she could do not to lean over and kiss him, to give in to that impulse to taste and touch that beautiful mouth once again—

Taking a quick breath, she dragged her eyes away from him, ignoring the sparks scattering over her skin.

'You said you wanted to finish this, Ram, but we can't,' she said hoarsely. 'Because it never started. It was just a one-night stand, remember?'

'Oh, I remember every single moment of that night. As I'm sure you do, Nola.'

His eyes gleamed, and instantly her pulse began to accelerate.

'But this isn't about just one night anymore. Our one-night stand has got long-term consequences.' He gestured towards her stomach.

'But not for you.' She looked up at him stubbornly, her blue eyes wide with frustration. 'Whatever connection we had, it ended a long time ago.'

'Given that you're pregnant with my child, that would seem to be a little premature and counter-intuitive,' he said softly. 'But I don't think there's anything to be gained by continuing this discussion now.' He grimaced. 'Or here. I suggest we leave it for a day or two. I can take you back to the city—I have an apartment there you can use as a base—and I'll talk to my lawyers, get some kind of intermediate financial settlement set up.'

Nola gazed at him blankly.

Apartment? Financial settlement?

What was he talking about?

This wasn't about money. This was about what was best for their child, and Ram was *not* father material. A father should be consistent, compassionate, and capable of making personal sacrifices for the sake of his child. But Ram was just not suited to making the kinds of commitment and sacrifices expected and required by parenthood.

She had no doubt that financially he would be generous, but children needed more than money. They needed to be loved. To be wanted.

Memories of her own father and his lack of interest filled her head, and suddenly she couldn't meet Ram's eyes. Her father had been a workaholic. For him, business had come first, and if he'd had any time and energy left after a working day he'd chosen to spend it either out entertaining clients or with one of his many mistresses. Home-life, his wife and his daughter, had been right at the bottom of his agenda—more like a footnote, in fact.

Being made to feel so unimportant had blighted her childhood. As an adult, too, she had struggled to believe in herself. It had taken a long time, her friendship with Anna, and a successful career to overcome that struggle. And it was a struggle she was determined her child would never have to face.

But what was the point of telling Ram any of that? He wouldn't understand. How could he? It was not as if he'd ever doubted himself or felt that he wasn't good enough.

'No,' she said huskily. 'That's not going to happen.' She was shaking her head but her eyes were fixed on his face. 'I don't want your money, Ram, or your apartment. And I'm sorry if this offends your *romantic sensibilities*, but I don't want you in my baby's life just because we spent eight hours on a sofa in your office.'

Recognising his own words, Ram felt a swirling, incoherent fury surge up inside him. Wrong, he thought savagely. She had *belonged* to him that night, and now she was carrying his baby part of her would belong to him for ever.

Leaning back, he let his eyes roam over her face, his body responding with almost primeval force to her flushed cheeks and resentful pout even as his mind plotted his next move.

What mattered most was keeping her in Australia, and losing his temper would only make her more determined to leave. So, reining in his anger, he stretched out his legs and gazed at her calmly.

'Sadly for you, that decision is not yours to make. I'm not a lawyer, but I'm pretty sure that it's paternity, not romantic sensibilities, that matters to a judge. But why don't you call your lawyer just to make sure?'

It wasn't true but judging by the flare of fear in her eyes, Nola's knowledge of parental rights was clearly based on law procedural dramas not legal expertise. Nola could hardly breathe. Panic was strangling her. Why was he suddenly talking about lawyers and judges?

'Wh-Why are you doing this?' she stammered. 'I know you're angry with me for not telling you about the baby, and I understand that. But you have to understand that you're the reason I didn't say anything.'

'Oh, I see. So it's *my* fault you didn't tell me?'

He was speaking softly, but there was no mistaking the dangerous undertone curling through his words.

'*My* fault that you deliberately chose to avoid me at the office today? And I suppose it'll be my fault, too, when my child grows up without a father and spends the rest of his life feeling responsible—'

He broke off, his face hardening swiftly.

She bit her lip. 'No, of course not. I just meant that from everything you said before I didn't think you'd want to know. So I made a choice.'

Ram could hear the slight catch in her voice but he ignored it. Whatever he'd said before was irrelevant now. This baby was real. And it was his. Besides, nothing he'd said in the past could excuse her lies and deceit.

'And that's what this is about, is it? *Your* choices? *Your* pregnancy? *Your* baby?' He shook his head. 'This is not *your* baby, Nola, it's *our* baby—mine as much as yours—and you know it. And I am going be a part of his or her life.'

Nola stared at him numbly, her head pounding in time with her heart. She didn't know what to say to him—hadn't got the words to defend herself or argue her case. Not that it mattered. He wasn't listening to her anyway.

Shoulders back, neck tensing, she looked away, her eyes searching frantically for some way to escape—and then her heart gave a jolt as she suddenly saw the time on the departures board.

The next second she had snatched her suitcase and was on her feet, pulse racing.

'What do you think you're doing?'

Ram was standing in front of her, blocking her way.

'I have to go!'

Her voice was rising, and a couple of people turned to look at her. But she didn't care. If she missed this flight she would be stuck in Sydney for hours, possibly days, and she had to get away—as far away from Ram as quickly as she could.

'They've called my flight so I need to check in my luggage.'

For a moment he stared at her in silence, and then his face shifted and, leaning forward, he plucked the suitcase handle from her fingers.

'Let me take that!'

He strode away from her and, cursing under her breath, she hurried after him.

'I really don't need your help,' she said through gritted teeth.

Tucking the suitcase under his arm, he smiled blandly. 'Of course not. But you have to understand I don't fly commercial, so all this rushing around is very exciting for me. It's actually better than watching a film.'

He sounded upbeat—buoyant, almost—and she glowered at him, part baffled, part exasperated by this sudden change in mood.

'That's wonderful, Ram,' she said sarcastically. 'But I'm not here to be your entertainment for the evening.'

'If you were my entertainment for the evening you wouldn't be getting breathless from running around an airport,' he said softly. And, reaching over, he took her arm and pulled her towards him.

Her breath stuttered in her throat, and suddenly all her senses were concentrated on his hand and on the firmness of his grip and the heat of his skin through the fabric of her shirt.

'You need to slow down. You're pregnant. And besides...' he gestured towards the seemingly endless queue of people looping back and forth across the width of the room '... I don't think a couple of minutes is going to make that much difference.'

Gazing at the queue, Nola groaned. 'I'm never going to make it.'

'You don't know that.' Ram frowned. 'Why don't we ask at the desk?'

He pointed helpfully to where two women in uniform were chatting with a group of passengers surrounded by trolleys and toddlers. But Nola was already hurrying across the room.

'Excuse me. Could you help me, please? I'm supposed to be on this flight to Edinburgh but I need to check in my baggage.'

Handing over her boarding pass, she held her breath as the woman glanced down at it, and then back at her screen, before finally shaking her head.

'I'm sorry, the bag drop desk is closed—and even if we rush you through it's a good ten minutes to get to the boarding gate.' She grimaced. 'And, looking ahead, all Edinburgh flights are full for the next twenty-four hours. You might be able to pick up a cancellation, but that would mean hanging around at the airport. I'm sorry I can't be more helpful...'

'That's okay,' Nola said stiffly. 'It's really not your fault.'

And it wasn't.

Turning away, she stalked over to where Ram stood, watching her unrepentantly.

'This is your fault,' she snapped. 'If you hadn't been talking to me I'd have heard it when they called my flight and then I would have checked in my luggage on time.'

He gazed at her blandly. 'Oh, was that your flight to Edinburgh? I didn't realise it was that important. Like I said, I don't fly commercial, so—'

Nola stared at him, wordless with disbelief, her nails cutting into her hands. 'Don't give me that "I don't fly commercial" rubbish. You knew exactly what you were doing.'

He smiled down at her serenely. 'Really? You think I'd deliberately and selfishly withhold a vital piece of information?' He shook his head, his eyes glittering. 'I'm shocked. I mean, who would *do* something like that?'

She was shaking with anger. 'This is not the same at all.'

'No, it's not,' he said softly. 'I stopped you catching a flight, and you tried to stop me finding out I was a father.'

'But I didn't do it to hurt you,' she said shakily. 'Or to punish you.

And she hadn't—only how could she prove that to Ram? How could she explain to him that she had only been trying to prevent her child's future from inheriting

her past? How could she tell him that life had taught her
that no father was better than a bad father.

She shivered. It was all such a mess. And she didn't
know what to do to fix it. All she knew was that she
wanted to go home. To be anywhere but at this noisy,
crowded airport, standing in front of a man who clearly
hated her.

Her eyes were stinging and she turned away blindly.

'Nola. Don't go.'

Something in his voice stopped her, and slowly, reluctantly, she met his gaze.

He was staring at her impassively, his eyes cool and
detached.

'Look, I don't think either of us was expecting to
have this conversation, and even though I think we both
know that we have a lot to talk about we need time and
privacy to do it properly. I also know that I need to get
home, and you need a plane. So why don't you borrow mine?'

She looked at him dazedly. 'Borrow your plane?'

He nodded. 'I have a private jet. Just sitting there, all
ready to go, thirty minutes from here. It's got a proper
bedroom and a bathroom. Two, in fact, so you can get
a proper night's sleep. I guess I *am* responsible in part
for making you miss your flight, so it's really the least
I can do.'

He looked so handsome, so contrite, and clearly he
wanted to make amends. Besides, all her other options
involved an effort she just couldn't summon up the energy to make right now.

Biting her lip, she nodded.

* * *

Exactly thirty-three minutes later, Ram's limo turned into a private airfield.

As the car slid to a halt, Nola glanced over to where Ram sat gazing out of the window in silence. 'Thank you for letting me use your plane,' she said carefully.

Turning, he looked over at her, his eyes unreadable in the gloom of the car.

'My pleasure. I called ahead and told the pilot where to take you, so you can just sit back and enjoy the ride.'

She nodded, her heart contracting guiltily as his words replayed inside her head. He was being so reasonable—kind, even—and like a storm that had blown itself out the tension between them had vanished.

Her pulse was racing. A few hours earlier she'd been desperate to leave the country, to get away from Ram. Only now that it was finally time to go something was holding her back, making her hesitate, just as she had three months ago when she'd crept out of his office in the early hours of the morning. It was the same feeling—a feeling that somehow she was making a mistake.

She held her breath. But staying was not an option. She needed to go home, even if that meant feeling guilty. Only she hadn't expected to mind so much.

Her heart was bumping inside her chest like a bird trapped in a room and, clearing her throat, she said quickly, 'I was wrong not to tell you about the baby. I should have done, and I'm sorry. I know we've got an awful lot to discuss. But you're right—we do need time and privacy to talk about it properly, so thank you for being so understanding about me leaving.'

His eyes were light and relaxed, and she felt another pang beneath her heart.

'I'm glad you agree, and I feel sure we'll see each other very soon.'

The walk from the car to the plane seemed to last for ever, but finally she was smiling at the young, male flight attendant who had stepped forward to greet her.

'Good evening, Ms Mason, welcome on board. My name is Tom, and I'll be looking after you on this flight with my colleagues, James and Megan. If you need anything, please just ask.'

Collapsing into a comfortable armchair that bore no resemblance to the cramped seats on every other flight she'd ever been on, she tried not to let herself look out of the window. But finally she could bear it no more and, turning her head, she glanced down at the tarmac.

It was deserted. The limo was gone.

Swallowing down the sudden small, hard lump of misery in her throat, she sat back and watched numbly as Tom brought her some iced water and a selection of magazines.

'If you could just put on your seatbelt, Ms Mason, we'll be taking off in a couple of minutes.'

'Yes, of course.'

Leaning back, she closed her eyes and listened to the hum of the air conditioning, and then finally she heard the engines start to whine.

'Is this seat taken?'

A male voice. Deep and very familiar.

But it couldn't be him—

Her eyes snapped open and her heart began to thump,

for there, staring down at her, with something very like a smile tugging at his mouth, was Ram.

She stared up at him in confusion. 'What are you doing here?'

'I thought you might like some company.'

Company! She frowned. Glancing past him at the window, she could see that they were starting to move forward, and across the cabin Tom and his colleagues were buckling themselves into their seats.

'I don't think there's time,' she said hurriedly. 'We're just about to take off.'

He shrugged. 'Well, like you said, we do have an awful lot to talk about.'

A trickle of cool air ran down her spine, and she felt a pang of uneasiness.

'Yes, but not now—'

She broke off as he dropped into the seat beside her.

'Why not now?' Sliding his belt across his lap, he stretched out his long legs. 'Just the two of us on a private jet...'

Pausing, he met her gaze, and the steady intensity of his grey eyes made the blood stop moving in her veins.

'Surely this is the perfect opportunity!'

CHAPTER SIX

NOLA STARED AT him uncertainly. Beneath the sound of her heartbeat she heard the plane's wheels starting to rumble across the tarmac. But she barely registered it. Instead, her brain was frantically trying to make sense of his words.

He couldn't possibly be intending to fly to Scotland with her, so it must be his idea of a joke.

Glancing up into his face, she felt her breath catch.

Except that he didn't look as if he was joking.

Taking a deep breath, trying to appear calmer than she felt, she forced herself to smile. 'I couldn't ask you to do that,' she said lightly. 'It's not as if it's on your way home.'

His grey gaze rested on her face. 'But you're not asking me, are you? Nor am I asking *you*, as it happens.'

Her face felt stiff with shock and confusion. Slowly she shook her head. 'But this isn't what we agreed. You said I could borrow your plane—you didn't say anything about coming with me.'

He gazed at her blandly. 'I thought you said we had a lot to talk about.'

'You know I didn't mean *now.*' Her voice rose.

This was madness. Total and utter madness.

Except madness implied that Ram was acting irrationally, and there was nothing random or illogical about his decision to join her on the plane. He was simply proving a point, and getting his own way just like he always did.

She felt as though she was going to throw up.

'You tricked me. You made me miss my flight and then you offered to let me use your plane just so you could trap me here.'

And, fool that she was, she had actually believed he was trying to make amends.

Her heart began to pound fiercely. Not only that, she'd apologised to him. *Apologised* for not telling him about the baby and *thanked* him for being so understanding.

But everything he'd said had been a lie.

How could she have been so stupid—so gullible?

Her cheeks felt as if they were on fire. 'Why are you doing this to me?' she whispered.

He shrugged. 'It was your choice. I didn't make you do anything. You could have waited for a regular flight.' His mouth hardened. 'Except that would have meant talking to me. So I made a calculated guess that you'd do pretty much anything to avoid that—including accepting the offer of a no-strings flight back to Scotland.'

'Except there *are* strings, aren't there?' she snapped. 'Like the fact that you never said you were coming with me.'

He looked at her calmly. 'Well, I thought it might be a little counterproductive.'

Her pulse was crashing in her ears. 'I can't believe you're doing this,' she said hoarsely.

Leaning forward, he picked up one of the magazines and began flicking casually through the pages. 'Then you clearly don't know me as well as you thought you did.' He smiled at her serenely. 'But don't worry. Now that we have the chance to spend some time alone, I'm sure we'll get to know each other a whole lot better.'

Her hands clenched in her lap. She was breathless with anger and frustration. 'But you can't just hijack this plane—'

'Given that it's my plane, I'd say that would be almost impossible,' he agreed.

'I don't care that it's your plane. People don't behave like this. It's insane!'

'Oh, I don't think so.' He gazed at her steadily. 'You're pregnant with my child, Nola. Insane would be letting you fly off into the sunset with just your word that you'll get in touch.'

'So you just decided to come with me to the other side of the world?' she snapped. 'Yeah, I can see that's *really* rational.'

For a moment she glared at him in silence, and then her pulse began to jerk erratically over her skin, like a needle skipping across a record, as he leaned over and rested his hand lightly on the smooth mound of her stomach.

'Whether you like it or not, Nola, this baby is mine

too. And until we get this sorted out I'm not letting you out of my sight. Where you go, I go.'

Blood was roaring in her ears. On one level his words made no sense, for she hardly knew him. He was a stranger, and what they'd shared amounted to so little. The briefest of flings. A night on a sofa.

And yet so much had happened in that one night. Not just the baby, but the fire between them—a storm of passion that had left her breathless and dazed, and eclipsed every sexual experience she'd had or would ever have.

She'd known that night that a part of her would always belong to Ram. She just hadn't realised then that it would turn out to be a baby. But now that he knew the truth was anything he'd done really that big a surprise? She was carrying his child, and she knew enough about Ram to know that he would never willingly give up control of anything that belonged to him.

Still, that didn't give him the right to trap her and manipulate her like this, bending her to his will as though being pregnant made her an extension of his life.

'You didn't have to do this,' she said hoarsely. 'I told you I was going to get in touch and I would have done.'

'I've saved you the trouble, then.' He gave her a small, taunting smile. 'It's okay—you don't need to thank me.'

She glowered at him in silence, her brain seething as she tried to think up some slick comeback that would puncture his overdeveloped ego.

But, really, why bother? Whatever she said wasn't

going to change the fact that they were stuck with each other for the foreseeable future.

Only just because he'd managed to trick her into getting on his plane, it didn't mean that he was going to have everything his own way. Remembering his remark back at the airport, she felt her breathing jerk, and she curled her fingers into the palms of her hands. She sure as hell wasn't going to spend the rest of this flight entertaining him.

'I'd love to keep on chatting,' she said coldly. 'But it's been a long, and exhausting day, and as you can imagine I'm very tired.'

Their eyes met—his calm and appraising, hers combative—and there was a short, taut silence.

Finally he shrugged. 'Of course. I'll show you to your room.'

Her room!

'No—' She lurched back in her seat.

She would have liked to brush her teeth, and maybe put on something more comfortable, but the thought of undressing within a five-mile radius of Ram made her heart start to beat painfully fast.

'Actually, I think I'd rather stay here,' she said quickly. 'These seats recline, don't they? And I'm not really sleeping properly at the moment anyway.'

He stared at her speculatively, and she wondered if he was going to demand that she use the bedroom.

But after a moment, he simply nodded. 'I'll get you a blanket.'

Five minutes later, tucked cosily beneath a soft cashmere blanket, Nola tilted back her seat and turned her head pointedly away from where Ram sat beside her, working on his laptop.

How was he able to do any work anyway? she thought irritably. After everything that had happened in the last few hours anybody else—her included—would have been too distracted, too agitated, too exhausted.

But then wasn't that one of the reasons she'd been so reluctant to tell him about the baby? Just like her father, he always put business first, pleasure second, and then the boring nitty-gritty of domestic life last. And, having offered to fly her home in his private jet, he probably thought he'd been generous enough—caring, even.

Stifling a yawn, she closed her eyes. Ram's deluded world view didn't matter to her any more than he did. He might have been her boss, and he might be calling the shots now. But that would change as soon as they landed in Scotland. Edinburgh was her home, and she wasn't about to let anyone—especially not Ram Walker—trample over the life she had built there. Feeling calmer, she burrowed further down beneath the blanket...

She woke with a start.

For a moment she lay there, utterly disorientated, trying to make sense of the soft wool brushing against her face and the clean coolness of the air, and then suddenly she was wide awake as the previous night's events slid into place inside her head.

Opening her eyes, she struggled to sit up, her senses on high alert.

Why did it feel as though they were slowing down? Surely she couldn't have slept for that long? Picking up her phone, she glanced at the screen and frowned. It didn't make sense. They'd only been flying a couple of hours, and yet the plane seemed to be descending.

'Good, you're awake.'

Her heart gave a jolt, and she turned.

It was Ram. He was standing beside her, his face calm, his grey eyes watching her with an expression she didn't quite recognise.

'I thought I was going to have to wake you,' he said coolly.

He was holding his laptop loosely in one hand, so he must have spent the last few hours working, and yet he looked just as though he'd had a full eight hours' sleep. She could practically feel the energy humming off him like a force field.

But that wasn't the only reason her pulse was racing.

With his dark hair falling over his forehead, and his crisp white shirt hugging the muscles of his chest and arms, he looked like a movie star playing a CEO. Even the unflattering overhead lights did nothing to diminish his beauty.

Was it really necessary or fair for him to be that perfect? she thought desperately. Particularly when her own body seemed incapable of co-ordinating with her brain, so that despite his appalling behaviour at the airport her senses were responding shamelessly to his blatant masculinity.

Gritting her teeth, hoping that none of her thoughts were showing on her face, she met his gaze.

'Why are we slowing down? Are we stopping for fuel?'

'Something like that.'

He studied her face for a moment, and then glanced back along the cabin. 'I just need to go and speak to the crew. I won't be long.'

Biting her lip, she stared after him, a prickle spreading over her skin. She sat in uneasy silence, her senses tracking the plane's descent, until she felt the jolt as it landed.

Something felt a bit off. But probably it was just because she'd never flown on a private jet before. Usually at this point everyone would be standing up and pulling down their luggage, chatting and grabbing their coats. This was so quiet, so smooth, so civilised. So A-list.

Glancing out of the window, Nola smiled. They might not be in Scotland yet, but the weather was doing its best to make her feel as if they were. She could hear the wind already, and fat drops of rain were slapping against the glass.

'Come on—let's go!'

Turning, she saw that Ram was standing beside her, his hand held out towards her.

She frowned. 'Go where? Don't we just wait?'

'They need to clean the plane and do safety checks. And then the crew are going off-shift.'

She gazed up at him warily.

'So where are we going?'

'Somewhere more comfortable. It's not far.'

Her heart began to thump. Maybe it would have been better after all if she'd just waited for another flight. But it was too late to worry about that now.

It was warm outside—tropical, even—but she still ducked her head against the wind and the rain.

'Be careful.'

Ram took hold of her arm and, ignoring her protests, guided her down the stairs.

'I can manage,' she said curtly.

But still he ignored her, tightening his grip as he walked her across the runway to an SUV that was idling in the darkness.

Inside the car, he leaned forward and tapped against the glass. 'Thanks, Carl. Just take it slow, okay?'

'I thought you said it wasn't far,' she said accusingly.

Turning back to face her, he shrugged. But there was a small, satisfied smile on his handsome face that made her heart start to bang against her ribs.

'It isn't. But this way we stay nice and dry.' His eyes mocked her. 'Despite what you may have heard, I can't actually control the weather.'

She nodded, but she was barely listening to what he said; she was too busy squinting through the window into the darkness outside.

Stopover destinations to and from Australia usually depended on the airline. It could be Hong Kong, Dubai, Singapore or Los Angeles. Of course flying on a private jet probably meant that some of those options weren't available. But, even so, something didn't feel right.

For a start there were no lights, nor even anything that really passed as a building. In fact she couldn't really see much at all, except a tangled, dark mass of trees and vegetation stretching away into the distance. Her heart began to beat faster, and she felt a rush of cold air on her skin that had nothing to do with the car's air conditioning.

She forced herself to speak. 'Where exactly are we?'

'Queensland—just west of Cairns.'

Turning, she stared at him in confusion, her mouth suddenly dry.

'What? We haven't even left Australia? So why have we stopped? We're never going to get to Scotland at this rate!'

'We're not going to Scotland,' he said quietly.

That prickling feeling had returned, and with it a sensation that she was floating—that if she hadn't been gripping the door handle so tightly she might have just drifted away.

'What do you mean? Of course, we're going to Scotland—' She broke off as he started to shake his head.

'Actually, we're not.'

His eyes glittered in the darkness, and she felt her breath catch in her throat.

'We never were. It was always my intention to bring you here.'

She stared at him in silence. Fury, shock, disbelief and frustration were washing over her like waves breaking against a sea wall.

Here? Here!

What was he talking about?

'There is no *"here"*,' she said shakily. 'We're in the middle of nowhere.'

He was mad. Completely mad. There was no other explanation for his behaviour. How could she not have noticed before?

'You and I need to talk, Nola.'

'And you want to do that in the middle of a jungle?' She was practically shouting now. Not that he seemed to care.

She watched in disbelief as calmly he shook his head.

'It's actually a rainforest. Only parts of it are classified as a jungle. And clearly I'm not expecting us to talk there. I have a house about three miles from here. It's very beautiful and completely private—what you might call secluded, in fact, so we won't be disturbed.'

Her head was spinning.

'I don't care if you have a palace with its own zoological gardens. I am not going there now or at any other time—and I'm definitely not going there with *you*.'

He lounged back against the seat, completely unperturbed by her outburst, his dark eyes locking onto hers. 'And yet here you are.'

She stared at him in shock, too stunned, too dazed to speak. Then, slowly, she started to shake her head. 'No. You can't do this. I want you to turn this car around now—'

Her whole body was shaking. This was far, far worse than missing her flight or Ram joining her on the plane.

Leaning forward, she began banging desperately on the glass behind the driver's head.

'Please—you have to help me!'

Behind her, she heard Ram sigh. 'You're going to hurt your hand, and it won't make any difference. So why don't you just calm down and try and relax?'

Her head jerked round. 'Relax! How am I supposed to relax? You're *kidnapping* me!'

Ram stretched out his legs. He could hear the exasperation and fury in her voice—could almost see it crackling from the ends of her gleaming dark hair.

Good, he thought silently. Now she knew how he felt. How it felt to have your life turned upside down. Suddenly no longer to be in charge of your own destiny.

'Am I? I'm not asking anyone for a ransom. Nor am I planning to blindfold you and tie you to the bed,' he said softly, his gaze holding hers. 'Unless, of course, you want me to.'

He watched two flags of colour rise on her cheekbones as she slid back into her seat, as far from him as was physically possible.

'All I want is for you to stop acting like some caveman.' She breathed out shakily. 'People don't behave like this. It's barbaric...primitive.'

'Primitive?' He repeated the word slowly, letting the seconds crawl by, feeling his groin hardening as she refused to make eye contact with him. 'I thought you liked primitive,' he said softly.

'That was different.' Turning her head sharply, she glowered at him. 'And it has nothing to do with any of this.'

'On the contrary. You and I tearing each other's clothes off has everything to do with this.'

'I don't want to talk about it,' she snapped, her blue eyes wide with fury. 'I don't want to talk to you about anything. In fact the only conversation I'm going to be having is with the police.'

She sounded breathless, as though she'd been running. He watched her pull out her phone and punch at the buttons.

'Oh, perhaps I should have mentioned it earlier… there's pretty much zero coverage out here.'

He smiled in a way that made her want to throw the phone at his head.

'It's one of the reasons I like it so much—no interruptions, no distractions.'

Fingers trembling with anger, she switched off her phone and pressed herself against the door. 'I hate you.'

'I don't care.'

The rest of the journey passed in uncomfortable silence. Nola felt as though she'd swallowed a bucket of ice; her whole body was rigid with cold, bitter fury. When finally the car came to a stop at his house she slid across the seat and out of the door without so much as acknowledging his presence.

Staring stonily at his broad shoulders in his dark suit jacket, she followed him through a series of rooms and corridors, barely registering anything other than the resentment hardening inside her chest.

'This is your room. The bathroom is through there.'

She glared at him. 'My room? How long are you planning on keeping me here?'

He ignored her. 'You'll find everything you need.'

'Really? You mean there's a shotgun and a shovel?'

His eyes hardened. 'The sooner you stop fighting me, Nola, the sooner this will all be over. If you need me, I'm just next door. I'll see you in the morning.'

'Unless you're going to lock me in, I won't be here in the morning.'

He stared at her impatiently. 'I don't need to lock you in. It would take you the best part of a day to walk back to the airfield. And there would be no point. There's nothing there. And if you want to get to civilisation that's a three-day walk through the rainforest—a rainforest with about twenty different kinds of venomous snakes living in it.'

'Does that include you?' she snarled.

But he had already closed the door.

Left alone, Nola pulled off her clothes and angrily yanked on her pyjamas. She still couldn't believe what was happening. How could he treat her like this?

Worse—how could he treat her like this and then expect her to sit down and have a civilised conversation with him?

She clenched her jaw. He could expect what he liked. But he couldn't make her talk or listen if she didn't want to.

Her eyes narrowed. In fact she might just stay in her room.

She would think about it properly in the morning. Right now she needed to close her eyes and, climbing into bed, she pulled the duvet up to her chin, rolled onto her side, and fell swiftly and deeply into sleep.

Ram strode into the huge open-plan living space, his frustration with Nola vying with his fury at himself.

What the hell was he doing?

He'd only just found out he was going to be a father. Surely that was enough to be dealing with right now?

But apparently not, for he had decided to add to the chaos and drama of the evening by kidnapping Nola.

Because, regardless of what he had said to her in the car, this *was* kidnapping.

Groaning, he ran a hand wearily over his face.

But what choice had she given him?

Ever since she'd forced him to meet her at that internet café she had challenged him at every turn. But she was pregnant with his child now, and her leaving the country was more than defiance. Even though she'd said she would be in touch, he hadn't believed her.

His face hardened. And why should he? She had kept the pregnancy secret for months, and even when she'd had the perfect opportunity to tell him about the baby she had chosen instead to avoid him. And then tried to run away.

But Nola was going nowhere now. She certainly wasn't going to Scotland any time soon.

He breathed out slowly. In fact, make that *never*.

If she moved back to Edinburgh, then he would be cut out of his baby's life. Not only that, his child would grow up with another man as his father—with another man's name instead of his. Worse, he or she would grow up believing themselves to be a burden not worth bearing, a mistake to be regretted.

He would do whatever it took to stop that from happening.

Crossing the room, he poured himself a whisky and downed it in one mouthful.

Even kidnapping.

His chest tightened.

What had he been thinking?

But that was just it. He hadn't been thinking at all—he'd just reacted on impulse, his emotions blindly driving his actions, so that now he had a woman he barely knew, who was carrying a child he hadn't planned, sleeping in the spare room in what was supposed to be his private sanctuary from the world.

Gritting his teeth, he poured himself another whisky and drank that too.

So why had he brought Nola here?

But he knew why. He hadn't been exaggerating when he'd said that the house was secluded. It was luxurious, of course, but it was completely inaccessible to anyone without a small plane or helicopter, and on most days communicating with the outside world was almost impossible.

Here, he and Nola would be completely alone and they would be able to talk.

His fingers twitched against the empty glass.

Except that talking was the last thing he wanted to do with her. Particularly now that they were alone, miles from civilisation.

A pulse began to beat in his groin.

For a moment he stared longingly at the bottle of whisky. But where Nola was concerned it would take a lot more than alcohol to lock down his libido. A cold shower might be better—and if that didn't work he might have to go and swim a few lengths in the pool. And then maybe a few more.

He'd do whatever was necessary to re-engage his brain so that tomorrow he could tell Nola exactly how this was all going to play out.

* * *

As soon as she woke Nola reached over to pick up her phone, holding her breath as she quickly punched in Anna's number. When that failed to connect she called the office, then Anna again, and then, just to be certain, her favourite takeaway pizzeria by the harbour. But each time she got the same recorded message, telling her that there was no network coverage, and finally she gave up.

Rolling onto her side, she gazed in silence around the bedroom. It was still dark, but unless she'd slept the entire day it must be morning. She wasn't planning on going anywhere, but there was no point in lying there in the dark. Sighing, she sat up. Immediately she heard a small click, and then daylight began filling the room as two huge blinds slid smoothly up into the ceiling.

She gasped. But it wasn't the daylight or the blinds or even the room itself that made her hold her breath. It was the pure, brilliant blue sky outside the window.

Heart pounding, she scrambled across the bed and gazed down at a huge canopy of trees, her eyes widening as a group of brightly coloured birds burst out of the dark green leaves. She watched open-mouthed as they circled one another, looping and curling in front of her window like miniature acrobatic planes, before suddenly plunging back into the trees.

She had been planning on staying in her room to protest against Ram's behaviour. But ten minutes later she had showered, dug some clean clothes out of her suitcase and was standing by her bedroom door.

Her pulse began to beat very fast. If she opened that

door she would have to face Ram. But sooner or later she was going to have to face him anyway, she told herself firmly.

And, not giving herself the chance to change her mind, she stalked determinedly out of her room.

In daylight, the house was astonishingly, dazzlingly bright. Every wall was made of glass, and there were walkways at different levels, leading to platforms actually within the rainforest itself.

No doubt it had been designed that way, she thought slowly. So that the wildlife could be watched up close but safely in its natural environment.

Her heart began to thump.

Only some of the wildlife clearly didn't understand the rules, for there on the deck, standing at the edge of an infinity pool, was one of the most dangerous animals in Australia—probably in the world.

Unfortunately there was no safety glass between her and Ram.

She was on the verge of making a quick, unobtrusive retreat when suddenly he turned, and her breath seemed to slide sideways in her chest as he began slowly walking towards her.

It was the heat, she thought helplessly. Although she wasn't sure if it was the sun or the sight of Ram in swimming shorts that was making her skin feel warm and slick.

She tried not to stare, but he was so unbelievably gorgeous—all smooth skin and golden muscles. Now he was stopping in front of her and smiling, as though yesterday had never happened, and the stupid thing was that she didn't feel as though it had happened either. Or at least her body didn't.

'Good morning.' He squinted up at the sky. 'I think it still qualifies as morning.' Tilting his head, he let his eyes drift casually over her face. 'I was going to come and wake you up. But I didn't fancy getting punched on the nose.'

She met his gaze unwillingly. 'So you admit that I've got a reason to punch you, then?'

He grinned, and instantly she felt a tug low in her pelvis, heat splaying out inside her so quickly and fiercely that she thought she might pass out.

'I'm not sure if you need a reason,' he said softly. 'Most of the time I seem to annoy you just by existing.'

She gazed at him in silence, trying to remember why that was.

'Not always,' she said carefully. 'Only some of the time. Like when you kidnap me, for instance.'

There was a short, pulsing silence, and then finally he sighed.

'We need to talk about this now, Nola. Not in a week or a month. And, yes, maybe I overreacted, bringing you here like this. But you've been building a life, a future, that doesn't include me.'

Her heart gave a thump. 'I thought you *wanted* that.'

'What if I said I didn't?'

His eyes were fixed on her face.

She breathed out slowly, the world shifting out of focus around her.

'Then I guess we need to talk.'

'And we will.' His gaze locked onto hers. 'But first

I'll give you the tour, and then you'd better eat something.'

The tour was brief, but mind-blowing. The house was minimalist in design—a stunning mix of metal and glass that perfectly offset the untamed beauty of the rainforest surrounding it.

Breakfast—or was it brunch?—took longer. A variety of cold meats, cheese, fruit and pastries were laid out buffet-style in the huge sunlit kitchen and, suddenly feeling famished, Nola helped herself to a plate of food and a cup of green tea while Ram watched with amusement.

'I have a live-in chef—Antoine. He's French, but he speaks very good English. If you have any particular likes or dislikes tell him. His wife, Sophie, is my housekeeper. She takes care of everything else. So if you need anything...'

Fingers tightening around her teacup, Nola met his gaze. 'Like what?'

He gave a casual shrug. 'I don't know. What about a bikini? You might fancy a swim.'

His eyes gleamed, and she felt something stir inside her as his gaze dropped over the plain white T-shirt that was just a fraction too small for her now.

'Unless, of course, you're planning on skinny-dipping.'

Ignoring the heat throbbing over her skin, she gave him an icy stare. 'I'm not planning on anything,' she said stiffly. 'Except leaving as soon as possible. I know we have a lot to talk about, but I hardly think it will take more than a day.'

He stared at her calmly. 'That will depend.'

'On what?'

He was watching her carefully, as though gauging her probable reaction to what he was about to say. But, really, given everything that he'd already said and done, how bad could it be?

'On what happens next. You see, I've given it a lot of thought,' he said slowly, 'and I can only think of one possible solution to this situation.'

Her nerves were starting to hum. She looked over at him impatiently. 'And? What is it?'

He stared at her for a long moment, and then finally he smiled.

'We need to marry. Preferably as soon as possible.'

CHAPTER SEVEN

Nola stared at him in stunned silence.

Marry?

As her brain dazedly replayed his words inside her head she felt her skin grow hot, and then her heart began to bang against her ribs. Surely he couldn't be serious.

She laughed nervously. 'This is a joke, right?'

For a moment he looked at her in silence, then slowly he shook his head.

She stared at him incredulously. 'But you don't want to get married.' Her eyes widened with shock and confusion. 'Everyone knows that. You told me so yourself.' She frowned. 'You said marriage was a Mobius strip of emotional scenes.'

Watching the pulse beating frantically at the base of her throat, Ram felt a flicker of frustration.

To be fair, her reaction wasn't really surprising. He'd spent most of the night thinking along much the same lines himself. But, as he'd just told her, marriage was the only solution—the only way he could give his child the *right* kind of life. A life that was not just financially secure but filled with the kind of certainty that came from *belonging*.

He shrugged. 'I agree that it's not a choice I've ever imagined making. But situations change, and I'm nothing if not adaptable.'

Adaptable! Nola felt her breathing jerk. What was he talking about? As soon as she'd shown the first signs of not wanting to do things his way he'd kidnapped her!

'Oh, I see—so that's what this is all about.' She loaded her voice with sarcasm. 'Dragging me out here, trying to coerce me into marrying you, is just your way of showing me how *adaptable* you are.' She gave a humourless laugh. 'You're about as adaptable as a tornado, Ram. If there's anything in your path it just gets swept away.'

'If that was true we wouldn't be having this conversation,' he said calmly.

'How is this a conversation?' Nola shook her head. 'You just told me we *need* to marry. That sounds more like an order than a proposal.'

His eyes narrowed. 'I'm sorry if you were hoping for something a little more romantic, but you didn't exactly give me much time to look for a ring.'

She glowered at him, anger buzzing beneath her skin. 'I don't want a ring. And I wasn't hoping for anything from you. In case you hadn't noticed, I've managed just fine without you for the last three months.'

His gaze didn't flicker.

'I wouldn't know,' he said softly. 'As you didn't bother telling me you were having my baby until last night.'

Pushing away a twinge of guilt that she hadn't told him sooner, she gritted her teeth. It had been wrong of her not to tell him that she was pregnant. But marrying him wasn't going to put it right.

Only, glancing at the set expression on his face, she saw that Ram clearly thought it was.

Forcing herself to stay calm, she said quickly, 'And I've apologised. But why does that mean we need to get married?'

Ram felt his chest grow tight. Did he *really* need to answer that? His face hardened and he stared at her irritably. 'I would have thought that was obvious.'

For a fraction of a second his eyes held hers, and then he glanced pointedly down at her stomach.

'Because I'm *pregnant*?' She stared at him in exasperation, the air thumping out of her lungs. How could he do this? It was bad enough that he'd tricked her into coming here in the first place. But to sit there, so handsome and smug, making these absurd, arrogant statements... And then assume that she was just going to go along with them.

'Maybe a hundred years ago that might have been a reason. But it is possible to have a baby out of wedlock. People do it all the time now.'

'Not *my* baby,' Ram said flatly, his stomach clenching swiftly at her words.

How could she be so casual about this? So dismissive? Did she really think that having a father was discretionary? A matter of preference? Like having a dog or a cat?

He studied her face, seeing the fear and understanding it. *Good.* It was time she realised that he was being serious. Marriage wasn't an optional extra, like the adaptive suspension he'd had fitted on his latest Lamborghini. It was the endgame. The obvious denouement of that night on his sofa.

Shaking his head, trying to ignore the anger pooling there, he said coolly, 'By any definition this situation is a mess, and the simplest, most logical way to clear it up is for us to marry. Or are you planning on buying a crib and just hoping for the best?'

Nola felt her heartbeat trip over itself. How *dare* he?

She didn't know what was scaring her more. The fact that Ram was even considering this as an option, or his obvious belief that she was actually going to agree to it.

Looking up into his handsome face, she felt her skin begin to prickle. She couldn't agree. She might not have planned this pregnancy, but she knew she could make it work. Marrying Ram, though...

How could that be anything *but* a disaster?

They barely knew each other, had nothing in common, and managed to turn every single conversation into an argument. She swallowed. And, of course, they weren't in love—not even close to being in love.

Her head was spinning.

All they shared was this baby growing inside her, and one passionate night of sex. But marriages weren't built on one-night stands. And, no matter how incredible that night had been, she wasn't so naive as to believe that a man like Ram Walker would view his wedding vows as anything but guidelines.

Her fingers curved into the palms of her hands. For

her—for most people—marriage meant commitment. Monogamy.

But Ram could barely manage five days with the same woman. So how exactly was he planning on forsaking all others?

Or was he expecting to be able to carry on just as he pleased?

Either way, how long would it be before he felt trapped…resentful?

Or, worse, bored?

Remembering the distracted look in her father's eyes, the sense that he was always itching to be somewhere else and her own panicky need to try and make him stay, she felt sick.

She knew instinctively that Ram would be the same.

Wanting Nola to be his wife was just the knee-jerk response of a CEO faced with an unexpected problem. But she didn't want her marriage to be an exercise in damage limitation. Surely he could understand that.

But, looking over at him, she felt a rush of panic.

He looked so calm, almost too calm, as though her opposition to his ludicrous suggestion was just a mere formality—some twisted version of bridal nerves.

And with any other woman he would probably be right in thinking that. After all, he'd almost certainly never met anyone who had turned him down.

Her heart began to pound.

Until now.

Slowly, she shook her head.

'I can't marry you, Ram. Right now, I'm not sure I ever want to be married. But if at some point I do, it will be because the man asking me *loves* me and wants me to be his wife.'

His face was expressionless, but his eyes were cool and resolute.

'And what happens if you don't marry? I doubt you'll stay single for ever, so how will that work? Are you going to live with a man? Is he just going to spend the occasional night in your bed?'

She felt her face drain of colour.

'I don't know. And you can't expect me to be able to answer all those questions now. That's not fair—'

His eyes were locked on hers.

'*I don't know* is not a good enough answer,' he said coldly. 'And the life you're planning for our child sounds anything but fair.'

'I'm not planning anything.' She stared at him helplessly.

'Well, at least we can agree on that,' he snarled. 'Believe me, Nola, when I tell you that no child of mine is going to be brought up by whichever random man happens to be in your life at that particular moment.'

'That's not—' She started to protest but he cut her off.

'Nor is my child going to end up with another man's name because its mother was too stubborn and selfish to marry its father.'

She stood up so quickly the chair she was sitting on flew backwards. But neither of them noticed.

'Oh, I see. So you marrying me is a *selfless* act,' she snapped. Her blue eyes flashed angrily up at him. 'A real sacrifice—'

'You're putting words in my mouth.'

'And you're putting a gun to my head,' she retorted. 'I'm not going to marry you just to satisfy your archaic need to pass on a name.'

'Names matter.'

She shivered. 'You mean *your* name matters.'

Ram felt his chest tighten. Yes, he did mean that. A name was more than just a title. It was an identity, a destiny, a piece of code from the past that mapped out the future.

His eyes locked onto hers. 'Children need to know where they come from. They need to belong.'

'Then what's wrong with *my* name?' she said stubbornly. 'I'm the mother. This baby is inside *me*. How could it belong to anyone more than to me?'

'Now you're just being contrary.'

'Why? Because I don't want to marry you?'

He shook his head, his dark gaze locked onto hers. 'Because you know I'm right but you're mad at me for bringing you here so you're just going to reject the only logical solution without a moment's consideration.'

Nola felt despair edge past her panic. His cavalier attitude to her objections combined with his obvious belief that she would crumble was overwhelming her.

'I have considered it and it won't work,' she said quickly. 'And it doesn't have to. Look, this is *my* responsibility. I should have been more careful. That's why this is on *me*.'

'This is *on you*?' He repeated her words slowly, his voice utterly expressionless.

But as she looked over at him she felt the hairs on

the back of her neck stand up. His eyes were narrowed, fixed on her face like a sniper.

'We're not talking about a round of drinks, Nola. This is a baby. A life.'

She flinched. 'Biology is not a determining factor in parenthood.'

He looked at her in disbelief. 'Seriously? Did you read that in the in-flight magazine?'

She looked at him helplessly. 'No, I just meant—'

He cut her off again. 'Tell me, Nola. Did you have a father?'

The floor seemed to tilt beneath her feet. 'Yes. But I don't—'

'But you don't what?' He gave a short, bitter laugh. 'You don't want that for your own child?'

She blinked. Tears were pricking at her eyes. But she wasn't going to lose control—at least not here and now, in front of Ram.

'You're right,' she said shakily. 'I don't want that. And I never will.'

And before he had a chance to reply she turned and walked swiftly out of the kitchen.

She walked blindly, her legs moving automatically in time to the thumping of her heart, wanting nothing more than to find somewhere to hide, somewhere dark and private, away from Ram's cold, critical gaze. Somewhere she could curl up and cradle the cold ache of misery inside her.

Her feet stopped. Somehow she had managed to find the perfect place—a window looking out into the canopy of the rainforest. There was even a sofa and, her legs trembling, she sat down, her throat burning, hands clenched in her lap.

For a moment she just gazed miserably into the trees, and then abruptly her whole body stilled as she noticed a pair of eyes gazing back at her. Slowly, she inched forward—and just like that they were gone.

'It was a goanna. If you sit here long enough it will probably come back.'

She turned as Ram sat down next to her on the sofa.

She stared at him warily, shocked not only by the fact that he had come to find her but by the fact that his anger, the hardness in his eyes, had faded.

'Did I scare it?'

Ram held her gaze. 'They're just cautious—they run away when something or someone gets too close.'

Watching her lip tremble, he felt his heart start to pound. She looked so stricken...so small.

His breath caught in his throat. In his experience women exploited emotion with the skill and precision of a samurai wielding a sword. But Nola was different. She hadn't wanted him to see that she was upset. On the contrary, she had been as desperate to get away as that lizard.

Desperate to get away from *him*.

An ache was spreading inside his chest and he gritted his teeth, not liking the way it made him feel, for he would never hurt her. In fact he had wanted more than anything to reach out and pull her against him. But of course he hadn't. Instead he'd watched her leave.

Only almost immediately, and for the first time in

his life, he'd been compelled to follow. He'd had no choice—his legs had been beyond his conscious control.

He stared at her in silence, all at once seeing not only the tight set of her shoulders and the glint of tears but also what he'd chosen to ignore earlier: her vulnerability.

Shifting back slightly, to give her more space, he cleared his throat.

'There's always something to see,' he said carefully. 'We could stay and watch if you want?'

He phrased it as a question—something he would never normally do. But right now getting her to relax, to trust him, seemed more important than laying down the law.

She didn't reply, and he felt an unfamiliar twitch of panic that maybe she never would.

But finally she nodded. 'I'd like that. Apart from the odd squirrel, I've never seen anything wild up close.'

'Too busy studying?'

It was a guess, but she nodded again.

'I did work too hard,' she agreed. 'I think it was a survival technique.'

Staring past him, Nola bit her lip. She'd spoken without thinking, the words coming from deep inside. Memories came of hours spent hunched over her schoolbooks, trying to block out the raised voices downstairs, and then—worse—the horrible, bleak silence that had always followed.

Ram stared at her uncertainly, hating the bruised sound of her voice. This was the sort of conversation he'd spent a lifetime avoiding. Only this time he didn't want to avoid it. In fact he was actually scared of spooking her, and suddenly he was desperate to say something—anything to make her trust him enough to keep talking.

'Why do you think that?' he asked gently.

She swallowed. 'My dad was often home late, or away, and my parents would always argue when he got home. He'd storm off, and my mum would cry, and I'd stay in my room and do my homework.'

The ache in her voice cut him almost as much as her words, for he was beginning to understand now why she was so determined to stay single, so vehemently opposed even to letting him know about the baby.

'Are they still together?'

She shook her head.

'They divorced when I was seven. At first it was better. It was calmer at home, and my dad made a real effort. He even promised to take me to the zoo in Edinburgh for my birthday. Only he forgot. Not just about the zoo, but about my birthday too.'

Ram felt as though he'd been punched hard in the face. He felt a vicious, almost violent urge to find her father and tell him exactly what he thought of him.

She breathed out unsteadily. 'About two months later I got a card and some money. The following year he forgot my birthday again. One year he even managed to forget me at Christmas. Of course when he remembered I got the biggest, glitziest present…'

Nola could feel Ram's gaze on her face, but she couldn't look at him. She couldn't let him see what her father had seen and rejected: her need to be loved.

Couldn't bear for him to guess her most closely guarded secret. That she hadn't been enough of a reason for her father to make the effort.

'I thought he'd stopped loving my mum, and that was why he left. But he didn't love me either, and he left me too.'

'And that's what you think I'd do?'

Turning her head, she finally met his eyes. 'You have to put children first. Only sometimes people just can't do that, and I'm not blaming them...'

His grey eyes were searching her face, and she felt a rush of panic. How could she expect Ram to understand? He wouldn't know what it was like to feel so unimportant, so easy to forget, so disposable.

'Sometimes you have to give people a chance too,' he said quietly.

Nola bit her lip. His voice sounded softer, and she could sense that he was if not backing down then backing off, trying to calm her. But her heart was still beating too fast for her to relax. And anyway... Her pulse shivered violently... It wasn't as though he was going to change his mind. He was just trying a different tactic, biding his time while he waited for her to give in.

Suddenly she could no longer rein in the panic rising up inside her. 'I can't do this, Ram. I know you think I'm just being difficult. But I'm not. I know what marrying the wrong person can do people. It's just so damaging and destructive. And what's worse is that even when the marriage ends that damage doesn't stop. It just goes on and on—'

'Nola.'

Her body tensed as he lifted a hand and stroked a long dark curl away from her face.

'I'm not going to behave like your father did. I'm not walking away from you, or our baby. I'm fighting to make it work. Why do you think I want to marry you?'

She shook her head. 'You want it *now*. But soon you'll start to think differently, and then you'll *feel* differently. And we hardly know each other, Ram. Having a baby won't change that, and there is nothing else between us.'

His gaze seemed to burn into hers. 'We both know that's not true.'

She swallowed. 'That was one night...'

'Was it?' Ram studied her face. He could see the conflict in her eyes, and with shock he realised that it mirrored what he was feeling himself—the longing, the fear, the confusion. The pain.

He didn't want to feel her pain, or his own. He didn't want to feel anything. And for a fraction of a second he was on the verge of pulling her into his arms and doing what he always did to deflect emotion—his own and other people's.

But something held him back—a sudden understanding that if he didn't allow himself to feel, then he would never be able to comfort Nola, and right now that was all that mattered.

Not himself, nor his business, the launch, or even getting her to agree to this marriage, but Nola herself.

In shock, clenching his hands until they hurt, he

gazed past her, struggling to explain this wholly un-characteristic behaviour.

Surely, though, it was only natural for him to care. Nola was carrying his child.

Turning, he breathed out slowly, staring down into her eyes. 'I know you don't trust me. And if I were you I'd feel exactly the same. I haven't exactly given you much reason to have faith in me, bringing you here like I have.'

He grimaced.

'I just wanted to give us some time and some privacy. I didn't think we could sort things out with everything else going on, and I still think that. But I'm not going to force you to marry me, Nola. Or even to stay here if you don't want to.'

Reaching into his pocket, he pulled out a phone and held it out to her, watching her eyes widen with con-fusion.

'I didn't lie to you. There is no coverage here. That's why I have this. It's a satellite phone. If you want to leave you can call the pilot. If you stay, I want it to be your choice.'

Nola stared at him, her tears beaten back by Ram's words. This was a concession. More than that, it was a chance to get her life back.

She glanced down at the phone, her brain fast-forwarding. They could handle this through their law-yers. There was probably no need even to see one another again. But was that really what she wanted? What was best for their baby?

'I'll stay.' She held his gaze. 'But I might ring Anna later, or tomorrow. Just to let her know I'm okay.'

He pocketed the phone and nodded, and then after the briefest hesitation he reached over and took her hand in his.

'I know this is a big step for both of us, Nola. But I think we can make it work if we compromise a little.'

Nola gazed at him blankly. 'Compromise?'

He frowned. 'That *is* a word, isn't it?'

She smiled weakly. 'It is. I'm just not sure you understand what it means. Maybe you're thinking of another word.'

His grey eyes softened, and she felt her pulse dip as he lifted her hand to his mouth and kissed it gently. 'Let's see... I think it means I have to stop acting like a tornado and listen to what you're saying.'

She felt her stomach drop. Ram might have been difficult to defy when he was angry, but he was impossible to resist when he was smiling.

'That sounds like a compromise,' she said cautiously. 'But what does it mean in real terms?'

'It means that I think we need time to get used to the idea of getting married and to each other.'

She bit her lip. 'How much time?'

'As long as it takes.' He met her gaze. 'I'll wait, Nola. For as long as it takes.'

Her pulse was jumping again. For a moment they stared at one another, breathing unsteadily, and then finally she gave him a hesitant smile.

'That could work.'

And maybe it would, for suddenly she knew that for the first time she was actually willing to consider marrying him.

* * *

They spent the rest of the morning together, watching lizards and frogs and birds through the glass. Ram knew a surprising amount about the various animals and plants, and she found herself not only relaxing, but enjoying herself and his company.

So much so that as she dialled Anna's number the following morning she found it increasingly difficult to remember that he was the same person who had made her feel so horribly trapped and desperate.

'So let me get this right,' Anna said slowly down the phone. 'You're staying with Ram Walker in his rainforest treehouse. Just you and him. Even though we don't work for him anymore. And you think that's normal?'

'I didn't say that,' Nola protested, glancing over to where Ram lay lounging in the sun, a discarded paperback on the table beside him. 'Obviously nothing he does is normal. He's the richest man in Australia. I just said that me being here is not that big a deal.'

Her friend gave a short, disbelieving laugh. 'Is that why I wasn't invited?'

Nola grimaced. 'You weren't invited because you're in Edinburgh. With a broken foot and a husband.'

'I *knew* it!' Anna said triumphantly. 'So there *is* something going on!'

'No!' Nola froze as Ram turned and glanced over at her curiously. Lowering her voice, she said quickly. 'Well, it's complicated…'

She badly wanted to tell her best friend the truth. Sooner or later she would have to. Her fingers gripped the phone more tightly.

'I'm pregnant, and Ram's the father.'

Her words hung in silence down the phone and she closed her eyes, equal parts of hope and fear rising up inside her. What if Anna was disgusted? Or never wanted to speak to her again?

'That's why I'm here. We're talking things through.' Breathing out shakily, she pressed the phone against her face. 'I wanted to tell you before, but—'

'It was complicated?'

Nola opened her eyes with relief. Her friend's voice was gentle, and full of love. It was going to be okay.

'I'm sorry. I just couldn't get think straight.'

Anna laughed. 'That's okay. I forgive you as long as you tell me everything now.'

She didn't tell Anna everything, but she gave her friend an edited version of the last few days. But even while she was talking she was thinking about Ram. Having finally stopped fighting him, all she wanted was to concentrate on the two of them building a relationship that would work for their child.

That was, after all, the reason she'd decided to stay.

The only reason.

Her cheeks grew hotter.

Try telling that to her body.

Her mouth was suddenly dry. Staring across the deck at Ram, she felt her breath catch fire. It was true, she *did* want a relationship with him that would work for their child. But that didn't mean she could deny the way her body reacted to his. Even now, just looking at him was playing havoc with her senses. And up close he seemed to trigger some internal alarm system, so that she felt constantly restless, her body shivering and tightening and melting all at the same time.

But her relationship with Ram was already complicated enough. So it didn't matter that no man had ever made her feel the way he had. Giving in to the sexual pull between them would only add another layer of complication neither of them needed.

Her mouth twisted.

Maybe if she told herself that often enough, she might actually start to believe it.

'So,' Ram said softly, as she sat down beside him and handed him the phone, 'is everything okay?'

She nodded. 'Yes. I told her about the baby. She was a little...' she hesitated, searching for the right word '...stunned at first, but she was cool about it.'

Ram studied her face. Since agreeing to stay, Nola had seemed more relaxed, but he couldn't shift the image from his head of her looking so small and crushed, and impulsively he reached out and ran his fingers over her arm.

'You need to be careful. Are you wearing enough sunblock?'

She grimaced. 'Loads. I used to try and tan, but it never works. I just burn and then peel, so now I am fully committed to factor fifty.'

'Is that right?' His gaze roamed over her face. 'Then I'm jealous. I only want you to be fully committed to *me*.'

Nola blinked. He must be teasing her, she decided. Ram might want to marry her in order to legitimise this pregnancy, but he didn't do commitment. And jealousy would require an emotional response she knew he wasn't capable of or willing to give. But knowing that didn't stop her stomach flipping over in response to the possessiveness in his words.

Hoping her thought process wasn't showing on her face, she said lightly, 'You've got bigger competition than a bottle of sunblock.'

His eyes narrowed. 'I do?'

He let his fingers curl around her wrist, and then gently he pulled her towards him so that suddenly their eyes were level.

'I thought you said you didn't have anyone missing you,' he said softly.

She bit her lip. 'I don't think he does miss me. He's quite self-sufficient...' Glancing up at the stubble shadowing his jaw, she smiled. 'A little prickly. A bit like you, really. Except he's green, and he's got this cute little pot like a sombrero.'

Ram shook his head. 'I can't believe you're comparing me to a cactus.'

She laughed. 'There's no comparison. Colin is a low-maintenance dream. Whereas you—'

His eyes were light and dancing with amusement. 'I'm what?'

She felt her pulse begin to flutter. 'You have a private jet and a house in the rainforest.'

'And you care about that?'

She glanced up. Something in his tone had shifted, and he was watching her, his grey gaze oddly intent.

'No, I don't,' she said truthfully. It might sound rude, or ungrateful but she wasn't going to lie just to flatter him. 'It's lovely to have all this, but it doesn't matter to me. Other things are more important.'

Her father had taught her that. His gifts had always been over the top—embarrassingly so in comparison to what her mother had chosen for her. But there had been no thought involved, nothing personal about his choice. Nothing personal about the money he'd sent either, except that it had grown exponentially in relation to his neglect.

'Like what?

Ram was gazing at her curiously, but just as she opened her mouth to reply, his phone rang.

Glancing down at it, he frowned. 'Excuse me. I have to take this.'

Standing up, he walked away, his face tight with concentration.

She caught bits of the conversation, but nothing that gave her any clue as to who the caller might be. Not that she needed any. It would be work-related, because of course, despite what he'd said and what she'd chosen to believe, work would always come first. She just hadn't expected to have it pointed out to her quite so quickly.

Finally he hung up.

'Sorry about that.' His face was impassive, but there was a tension in his voice that hadn't been there before.

Looking up, she forced herself to smile casually, even though she felt flattened inside. 'When do they want you back?'

'Who?' He stared at her blankly.

'Work. Do you need to leave now?'

Ram didn't answer. He was too busy processing the

realisation that since getting off the plane he hadn't thought about work once. Even the launch seemed to belong to another life he had once lived. And forgotten.

He shook his head.

'It wasn't work. It was Pandora. My mother. I was supposed to have lunch with my parents today, only with everything that's happened I forgot.'

Catching sight of Nola's face, he shrugged.

'It's fine—honestly. My mother's portions are so tiny it's hardly worth the effort of going, and besides it gives Guy, my father, a chance to complain about me, so—'

'You could still go,' she said hastily. 'I can just stay here and—'

She stopped mid-sentence as his eyes locked onto hers.

'Why would you stay here?

'I don't know.' She hesitated. 'I just thought… I mean, obviously I'd like to meet them.'

Was that true? Her pulse jumped.

She was still wary of escalating their relationship too fast. But was that because her perception of marriage was so skewed by the past? Maybe lunch with Ram's family would help balance out her point of view. And, more importantly, it might give her some insight into the father of her child, for while she had talked a lot— about herself, her parents, even her cactus—Ram was still a mystery to her.

Take his parents. She didn't know anything about them. If she'd been shaped by her mother and father, then surely it was logical to assume that Ram had been shaped by his parents too. So why not take this opportunity to see what they were like? For the sake of their child, of course.

She glanced up at him hesitantly. 'Would you like me to meet them?'

Ram stared at her in silence, wondering how best to answer that question. Nola meeting his parents had not been part of the equation when he'd brought her here. Yet clearly she was trying to meet him halfway, and as it had been he who had suggested they get to know one another better it seemed churlish to refuse.

But going to lunch with them would mean leaving the rainforest, and he didn't want to do that.

He wanted to stay here with Nola. For it to be just the two of them. There was no need to involve Pandora and Guy. Only how could he explain that without having to explain who he was and *what* he was…?

His chest tightened.

Lifting his face, he smiled coolly. 'Of course. It will give me a chance to drop in at the office. There are a couple of papers I need. I'll ring her back and see if she can do tomorrow.'

CHAPTER EIGHT

THEY FLEW BACK to Sydney the next day.

Gazing out of the window, Nola wished her thoughts were as calm as the clear blue sky beyond the glass. It was hard to believe that only a few days ago she'd fled from the RWI building. So much had happened since then. So much had changed. Not least her perception of Ram.

She had believed him to be domineering, insensitive and unemotional, but as she glanced across the aircraft to where he stood, joking with the cabin crew, she knew that he was a different man than she'd thought.

Yes, he had as good as abducted her from the airport but, seeing her upset, he had backed down, given her the option of leaving. And he'd been unexpectedly gentle and understanding when she'd told him about her father.

Shifting in her seat, she bit her lip. She still didn't really understand why she had confided in Ram. The words had just spilled out before she'd been able to stop them. But she didn't regret it, for they had both learnt something about one another as a result.

Yet now she was about to meet *his* parents, and she

could feel all her old nervousness creeping over her skin. Glancing down at her skirt, she pressed her hands against the fabric, smoothing out an imaginary crease.

If only they could just stay here on the plane, circling the earth for ever...

She jumped slightly as Ram sat down beside her, and plucked her hand from her lap. Threading his fingers through hers, he rested his grey eyes on her face.

'So, what's bothering you, then?'

'Nothing,' she protested.

'You haven't said more than two words since we got on the plane. And you're fidgeting. So let's start with the obvious first. What have I done?'

She shook her head again. 'You haven't done anything.'

'Okay. What have I said? Or not said?'

Despite her nerves, she couldn't help smiling.

'It's not you...it's nothing—' She stopped, suddenly at a loss for words. 'It's just been such a long time since I've done a family lunch, and spending time with my mum and dad was always so stressful.'

'Then you don't need to worry,' he said dryly. 'My parents are the perfect hosts. They would never do anything to make a guest feel uncomfortable.'

She frowned. There was an edge to his voice that hadn't been there before.

'Are you sure they don't mind me coming along too? I don't want to put them to any trouble.'

He smiled—an odd, twisted smile that made her heart lurch forward.

'Pandora is the queen of the charity dinner and the

benefit dance. She loves entertaining, and Guy does as he's told, so you coming to lunch will be absolutely no trouble at all.'

Her heart felt as if it were high up in her chest.

'And who do they think I am? I mean, in relation to you?' She hesitated. 'Have you told them about the baby?'

His face was expressionless. 'No. They don't need to know. As to who you are—I told them you used to work for me, and that now we're seeing one another.'

As she opened her mouth to protest, he shrugged.

'You're the first woman I've ever taken to meet them.' His grey eyes watched her steadily, his mouth tugging up at the corners. 'It was either that or pretend you were coming to fix the hard drive.'

They landed in Sydney an hour later. Ram's limo was waiting for them at the edge of the private airfield, and soon they were cruising along the motorway.

But instead of turning towards the city centre, as she'd expected, the car carried on.

'Didn't you want to go to the office first?' Frowning, Nola glanced over to where Ram was gazing down at his phone.

'I changed my mind.' He looked up, his face impassive. 'I thought you might like to freshen up, and I need to pick up a car.'

'Where are we going?'

He smiled. 'We're going home.'

She frowned. 'I thought you had a penthouse in the city?'

He shrugged. 'I do. It's convenient for work. But it's not my home.'

Home.

The word made her think of her flat in Edinburgh, her shabby sofas and mismatched crockery. But home for Ram turned out to be something altogether grander—a beautiful white mansion at the end of a private drive.

Stepping dazedly out of the car, Nola felt her heart jump. She'd recognised the name of the road as soon as they'd started to drive down it. How could she not? It was regularly cited as being the most expensive place to live in the country, and Ram's house more than lived up to that reputation.

'Welcome to Stanmore.' He was standing beside her, smiling, watching her face casually, but she could sense a tension beneath his smile, and suddenly she knew that he cared what she thought—and that fact made her throat tighten so that she couldn't speak.

'It's incredible,' she managed finally.

A couple of hours ago she'd denied being intimidated by his wealth, but now she wasn't sure that was still true. For a moment she hesitated, caught between fear and curiosity, but then his hand caught hers and he tugged her forward.

'I'm glad you think so. Now, come on. I want to show you round.'

As they wandered through the beautiful interior Nola caught her breath, her body transformed into a churning mass of insecurity. How could Ram seriously expect them to marry? This was a different world from hers. And no doubt his parents would realise that the moment she walked through their door.

'My great-great-grandfather, Stanley Armitage, bought this land in 1864,' Ram said casually as he led her into a beautiful living room with uninterrupted views of the ocean. 'I'm the fifth generation of my family to live here.'

Nola nodded. 'So you grew up here?'

His face didn't change but his eyes narrowed slightly.

'My mother moved out when she got married. They live just along the road. But I spent most of my holidays here, aside from the odd duty dinner with my parents.' He paused. 'Which reminds me… We should probably think about getting ready.'

Nola gazed down at her skirt and blouse in dismay. They had looked fine when she'd put them on that morning, but after two hours of travelling she felt sticky and dishevelled.

'I can't meet your parents looking like this.'

'So don't,' he said easily.

'But I don't have anything else.'

'Yes, you do.'

Before she had a chance to reply, he was towing her upstairs, through one of the bedrooms and into a large dressing room.

'I know you acted cool about it, but I thought you might worry about being underdressed, so I spoke to my mother's stylist and she sent these over this morning.'

Hanging from a rail were at least twenty outfits in clear, protective wrappers.

Nola gazed at them speechlessly.

He grinned, obviously pleased by her reaction. 'Pick something you like. I think there are shoes as well. I'm just going to go change.'

She nodded. But picking something was not as easy as Ram's throwaway remark had implied. The clothes were all so beautiful… Finally she settled on a pale blue dress with a pretty ribbon-edged cardigan that cleverly concealed her bump. Her cheeks were already flushed, so she didn't bother with any blusher, but she brushed her hair until it lay smoothly over her shoulders, and then added a smudge of clear lip gloss.

'You look beautiful.'

Turning, she caught her breath. Ram was lounging in the doorway, his grey eyes glittering with approval.

'So do you,' she said huskily, her gaze drifting over his dark suit and cornflower-blue shirt.

Holding out his hand, he grinned. 'Who? Me? I'm just here to drive the car.'

The car turned out to be a Lamborghini, low to the ground and an eye-catching bright blue.

As they drove the short distance to his parents' house she couldn't resist teasing him about the colour. 'Did you choose the car to match your shirt?'

He gave her a heartbreaking smile. 'No, your eyes,' he said softly. 'Now, stop distracting me.'

She bit her lip, her expression innocent. 'I distract you?'

Shaking his head, he grimaced. 'More like bewitch me. Since I met you in that café I haven't been able to concentrate on anything. I've hardly done any work for months. If I wasn't me, I'd fire myself.'

Glancing out of the window, with his words humming inside her head, she felt suddenly ridiculously happy—even though, she reminded herself quickly, Ram was really only talking about the sexual chemistry between them.

Two minutes later he shifted down a gear and turned into a driveway. Nola could see tennis courts and a rectangle of flawless green grass.

'It's a putting green,' Ram said quietly. 'Guy is a big golf fan.'

She nodded. Of course it was a putting green.

But then the putting green was forgotten, for suddenly she realised why Ram had taken her to his house first.

As he switched off the engine she breathed out slowly. 'You thought all this would scare me, didn't you? That's why we went to Stanmore first.'

He shrugged, but the intensity of his gaze told her that she was right.

Reaching out, she touched his hand tentatively. 'Thank you.'

He caught her fingers in his, his eyes gently mocking her. 'I was a little concerned at how you might react. But, as you can see, I'm way richer than they are...'

She punched him lightly on the arm.

'I can't believe you said that.'

Leaning forward, he tipped her face up to his. 'Can't you?' he said softly. 'Then your opinion of me must be improving.'

For a moment time seemed to slow, and they gazed at one another in silence until finally she cleared her throat.

'Do you think we should go in?'

'Of course.' He let go of her chin. 'Let's go and eat.'

Walking swiftly through the house, Ram felt as though his chest might burst. He couldn't quite believe that he'd brought Nola here. One way or another it was asking for trouble—especially as his relationship with her was still at such a delicate stage. But avoiding his parents wasn't an option either—not if he was serious about getting Nola to trust him.

Aware suddenly that she was struggling to keep up with him, he slowed his pace and gave her an apologetic smile. 'Sorry. I think they must be in the garden room.'

The garden room! Was that some kind of conservatory? Nola wondered as she followed Ram's broad back.

Yes, it was, she concluded a moment later as she walked into a light, exquisitely furnished room. But only in the same way that Ram's rainforest hideaway was some kind of treehouse.

'Finally! I was just about to ring you, Ramsay.'

Pulse racing, Nola swung round. The voice was high and clear, and surprisingly English-sounding. But not as surprising as the woman who was sashaying towards them.

Ram smiled coolly. 'Hello, Mother.'

Nola gazed speechlessly at Pandora Walker. Tall, beautiful and blonde, wearing an expensive silk dress that showed off her slim arms and waist, she looked more like a model than a mother—certainly not one old enough to have a son Ram's age.

'You said one o'clock, and it's two minutes past,'

Ram said without any hint of apology, leaning forward to kiss her on both cheeks.

'Five by my watch.' She gave him an indulgent smile. 'I'm not fussing on my account, darling; it's just that you know your father hates to be kept waiting.'

Glancing past them, she pursed her lips.

'Not that he has any qualms about keeping everyone else hanging around. Or ruining the food.'

Nola stilled. Goosebumps were covering her arms. For a fraction of second it could have been her own mother speaking.

But that thought was quickly forgotten as, shaking his head, Ram turned towards Nola and said quietly, 'The food will be perfect. It always is. Nola, this is my mother, Pandora. Mother, this is Nola Mason. She's one of the consultants I hired to work on the launch.'

Smiling politely, Nola felt a jolt of recognition as she met Pandora's eyes—for they were the exact same colour and shape as Ram's. But where had he got that beautiful black hair?

'Thank you so much for inviting me,' she said quickly. 'It's really very kind of you.'

Pandora leaned forward and brushed her cheek lightly against Nola's.

'No, thank *you* for coming. I can't tell you how de-lightful it is to meet you. Ram is usually so secretive. If I want to know anything at all about his private life I have to read about it in the papers. Ah, finally, here's Guy. Darling, we've all been waiting...'

Nola felt another shiver run over her skin. Pandora was still smiling, but there was an edge of coolness to her voice as a tall, handsome man with blond hair and light brown eyes strolled into the room.

'Ramsay, your mother and I were so sure you'd forget I booked to have lunch with Ted Shaw at the club. Just had to ring and cancel.' He turned towards Nola. 'Guy Walker—and you must be Nola.'

'It's lovely to meet you, Mr Walker.'

He smiled—a long, curling smile that reached his eyes.

'Call me Guy, please, and the pleasure is all mine.'

Ram might get his grey eyes from his mother, Nola thought as she followed Pandora out of the room to lunch, but he'd clearly inherited his charm from his father.

To her relief, she quickly discovered that Ram had been telling the truth about his parents. They were the perfect hosts: beautiful, charming and entertaining. And the food was both delicious and exquisitely presented. And yet somehow she couldn't shift the feeling that there was an undercurrent of tension weaving unseen beneath the charm and the smooth flow of conversation.

'So what is it you did, then, Nola? For RWI, I mean?' Leaning forward, Guy poured himself another glass of wine.

'I'm a cyber architect. I designed and installed the new security system.'

He frowned. 'That's a thing now, is it?'

Nola opened her mouth, but before she could reply Ram said quietly, 'It's been a "thing" for a long time now. All businesses have cyber security teams. They have to. Big, global companies like RWI even more so.

They're a prime target for hackers, and if we get hacked we lose money.'

Guy lifted his glass. 'By *we* you mean *you*.' He smiled conspiratorially at Nola. 'I might have given him my name but it's not a family business.'

She blinked. Taken at face value, Guy's comment was innocuous enough: a simple, statement of fact about who owned RWI. So why did his words feel like a shark's fin cutting through the surface of a swimming pool?

'Actually, I think what Ram is trying to say is that hacking is like any other kind of theft,' she said hurriedly. 'Like shoplifting or insurance fraud. In the end the costs get passed on to the consumers so everyone loses out.'

Feeling Ram's gaze on the side of her face, she turned and gave him a quick, tight smile. He nodded, not smiling exactly, but his eyes softened so that for a fraction of a second she almost felt as if they were alone.

Watching the faint flush of colour creep over Nola's cheeks, Ram felt his throat tighten.

He couldn't help but admire her. She was nervous—he could hear it in her voice. But she had defended him, and the fact that she cared enough to do that made his head spin, for nobody had *ever* taken his side. He'd learnt early in life to rely on no one but himself. Some days it felt as though his whole life had been one long, lonely battle.

Not that he'd cared.

Until now.

Until Nola.

But spending time with her over the last few days had been a revelation. Having never cohabited before, he'd expected to find it difficult—boring, even. But he'd enjoyed her company. She was beautiful, smart, funny, and she challenged him. And now she had gone into battle for him, so that the solitude and independence he had once valued so highly seemed suddenly less important. Unnecessary, unwelcome even.

'I'll have to take your word for it.' Guy laughed. 'Like I said, I might be a Walker but I'm not a hotshot businessman like my son.'

Draining his glass, he leaned forward towards Nola.

'A long time ago I used to be an actor—quite a good one, actually. Right now, though, I'm just a party planner!'

Nola stared at him confusedly. 'You plan parties?'

'Ignore him, Nola, he's just being silly.' Pandora frowned at her husband, her lips tightening. 'We're having a party for our thirtieth wedding anniversary, and Guy's been helping with some of the arrangements.'

'Thirty years!' Nola smiled. 'That's wonderful.'

And it was. Only as Ram reached out and adjusted his water glass she felt her smile stiffen, for how did that make him feel? Hearing her sound so enthusiastic about his parents' thirtieth wedding anniversary when she'd been so fiercely against marrying him.

But then Ram only wanted to marry her because he felt he should, she thought defensively. His parents, on the other hand, had clearly loved each other from the start, and they were still in love now, thirty years later.

'Oh, you're so sweet.' Pandora gave her a pouting

pink smile. "It's going to be a wonderful evening, but there's still so much to sort out. Only apparently *my* input is not required.'

So that was why she and Guy were so on edge.

Glancing over to see Guy was pouring himself another glass of wine, Nola felt a rush of relief at having finally found an explanation for the tensions around the table.

Guy scowled. 'You're right—it's not.' He picked up his glass. 'Doesn't stop you giving it, though. Which is one of the reasons why there's still so much to sort out.'

For perhaps a fraction of a second Pandora's beautiful face hardened, and then almost immediately she was smiling again.

'I know, darling. But at least we have one less thing to worry about now.' As Guy gazed at her blankly, she shook her head. 'Ram's guest. You *are* bringing Nola to the party, aren't you, Ramsay?'

There was a tiny suspended silence.

Nola froze. That aspect of the party hadn't even occurred to her. But obviously Ram would be going. Her heartbeat resonated in her throat as he turned towards her.

'Of course.'

Breath pummelled her lungs as he held her gaze, his cool, grey eyes silencing her confusion and shock.

'She's looking forward to it—aren't you, sweetheart?'

She gazed at him in silence, too stunned to reply. Over the last few days she had spent some of the most intense and demanding hours of her life with Ram. She had revealed more to him about herself than to any other person, and she had seen a side to him that few people knew existed.

But his parents' party was going to be big news, and although it was unlikely anyone would be interested in her on her own, as one half of a couple with Ram...

Her pulse fluttered.

She knew enough about his private life to know that it wasn't private at all, and that as soon she stepped out in public with him there would be a feeding frenzy—and that wasn't what she wanted at all.

Or was it?

Suddenly she was fighting her own heartbeat. Definitely she didn't want the feeding frenzy part, but she would be lying if she said that she didn't want the chance to walk into a room on his arm. And not just because he was so heart-stoppingly handsome and sexy.

She liked him.

A lot.

And the more she got to know him the more she liked him.

Looking up, she met his gaze, and nodded slowly. 'Yes, I'm really excited.'

Pandora clapped her hands together. 'Wonderful,' she purred. 'In that case I must give you the number of my stylist...'

After lunch, they returned to Stanmore.

Ram worked while Nola sat watching the boats in the harbour. After a light supper he excused himself, claiming work again, and she went upstairs to shower and get ready for bed.

Standing beneath the warm water, she closed her eyes and let her mind drift.

The drive home had been quiet—supper too. But then both of them had a lot to think about. Introducing her to his parents had probably been about as a big deal for Ram as meeting them had been for her.

Turning off the shower, she wrapped a towel around herself. And then, of course, there was the party. Her heart began to thump loudly inside her chest. Was that why he'd been so quiet? Was he regretting letting himself be chivvied into taking her as his guest?

But as she walked back into the bedroom that question went unanswered, for there, sitting on her bed, was Ram.

She stopped, eyes widening with surprise. 'I thought you were going to do some work?'

Glancing past her, he shrugged. 'I was worried about you. You seemed…' He hesitated, frowning. 'Distracted.'

There was an edge to his voice that she couldn't quite pinpoint.

'I'm just tired.'

His eyes on hers were dark and filled with intent. 'That's all? Just tired?'

For a moment she considered leaving it there. It had been a long day, but for the first time they seemed to be edging towards a calm she was reluctant to disturb. Although if she didn't tell him what she was really thinking, what would that achieve? Okay, it might just be one night in their lives, but if it was bothering her… bothering him…

She took a deep breath. 'I just want you to know that you don't have to take me to the party,' she said quickly.

His eyes narrowed. 'I know I don't. But I want to.' He studied her face. 'Is that really what this is about? What *I* want. Or is it about what *you* want?'

Nola looked at him uncertainly. 'What do you mean?'

He cleared his throat. 'Are you saying you don't want to go with me?'

She shook her head. 'No, but you only— I mean, your mother—'

He interrupted her, his voice suddenly blazing with an emotion she didn't recognise.

'Let me get one thing clear, Nola. *I want you to be there with me*. And my mother has got nothing to do with that decision.'

She nodded—for what else could she do? She could hardly demand proof. And she wanted to believe him. Of course she did. Besides, if they were going to work even at the simplest level, wasn't it time to move on? To put all the doubt and suspicion and drama behind them and start to trust one another?

Drawing in a deep breath, she lifted her chin and looked into his eyes.

'Thank you for telling me that,' she said simply. 'And thank you for taking me to lunch. It was lovely.' Remembering the strange tension around the table, those odd pointed remarks, she hesitated. 'What about you? Did you enjoy yourself?'

Ram stared at her in silence. Her question was simple

enough but it stunned him, for he couldn't remember anyone ever asking him that before.

'I suppose,' he said finally. 'Although they were a little tense. But there's a lot going on—I mean, with the party coming up—'

She nodded slowly. 'Thirty years together is an amazing achievement.'

'Yes, it is.'

He watched her bite her lip, glance up, try to speak, then look away. Finally she said quietly, 'I get that it's why you wanted me to meet them.'

His heart seemed to still in his chest. 'You do?'

She nodded. 'You wanted me to understand why you want us to marry. And I do understand. I know you want what they have.'

Her blue eyes were fixed on his face, and he stared back at her, his breath vibrating inside his chest.

You want what they have…

He tried to nod his head, tried to smile, to do what his mother had always required of him.

But he couldn't. Not anymore. Not with Nola.

Slowly he shook his head. 'Actually, what they have is why I've always been so *against* marriage.'

He watched her eyes widen with incomprehension, and it made him feel cruel—shattering her illusions, betraying his mother's confidences. But he was so tired of lying and feeling angry. His chest tightened. Nola deserved more than lies, more than his anger—she deserved the truth.

He cleared his throat. 'You see, Guy has a mistress.'

Confusion and shock spread out from her pupils like shock waves across a sea.

There was a thick, pulsing silence.

'But he can't have—' Nola bit her lip, stopped, tried again. 'Does your mother know?'

As she watched him nod slowly the room seemed to swim in front of her eyes.

There was another, shorter silence.

'I'm so sorry, Ram,' she whispered at last. 'That must have been such a shock.'

He stared past her, his eyes narrowing as though he was weighing something up.

'Yes, it was,' he said quietly. 'The first time it happened.'

The first time?

'I—I don't understand,' she said slowly. 'Isn't this the first time?'

His mouth twisted. 'Sadly not. That honour went to an actress called Francesca. Not that I knew or cared that she was an actress.' An ache of misery was spreading inside him. 'I was only six. To me, she was just some woman in my mother's bed.'

Nola flinched. *Six!* Still just a child.

Watching her reaction, Ram smiled stiffly. 'Guy told me it would upset my mother if I said anything. So I didn't.'

He was speaking precisely, owning each word in a way that made her feel sick.

'I thought if I kept quiet, then it would stop,' he continued. 'And it did with Francesca. Only then there was Tessa, and then Carrie. I stopped learning their names after that. It was the only way I could face my mother.'

'But you weren't responsible!' Nola stared up him, her eyes and her throat burning. 'You hadn't done anything.'

His skin was tight over his cheekbones.

'You're wrong. It *was* my fault. All of it.'

She shook her head. Her heart felt as if it was about to burst. 'You were a little boy. Your father should never have put you in that position.'

He was looking past her, his eyes dull with pain. 'You don't understand. *I'm* the reason they had to marry.'

She shivered. 'What do you mean?'

'My mother got pregnant with me when she was sixteen. In those days girls like her didn't do so well on their own.'

Nola blinked. She had imagined many reasons for what had made him the man he was, but nothing like this. No wonder he was so confused—and confusing—when it came to relationships.

'But that's not *your* fault,' she said quietly. 'I know it must have been hard for both of them. But just because Guy became a father too young, it doesn't mean you're responsible for his affairs.'

He shook his head, his mouth twisting into a smile that had nothing to do with laughter or happiness.

'Guy's not my father. My biological father, I mean.'

She stared at him in silence, too shocked to speak, the words in her mouth bunching into silent knots.

He looked away. 'My mother was staying with a friend and they heard about a party. A real party, on

the wrong side of town, with drink and boys and no supervision. That's where she met my father. They were
drunk and careless and they had sex.'

'Who is he?' she whispered. 'Your real father?'

Ram shrugged. 'Does it matter? When he found out
she was pregnant he didn't want anything to do with
her—or me.'

His eyes were suddenly dark and hostile, as though
challenging her to contradict him.

She swallowed. 'So how did she meet Guy?'

He breathed out unsteadily.

'My grandparents knew his family socially. His father had made some bad investments. Money was tight,
and Guy's never been that interested in working for
a living, so when Grandfather offered him money to
marry my mother he accepted.'

Nola didn't even try to hide her shock.

'That's awful. Your poor mother. But why did she
agree to it?'

Ram's face was bleak. 'Because my grandfather told
her he'd cut her off, disown her, cast her out if she
didn't.'

A muscle pulsed in his cheek.

'She couldn't face that, didn't think she could survive without all this, so she gave in. Guy got a generous
lifetime monthly allowance, my mother preserved her
reputation and her lifestyle and my grandparents were
able to keep their dirty linen private.'

The misery in his voice almost overwhelmed her.

She took a breath, counted to ten. 'How did you
find out?'

'My mother told me.' This time his smile seemed to slice through her skin like a mezzaluna. 'We were arguing, and I compared her unfavourably to my grandparents. I hurt her, so I guess she thought it was time I knew the truth.'

Nola could feel her body shaking. How could his mother have done that? It had been needlessly cruel. She had to swallow hard against the tears building in her throat before she could speak.

'How old were you?'

He shrugged. 'Eleven...twelve, something like that.'

Her eyes held his as she struggled to think of something positive to say. 'But you get on with Guy?'

He shrugged. 'When I was a child he more or less ignored me. Now I'm older I just avoid him. After my grandfather died he made a big scene about needing more money, so I give him an allowance and in return he has to be devoted to my mother—in public, at least. And discreet about his affairs. Or he's supposed to be.'

Nola looked up into his face. There was nothing she could say to that.

'What about your real father?' she asked carefully. 'Do you have any contact with him?'

His eyes hardened. 'I know who he is, and since he knows who my mother is, he must know who *I* am, and how to find me. But he hasn't, so I guess he's even less interested in me than Guy.'

His face was expressionless but the desolation in his voice made her fists clench.

'It's his loss,' she said fiercely.

He gave a small, tight smile.

'Are you taking my side, Ms Mason?'

His words burned like a flame. Was she?

For months there had been an ocean between them. Then, for the last few days, she'd been fighting to keep him at a distance. Fighting to keep her independence. Fighting the simmering sexual tension between them. Her mouth twisted. In fact just fighting him.

Only now the fight had drained out of her, and instead she wanted nothing more than to wrap her arms around him, ease the desperate ache in his voice and that terrible tension in his body. Her breath seemed to swell in her throat as she reached out and tentatively touched his hand. For a moment he stared at her hand in silence, then finally he reached out and pulled her against him.

Burying her face against his body, she let out a shuddering breath. Being here in his arms felt so good, so right. If only she could stay this way for ever. But this wasn't about her, it was about Ram—*his* pain and his anger, his past. A past that still haunted him. A past she was determined to exorcise now.

Lifting her head, she looked up into his face. 'Your mother was so young. Too young. And she was scared and hurt and desperate. People don't always do the right thing when they're desperate. But they can do the wrong thing for the right reasons.'

Their eyes met, and they both knew she wasn't just talking about his mother.

Breathing out shakily, he shook his head. 'I've been struggling to figure that out for nearly twenty years. It's taken you less than half an hour.'

She smiled a little. 'It's all those in-flight magazines I read.'

Mouth twisting, he clasped her face, his thumbs gently stroking her cheeks.

'I'm sorry for what I did. Lying to you, dragging you off to the rainforest like that. It was completely out of order.'

Ram was apologising.

Her throat ached. She could hardly breathe.

'We both behaved badly,' she said shakily. 'And we both thought the worst of each other. But I'm glad you did what you did, otherwise we might never have got this far.'

Her gaze fastened on his face.

'But now we're here, and I think it's about time we started figuring things out. If we're going to make it work, I mean.'

The words were out of her mouth before she even understood what it was she wanted to say. What it was she really wanted. Her heart began to beat fiercely as his grey eyes searched her face.

'Make what work?'

It wasn't too late. There was still time to backtrack. Ram couldn't read minds, and she'd said nothing damning or definitive. But she didn't want to backtrack—for wasn't that their problem in a nutshell? Both of them looking back to the past, and in so doing threatening to ruin the future—their child's future? 'Our marriage,' she said after a moment.

'Are you asking me to marry you?'

He looked tense, shaken, nothing like the cool, sophisticated Ramsay Walker who could stop meetings with a raised eyebrow. It scared her a little, seeing him so uncertain. But it made her feel stronger, more determined to tell him how she felt—and maybe, just maybe, get him to do the same.

She hesitated. 'Yes, I am.'

He had confided in her, and she knew what each and every word had cost him. Knew too why he was so conflicted, so determined to do his duty as a father even as he pushed away any hint of love or commitment.

'Is this what's changed your mind?' he asked slowly.

She bit her lip. 'Yes, but also it was that night we spent in your office—I've tried not to think about it, but I can't stop myself. It was so different...so incredible. I've never felt like that with anyone, and I wanted to tell you that. I wanted to stay, but I was too scared—scared of how you'd made me feel.'

'I felt the same,' he said hoarsely.

She felt a sudden twinge of panic. 'But it was a long time ago. Maybe we don't feel that way anymore.'

His grey eyes locked onto hers.

'We do feel it, Nola. We've felt it and fought it.'

The heat in his voice made blood surge through her body.

'But I don't want to fight you anymore. In fact fighting is the opposite of what I want to do with you.'

She held her breath as he stared down into her eyes. Chaos was building inside her.

'What is it you want to do?' she whispered.

His gaze moved from her face down to the slight V of her cleavage.

'This…'

Holding her gaze, he reached out and slowly unwrapped the towel from around her body. As it dropped to the floor she heard his sharp intake of breath.

She swallowed, her imagination stirring.

His mouth was so close to hers—those beautiful curving lips that had the power to unleash a blissful torment of heat and oblivion. For a moment she couldn't speak. All she could think about was how badly she wanted to kiss him, and how badly she wanted him to kiss her back.

And then her breath lurched in her throat as, lowering his hand, he began stroking her breast in a way that made her quiver inside.

'I want you, Nola,' he said softly.

'For ever?' She couldn't help asking.

His gaze held hers, then his hands dipped lower to caress her stomach and her thighs and the curve of her bottom.

'For the rest of my life.'

She pressed her hands against his chest, feeling his heart beneath her fingertips, and then she was pushing him backwards onto the bed, and he was pulling her onto his lap so that she was straddling him.

Fingers trembling, she undid the button of his jeans, tugging at the zipper, freeing him. His ragged breathing abruptly broke the silence as she ran her hand gently up the length of him and guided him inside her.

He groaned, his body trembling. Leaning forward, she found his mouth and kissed him desperately. And then his hands were tightening on her thighs, and she was lifting her hips, heat swamping her as he shuddered inside her, pulling her damp, shaking body against his.

But it wasn't just desire that was rocking her body—it was shock. For mere sex, no matter how incredible, could not make you want to hold a person for ever.

Only love could make you feel that way.

It was like a dam breaking inside her, but even as she acknowledged the truth she knew it was not a truth she was ready to share with Ram. Or one he was ready to hear. But wrapped in his arms, with his heart beating in time with hers, it didn't seem to matter. For right now this was enough.

CHAPTER NINE

THE NEXT MORNING Ram woke early, to a sky of the palest blue and yellow.

Next to him Nola lay curled on her side, her arm draped across his chest. For a moment he lay listening to her soft, even breathing, his body and his brain struggling to adjust to this entirely new sensation of intimacy.

Waking beside a woman was something he'd never done before. In the past, even the thought of it would have made his blood run cold.

But being here with Nola felt good.

Better than good, he thought, breathing in sharply as she shifted against him in her sleep.

After last night there could be no doubt that they still wanted one another. They had made love slowly, taking their time, holding back and letting the pleasure build. And, unlike that first time in his office, there had been tenderness as well as passion.

Forehead creasing, he stared out of the window. But last night had not just been about sex. Exploring the lush new curves of her body had eased an ache that was more than physical.

He froze as Nola stirred beside him, curling closer, and suddenly the touch of her naked body was too great a test for his self-control. Gritting his teeth against the instant rush of need clamouring inside him, he gently lifted her arm and slid across the bed, making his way to the shower.

Turning the temperature to cool, he winced as the water hit his body.

For years he'd never so much as hinted at his parents' unhappiness to anyone. Even imagining the pity in someone's eyes had been enough to ensure his silence. But last night—and he still wasn't quite sure why or how—he'd ended up telling Nola every sordid little detail about his life. Not just his mother's miserable marriage of necessity, but Guy's serial affairs too.

The words had just tumbled out.

Only Nola hadn't pitied him. Instead she had helped him to face his past. More than that, she'd finally agreed to build a future with him.

Tipping back his head, he closed his eyes, remembering how she'd asked him to marry her. His mouth curved. Of course she had—and wasn't that as much of an attraction as her glorious body? The way she kept him guessing, and her stubborn determination to do things her way and at her pace.

Switching off the water, he smoothed his dark hair back against the clean lines of his skull. It ought to drive him crazy, yet it only seemed to intensify his desire for her. And now that Nola had finally come round to his point of view he was determined that nothing would get in their way.

Whatever it took, they were going to get married—and as soon as possible.

'I need to drop by the office later, so I was wondering if you'd like to go into town?'

They had just finished breakfast and Ram was flicking through some paperwork.

Looking over at him, Nola frowned. 'Is there a problem?'

He shook his head. 'I just need to show my face—otherwise there might be a mutiny.'

'I doubt that. Your staff love you.'

He laughed. '*Love* might be pushing it a little. They respect me—'

'Yes, and respect is a kind of love,' she said slowly. 'Like duty and faith. Love isn't just all about passion and romance—it's about commitment and consideration, and sacrifice too.'

He leaned back in his chair. 'Then I take it back. I must be very loved. So must you.'

She felt her skin grow hot. Of course he wasn't talking about their relationship but his staff, and probably her friendship with Anna. Aware, though, of his sudden focus, she grasped helplessly towards his earlier remark.

'When are you thinking of going into the office, then?'

'Whenever suits you.'

'In that case, maybe I'll stay here. It's not as if I really need anything.'

He was silent a moment, and then he said quietly, 'Apart from a dress?'

A dress?

She stared at him. 'Oh, yes, of course—for the party.'

His gaze rested on her face. 'Are you having second thoughts?'

His tone was relaxed, but there was an intensity in his grey eyes that made her heart beat faster.

'About the party?'

'About agreeing to marry me?'

Looking up, she shook her head. 'No. Are you?'

Gently he reached over and, smoothing her hair back from her face, he gave her one of those sweet, extraordinary smiles that could light up a room.

'If I could walk outside and find a registrar and a couple of witnesses, you'd be making an honest man out of me right this second!'

She burst out laughing. 'I thought the bride was supposed to be the pushy one?'

His face grew serious. 'I don't want to push you into anything, Nola. Not anymore. I just want you to give me a chance—to give us a chance.'

Heart bumping into her ribs, she nodded. 'I want that too.' Taking a quick breath, she smiled at him. 'So what happens next?'

There was a fraction of a pause.

'I suppose we make it official,' he said casually. 'How do you feel about announcing our engagement at the party?'

Her pulse darted forward. *Engagement?*

But of course logically their getting engaged was the next step.

Only up until yesterday marrying Ram had been more of a hypothetical option than a solid, nuts and bolts reality. And now he wanted to announce their engagement in three days.

Three days!

Ram watched with narrowed eyes as Nola bit her lip. Taking her to the party was a statement of sorts, but announcing their engagement there would escalate and consolidate their relationship in the most public way possible. Clearly Nola thought so too, for he could see the conflict in her eyes. Only instead of making him question his actions, her doubt and confusion only made him more determined than ever to make it happen.

But he'd learnt his lesson, and he wasn't about to make demands or start backing her into a corner.

'It does make sense,' she said finally.

And it did—but that didn't stop the feeling of dread rising up inside her. For how was everyone going to react to the news? Her heart gave a shiver. She might have finally come to terms with the idea of marrying Ram, but this was a reminder that their marriage was going to be conducted in public, with not only friends and family having an opinion but the media too.

'What is it?'

The unexpected gentleness of his voice caught her off guard, and quickly she looked away—for how could she explain her fears to him? Ram didn't know what it felt like to be hurt and humiliated in public, to have his failures held up and examined.

A lump filled her throat as she remembered the first time her father had let her down in front of other people. She'd been on a school trip, and he'd promised to collect her in his new car. She had been so convinced that he would pick her up, adamant that he wouldn't forget her. In the end one of the mothers had taken pity on her and driven her home, but of course the next day at school everyone had known.

She clenched her fists. And then there was what had happened with Connor. It had been bad enough splitting up with him. To do so under the microscope of her colleagues' curiosity and judgement had been excruciating.

Even thinking about it made her feel sick to her stomach.

She took a breath. 'It's just...once we tell everyone it won't be just the two of us anymore.'

'Yes—but, like I said, if we go to the party together then they'll know about us anyway.' He frowned. 'I'm confused—I thought you *wanted* to get married.'

'I do. But what if our marriage doesn't work?' The words were spilling out of her—hot, panicky, unstoppable. 'What happens then? Have you thought about that? Have you any idea what that will feel like—?'

She broke off as Ram reached out and covered her hands with his.

'Slow down, sweetheart. At this point I'm still trying to get you down the aisle. So right now I'm not thinking about the end of our marriage.'

Gently, he uncurled her fingers.

'Is this about your father?' he said quietly.

She shook her head, then nodded. 'Sort of. Him and Connor. He was my last boyfriend. We worked together. He told a couple of people in the office some stuff about us, and then it all got out of hand.'

'What stuff? And what do you mean by "out of hand"?'

She couldn't meet his eyes. 'Some of my colleagues went to the pub after work. Connor had been drinking, and he told them—well, he told them things about us. You know…what we'd done together, private things. The next day everyone was talking about me. It was so embarrassing. Even my boss knew. People I thought were my friends stopped talking to me, I was overlooked for a promotion, and then Connor dumped me.'

'Then, quite frankly, he was an idiot,' Ram said bluntly. Cupping her chin in his hand, he forced her face up to his. 'Correction. He's an idiot and a coward, and if ever I meet him I'll tell him so—shortly after I've punched him.'

She couldn't stop herself from smiling. 'You don't need to worry about me. I can fight my own battles.'

His gaze rested on her face, and he gripped her hand so tightly she could almost feel the energy and strength passing from his body into hers.

'Not anymore. You're with me now, Nola. Your battles are my battles. And, engaged or not, nothing anyone says or does is going to change that fact, so if you don't want to say anything, then we won't.'

Nola stared at him in silence. She knew how badly he wanted to get married, but he was offering to put his needs and feelings behind hers. Neither her father nor Connor had been willing to do that.

She couldn't speak—not just because his words had taken her by surprise, but because she was terrified she would tell him that she loved him.

Finally, she shook her head. 'I do want to announce it. But I think I should ring my mum and Anna first. I want them to know before anyone else.'

He dropped a kiss on her mouth. 'Good idea. Why don't you call them now? And then you'd better come into town with me after all, so you can choose a dress.'

It was the afternoon of the party.

Slipping her feet into a pair of beautiful dark red court shoes, Nola breathed out softly. She could hardly believe that in the next few hours she would be standing beside Ram as his fiancée. Just days ago they had been like two boxers, circling one another in the ring. But all that had changed since they'd made peace with their pasts, and she had never felt happier.

Or more satisfied.

Her face grew hot. It was crazy, but they just couldn't seem to keep their hands off one another. Even when they weren't making love they couldn't stop touching—his hand on her hip, her fingers brushing against his face. And on the odd occasion when she forced Ram to do some work he'd stay close to her, using his laptop and making phone calls from the bed while she slept.

In fact this was probably the first time they'd been apart for days, and she was missing him so badly that it felt like an actual physical ache.

Her breath felt blunt and heavy in her throat. It was an ache that was compounded by the knowledge that, even though she loved him, Ram would never love her. She lifted her chin. But he did *need* her, and he felt responsible for her and the baby—and hadn't she told him that duty was a kind of love?

But she couldn't think about that now. There were other more pressing matters to consider and, heart pounding, she turned to face the full-length mirror. She stared almost dazedly at her reflection. It was the first time she had seen herself since having her hair and make-up done, and the transformation was astonishing. With her dark hair swept to one side, her shimmering smoky eye make-up and bright red lips, she looked poised and glamorous—not at all like the anxious young woman she was feeling inside.

Which was lucky, she thought, picking up her clutch bag with a rush of nervous excitement, because soon she would be facing Sydney's A-listers as Ram's bride-to-be.

Downstairs, Ram was flicking resignedly through the pages of a magazine. If Nola was anything like Pandora he was going to be in for a long wait. Or maybe he wasn't! Already Nola had surprised him, by being sweetly excited by the party, whereas Pandora was just too much of a perfectionist to truly enjoy *any* public appearance. She saw only the flaws, however tiny or trifling. And of course that led inevitably to the reasons for those flaws.

His mouth tightened. Or rather *the* reason.

There was a movement behind him and, turning round, he felt his heartbeat stumble.

Nola was standing at the top of the stairs, wearing a beautiful pleated yellow silk dress that seemed to both cling and flow. It perfectly complemented her gleaming dark hair and crimson lips and, watching her walk towards him, he felt his breath catch fire as she stopped in front of him. She met his gaze, her blue eyes nervous, yet resolute.

'You look like sunlight in that dress,' he said softly and, reaching out he pulled her towards him. 'You're beautiful, Nola. Truly.'

'You look pretty damn spectacular too,' she said huskily.

The classic black dinner jacket fitted his muscular frame perfectly, and although all the male guests at the party would be similarly dressed, she knew that beside Ram they would look ordinary. His beauty and charisma would ensure that.

He glanced down at himself, then up to her face, his grey gaze dark and mocking. 'I doubt anyone's going to be looking at me.'

She shivered. 'Hopefully they won't be looking at me either.'

'They can look. But they can't touch.'

His arm tightened around her waist and she saw that his eyes were no longer mocking but intent and alert. Tipping her chin up, he cupped her face in his hand.

'You're mine. And I want everyone to know that. After tonight, they will.'

She felt her heart slip sideways, like a boat breaking free from its moorings. But of course he was just getting into the mood for the evening ahead, and it was her cue to do the same.

'I'll remind you of that later, when we're dancing and I'm trampling on your toes,' she said lightly. 'You'll be begging other men to take me off your hands.'

His face shifted, the corners of his mouth curving upwards, and his arms held her close against him.

'And what will you be begging *me* to do?'

Their eyes met, and she felt her face grow warm. She hadn't begged yet, but she hadn't been far off it. Remembering how frantic she had felt last night, how desperate she had been for his touch, the frenzy of release, she swallowed.

'We shouldn't—'

He nodded. 'I know. I just wish we could fast-forward tonight.'

She could hear the longing in his voice. 'So do I. I wish it was just the two of us.'

'It will be.' He frowned. 'I know you're nervous. But I'll be there with you, and if for some reason I'm not—well, I thought this might help. I hope you like it.'

He lifted her hand and Nola stared mutely as he slid a beautiful sapphire ring onto her finger.

A sweet, shimmering lightness began to spread through her body. 'It—It's a ring,' she stammered.

His eyes glittered. 'You sound surprised. What were you expecting?'

'Nothing. I wasn't expecting anything.'

'We're getting engaged tonight, sweetheart. There has to be a ring.'

She nodded, some of her happiness fading. He was right: there did have to be a ring.

'Of course,' she said quickly. 'And it's lovely. Really...'

'Good.' Pulling out his phone, he glanced down at the screen and grimaced. 'In that case, I guess we should be going.'

* * *

Bypassing the queue of limousines and sports cars in the drive, Ram used the service entrance to reach the house. As they walked hand in hand towards the two huge marquees on the lawn Nola shivered. There were so many guests—several hundred at least.

'Do your parents really know this many people?' she asked, gazing nervously across the lawn.

He shrugged. 'Socially, yes. Personally, I doubt they could tell you much more than their names and which clubs they belong to.'

He turned as a waiter passed by with a tray of champagne and grabbed two glasses.

'I'm not drinking.'

'I know. But just hold it—otherwise somebody will wonder why.'

He smiled down at her and she nodded dumbly. He was so aware, so in control of everything. In that respect this evening was no different for him than any other.

If only she could let him know how different it was for *her*.

But, much as she longed to tell him that she loved him, she knew it wasn't the right time. For there was a tension about him, a remoteness, as though he was holding himself apart. It was the same tension she'd felt at lunch that day with his parents. And of course it was understandable. This was a big moment for him too.

The party passed in a blur of lights and faces. She knew nobody, but it seemed that everybody knew Ram, and so wanted to know her too. Clutching her glass of champagne, she smiled and chatted with one glamorous couple after another as Ram stood by her side, looking cool and absurdly handsome in his tuxedo as he talked in French to a tall, elderly grey-haired man who turned out to be the Canadian Ambassador.

Later, ignoring her protests, he led her onto the dance floor and, holding her against his body, he circled her between the other couples.

'Are you having fun?' he said softly into her ear.

She nodded. 'Yes. I thought people might be a bit stiff and starchy. But everyone's been really friendly.'

His eyes glittered like molten silver beneath the soft lights. 'They like you.'

She shook her head. 'They're curious about me. It's *you* they like.

'And what about you? Do *you* like me?'

Around them the music and the laughter seemed to fade, as though someone had turned down the volume, and the urge to tell him her true feelings welled up inside her again. But she bit it down.

She smiled. 'Yes, I like you.'

'And you still want to marry me?' He met her gaze, his grey eyes oddly serious. 'It's not too late to change your mind…'

She shook her head. 'I want to marry you.'

'Then maybe now is a good time to tell everyone that.' Glancing round, he frowned. 'We need my parents here, though. Let's go and look for them.'

His hand was warm and firm around hers as he pulled her through the dancing couples and onto the lawn, but after ten minutes of looking they still hadn't found Guy and Pandora.

Nodding curtly at the security guards, he led her into the main house.

'My mother probably wanted to change her shoes or something. I'll go and find them.'

His eyes were fixed on her face and, seeing the hesitancy there, she felt her heart tumble inside her chest.

Taking his hands in hers, she gave them a squeeze. 'Why don't I come with you? We can tell them together.'

There was a brief silence as he stared away across the empty hallway. Then his mouth twisted, and he shook his head. 'It's probably better if I go on my own.'

She nodded. 'Okay. I'll wait here.'

He kissed her gently on the lips. 'I won't be long.'

Walking swiftly through the house, Ram felt his heart start to pound.

He could hardly believe he'd managed to get this far. Bringing Nola to the party had felt like a huge step but this—this was something almost beyond his comprehension, beyond any expectations he'd had up until now.

It hardly seemed possible, but by the end of the night he would be officially engaged to Nola. Finally, with her help, he had managed to bury his past, and now he had a future he'd never imagined, with a wife and a baby—

Abruptly, his feet stilled on the thick carpet and his thoughts skidded forward, slamming into the side of his head with a sickening thud.

His heartbeat froze. Beneath the throb of music and laughter, he could hear raised voices. Somewhere in the house a man and woman were arguing loudly.

It was Guy and his mother.

His heart began beating again and, with the blood chilling in his veins, he walked towards the doorway to his mother's room. The voices grew louder and more unrestrained as he got closer.

And then he heard his mother laugh.

Only it wasn't a happy sound.

'You just can't help yourself, can you? Couldn't you have a little self-control? Just for one night?'

'Maybe you should have a little *less*, darling. It's a party—not a military tattoo.'

Ram winced. Guy sounded belligerent. And drunk.

For a moment he hesitated. There had been so many of these arguments during his life. Surely it wouldn't matter if he walked away from this one? But as his mother started to cry he braced his shoulders and walked into the bedroom.

'Oh, here's the cavalry.' Turning, Guy squinted across the room at him. 'Don't start, Ram. You don't pay me enough to take part in that gala performance downstairs.'

'But I pay you enough to treat my mother with respect,' he said coolly. 'However, if you don't think you can manage to do that, maybe I'll just have to cut back your allowance. No point in paying for something I'm not actually getting.'

For a moment Guy held his gaze defiantly, but then finally he shrugged and looked away. 'Fine. But if you think I'm going to deal with her in this state—'

'I'll deal with my mother.' Ram forced himself to stay calm. 'Why don't you go and enjoy the party? Eat some food…have a soft drink. Oh, and Guy? I meant what I said about treating my mother with respect.'

Grumbling, still avoiding Ram's eyes, Guy stumbled from the room.

Heart aching, Ram stared across the room to where his mother sat crying on the bed. Crossing the room, he crouched down in front of her and stroked her hair away from her face.

'Don't worry about him. He's been drinking, that's all. And he's had to get up before noon to make a couple of phone calls so he's probably exhausted.'

She tried to smile through her tears. 'That must be it.'

'It is. Now, here. Take this.' Reaching into his pocket, Ram pulled out a handkerchief and held it out to her. 'It's clean. I promise.'

Taking the handkerchief, Pandora wiped her eyes carefully. 'I just wanted it to be perfect, Ramsay. For one night.'

'And it is. Everyone's having a wonderful time.'

She shook her head, pressing her hand against his. '*You're* not. You'll say you are, but I know you're not.'

Ram swallowed. Whenever his mother and Guy argued there was a pattern. She would get angry, then cry, and then she would redo her make-up and carry on as if nothing had happened. But tonight was different, for he could never remember her talking about him or his feelings.

He looked at her uncertainly. 'You're right—normally. But it's different tonight. I really am enjoying myself.'

His mother smiled.

'That's because of Nola. *She's* the difference and you're different with her. Happier.' She squeezed his hand. 'I was happy like that when I found out I was pregnant with you. I know it sounds crazy, but when that line turned blue I just sat and looked at it, and those few hours when it was just you and me were the happiest of my life. I knew then that you'd be handsome and smart and strong.'

A tear rolled down her cheek.

'I just wish I'd been stronger.'

Ram dragged a hand through his hair. He felt her pain like a weight. 'You *were* strong, Mother.'

Shaking her head, she let the tears fall. 'I should never have married Guy. I should have had the courage to stand up to your grandfather. I should have waited for someone who wanted me and loved me for who I was.'

Looking up into Ram's eyes, she twisted her lips.

'But I was scared to give all this up. So I settled for a man who was paid to marry me and a marriage that's made me feel trapped and humiliated for thirty years.'

She bit her lip.

'I'm sorry, darling, for acting so selfishly, and for blaming you.'

Ram couldn't breathe.

His mother was apologising.

For so long he'd been so angry with her. Never to her face, because despite everything—the hysterics, the way she lashed out at him when she was upset—he loved her desperately. Instead he'd deliberately, repeatedly, and publicly scorned the very idea of becoming a husband and a father.

And he'd done that to punish her. For giving him a 'father' like Guy, for making choices that had taken away *his* choices, even though she'd been little more than a child herself.

'Don't,' he whispered. 'It wasn't your fault.'

'It was. It *is*.' Reaching out, Pandora gently stroked his face. 'And I can't change the past. But I don't want you to repeat my mistakes. Promise me, Ramsay, that you won't do what Guy and I did. Relationships can't be forced. There has to be love.'

'I know.'

He spoke mechanically, but inside he felt hollow, for he knew his mother was right. Relationships couldn't be forced—and yet wasn't that exactly what he'd done to Nola? Right from the start he'd been intent on having his own way—overriding her at every turn, kidnapping her at the airport, pressuring her to get married.

He'd even 'persuaded' her into announcing their engagement tonight, despite knowing that she was nervous about taking that step.

His breath felt like lead in his throat. Whatever he might like to believe, the facts were undeniable. Nola wasn't marrying him through choice or love. Just like his mother, for her it would be a marriage of convenience. A marriage of duty.

Gazing into his mother's tear-stained face, he made up his mind.

He'd never wanted anything more than to give his

child a secure home, a future, a name. But he couldn't marry Nola.

Now all he needed to do was find her and tell her that as soon as possible.

Glancing up, Nola saw Ram striding down the stairs towards her. Her heart gave a lurch. He didn't look as if news of his engagement had been joyfully received.

Standing up, she walked towards him—but before she had a chance to speak Ram was by her side, grabbing her hand, towing her after him, his grip on her hand mirroring the vice of confusion and fear squeezing her heart.

'What did they say?' she managed as he wrenched open the door, standing to one side to let her pass through it.

'Nothing,' he said curtly. 'I didn't tell them.'

She gazed at him in confusion.

'So what are we doing?'

'There's been a change of plan. We're leaving now!'

Five minutes later they were heading down the drive towards the main road. Cars were still arriving at the house, but even though Ram must have noticed them, he said nothing.

Several times she was on the verge of asking him to stop the car and tell her what had happened. But, glancing at his set, still profile, she knew that he was either incapable of telling her or unwilling. All she could do was watch and wait.

She was so busy watching him that she didn't even notice when they drove past Stanmore. In fact it wasn't until he stopped the car in front of a large Art Deco—style house that she finally became aware of anything other than the terrible rigidity of his body.

He had switched off the engine and was out of the car and striding round to her door, yanking it open before she even had a chance to take off her seatbelt.

'This way!'

Taking her hand, he led her to the front door, unlocking and opening it in one swift movement. Inside the house, Nola watched confusedly as he marched from room to room, flicking on lights.

'What is this place?' she said finally.

'It's a property I bought a couple of years ago as an investment. I lived here when Stanmore was being renovated.'

'Oh, right...' It was all she could manage.

Maybe this was some kind of bolthole? She flinched as he yanked the curtains across the windows. If so, he must have a good reason for coming here now. But as she stared over at him anxiously she had no idea what that reason might be. All she knew was that she wanted to put her arms around him and hold him tight. Only, he looked so brittle, so taut, she feared he might shatter into a thousand pieces if she so much as touched him.

But she couldn't just stand here and pretend that everything was all right when it so clearly wasn't.

'Are you okay?' she asked hesitantly.

'Yes. I'm fine.'

He smiled—the kind of smile she would use when sharing a lift with a stranger.

'I'm sure you're tired. Why don't I show you to your bedroom?'

'But don't you want to talk?'

Watching his expression shift, she shivered. It was like watching water turn to ice.

'No, not really.'

'But what happened? Why did we leave the party?' She bit her lip. 'Why didn't you tell them about the engagement?'

He stared at her impatiently, then fixed his eyes on a point somewhere past her head.

'I'm not having this conversation now. It's late. You're pregnant—'

'And you're upset!' She stared at him in exasperation. 'Not only that, you're shutting me out.'

His eyes narrowed. 'Shutting you out? You sound like you're in a soap opera.'

She blinked, shocked not so much by his words but by the sneer in his voice.

'Maybe that's because you've behaving like a character in a soap opera. Dragging me from the party. Refusing to talk to me.'

'And what exactly do you think talking about it will achieve?'

'I don't know.' Her breath felt tight inside her chest. 'But I don't think ignoring whatever it is can be the solution.'

He gave a short, bitter laugh. 'You've changed your tune. Not so long ago you managed to ignore me for three months without much problem.'

Nola felt her whole body tighten with shock and

pain. Then, almost in the same moment, she knew he was lashing out at her because he was upset, and even though his words hurt her she cared more about *his* pain than her own.

'And I was wrong.'

'So maybe in three months I'll think I was wrong about this. But somehow I don't think so.'

She gritted her teeth. 'So that's it? You just want me to shut up and go to bed?'

His face hardened. 'No, what I want is for you to stop nagging me, like the wife you've clearly never wanted to be.'

'I *do* want to be your wife.' The injustice of his words felt like a slap. 'And I'm not nagging. I'm trying to have a conversation.'

He shook his head. 'This isn't a conversation. It's an interrogation.'

'Then *talk* to me.'

His jaw tightened. 'Fine. I was going to wait until the morning, but if you can't or won't wait, we'll do it now.'

'Do what?'

'Break up. Call it off.' His voice was colder and harder than his gaze. 'Whatever one does to end an engagement.'

Watching the colour drain from her face, he felt sick. But knowing that he could hurt her so easily only made him more determined to finish it there and then—for what was the alternative? That she spent the next thirty years trapped with him in a loveless marriage?

A marriage that would force their child to endure the same dark legacy as him.

No, that wasn't going to happen. His child deserved more than to be a witness to his parents' unhappy marriage. And Nola deserved more than him.

Across the room Nola took a breath, tried to focus, to make sense of what Ram had just said.

'I don't understand,' she said finally.

But then, staring at him, she did—for the man who had held her in his arms and made love to her so tenderly had been replaced by a stranger with blank, hostile eyes.

'You want to end our engagement? But you were going to announce it tonight...'

He shrugged. 'And now I'm not.'

But I love you, she thought, her heart banging against her ribcage as though it was trying to speak for itself. Only it was clear that Ram had no use for her love, for any kind of love.

'Why?' she whispered. 'Why are you doing this?'

'I've changed my mind. All this—us, marriage, becoming a father—it's not what I want.'

'But you said that children need to know where they come from. That they need to belong.' His words tasted like ash in her mouth.

His gaze locked onto hers. 'Don't look so surprised, Nola. You said yourself I'm not cut out to be a hands-on daddy. And you're right. I'm not. What was it you said? No father is better than a bad father. Well, you were right. You'll do a far better job on your own than with me messing up your life and our child's life. But you don't need to worry. I fully intend to take care of you and the baby financially.'

Nola stared at him in silence.

He was talking in the same voice he used for board meetings. In fact he might just as easily have been discussing an upcoming software project instead of his child.

Her heart was beating too fast. Misery and anger were tangling inside her chest.

'Is that what you think matters?' she asked, reining in her temper.

He sighed. 'Try not to let sentiment get in the way of reason. Everything that baby needs is going to cost money so, yes, I think it *does* matter.'

'Not everything,' she said stubbornly. 'Children need love, consistency, patience and guidance, and all those are free.'

His mouth curled. 'Tell that to a divorce lawyer.'

Reaching into his pocket, he pulled out his car keys.

'There's no point in discussing this now. You can stay here, and I'll call my lawyers in the morning. I'll get them to draw up the paperwork and they can transfer this house into your name tomorrow.'

'What?' She stared at him, struggling to breathe.

'I'll work out a draft financial settlement at the same time. As soon as that's finalised we can put all this behind us and get back to our lives.'

Her skin felt cold, but she was burning up inside.

So was that it? Everything she had been through, that *they* had been through, had been for this? For him to pay her off. Just like her father had done with his ostentatious but impersonal presents.

Anger pounded through her. And, just like those

presents, giving her this house and an allowance were for *his* benefit, not hers. He was offering them as a means to assuage his conscience and rectify the mistake he clearly believed he'd made by getting her pregnant.

'I don't want your house or your money,' she said stiffly.

He frowned. 'Please don't waste my time, or yours, making meaningless remarks like that. You're going to need—'

She shook her head. 'No, you don't get to offer me money. Aside from my salary, I've never asked for or expected any money from you, and nothing's changed.'

His eyes narrowed. 'Give it time.'

She felt sick—a sickness that was worse than anything she'd felt in those early months of pregnancy. For that nausea had been caused by the child growing inside her, a child she loved without question, even when she felt scared and alone.

Now, though, she felt sick at her own stupidity.

Ignoring all her instincts, she had let herself have hope, let herself trust him. Not just trust him—but love him too.

And here was the proof that she'd been wrong all along.

Ram was just like her father, for when it came to sacrificing himself for his family he couldn't do it.

He was weak and selfish and he was not fit to be a father to her child.

Wide-eyed, suddenly breathless with anger, Nola stepped forward, her fingers curling into fists.

'Get out! You can keep your stupid financial settlements and your paperwork. As of this moment I never want to see or speak to you again, Ramsay Walker. Now, get out!'

He stared at her in silence, then, tossing the house keys onto one of the tables, he turned and walked swiftly across the room.

The door slammed and moments later she heard his car start, the engine roaring in the silence of the night and then swiftly fading away until the only sound was her ragged breathing.

It was then that she realised she was still wearing his ring. Unclenching her fingers, she gazed down at the sapphire, thinking how beautiful it was, and yet how sad.

And then her legs seemed to give way beneath her and, sliding down against the wall, she began to sob.

CHAPTER TEN

FINALLY IT WAS time to stop crying.

Forcing herself to stand up, Nola walked into the kitchen and splashed her face with cold water. Her mascara had run, and she wiped it carefully away with her fingertips. But as she tried to steady her breathing she knew it would be a long time—and take a lot more than water—to wash away Ram's words or that look on his face.

Her chest tightened, and suddenly the floor seemed to be moving. She gripped the edge of the sink.

Ram giving up like that had been so shocking—brutal, and cruel.

Like a bomb exploding.

And she still didn't really understand what had happened to make him change his mind—not just about the engagement but about everything. For her, cocooned in her newly realised love, it had begun to feel as though finally there was a future for them.

She felt anger scrape over her skin.

But what use was love to a man like Ram?

A man who measured his feelings in monthly maintenance payments?

Steadying herself, she lifted her shoulders. She wasn't going to fall apart. For what had she really lost?

Even before she'd thrown him out she had felt as though the Ram she loved had already left. He'd been so remote, so cold, so ruthless. Changing his mind, her life, her future and their child's future without batting an eyelid, then offering her money as some kind of consolation prize.

Her throat tightened, and suddenly she was on the verge of tears again.

And now he was gone.

And she knew that she would never see him again.

Somewhere in the house a clock struck two, and she felt suddenly so tired and drained that standing was no longer an option. There were several sofas in the living room, but she knew that if she sat down she would never get up again, and lying on a sofa in a party dress seemed like the worst kind of defeat. If she was going to sleep, she was going to do it in a bed.

Slipping off her shoes, she walked wearily upstairs. There was no shortage of bedrooms—she counted at least seven—but as she opened one door after another she began to feel like Goldilocks. Each room was beautiful, but the beds were all too huge, too empty for just her on her own.

Except that she wasn't on her own, she thought defiantly, stroking the curve of her stomach with her hand. Nor was she going to lie there worrying about the future. Her mother had more or less brought her up on her own and, unlike her mother, *she* was financially independent. So, with or without Ram, she was going to survive this *and* flourish.

Getting undressed seemed like too much of an effort, though, and, stifling a yawn, she crawled onto the next bed and slid beneath the duvet.

She didn't remember falling asleep, but when she opened her eyes she felt sure that she must have dozed off only for a couple of minutes. But one glance at the clock on the bedside table told her that she had been asleep for two hours.

Her skin felt tight from all the crying, and her head was pounding—probably from all the crying too. Feeling a sudden terrible thirst, she sat up and wriggled out from under the duvet.

The house was silent and still, but she had left some of the lights on during her search for a bedroom. Squinting against the brightness, she made her way towards the stairs. It was dark in the living room, but her head was still so muddied with sleep that it was only as she began to grope for a light switch that she remembered she had also left the lights on downstairs.

So why were they off now?

In the time it took for her heart to start beating again she had already imagined several nightmare crazed intruder scenarios—and then something, or someone, moved in the darkness and her whole body seemed to turn to lead.

'It's okay…it's just me.'

A lamp flared in the corner of the room, but she didn't need it to know that it was Ram sitting in one of the armchairs. She would recognise that voice any-where—even in darkness. And even had he lost his voice she would still have known him, for she had traced the pure, straight line of his jaw with her fingers. Touched those firm, curving lips with her mouth.

She felt a sudden sharp stab of desire, remembering the way his body had moved against hers. Remembering too how much she'd loved him. How much she still loved him. But with loving came feelings, and she wasn't going to let herself feel anything for this man anymore, or give him yet another chance to hurt her.

'How did you get in?' she asked stiffly.

'I have a spare key.'

Her heart began to race with anger, for his words had reminded her of the promise he'd made only a few hours ago. Not to love her and his child, but to take care of them financially, provide a fitting house and lifestyle.

Glancing round, she spotted the keys he'd left behind earlier, and with hands that shook slightly she picked them up.

'Here, you can have these too.' She tossed them to him. 'Since I'm not planning on staying here I won't be needing them. In fact...' She paused, tugging at the ring on her finger. 'I won't be needing this either.'

'Nola, please—don't do that.' He struggled to his feet, his mouth twisting.

'Don't do *what*, Ramsay?' She stared at him, a cloud of disbelief and anger swirling inside her. 'Why are you even here? I told you I never wanted to see you again.'

'I know. But you also said that ignoring this wasn't the solution.'

His voice was hoarse, not at all like his usual smooth drawl, but she was too strung out to notice the difference.

'Well, I was wrong. Like I was wrong to give you a chance. And wrong to think that you'd changed, that you could change.' Meeting his gaze, she said quickly, 'I know I've made a lot of mistakes, but I'm not about to repeat them by wasting any more of my time on you, so I'd like you to leave now.'

He sucked in a breath, but didn't move. 'I can't do that. I know you're angry, but I'm not leaving until you've listened to me.'

Her eyes widened, the pulse jerking in her throat. She didn't want to listen to anything he had to say, but she could tell by the set of his shoulders that he had meant what he said. He was just going to stand there and wait— stand there and wait for her to grow tired of fighting him and give in. Just as she always did, she thought angrily.

Blood was beating in her ears.

Taking a step backwards, she folded her arms protectively around her waist and looked at him coldly. 'Then say whatever it is and then I want you to leave.'

Ram stared at her in silence.

Her face was pale and shadowed. She was still wearing her dress from last night, and he knew that she must have slept in it, for it was impossibly crumpled now. But he didn't think she had ever looked more beautiful, or desirable, or determined.

Or that he had ever loved her more.

He stood frozen, his body still with shock. But inside the truth tugged him down and held him fast, like an anchor digging into the seabed.

He loved her.

He hadn't planned to. Or wanted to. But he knew unquestioningly that it was true.

And, crazy though it sounded, he knew it was the reason he'd broken up with her.

He'd told himself—told her—that he had never wanted to marry or have children. That he wasn't a good bet. That he would only ruin everything. And all of that had been true.

But it wasn't the whole truth.

He loved her, and in loving her he couldn't force her into a marriage of convenience. For, even though she had agreed to be his wife, he knew that she didn't love him. And he'd seen with his own eyes the damage and misery that kind of relationship could cause. He only had to look at his mother or look in the mirror for proof.

No, he didn't wanted to trap her—only he couldn't bear a life without Nola, a life without his child.

But how he could salvage this?

He took a deep breath. 'I know I've messed up. And I know you don't have any reason to listen to me, let alone forgive me, but I want a second chance. I want us to try again.'

For a moment she couldn't understand what he was saying, for it made no sense. Only a couple of hours ago he had said that he wanted to break up with her, to go back to his old life, and yet now he was here, asking her for a second chance.

But even as her brain raged against the inconsistency of his words her heart was responding to the desperation in his voice.

Only she couldn't do this again. Couldn't start to believe, to hope.

Ignoring the ache in her chest, she shook her head. '*You* gave up on *me*. And on our baby. Or have you forgotten that you were supposed to announce our engagement last night—?' She broke off, her voice catching in her throat as pain split her in two.

He took a step towards her, and for the first time it occurred to her that he looked as desperate as he sounded. There were shadows under his eyes and he was trembling all over.

'I haven't forgotten, and I'm sorry—'

'You're *sorry*!'

She shook her head. Did he really think that saying sorry was somehow going to make everything right again? If so, she had been right to throw him out.

'Well, don't be—I'm not. You know what? I'm *glad* you broke it off, because there's something wrong with you. Something that means that every time we get to a place of calm and understanding you have to smash it all to pieces. And I can't—I don't want to live like that.'

'I know, and I don't want to live like that either.'

He sounded so wretched. But why should she care? In fact she wasn't going to care, she told herself.

Only it was so hard, for despite her righteous anger she still loved him. But thankfully he would never know that.

'Then it's lucky for both of us that we don't have to,' she said quickly. 'As soon as I can get a flight back to Scotland I'm going home.'

She watched as he took a deep breath, and the pain

in his eyes tugged at an ache inside her, so that suddenly she could hardly bear looking at his stricken face.

'But this is your home…'

She shook her head. 'It's *not* my home. It's a payoff. A way for you to make yourself feel better. I don't want it.'

Ram stared at her in silence. The blood was roaring in his ears.

He was losing her. He was losing her.

The words echoed inside his head and he could hardly speak through the grief rising up in his throat. 'But I want you. And I want to marry you.'

Her heart began to beat faster. It was so tempting to give in, for she knew that right now he believed what he was saying. But now was just a moment in time: it wouldn't last for ever. And she was done with living in the moment.

Slowly she shook her head. 'Only because you can't have me. I don't know *what* you want, Ram. But I do know that you can't just break up with me and then two hours later come and tell me that you want me back and expect everything to be okay again. Maybe if this was a film we could kiss, and then the credits would roll, and everyone in the cinema would go home happy. But we're *not* in a film. This is real life, and it doesn't work like that.'

Tears filled her eyes.

'You hurt me, Ram…' she whispered.

'I know.'

The pain in his voice shocked her.

'I wish I could go back and change what I did and what I said. I panicked. When I went to find my mother she told me not to make the same mistake that she had. That relationships can't be forced. That they need love. That's why I couldn't go through with it.'

She nodded. 'Because you don't love me—I know,' she said dully.

'No!' He let out a ragged breath. 'I broke up with you because I *do* love you, Nola, and I didn't want to trap you in a marriage that you didn't want. That you never wanted.'

He took a step towards her, his hands gripping her arms, his eyes glittering not with tears but with passion.

'I *love* you, and that's why I want to marry you. Not out of duty, or because I want the baby to have my name. But I know you don't love me, and I've hurt you so much already. Only I couldn't just walk away. I tried, but I couldn't do it. That's why I came back—'

He stopped. There were tears in her eyes.

Only she was smiling.

'You love me? *You love me?*'

He stared at her uncertainly, his eyes burning, wishing there was another way to tell her that—to make her believe. But even before he'd started to nod she was pressing her hand against her mouth, as though that would somehow stop the tears spilling from her eyes.

'You're so smart, Ram. Easily the smartest person I've ever met. But you're also the stupidest. *Why* do think I agreed to marry you?'

'I don't know...' he whispered.

'Because I love you, of course.'

Gazing up into his face, Nola felt her heart almost stop beating as she saw that he too was crying.

'Why would you ever love me?'

His voice broke apart and she felt the crack inside her deepen as his mouth twisted in pain.

'How could you love me? After everything I've said and done? After how I've behaved?'

'I don't know.' She bit her lip. 'I didn't want to. And it scares me that I do. But I can't help it. I love you.' Her mouth trembled. 'I love you and I still want to marry you.'

His hands tightened around her arms, his eyes searching her face. 'Are you sure? I don't want to trap you. I don't want to be that kind of man—that kind of husband, that kind of father.'

Her heart began to beat faster. 'You're not. Not anymore. I don't think you ever were.'

Breathing out unsteadily, he pulled her close, smoothing the tears away from her face. 'Your parents married because it was the next step,' he said slowly. 'My mother married Guy out of desperation. They didn't think about what they were doing…it just happened. But we're different. We've fought to be together, and our marriage is going to work just fine.'

She breathed out shakily. 'How do you know?'

His eyes softened. 'Because you know me,' he said simply. 'You know everything about me—the good and the bad. And you still love me.'

Her lip trembled. 'Yes, I do.'

'It scares me, you knowing me like that.' He grimaced. 'But I trust you, and I love you, and I always will.'

Gently, he uncurled her arms from around her body, and as one they stepped towards each other.

Burying her face against his chest, Nola sighed with relief as Ram pulled her close.

'I love you, Nola.'

She lifted her head. 'I love you too.'

For several minutes they held each other in silence, neither wanting to let go of the other, to let go of what they had come so close to losing.

Finally Ram shifted backwards. 'Do you think it's too late to tell my mother?'

Tracing the curve of his mouth with her fingers, she laughed. 'I think it might be better for us to get some sleep first. Besides, what's a couple of hours when we have the rest of our lives together?'

'The rest of our lives together...' He repeated it softly, and then laying one hand across the swell of her stomach, he pulled her closer still, so that he and Nola and the baby were all connected. 'That's a hell of a future,' he whispered, kissing her gently on the forehead.

Looking up into his handsome face, Nola felt her heart swell with happiness. All the hardness and anger had gone and there was only hope and love in his grey eyes.

'Although, from where I'm standing, the present looks pretty damn good too.'

She bit her lip, her mouth curling up at the corners. 'I think it would look even better lying down.'

'My thoughts exactly,' he murmured, and with his heart beating with love and joy he scooped her up into his arms and carried her towards the stairs.

EPILOGUE

STEPPING UNDER THE shower head, Nola switched on the water and closed her eyes. If she was lucky, she might actually get to wash her hair today. Yesterday Evie, who was four months old today, had woken just as she'd stepped under the water. Not that she really minded. Her tiny daughter was the best thing in her life. The joint best thing, she amended silently.

Tipping her face up to meet the hot spray, she smiled as she thought back to the day of Evie's arrival. Ram had not only turned into a hands-on daddy, he'd practically taken over the entire labour ward.

It had been a small and rare reminder of the old work-hard, play-hard Ram, for nowadays she and Evie were the focus of his passion and devotion. He still loved his job, and the launch had been the most successful in the company's history—but he was happiest when he was at home.

And she was happy too. How could she not be?

She had a handsome, loving husband, a job working with her best friend, and a baby she adored.

Evie was beautiful, a perfect blend of both her parents. She'd inherited her pale skin and loose dark curls from Nola, but she had her father's grey eyes—a fact which, endearingly, Ram pointed out to everyone.

Her skin prickled as the fragrant warm air around her seemed to shift sideways, and then she gasped, her stomach tightening as two warm hands slid around her waist.

'Hi!'

Ram kissed her softly on the neck and, breathing out unsteadily, she leaned back against his warm naked body.

'Hey! That was quick.'

'I haven't done anything yet.'

The teasing note in his voice matched the light, almost tormenting touch of his fingers as they drifted casually over her flat stomach. Turning, she nipped him on the arm, softening it to a kiss as he pulled her closer.

'I meant the interview. I thought you were seeing that super-important woman from the news network?'

Tugging her round to face him, he looked down into her eyes, his mouth curving upwards into one of those sexy smiles she knew would always take her breath away.

'I talked really fast. Besides, I have two far more important women right here!'

'And in about half an hour you'll have three.' She pulled away slightly and smiled up at him. 'Pandora rang. She went shopping yesterday, and she wants to drop off a few things for Evie.'

Ram groaned. 'I presume she went shopping overseas? There can't be anything left in Australia for her to buy.'

Since the night of her anniversary party Pandora had been working hard to rebuild her relationship with her son, and Nola knew that, despite joking about her shopping habits, Ram was touched by his mother's efforts to make amends. She had separated from Guy, and now that they were no longer forced to live together the two of them had begun to enjoy each other's company as friends.

Nola laughed. 'You can talk. Every time you go out of the door you come back with something for me or Evie.'

'She deserves it for being so adorable,' Ram said softly as she glanced down at the beautiful diamond ring he'd given her when Evie was born. 'And you deserve it for giving me such a beautiful daughter.'

And for giving him a life, and a future filled with love.

Gently he ran his hand over her stomach. 'I miss your bump. I feel like I'd just got used to it, and then she was here. Not that I'm complaining.' His eyes softened. 'I can't imagine my life without her *or* you.'

Nola felt a pang of guilt. She knew how much he regretted not being there for the early stages of her pregnancy, for they had no secrets from one another now. That was one of the lessons they'd learnt from their past—to be open with one another.

'I miss it too. But there'll be other bumps.'

'Is that what you want?'

His face had gentled, and she loved him for it, because now everything was about what they *both* wanted.

'It is. It all happened so quickly last time.'

She hesitated, and then, leaning closer, ran her hand slowly over his stomach, her heart stumbling against her ribs as his skin twitched beneath her fingers.

His eyes narrowed, and a curl of heat rose up inside her as he pulled her against his smooth golden body.

'I'm happy to go slowly. On one condition.'

The roughness in his voice made her blood tingle.

'And what's that,' she asked softly.

'That we start right now.'

And, tipping her mouth up to his, he kissed her hungrily.

* * * * *

Keep reading for an excerpt of a new title
from the Modern series,
THE SICILIAN'S DEAL FOR 'I DO' by Clare Connelly

PROLOGUE

Twelve months earlier

BENEATH THE CHAPEL WINDOW, in the small square tucked deep in the ancient heart of Palermo, the world kept turning. Children ran by, gelatos in hand, sun on their chubby cheeks, parents walking behind them arm in arm, smiling, doting, adoring.

Mia watched as a boy of about nine tucked behind a wall, grinning, waiting until his sister, perhaps six, walked near to him, when he jumped out and shouted something. Though the chapel glass was thin and rippled by age, Mia couldn't hear through it, but she guessed it was something like, 'Boo!' The girl jumped, then both keeled over, laughing.

Despite the anxiety building inside Mia's gut over her own situation, she smiled. A weak, distracted smile, before she turned her back on the outside world with deep reluctance.

'Surely he's just been delayed.'

She caught sight of herself in an ancient mirror. Like the windows, it too was damaged by the passage of time, so it distorted her slightly, but that didn't matter. The ludicrousness of this was all too apparent, even without a clear reflection.

Had she really thought this would happen?

That today would be her wedding day?

That Luca Cavallaro would *actually* marry her?

Flashes of their brief, whirlwind courtship ran before her eyes. Her bewilderment at the idea of marriage, her parents' explanation that it was best for the family, for the business, and then, meeting Luca, who had swept her away with a single look, a brooding, fulminating glance that had turned her blood to lava and made her wonder if she'd ever really existed before knowing him.

Every time they'd been together, she'd felt that same zing. When they'd touched—even just the lightest brushing of hands—it had been like fireworks igniting in her bloodstream, and their kiss, that one, wild kiss, had left Mia with the certainty that she was born to be held by him.

The hot sting of tears threatened but Mia sucked in a calming breath, refusing to give into the temptation to weep. Not here, not now, certainly not in front of her parents, who were staring at Mia with expressions of abject disappointment, and, worse, a lack of surprise. As if they had almost expected this, for her to fail them.

'What did you say to him?' Jennifer Marini pushed, arms crossed over her svelte frame. 'You were alone with him, by the car the other night. What happened?'

Unlike Mia, Jennifer was tall and willow thin—a difference Jennifer never failed to highlight. Instead of growing into a stunning, svelte woman, like Jennifer, Mia had stopped growing a little over five feet, and had developed lush, generous curves. *Just like your mother*, Jennifer had never failed to condemn, as if bearing a resemblance to the woman who'd birthed Mia was a sin.

Reluctantly, Mia's eyes were drawn back to her own reflection. To the frothy white dress and ridiculous hairstyle. She'd been primped and preened and pulled in a thousand directions since first light. An army of women had worked on getting her 'bride ready'. She thought of the waxing with heated cheeks and blinked again quickly now.

Despite their efforts, Mia couldn't help thinking how far this was from her best look. She was under no illusions as to her beauty. She was pretty enough, she supposed, in the right light and to the right person, and as long as she could remember her biological mother's eyes and smile, Mia felt glad that they lived on in her own face. But she liked pasta far too much and disliked sweating generally, which ruled out a vast array of cardio exercises. She was never going to be reed thin like her adoptive mother, nor did she want to be. There was a sternness to Jennifer, and a general lack of *joie de vivre* that Mia had always associated with her restrictive diet: far better to eat the pasta—and the gelato and the focaccia and the mozzarella—and be happy, Mia always thought.

'I—nothing,' she said, quickly, even though memories of those snatched moments were making her pulse rush now.

'I did everything I could for you,' Jennifer said with a ticking of her finger to her palm, the harsh red of her manicure catching Mia's eye. 'I did everything I could to pave the way for this marriage. You must have said something.'

'I haven't spoken to him in a week,' Mia denied. Perhaps it was strange not to talk to your fiancé for so long, but then, this was far from a normal marriage, and her situation was far from normal. Marriage to Luca Cavallaro wasn't a love match. Not for him, anyway. She frowned, and her heart began to beat faster, to race, as she remembered their first meeting. The way their eyes had locked, and something had shifted inside her, a part of Mia she hadn't known existed, the part of her she'd always wondered about.

Whatever physical beauty she lacked, he made up for, with abundance.

Like a specimen from a gallery or a famous actor or a pristine example of what the male species *should* be. Tall, sculpted, muscular without being bulky, strong, and when he'd looked at her, she'd felt this giddy sense of disbelief that *he* was actually going to be her husband.

They'd only seen each other a handful of times after that, always with Mia's parents until that last night, and the conversations had revolved around the businesses. The sale of Mia's father's old family corporation to Luca Cavallaro and his newly minted multibillion-dollar fortune. Just what the world needed: another beyond handsome, alpha-male billionaire!

But then there'd been *that* kiss, when he'd been leaving one evening and Jennifer had hastily told Mia to walk him out. The moon had been high in the sky above her parents' estate in the countryside surrounding Palermo, the sound of the ocean drowned out by the rushing of her blood as he'd pulled her into his arms, stared down at her, frowned for a moment and then, he'd simply kissed her, as though it were the most natural thing in the world.

Perhaps it was. They'd spent hours in each other's company over the course of their engagement—maybe he'd expected more kissing, more of everything? Mia didn't know. That night, he'd taken matters into his own hands... She'd expected it would turn out like a movie, a three-second kiss, maximum, but his lips had lingered, and the world had slowed right down along with it. She'd moaned, because he'd smelled so good but tasted better; the kiss was by far the best thing she'd ever felt. Like coming home—except, Mia had never really felt at home anywhere since her parents had died.

And then his arms had tightened around her back, melding her curvy body to his, and he'd deepened the kiss, his passionate inspection of her mouth leaving her shaking, writhing wantonly against him, until he'd pulled away and stared down at her once more. Was that surprise in his features? At the time, Mia had thought so, but, like all memories, it shifted and morphed so she couldn't have said with any confidence the next morning that it hadn't been boredom. Or worse, disgust. After all, Mia had very limited experience with kissing men.

That had been one week before their wedding. They hadn't seen nor spoken to one another afterwards, but she'd had no reason to doubt him.

No reason to doubt this would come to pass. If anything, the kiss had cemented his intentions for Mia. How could he make her feel like that and then walk away?

She could have wept when she thought of her childish fantasies, the dreams that had kept her awake at night and stirred her body to a fever pitch of wanting.

When her parents had first told her about the wedding, she'd been unsure about the idea. They'd wanted to know a Marini would still work in the family business, and also that Mia would be taken care of once they'd sold off such a valuable asset. But it didn't take long for Mia to warm to the idea.

Of no longer being a Marini, which, in some ways, she'd never really felt herself to be.

Of no longer being alone.

Of being a wife, married—and to someone like Luca. Putting aside his physical beauty, he was rich and powerful and she was sure she'd be able to lead her own life while living under his roof, that he wouldn't trouble himself with her comings and goings. But also, there would be children, and that thought alone had made her a very willing accomplice to the whole scheme. Children, a family of her own, something she'd so desperately wanted since losing her parents and the sense of security that came from knowing she was loved.

Though she was outwardly compliant with her adoptive parents, a streak of rebellion had been growing inside Mia, and marrying Luca Cavallaro seemed like a brilliant way to exercise her independence, finally.

'He's probably just late,' Mia murmured, trying to reassure herself.

'To his own wedding?' Jennifer demanded, moving one of the red-taloned hands to her hips. 'He is supposed to be out there, waiting for you, Mia. That's the way it works.'

'He's a very busy and important man,' Mia pointed out. 'That's why we're here, isn't it?'

Gianni Marini shook his head, his rounded face showing obvious impatience. 'All you had to do was sit in the corner and smile from time to time.'

Something sparked in Mia's chest. Had she done something wrong? Had she been the one to ruin this? Had the kiss been so bad? She spun away again quickly, trying to find the same family with the brother and sister playing hide and seek, but they were gone. The light danced off the large tree in the centre of the square. Mia had always loved the light of Palermo. She'd hated leaving it to go to milky grey England, but

Jennifer had insisted that her daughter attend her alma mater, so boarding school it had been. How she'd missed the sunshine and sea salt.

'Oh, God.' Jennifer's voice crackled in the air. Mia closed her eyes without turning around. She'd been holding onto hope, remembering Luca's eyes, absolutely certain that someone with such beautiful eyes and the ability to truly look at someone and *see* them could never do anything quite so callous as this. But then, she also knew. Even as the hairdressers had worked and the make-up artist had glued false lashes in place and her nails had been painted and made hot beneath a UV light, Mia had somehow *known* it would all come to nothing.

'What is it?' Gianni asked loudly.

'He's not coming.'

'How do you know?'

'The whole world knows,' Jennifer snapped. 'Look.' Mia kept her eyes shut, back to the room, breath silenced despite the heaviness of her heart.

Gianni read aloud, quickly, '*"Runaway Groom"*—that's the headline. *"It appears Luca Cavallaro preferred the idea of an airport runway to that of a wedding aisle after all. The billionaire bachelor was spotted leaving Italy last night despite his planned wedding, which was to take place today, to Mia Marini, daughter of steel magnate Gianni Marini. Trouble in corporate merger paradise? Watch this space.'"*

Mia groaned, the last sentence almost the hardest to hear of all, because she realised that the whole world knew their marriage was just a corporate merger. And it was. But was it so implausible to think a man like Luca might actually want to marry Mia for herself?

A single tear slid down her cheek.

'He left last night!' Jennifer barked, her voice trembling with rage. 'And didn't have the decency to tell us. All of this, all of this trouble, and not even a chance to save face. How could he do this to us, Gianni?'

To you? Mia wanted to scream. She was the one in the ridiculous dress with awful hair and over-the-top make-up. Suddenly, she was claustrophobic and couldn't breathe. Could barely stand up. Stars danced behind her eyes and she spun wildly, staring at her parents without seeing them, then locating the door to the small room.

'I have to go.'

'Go where, Mia?' Jennifer asked sharply.

'Outside. Anywhere. I don't care. I just—I can't breathe.'

'Mia, don't,' her mother warned, but too late. Mia burst into the chapel, to a packed room of people, all there for the spectacle of this. Most were on their phones, but when she appeared, they looked up, almost as one, some with pity, others with a delighted sense of *schadenfreude*. Mia barely noticed any of it. She scrambled along the back of the church, past the guests who'd not been able to find seats, ignoring their words, their voices, throwing open the heavy, old timber doors so the beautiful Palermo light bathed her. She closed her eyes and let it make her strong for a moment, then ran down the stairs and across the square, right into a child who smeared strawberry gelato against the horrible white dress.

And all Mia could do was stand still, in the middle of the square, hands on her hips, head tilted to the sky, and laugh. There was nothing else for it.

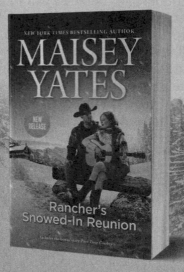